Penguin Books

Rubicon

John Hooker was born in New Zealand and has lived
in Australia since 1963. For many years he was a
publisher then turned to full-time writing in 1985.

His previously published books include *Jacob's
Season, The Bush Soldiers, Standing Orders,
Captain James Cook* (from a screenplay by Peter
Yeldham) and *Korea: The Forgotten War.*

He lives on the south-west coast of Victoria and is
currently working on a satirical novel covering the
last forty years of the Cold War.

By the same author

Jacob's Season

The Bush Soldiers

Standing Orders

Captain James Cook (with Peter Yeldham)

Australians at War: Korea, the Forgotten War

Rubicon

John Hooker

Penguin Books

For Patrick Coyle

Penguin Books Australia Ltd
487 Maroondah Highway, PO Box 257
Ringwood, Victoria, 3134, Australia
Penguin Books Ltd
Harmondsworth, Middlesex, England
Viking Penguin, A Division of Penguin Books USA Inc.
375 Hudson Street, New York, New York 10014, USA
Penguin Books Canada Limited
10 Alcorn Avenue, Toronto, Ontario, Canada M4V 1E4
Penguin Books (N.Z.) Ltd
182-190 Wairau Road, Auckland 10, New Zealand

First published in Viking by Penguin Books Australia, 1990
Published in Penguin, 1991
10 9 8 7 6 5 4 3 2 1
Copyright © John Hooker, 1990

Typeset in Garamond by Midland Typesetters, Maryborough, Victoria
Printed and bound in Australia by The Book Printer, Maryborough, Victoria

National Library of Australia
Cataloguing-in-Publication data:
Hooker, John, 1932-
Rubicon
ISBN 014 014 976 7
I. Title
A 823.3

If a man own land, the land owns him.

R.W. Emerson

One

As he drove past the deserted farms, the collapsing sheds and barns, and the crops withered upon the earth, it seemed to Frank Cameron that no matter how hard some men worked, how long families stuck together, there were devilish forces beyond their control. He wasn't thinking of the weather – although it had been bad enough, with no rain for over a year, dry thunderstorms and dust clouds – he was thinking of inexplicable falls in prices for produce, collapses in the stock markets, sudden poverty and evictions and skilled men walking the roads for jobs. Now, these men were everywhere: shabby, grey-faced, looking for a hand-out and wandering. Now, it appeared as though hard work was of no account.

At times, the journey north had been a nightmare: in one town there was a procession and violence. Policemen armed with truncheons and mounted troopers were struggling with unemployed miners in the dusty streets; a horse had its fetlocks slashed with a knife and fell screaming; buildings were ablaze and some men were carrying the Eureka flag. Frank had heard that American unionists from the Industrial Workers of the World were about, and it seemed that the country was drifting into anarchy.

In some parts, the road was lined with men and youths pushing bicycles and carts through the gravel. It appeared as if the living in the country might be better, that work was there, but Frank was beginning to doubt that. He gave lifts to several, but when he found he was being slowed down and scuffles developed, he gave up and pressed north toward the plains.

Now the road ran straight to the horizon and each side the country was vast and flat; the last wheat crop had failed and the light was hard. In the heat, the tree-lines shimmered; the journey seemed endless and the townships and settlements lay boiling in the sun – a general store, a pub, a post office, a district hall – the paint blistered and peeling, and old men dozing on cluttered front verandahs. This season, the drought was so bad that even the ancient pepper trees were dying.

The dust from the road billowed up between the floorboards of the Chevrolet; now and again another truck or car passed, but no one saluted. It was as though everyone was infected and wanted to avoid contact. As he drove and watched the petrol gauge, Frank remembered something about a plague he had read of in school. Was it the Black Death? What sheep were left were huddled on the mounds by the empty dams and crows and magpies sat on the corner fenceposts. The power lines looped and sagged to the north, and the starlings and sparrows wheeled and flew in droves in the cloudless, glaring sky.

When he knew he had been granted a lease, Frank had taken down his father's old red-bound atlas to get a picture of the country in his mind. He had seen that the land here was so flat there were no contours marked; but now he found there were depressions – so vast that the smudge of the bush on the other side looked like a range of mountains. He also learned that forty million years ago this area was covered by the sea, but this had receded, leaving great beds of marine limestone, overlaid with clay and topped with sand. These grey plains were taken up by the squatters whose sheep wandered across the soundless landscape and where the shepherds slept in outstations of corrugated iron and portable boxes. In the 1890s, the land was opened up to crop farmers and was now given over to wheat. But in this year of Our Lord 1932, crop prices had collapsed, banks had withdrawn their credit – some already had closed – and a drought had settled on the northern plains like some pestilence from the Old Testament.

When he stopped for petrol, it was almost half-past midday and he guessed the temperature was in the nineties. The north wind was stronger than he had thought and thistles and paper were blowing about the yard where an old Ford truck sat up on bricks, its canvas hood torn and flapping. Two boys with scabby knees were playing marbles in the dirt; otherwise nobody seemed to be around. Frank got his hat from the front seat, put it on, looked at the hard country and went inside the pub for a drink. He had another hundred miles to go, and it didn't look too promising.

Three men were at the bar, but didn't look up: this was the habit now. The window screens were missing and the room was full of flies. Old football photographs lined the walls, and a golf trophy made from a bent club sat over the vacant fireplace. Were there golf courses in these parts? The man behind the bar came up and looked.

'I'll have a beer,' Frank said.

'Right.'

'Are you selling petrol?'

'Yep.'

'You can fill up that truck outside.'

'Okay.' The barman studied the big, fair-haired man with a limp.

'Travelling through?'

The beer was cold and good and Frank rolled a cigarette. 'That's right.'

'Where to?'

'Rubicon.'

'Rubicon?'

'That's right. It's about a hundred miles north-west.'

'I didn't know there was a town up there,' the barman said. 'It's all uncleared.'

'It may be uncleared, but there's a town up there.' Frank slid another shilling across the counter. 'Same again.'

The barman stole another look at Frank's gammy leg. 'You going farming?'

'That's right.'

'You haven't chosen much of a time. The whole country's as dry as buggery.'

'I didn't choose it,' Frank said. 'The Repatriation Department did.'

'Well, they wouldn't know, would they?'

'I don't think the drought's their fault. What about filling my truck?'

Outside, in the glare, the barman pinched out his cigarette, put it behind his ear and worked the pump. 'It's a wonder you haven't picked anybody up, or don't you risk that?'

'I risk it,' Frank answered, 'but I haven't seen anyone for a bit.'

'Aw Christ, they're around. The weather's that hot they're probably laying under the trees. A lot of them move on at night. They're around. Fucking vagrants and Bolshies – a woman was raped up here last month and the pub's been broken into twice. Christ knows what blokes like you fought for! You watch out for yourself, digger!'

Frank pulled out his wallet and gave the man his money.

'I will,' he said. 'Too bad you've never heard of Rubicon.'

'No, I never have.' The barman watched Frank as he climbed up easily into the cab and slammed the door. 'Good luck, digger.'

'Thanks. I might need it.' He pulled at the starter, shoved the engine into gear and drove out on to the highway.

At half-past four, Frank decided to pick up another man who was sitting on the side of the road. He was wearing a greatcoat even though it was still hot. Frank knew the trick: the nights here were cold and you put your coat on while you were still warm.

'Thanks, mate,' the man said as he tossed his old Gladstone bag into the back and climbed in. 'You're only the third I seen all day. The other two bastards didn't stop.'

'There's a lot of them about.' Frank looked at the faded marks on the man's greatcoat sleeve and swung out through the gravel on to the road. He had been a corporal, or the owner had. And he was wearing heavy dole boots.

'You can say that again.' The man took off his felt hat and wiped his bald head. 'Going far?'

Frank thought before he answered: he didn't want company for too long. 'About fifty miles.'

'That'll do me.' The stranger cocked his head. 'The motor doesn't sound too good.'

'It'll do, it's always sounded like that.'

'It sounds like a piston.'

'Frank moved into top and wound the truck up to sixty. 'Are you a mechanic?'

'Nah, bricklayer. Christ, if you don't mind me saying so, you can drive alright.'

'I've had fourteen years' experience.'

'Mind you, I reckon these Chevs go anywhere.'

Frank wondered if the man had eaten during the day. He was wiry and pinched, with a face like a bird. 'So you're a brickie?'

'I sure am.' The man's thin face brightened. 'Do you want a house built.'

Frank laughed. 'I don't think so. Not of brick, anyway.' He thought of the story of the Three Little Pigs and his mother reading to him in the candle-light.

'They're still putting buildings up, ain't they? In some of the country towns? I'm qualified. They reckon the Catholics are putting up schools because of the cheap labour.'

'They might be. You never know.'

After an hour or so, the sun was sinking and kept shining in his face; the visor was missing and driving became awkward. Dust and dead insects were stuck to the windscreen and Frank started to look for a suitable place to doss down for the night. The country looked bleak in the yellow light and the sun hung, crimson, in the evening sky. Then he saw the evening star rising and asked: 'Have you eaten today?'

'Aw, had a few scraps.'

'I'll be stopping in half an hour. Do you want a meal with me?'

The man looked gratefull. 'That's white of you, mate. The name's Bill.'

'Cameron, Frank Cameron. It's going to be cold.'

'Don't I know it.'

'We could sleep in the back of the truck, but it's full of gear.'

'That's okay, mate. As I said: you're a white man.'

In the moonlight, Frank saw a stone cottage near the road, stopped, turned off the motor and said: 'I reckon that will do.'

When he got out, Frank felt the cold rising through his boots. The moon was higher and the planets gleamed. Venus, Mars, Jupiter, Saturn: he remembered them from his childhood. In a few minutes he would see the Southern Cross. The wind was a whisper and the crickets sang; somewhere a sheep bleated, then all was silent. They would make a fire and spend the night in the stone house. Frank looked at the bricklayer: he was a little man in that greatcoat, but strong – he was sure of that. He pulled the keys from the dash, reached under the seat and got out his torch. 'You stay here, Bill, I'll have a look and see what's what.'

'Right you are, Frank. Do you want me to get anything out of the back?'

'No, I'll do that. You wait here, I shan't be a moment. There might be some other jokers in there.' He climbed over the fence and was gone.

Bill watched the torch flickering over the rough ground, then walked around the back of the Chevrolet. It was a 1930 model with a canvas hood; he wondered what was inside – he pulled at the ropes, but they were cleated down tight. There had to be something in there worth a few bob – he would find out when the time was right. Frank Cameron was a big bugger, but he had that limp. He opened his trousers and pissed on the gravel, then rolled a cigarette, lit it and leaned against the fender. This time, maybe he was in luck. The stars glittered and the breeze moved in the dry and broken grass.

'There's no one there.'

The bricklayer started and turned to see Frank Cameron in the gloom, his torch out. He was a silent bugger, too. 'Right-oh, mate, I'll bring me bag.'

'I've got some beans,' Frank said. 'I'll get the gear.' He let down the tailboard, ducked under the flap and climbed inside.

'Do you want a hand?' Bill asked.

'No, it's okay.'

When Frank jumped down, he was carrying an army kitbag. Then the two men walked through the dewy grass, climbed the fence and strode toward the house.

There was plenty of wood; they cleared off the broken glass, made a fire, sat on the earth floor and warmed their hands. Frank would have preferred to be by himself, but this little bloke wasn't that bad, although he was unshaven, his fingernails split and black and he smelt of stale sweat. He had been on the road for several weeks. When Frank had found two cans of beans, he opened them and said: 'Where are you going?'

'Anywhere I can get a job. I've heard things ain't so bad in the country. Is that right?'

'They're patchy. Good places, bad places.'

'They'd better be good for me – I've got six kids at home. Have you got any kids?'

'No.' Frank got a stick, cleared a space in the embers and put on the beans.

'Did you fight in the War?'

'Yes.'

'Whereabouts?'

'France and Belgium. And you?'

'Me? Palestine.'

Frank knew the man was lying – he was no horseman. 'I reckon those beans won't take long.'

'They smell good. Are you from around here?'

'No.'

'Do you reckon there are any blackfellows further north?' Frank spooned the beans out on to the tin plates. 'Probably.'

Bill ate quickly. 'I don't like them bastards.' He dropped some beans on his trousers, scraped them off and put them in his mouth.

'Why?'

'They're sneaky and cunning.'

'They're okay,' Frank said, 'if you leave them alone.'

'Christ, I could do with a drink.'

Frank thought of the bottle of whisky in his kitbag: he wouldn't share it with this fellow. 'There's tea.'

'That'll have to do. Them beans was good.' Bill rolled a thin cigarette and stuck it on his lower lip. 'Do you want one?'

'It's okay, I've got my own.' Frank buttoned up his jacket and felt the lump of his wallet next to his chest.

'What do you reckon's happened?'

'To what?'

'To us. More jobs than you could poke a stick at one year, then, bingo, none the next.'

'I don't know. Good times, bad times.' The fire was getting low now and Frank considered getting more wood, then decided against it: he would get some sleep.

'It beats me.'

'I'm going to turn in,' Frank said as he put down his mug. 'I'll see you in the morning.'

'Okay.'

'Watch that fire, Bill. We don't want to be roast pigs.'

'Okay. What could I do with a couple of pork chops.'

Frank got up, didn't reply, chose a place against the wall where he would be safer, spread out his blanket and shoved his kitbag under his head. Tomorrow, he would be at Rubicon and the work would begin. He was looking forward to that.

It must have been about the false dawn when Frank heard the sound of the man moving. A few moments later, he felt the man's fingers inside his jacket. He let him take out the wallet, then grabbed him by the throat, twisted his windpipe and saw the blade of the knife gleaming. 'If you don't drop that knife,' Frank whispered, 'I'll break your neck.'

'Jesus,' Bill gasped, 'you're choking me.'

'That's the idea. Drop the knife.'

'Okay, okay.'

The knife fell, but the little man was quick and strong; he

thrust his knee into Frank's groin and slipped away into the darkness. Neither man knew where the knife was. Frank cursed, clutched himself and stood still in the room. He listened – it was like hunting at night, when the animal had to make the first move. As the minutes went by, Frank thought of the man's heavy dole boots; he tugged at the laces of his own, eased them off and stood in his socks. He took his time and waited. You little bastard, he thought, you only have to move in those boots, and I'll get you. Outside the wind moved in the trees, an owl hooted and sheep bleated. He thought of night watch in the trenches and the accordian music drifting over the pitted landscape. Be patient, outlast the other man. At last, in the blackness, he heard the sound of boots on gravel and knew the man was near the far wall, making for the door. Like a fish taking the bait, Frank let him move, heard the boots again and leapt: he got him by the waist in a tackle, brought him down hard and tore his arms up his back. 'I'll tear your fucking arms from their sockets, then I'll break your back.'

'Jesus Christ, you're killing me.'

'Too right I will,' Frank said. He heaved him round and hit him in the mouth, felt blood on his knuckles and hit him again on the bridge of the nose. The bone broke, the man screamed and fell. Frank knew his little mate was done for, found the torch, switched it on and shone it in the man's face. His front teeth were loose, his nose broken and blood ran down his face and chin. 'Lying is one thing,' he said. 'You aren't a returned man's arsehole, but stealing from a mate is another. You're in big trouble, my friend.'

'You ain't going to kill me?'

Frank thought of the last time he had killed a man. 'No.' He found the knife, it was spring-loaded and he put it in his trouser pocket. The real dawn was breaking now and the birds were starting to sing. Somewhere to the south came the sound of a train whistle. It was cold and Frank stamped his feet. 'Pick up all this gear and take it down to the truck.'

'What are you going to do?'

'Pick up the gear.'

'Okay.'

The man spat out blood, grabbed his Gladstone bag and Frank's kit and blanket. When he started to argue, Frank pushed him hard in the back. 'Keep moving, my friend.'

'You're not going to turn me in, are you?'

'You'll see.'

When they got to the road, a car passed, its headlights gleaming and the dust swirling. Frank opened the flap of the truck. 'Chuck the kit in here. You can keep your bag.'

'If you turn me in, I'm finished.'

'Take off your boots.'

'What?'

'Take off your boots.'

'Jesus.' Bill stooped and picked at the laces.

'Give them to me,' Frank said as he opened the truck door. He pulled the starter, gunned the motor and hung the boots on the outside driving mirror. 'Have a pleasant walk.'

After he had driven about ten miles, Frank reached out the window and tossed the boots on to the road. If this was what was happening up here, he didn't like it much. He drove north into the morning.

Two

Maria Hoffmayer had started to mark the days off on the calendar: this was the fifteenth month without rain. Now and again, black clouds would bundle in from the south-west, thunder would boom and spots of water, the size of pennies, would fall. The lightning flashed in the dark sky; there was the sound of cannon fire, and spots fell as heavy as birds' droppings in the red dust. The farmers and townsfolk looked heavenwards, their spirits lifting yet again – but that was all. The clouds moved away to the north; the thunder became distant; the lightning struck somewhere in the uncleared bush and the sun shone once more – hard, brassy and blinding the eye. The farmers squinted beneath their battered, broad-brimmed hats and went inside to their stifling, dusty kitchens to drink tea and wait for the cool of the evening. For many, there was no more milking to be done: the cows were skin and bone, no fresh feed was to be had, and the spiders spun their webs in the silent, dusty dairies.

For reasons she was starting to understand, Maria had stopped using her book of devotions at the start of the summer, and now used her Bible alone. It was leather-bound and the inscription on the flyleaf read: *August Adolph Hoffmayer, his book, 18th February, 1872.* It was in fine condition – Julius's father had not used it much, especially in his adult years. She sometimes wondered why Julius allowed it to be used – but it was the Holy Book and the message stood forever no matter the sins of the owner.

After she had read a few verses, Maria thought over what she had read and then tried to compose a prayer of her own. *O Lord, in your infinite wisdom, bring forth the rain.* She remembered when, as a child, she used to open her Bible

11

at random, close her eyes, point with her finger and begin reading at that place. But that was a childish habit and not the way to get the most benefit from daily Bible reading. There had to be some purpose in it, some connection between the daily readings, some plan to be followed. God's plan. Now, with the drought, the drop in wheat prices and, most of all, her strange restlessness, was there no plan? Maria was starting to admit such a possibility.

Because of the strange portents – the drought, the dust storms, the bankruptcies and the plagues of mice and sparrows – Maria had turned to The Revelation of St John the Divine. It was difficult to understand and she thought of the four horsemen of the Apocalypse, the seven angels and the seven plagues. Last week there was a sudden hailstorm with stones the size of pebbles; the starving cattle and horses had panicked, running themselves into fences and gates; then the sun shone once more, the ice stones disappearing into the dust. Two days later, two men were struck dead by bolts of lightning in separate parts of the district. What kinds of signs were these? Maria's grandmother was supposed to have had the gift of prophecy, but few people ever knew as many said that was the work of the Anti-Christ.

Today was Tuesday and Maria had tried to pray according to the plan: for Christian homes, for parents and children. As she put August's Bible back on the sideboard, she heard the wind whispering under the kitchen door; the dust hung in shafts of light from the windows and something moved in the wainscot. Was it mice? Would they return? She remembered the stench of the strychnine and the buckets of small, furry carcasses. The clock struck midday: Julius and Carl would soon be home for their dinner. She went to the stove and stirred the mutton stew as the wind grew stronger and growled around the house.

Outside in the yard, a horse sneezed and stamped in the dust. Please God, Maria thought, let no one come begging to the door today. As with the days of drought, she had started to keep count: eight men had come during the past month.

She gave them a piece of bread and mutton fat, sent them on their way and had not told Julius. Many of the men were from the cities, in old suits, with badly sunburned faces and cut and bloodied hands. Why did they come to the country? There was nothing for them here, especially at Rubicon. Maria often wondered what was happening in the towns and asked Farozi, the Indian hawker, when he called. But all he said was that times were bad, and had no explanation. The Indian was a mean and tricky man who tried to sell her pickled eggs when the fowls were off laying. Although he was insistent, she would never let him inside. Last year, Julius had threatened the hawker with a shotgun; but the Indian had started to come back with his tired old pony and his waggon stacked with haberdashery, ribbons, silks and perfumed soap. The Hindus were only good for picking up stumps, and not much good for that.

The German clock struck the quarter-hour as Maria went to the safe, took out the bread and cut three slices. Then, her boots echoing on the wooden floor, she went to the trapdoor, opened it and climbed down into the cellar for the scalded milk. Only two cows were left now: the others were dry and she had made no cheese for months. The bacon hung in its muslin bag and the barrel of pickled pork was almost empty. She inspected the jars of preserved fruit, wiped the dust off them with her apron, stamped on a spider and climbed the ladder back into the kitchen.

When Maria opened the back door, the sun beat on her head like a hammer; the wind caught at her long black dress and the parakeets were screeching in the branches of the trees. The horse was standing in the bare and pitted yard, its head down, and the chickens were crouched in the shade of the dead and broken hedge. She took the bucket from the stand and walked over to the tank, turned the tap and listened to the water dribbling and splashing onto the hot metal. The first drops fizzed and disappeared, then the water ran, cloudy and tepid. As always, Maria banged on the rim of the tank and listened to the hollow sound. When this was gone, it was

13

water from the bore and after that Julius would have to go into town with the tank on the cart and pay for it. He had never had to do that yet, but needs must when the devil drives.

When she was back inside the kitchen, Maria poured some water carefully into the teapot, set it on the hot plate and tossed a few logs into the range. Sweat and dust stuck to her back, her eyes were gritty and thistle seeds floated in the hot gloom. Was that a sound? She opened the hall door and went down the passage to Louisa's room and listened at the door. All was silent: the north wind ghosted and the threadbare curtains floated and billowed; the dust crunched beneath her boots, then she heard the heavy sound of men walking on the boards of the verandah. It was Julius and Carl.

Her husband was tapping at the barometer on the wall beside the dresser, and Carl was sitting at the table, already waiting for his midday meal. 'It is hotter than this outside,' Julius said, looking at her with his black eyes, 'much hotter.'

There was no need to reply and she took the plates from the dresser and started to serve the mutton. The bread was cut and Julius sat at the head of the table. 'For what we are about to receive, we give thanks to the Lord, and are truly grateful.'

'It feels as though a fire is coming,' Maria said.

Although Carl was hungry, he always ate carefully in front of his father. He had been working since five. 'I do not think so. Not today. Tomorrow, perhaps?'

The three of them ate the mutton stew and when he had finished, Julius picked out the marrow with his fork. 'This mutton is stringy, but we are better off than most. We are better off than all of them.' He pushed his plate back and started to fill his pipe. 'And that is how it shall be.' He drank his tea. 'They are re-opening the Kurnbrun block to soldier-settlers. I was told that in Rubicon. Those fellows will not last – the banks will see to that.'

This was news, indeed, as the nearest Kurnbrun block was but one mile away. 'Do you want some more tea?' she said.

Carl, too, was filling his meerschaum. 'No thank you, Stepmother.' He rose from the table and took up his hat. He was growing a beard, his shoulders were broad and his arms were scarred.

'We will be back at six,' Julius said. 'We will not have afternoon tea.'

The two men rose, put on their hats, opened the door and were gone. Maria sat at the table: the clock struck the quarter-hour. As usual, her husband and stepson had been home for dinner precisely one hour. Suddenly, Louisa screamed in the darkness of her room and Maria ran down the hall. But when she got there and opened the door, her stepdaugher was asleep.

On the wall above the dresser in the empty drawing-room was the Hoffmayer family tree; but this looked like a kind of exploding sun with the great-great-grandparents, Elvira and Johannes Hoffmayer, as the nucleus. When Maria married Julius and he had taken her into his house, the chart was already on the wall. Although it looked like the work of an astrologer, it was not: since they had emigrated to Australia in 1849, the Hoffmayer family and their issue had increased, but now only Julius and his two children were left.

Elvira and Johannes were rye and barley farmers in Neukirch, Saxony. There, the farmers grew mangels, oats and peas; and from pictures Maria had seen, the surrounding countryside looked like a Chinese garden, with its roads ornamented with apple trees, pear trees and cherries. The area was hilly with forests and streams. In the village of Neukirch, artisans made porcelain, glassware, earthenware and tweed. Iron was manufactured and charcoal burners lived in the hills. The town was surrounded by medieval walls until they were destroyed by Napoleon's troops in 1813. The farm was in the hands of the Hoffmayers for five generations, and year after year they prospered. But in the 1830s, factories sprang up in the cities, unemployment grew; there was famine in some places; strange men preached revolution and civil war; and, worst of all, came the prospect of compulsory military service

15

and religious persecution. In the winter of 1849, Johannes, Elvira and their six children boarded a five-hundred-ton barque in Hamburg and sailed for Australia. Now, in 1932, Julius Hoffmayer and his second wife, Maria, grew wheat, peas and rye, and raised sheep on a thousand-acre block near Rubicon in north Victoria, Australia. But the land did not look like a Chinese garden.

Louisa and Carl were from Julius's first wife, Sophie, who had died of tuberculosis in 1916. Louisa was seventeen – she was always a strange child and had been ill since the beginning of the drought. Julius forbade the doctor: he said no one was to come near her as there was nothing wrong with her and that God would have His way. But something was wrong with her, and Maria wondered yet again how long this sickness was going to last.

Next to the Hoffmayer chart were photographs of the family. Julius's forebears were seated on bentwood chairs in their struggling gardens – the women in their long, black dresses; the bearded men with their wing collars and watch chains; the boys in knickerbockers and buttoned boots and the girls with their lace aprons and straw hats. All were proud and unsmiling among the wicker furniture and spindly fruit trees.

Despite Julius, Maria was proud of these people – these men and women were tenacious in body and spirit. They worked all hours God gave them. Ignoring the reports of terrible droughts, the German settlers came north to occupy their bush blocks: to fence their land with sticks, to build their church with limestone, to put up their pine-slab cottages, to establish their gardens and hold the land in perpetuity.

The Germans were a restless and independent people. But despite the work of the surveyors with their theodolites and chains, the map further to the north was blank: there were almost twelve million acres of useless land – silent and lifeless, where the soil was loose, sandy and porous, where the lakes were dry and the salt pans gleamed, where the fires burned all summer and the stunted bush grew, its pre-historic roots clinging to the waterless earth. It was this country the settlers wanted to tame, where they wanted to grow wheat, to hold the land in their own right and pass it on to their children, their grandchildren and their issue forever.

On a thousand acres of partly cleared land, Julius Hoffmayer grew wheat, barley, rye, sorghum and stock peas. And two years after his father died in 1924, the farm was made to pay: prices were good and every penny was put to paying off the debts to the banks, his father's clubs, wine merchants and fashionable Melbourne stores. Then, suddenly, in 1931, prices collapsed and the winter rains did not come.

Before the drought, Julius owned fifteen Clydesdale horses, a team of eight bullocks, a dozen pigs, fifty fowls, eight cows and a bull. There were three other horses and the mare was serviced by a leased stallion. Now, the Clydesdales and the bull were gone to the slaughterhouse and the fowls reduced to a dozen.

Since Maria had come to the house in 1922, the daily routine was always the same. They all, save Louisa, rose at six – no matter the season or the weather. In the winters, the ice in the puddles cracked beneath her boots as she went to the tank for the water; and in the summers, the hot north wind was often blowing as the sun was rising behind the pine trees.

In the hot weather, Julius watered the big vegetable garden and weeded the beds while Carl fed and combed the horses. In good times, Maria served the men porridge, eggs and bacon and home-made bread; but now breakfast was reduced to stale *schwartzbrot*, tea and dripping. Then Julius and Carl yoked the oxen and went to work in the bush.

No matter how hard Maria cleaned and scrubbed, the kitchen always smelt of cinders, kerosine and candle grease. Every room in the house was dark and when she went down the hall to sweep and dust the bedrooms, Maria was aware of mothballs and ageing lavender.

The routine of the Hoffmayer house was as unchanging as a church service. Each morning upon waking, Julius wound his silver watch, cleaned his steel-framed spectacles, put them

17

on and read his Bible for five minutes. Then he dressed, pulling his moleskin trousers and collarless shirt over his longjohns, opened the bedroom door and walked down the hall in his stockinged feet to put on his boots and inspect the horses. There were three things necessary to run a profitable farm, Julius said: God, hard work and horses. Tractors and petrol-driven machinery, he said, were the work of the devil. But Maria thought another thing was essential – and that was love.

The Hoffmayers' was a silent house: Julius had sold his father's piano and there was no electricity, either for light or a radio. During the day when she was in the house by herself, all Maria heard was the sound of the crows and parakeets calling in the trees, and the thunder echoing in the late afternoon.

It was the summer before last when Julius started to go to Louisa's room late at night. That was an uncertain season, with days so hot the shingles would split and crack on the roof like pistol shots; the milk went sour in less than an hour and swarms of flies beat against the windowpanes. Then the weather would turn south-west with sudden squalls, heavy rain, puzzling clear spells, quick thunderstorms and fierce winds that brought down trees and raised the dust from the fallowed paddocks. That year, the roses died in the garden and never recovered. It was the summer of the mice plague and Louisa found it hard to sleep after that.

When Louisa fell ill, Julius, for some reason Maria could not fathom, moved her into a bedroom at the back of the house. This room had not been renovated and was still papered with pages from the *Illustrated London News* – on the walls were steel engravings of General Gordon at Khartoum, a textile factory at Lucknow and Paris fashions for April 1870. This was the room where Maria's stepdaughter slept and where her husband visited in the darkness of the night.

Now, with the drought, the nights seemed longer than any other season and Maria often lay awake long after Julius returned to bed, silently and with no explanation. She knew his secret, but it would never be discussed.

Her Aunt Matilde never tired of telling her the story. In the winter of 1841, her grandparents, Erich and Else Ampt, decided to emigrate to South Africa. They boarded the small sailing barque, the Alfred, *at Hamburg. They stopped at Plymouth and then at Rio de Janiero, where for the first time, they tasted oranges. After Rio, the voyage seemed very long – three adults and seven children died – and, after six months, they climbed down a rope ladder and were rowed ashore to a small town at the head of a river. The land was flat and fires burned in the hinterland. Grandfather Erich stood on the beach and said: 'Where is the jungle? Where are the brightly coloured birds? This is not Africa.' They were on the south coast of Australia at a place called Adelaide.*

Grandmother Else was fiercely devout – she prayed three times a day and read the lesson at the Sunday services. As the baggage was thrown ashore and the men stood idle and confused, she said: 'Let's get on with it: this is our new land and there is much to do.'

The men stayed behind with the ship and, that evening, the women and their belongings were put on to a horse-drawn dray and taken to a settlement called Klemsig. In the morning, they found they were in a two-roomed house in the middle of a paddock where the grass was long and dry. The temperature was over a hundred degrees and they knew nobody. A well-meaning neighbour gave Else a skinned ox head with its eyes still in its sockets. She screamed and fell down in a faint.

'That,' her aunt said, 'was how your family began in Australia.'

But that night, as she lay in bed, she thought: I have no family.

Three

When Frank got further north, he found the country was broken and undulating with sandhills glistening on the sky line and the bush creeping back. It looked to Frank as though the settlers had stopped clearing: there was no point in bringing in any more country now. When he stopped to have a spell and stretch his legs, he saw that weeds and thistles were growing in the gravel: the fences were down, the road rutted, the sun as hard as brass and the silence was unnerving. As there were no petrol garages, he had to lug one of the ten-gallon cans down from the truck and fill the tank. During one four-hour spell of driving, he saw only one car, loaded with luggage and furniture, going south. There was no one else and the barren, empty country seemed lifeless, except for the crows and the sparrows – and now and again, he saw eagles hovering in the updraughts.

At the railway sidings, stacks of wheat were piled high like the walls of great redoubts in the war. The waggons lay empty, weeds growing through the wheel spokes and ragged washing flapped from lines strung up between the boxcars. A dust storm loomed on the horizon and the wind swung around to the north. The earth was grey and although Frank knew the drought was bad, he was not prepared for this.

At Dimboola, gangs of tired men were working on some kind of public project. The earth was piled high; lines of horses and carts waited; a donkey engine threw cinders and black smoke into the air; the men sweated in the heat. Frank had to stop while a waggon of rock crossed the road, but nobody greeted him, and he could see no purpose in the activity. Once he was past the road block, he entered the main street with its ornate pubs and closed shops, but decided to keep going. The petrol gauge measured half-full, and he had ten gallons in the back. Grit was in his eyes, his shirt was stuck to his back and his feet sweated inside his boots. He pulled out his watch, saw it was almost half-past four, and wondered if he should turn round and go back for a beer. It was too late for that now; he saw the signpost, Rubicon 65 miles, and swung off the highway on to a narrow road. He would be there in a couple of hours, and he would see the stock and station agent in the morning.

In the hot west light, the dun green bush closed in around the cleared ground and he came upon salt lakes, black and gleaming. The tree stumps looked like military cemeteries and the country like a battlefront. There were no buildings – no sign of habitation – and Frank started to wonder if there was a settlement in this menacing wilderness. Of water, there was no evidence and no windmills turned.

When next he stopped, Frank pissed into the bracken and kicked at the soil with his boots. The blood-red earth was as fine as talcum powder, and drifted away on the late afternoon breeze. Would anything of any value, he wondered, grow up here? The sun was as red as the soil and hung in the western sky; it was huge and looked as though it would devour the entire earth as he swung up, slammed the truck door and continued north. Even he had misgivings now.

By six, he was very tired and it was obvious he would not get to Rubicon that night: he was starting to doze at the wheel; the dust in the cab was as thick as a fog and his stomach was starting to grip with hunger. The dirt road was endless, the sun low and he looked for a place to spend the night. There was no point in driving further, but at least he was alone and there was no one to steal his money. Where was the bricklayer now? There were thousands like him, tramping the country and thieving off their mates.

He saw a tall palm tree next to a gutted corrugated-iron house, and this gave him comfort: it was a sign that men did live and work here. The wire fences were tangled and an old dray lay in the front paddock. He stopped the Chev, climbed down and rolled a cigarette. The only sound was the wind, still warm and uncomfortable. Frank took off his shirt, hung it over the rear-vision mirror and watched the spindleweeds rolling across the road. Then he saw the windmill behind the house, but its blades were still, despite the breeze. There was no sound of the pump grinding and he knew the stock trough would be empty, the lizards sleeping in the dust. As he climbed through the fence, the starlings flew in and perched on the sagging power lines. The sun was behind the bush now and the light through the trees was as red as blood as Frank walked through the weeds and thorns.

This place, with its shallow depressions and salt lakes, looking like the drowned trenches at Polygon Wood, reminded him of northern France. *Keep to the high ground.* But there was no high ground here.

The iron house was unlined and the fireplace full of blackened rubble; the flies buzzed and the building was hot from the heat of the day. Frank cleared a space on the hearth with his boot, went outside, gathered some wood, tossed it inside and strode back to the truck. In the gathering dark, he shouldered his kit and pulled on his shirt. It reeked of sweat and he found the water can – at least he would have a shave in the morning. As he went back up the track, he saw a horse standing by the windmill. And next to the animal, he thought he could see a man.

The man strolled easily through the bush and, as he came up, Frank saw he was carrying a rifle. He put his kit and water can on the ground and waited. He had left his shotgun in the truck.

'G'day,' the man said. 'Do you need a hand?'

He was tall and thin – over six feet – and was wearing a waistcoat, moleskin trousers, riding boots and a slouch hat; and he was black-skinned, his curly hair falling down to his shoulders.

'G'day,' Frank answered. 'I'm okay.'

They faced each other in the twilight and the aborigine put the stock of his rifle on the ground. Frank thought all the blacks had been driven away. The man grinned and said: 'Time for a beer, eh?'

'Maybe.' Frank picked up his kit: he didn't want company.

'You going to Rubicon?' The aborigine's voice was as soft and quiet as running water.

'That's right.'

'There's no other place to go, is there?'

'It doesn't look like it.'

'Not up here.' The black took up the water can and put it on his shoulder. 'I'll give you a hand anyway.'

When they got to the house, the aborigine tossed the wood into the fireplace and started a fire. Frank lit the hurricane lamp and foraged in his kit, feeling for his sheath knife and the hard lump of the whisky bottle. He looked at the rifle propped against the wall by the door: it was an old Martini-Henry, well oiled and in good repair. This man had European blood and the odd thing was that he was not apprehensive. In some strange way it was as though they were already mates. He had known several blacks before and they were a shiftless, drunken mob – not like the Indians and Afghans who worked hard for all their strange ways. This man moved silently as he put the wood on the fire – he was as thin and as strong as a tree. Would he hang about for a free feed? Frank thought he would, but he could go when he wanted as he had that horse. Then the aborigine reached inside his jacket and pulled out a bottle.

'Do you want a drink?'

'Okay.' This man was no ordinary rouseabout, nor was he your ordinary black: he was confident and upright.

'It's brandy.' He passed the bottle over and watched Frank to see what he would do.

'That'll do.' He looked at the label: it was French. Where would a black get that? He pulled the cork, drank and passed the bottle back.

The aborigine wiped the neck, drank and set it down on the floor between them. 'That settles the dust, don't it?' Then he came over, stuck out his hand and said: 'The name's Ray

Stark.' His hand was hard and his fingers strong.

'Cameron, Frank Cameron.'

'Did you get a surprise, seeing me?' Ray sat down in the firelight, pushed the bottle over and rolled a cigarette.

'It's not exactly crowded around here.' Frank took another shot of brandy and didn't bother to wipe the neck of the bottle.

'And I'm a black man as well.'

'I thought you lot had moved on.'

Ray laughed. 'You mean driven on, shot out.'

Frank didn't want to get involved – every man to himself, he thought. 'That's progress.'

'I got some tucker in me saddlebag.' Ray said. 'Do you want some? It's regular stuff – not grubs or anything like that.'

Frank thought. 'Okay.'

'Right,' Ray said as he got up. 'See you in a moment.' And he disappeared like a shadow.

Frank went over and looked at the rifle. Stark was a hunter and trapper and knew what he was doing. He picked it up, put it to his shoulder, put it back then spread out his bed roll. The moths were fluttering against the lamp as he dragged on his pullover and lit a cigarette. It was night now and the cold was coming down. He picked up Stark's battered tobacco tin, opened it and smelt: it was pipe tobacco. What was a black man doing around these parts? He had heard stories of blacks stealing sheep and molesting white women, but those days were over now. Frank also knew the aborigines were unpredictable, living off the land, coming and going, melting away and reappearing. But his father had employed Henry for ten years and there was never any trouble; and when the neighbours objected, the old man stuck to his guns. Each man to his deserts. This time tomorrow night, he would be on the block and the work would begin – the drought, he thought, had to break sooner or later.

'It's bully beef and tinned beans.' Ray stood in the doorway. 'And I got some bread.' He put the food down and crouched in front of the fire. 'What brings you around here?'

'I'm leasing a block.'

'The farmers are having it tough,' Ray said. 'Something's happened.'

'It doesn't affect you, does it?'

'Nah.' Ray laughed. 'Blackfellows like me don't own property, we live by our wits. If you don't own nothing, they can't take it away from you, can they?'

'That's one way of looking at it.'

'It's the only way – fellows like me ain't got a choice, but I don't mind. I've got me ways.' Ray opened the tin and cut the bread while Frank put the beans on the coals. 'Where's the block?'

'Kurnbrun.'

'There's Germans out there.'

'There's a few up north.'

'Tough bastards.'

'They are.'

Ray passed over the bread and bully beef. 'You a returned man?'

'Yes.'

'I thought they'd stopped dividing up them blocks for returned soldiers.'

'They have,' Frank replied. 'I got mine from some poor bugger who didn't make it.'

'There's plenty of those around these parts. I reckon the beans are about done.'

They ate the food by the fire as the soft wind blew around the old house; the iron creaked and the dead trees scraped against the rusted walls.

'Why did you stop and give me a hand?' Frank asked.

'Aw, I like to see who's coming and going.' Ray grinned. 'Some of them call me the Shadow – and other things.'

'And what do you do?'

The aborigine pointed to the rifle. 'I'm a hunter and trapper, and there's no shortage up here. Rabbits, dingoes, sparrows – we've got them all. I'm the last of the Mohicans, they won't ever get Ray Stark. Do you know where the block is?'

'No, I'm seeing the agent in the morning.' Frank felt stiff and tired now. 'I think I might turn in.'

'Okay, I'll get meself going.'

As Ray got up, Frank said: 'Don't forget your brandy.'

'Jesus, no, I wouldn't do that. Do you want one for the road?'

'No thanks.'

Ray took up his rifle and moved toward the door. 'I'll see you around, Mr Cameron.'

The door creaked and he was gone.

When Frank stretched out on his bed roll and watched the fire, he found he couldn't sleep. The bush seemed noisy; the wind blew up; he sweated and, somewhere outside, the branch of a tree snapped. As he lay awake, he thought he heard the sound of the rustling of grass and the cracking of dry sticks. Was Ray Stark outside? The truck was locked, but he had still forgotten to bring the shotgun in. He reached over for his knife and pushed it under his kit. But when nothing happened, he felt easier and slept.

His father's house was set among trees as high as church steeples; the stumps around the building looked like sawn-off elephants' feet and oozed gum that ran in glistening rivulets down the bark where the bull-ants ran; at the back, the ring-barked trees stood like black skeletons. The trees of the bush were as slender as flagpoles, and ferns grew along the shady creeks with the wildflowers, where the honeyeaters, golden whistlers and crimson rosellas flew. At night, the bush owls hooted, the possums' eyes gleamed in the moonlight and the gentle rain fell.

Henry, the black, lived in a shed away from the house.

He and his brother caught freshwater crayfish and eels in the streams; they built a tree house, played marbles with the stoppers from soft-drink bottles and shot rabbits with the .22.

On washing days, his mother was often attacked by swooping magpies and the smoke from the wash-house chimney rose straight up to God in the breathless sky. She was a strong and beautiful woman, who wore her hair pinned up: she had a wide mouth and grey-green eyes, and he loved her very much.

In the house there were but three books: Great Expectations, *the Holy Bible and the* Poems of Alfred, Lord Tennyson. *When the day's work was done and the candles were flickering and he lay in his bed, his mother would kneel beside him, her hands red and raw from working in the bush, and read to him:*

When will the clouds be aweary of fleeting?
When will the heart be aweary of beating?
And nature die?
Never, oh! never, nothing will die;
The stream flows,
The wind blows,
The cloud fleets,
The heart beats,
Nothing will die.

All that summer, they cleared the trees, his father and Henry with the broadaxe, his mother firing the stumps with saltpetre and his brother dragging the bush into piles. They owned eight cows, two horses, six pigs and a dozen fowls, which he fed bran and pollard night and morning. The nearest church was fifteen miles away and each Sunday they held their own services in the front room, his mother playing the button accordian and his father saying the prayers. She had a fine soprano voice and his favourite hymn was Onward Christian Soldiers.

That winter it rained for three months. The creeks overflowed, the flour went mouldy, his father's boots fell apart, the shingle roof leaked and his bedclothes were always damp. His mother started to cough and fell ill; she worked until she dropped and his father put her to bed under the hand-embroidered quilt in the smoky bedroom. She lay there for three weeks; her face became as white as parchment; she coughed blood into a saucepan, prayed to God and died.

His father made a coffin from hand-split timber and she

was taken away. He was left alone to look after the house as the rain continued to fall: he lit a kerosine lamp and wept until they returned.

The magpies and parrots woke him in the morning, and as he packed his gear he thought of Ray Stark.

Rubicon lay in a shallow depression, where the country was cleared and the dust billowed. The mirages shimmered and the grey bush lay like a dark stain on the horizon. To the south a fire was burning, but Frank reckoned the north wind would keep it away. The first building he saw was the water tank, standing on a lattice tower in the brush, then a shingled church steeple among the pine trees. To the east, the country was as flat as a billiard table and the sun glared from the roofs of tin sheds and barns. Twice, the road crossed the railway line where the tracks ran north and empty waggons stood on the side tracks: there would be a water train once a week, as he had no doubt that the town reservoir was empty. As for bores and wells, Frank was not sure how long they would last. The sun was high and, despite the heat, several farmers were harrowing, the dust thick behind their tractors and the starlings wheeling.

In some paddocks he saw stone chimneys standing like ransacked tombs and hay sheds staggering sideways before the prevailing wind. There were several small wooden churches surrounded by ancient pines and yellow cypresses, but the cemeteries were overgrown and the windows covered with corrugated iron. Patches of bush still grew, the trees stunted, their grey and gnarled roots exposed as the soil had blown away to the south. Sometimes it had even drifted and settled on the cottage and factory roofs of Melbourne. This country, some men said, was blowing away, but Frank did not believe that.

To the west, he saw a farmer clearing: he was smashing the bush down with a huge roller on a timber frame mounted on waggon wheels. To Frank's surprise, this man was using bullocks. This farmer would be lucky to clear eight acres a day and this was how the land had been brought in until tractors. Were there farmers so poor, they could not borrow the money for modern machinery? Then Frank remembered: the banks were repossessing property all over Australia now. He crossed the railway lines once more and drove down a straight road toward a row of wooden cottages where washing hung on the front verandahs and wireless masts stood, fragile, against the dusty sky.

As Frank drew close to the settlement of Rubicon, he passed a man mounted on a tall brown horse and wearing a slouch hat. This time, Frank *was* saluted, but the man was carrying a double-barrelled shotgun.

Four

On Federation Street, the tar bubbled in the heat, and the roses in the centre garden strip were dying. Frank drove slowly and thought about the armed man on the horse. Cars and buggies were parked at the kerb-side and horses stood at the drinking troughs. It was noon and few people were about, some standing in the shade of the wide verandahs and others in the entrance to the post office. The kerb-stones were about a foot high and some shops were boarded up and vacant. He saw the stock and station agent's building, drove on and stopped at the Royal Hotel, where three old men were sitting outside drinking beer. The building was made of sandstone; its paint was yellow and peeling and washing hung in the dark verandahs above. The men's faces were as old and as wrinkled as the bark of a tree; they wore threadbare waistcoats and stained, broad-brimmed hats. One had a walking stick between his knees and they all looked up as Frank got out and slammed the truck door.

The heat from the pavement burned through the soles of his boots as he stepped into the shade. A dog lay stretched out in a bricked-up doorway and a horse and waggon clattered past. Frank raised his hand to his hat to the locals, opened the hotel door and went inside. The carpet in the lobby was worn down by farmers' boots and the room smelt of ten thousand cigarettes; from the kitchen came the odour of boiled vegetables and fried onions. From the bar door came the sound of men's voices. A dog-eared hotel register lay on the office counter and a pencil dangled. The narrow stairs led to the dark rooms above, and somewhere a wireless played.

By the front window, a man was asleep in an armchair; his hat was over his face and a Winchester shotgun lay propped against the wall. A door banged, and from the back of the building came the sound of whistling. The sleeping man shifted and snorted and his hat fell to the floor – he was young and unshaven, his face grimy. He was an itinerent worker, a shooter – the country was full of them. Frank crossed the hall and went into the bar. The place was cavernous, the walls lined with sporting photographs and trophies; the floor was bare and a Union Jack was draped on the shelves above the counter. Three men were drinking and talking to the barman.

'G'day,' the barman said as he came over. 'What can I do for you?'

The men at the bar turned to look at the newcomer. 'I'll have a beer,' Frank answered.

The barman turned the spiggot on the barrel. 'Just travelling through?'

'I've leased a block up here.'

'Have you? Whereabouts?'

'Kurnbrun.'

'Pretty, shitty country, if you don't mind me saying so.'

Frank drank his beer down. 'I think it'll do.'

'Are you a returned man?'

'That's right.'

The man stuck out his hand over the bar. 'Welcome to Rubicon.'

'Thanks.'

'You might have a tough time – it's all uncleared up there.'

'I've got plenty of time,' Frank replied. 'There's only me.'

The barman filled the empty glass. 'Have this one on the management.'

'Thanks.' Frank fished out his tobacco tin. 'When did it last rain?'

'Jesus, I don't remember. Over twelve months. Things aren't so good up here, but it's the same all over, isn't it? We can always do with returned men.'

'Where can I get a tractor?'

'That's no worries,' the barman said. 'You can get one real cheap at Farrar's up the street. There's dozens of them – all repossessed.' He leaned over the counter. 'There's Huns at Kurnbrun, I suppose you know that.'

'That won't worry me.'

'My name's Jim Banks, by the way. I'm the owner.' He considered Frank. 'No, I don't think that would worry you. You fought the bastards and lived to tell the tale, didn't you?'

'That's one way of putting it.' He thought of the sisters in the German field hospital.

'Do you want to meet some of the locals?'

'Thanks,' Frank answered, 'but I'd better be going, I've got a lot to do.'

'Right. You didn't tell me your name.'

Frank told him, drained his glass and asked, 'Where can I get some groceries?'

'At Ballantine's over the road. George will fix you up.'

'Thanks,' Frank said. 'I'll see you later.'

'Good luck, mate, and mind them Huns.'

Frank turned on his boot heels and didn't reply.

When Frank got outside, he saw another armed man riding up the street by the war memorial, noticed the flag flying at the post office and thought about leaving his name there. But what was the point? There was nobody to write to him, except a cousin who, he had last heard, was droving cattle in the Diamantina. He walked down to the estate agents, got a sketch map of the whereabouts of the block, paid three months' lease in cash and thought about opening a bank account. He was on the point of going into the bank, but decided not: his money was safer on him these days.

He crossed the street, paused by the war memorial, looked at the unfamiliar names on the bronze plaque and walked down to Ballantine's emporium. After the dust and heat, the store seemed cool and the boards creaked under his boots. The place was huge and packed with merchandise. He guessed the bald man behind the counter was George Ballantine.

Every night after tea and when the day's trading was over,

George Ballantine drank three whiskies and read or listened to the wireless. He always drank Dewar's, poured from a cut-glass decanter which had belonged to his father. Hector Ballantine had been given it by the Rubicon Progress Association for twenty-five years' faithful service – that and a gold fob watch, which George always wore in the right-hand pocket of his waistcoat.

Although George left school at the age of fourteen, he was well read: he liked the novels of Sir Walter Scott, Jeffrey Farnol, Arthur Conan Doyle and Rider Haggard. He had a sizeable library of his own, but was a regular customer of the Mechanics' Institute where, on Friday afternoons, he sometimes played billiards with John Carver. But, unlike Carver, George had never been in the bar of the Royal Hotel. Carver also read Rider Haggard and, between breaks, they would talk about books.

As he owed no money, the Depression did not immediately affect George, but now trade in the emporium was slack – sometimes no more than half a dozen people in a day came in to buy anything. The stock was becoming dusty; cobwebs festooned the hardware; sometimes weevils were found in the flour; the jam went sugary; the candles melted in the summer heat; and silverfish were eating the bond stationery, the school exercise books and the funeral cards.

George did not offer the specials which customers could get at Withers', nor was his store as modern, but he gave informal credit and did not charge interest. He had no precise figure of what he was owed, but guessed it was probably around £2000. By the late summer of 1932, it seemed he could not move around the building for stock, but he was sure the bad times would pass.

'G'day,' Frank said, 'I've got a block up here and I want to open an account.'

Ballantine was polite enough and fingered his big white moustache. 'Do you have any identification? I hope you don't mind, but there's all kinds coming through these days.'

'That's okay.' Frank showed him his driver's licence and the sketch map from the agent. He bought some tea, flour, oatmeal, sugar, matches and tinned food. He signed the docket and said: 'Thank you, Mr Ballantine.'

'Thank you, Mr Cameron.' The store-keeper's armbands gleamed in the half-light. 'I wish you luck out there. If you want any help, let me know.'

'I'll do that,' Frank said as he carried the box toward the door.

'Friday's the big day in town,' George Ballantine called. 'But I expect you know that.'

'It usually is,' Frank replied. 'I'll see you.'

After he put the groceries in the back of the Chev, Frank decided to walk up Federation Street and take in the sights. Why were there armed men on horseback? The place looked quiet enough. As he walked up the street toward the railway station, he saw children playing in the dusty alleys: they were ragged and should have been at school. A few people were moving in the darkness of the shops; cats slept in several front windows; he heard the sound of the hammer and anvil at the blacksmith's and looked at the horses in the yard. He would have to buy a good animal and studied the stock. There was a big, strong gelding that might do. Then he stood on the kerb as a big Hupmobile straight-8 drove past: someone in town had money. The butcher, a big man with a bloodied apron, was standing outside his shop where the carcasses hung. The man looked at Frank: this fellow examined every newcomer.

'G'day,' the butcher said.

Frank acknowledged, and continued up the street as the dust clouds loomed in the west.

At the station, Frank stood about, looked at the storage sheds and watched the farmers filling the tanks on their trucks and drays from the water train. He would be doing that soon if the well on the block was dry. The stores on the other side of the street were vacant, but the town lawyer was still there. Frank read the notice – he was in attendance Tuesdays and Fridays. Then he stopped in front of the Regal Cinema; he hadn't been to the pictures for months. The torn posters flapped in the wind as he looked to see what was on. It was a double feature: *The Cisco Kid* followed by *The Return of Dr Fu Manchu.* As he stood there, a tall man who looked like John Barrymore opened the glass doors and walked over to the Royal. Before six months were out, he would know all these people.

On the way back to the truck, Frank saw a well-dressed man getting out of the back of the Hupmobile and, to his surprise, he saw a uniformed chauffeur sitting in the front. The man was wearing a homburg hat and sported a big Victorian moustache. As he disappeared inside the building, Frank noted the sign: Withers Emporium. That, Frank guessed, was the boss. He smiled – every small town had one, someone who made money no matter how bad the times. He got to the Chev, climbed in, started the motor and looked at the sketch map. Kurnbrun was due west, over the railway tracks. He left town and took a straight narrow road which disappeared into the bush. The country was grey and all the ponds and dams dry. He thought of a poem by Henry Lawson – this was the Never-Never Land. After twenty minutes or so, he passed a man on a horse. When he looked back in the driving mirror, he saw it was Ray Stark.

Frank had little trouble finding the block. He drove the truck down the narrow track from the road and stopped outside the cottage: it was wooden and two-roomed, with a tin chimney and the remains of a vegetable garden where thistles grew among the junk. The windmill was immobile and the tank stand had collapsed. The white parakeets watched him from the dead trees as he fossicked around the abandoned yard. The previous owner had been beaten by the uncertain seasons and the bank, but he would not be. The world needed wheat and he would grow it, despite the slump and the chaos in the cities.

The hut was made of hand-split timber with corrugated iron at the back; the roof shingles were narrow and held down with branches and pegs. The last man had known what he was doing, despite the outcome. He kicked at the earth, bent down, picked it up and let it run through his fingers. It was rich and red: all that was needed was a little rain. Frank pulled the wooden peg from the latch and went inside. The floor was of stamped earth; the place smelled of kerosine and candle grease; spiderwebs drifted from the rafters and some of the hand-adzed walls were lined with old newspapers. In the gloom, he peered at the news for August 1914: 'Angel Appears at Mons'. He smiled and went into the other room. There, he found an old meat safe in disrepair and a hand-made broom. In the back corner something on the floor caught his eye: it was a child's teddy bear. Frank was about to toss it outside, but changed his mind and placed it on the rough shelf above the fireplace. Children had been in this place and that comforted him.

By six, Frank had brought most of his gear in: the bags of flour and sugar, the biscuit tins and the canned food were neatly stacked and the kerosine lamp stood on the table. He gathered some wood, lit the fire and poured out some water for his billy tea. First thing in the morning, he would look at the windmill and the pump. Somewhere near there would be a creek, but that no doubt was dry. It was time for a drink, but he remembered the armed man on the road into town, picked up his shotgun, broke it, oiled the breech and pulled the barrels through. He loaded it and propped it against the wall near the fireplace.

After the hot day, the night was cold and Frank sat in front of the fire. Now he was a dry-farmer: maybe his luck would change. But the depression had descended and he thought of the unemployed miners, armed with axe-handles, shouting at the police in their frustration; of the bricklayer with the knife; and of Ray Stark emerging from the bush by the tin house. Then he thought of Jim Banks, the publican. *Mind them Huns.*

When he was thirteen, the war between the English and the

Boers began. His brother had been given three lead soldiers – a grenadier guardsman, a Scottish piper and a machine-gunner. Even at the age of nineteen, he still put them on his dressing table, next to his shaving mug and a picture of his mother. Fred was a strong lad, with broad shoulders, sandy hair and bright blue eyes: he could work ten hours a day in the bush and never complained; he had muscles as hard as steel and could lift an eighty-pound cream can as though it were a baby. On Saturday nights, he rode his horse to the town dances, flirted with the girls and chatted with the locals. Fred was popular, played cricket and football and was the Best and Fairest in the season of 1898.

One hot Sunday evening, Fred told his father he was going to join up and fight the Boers, for Queen and Country. His father looked up, stroked his grey moustache, and said: 'I want you to stay and help me and Frank, but if you want to go, I cannot stop you.'

Fred said he did, he said that was what he most wanted to do. One week later, they drove him into town to the railway station. There were lots of lads on the platform; they were holding their portmanteaux and Gladstone bags as the engine hissed and steamed and their mothers wept. His father drove back to the farm, and they milked the cows night and morning, separated the cream, fed the pigs, dug the vegetable garden and split the logs for the stove.

Each Saturday, he drove into town for the paper and by the light of the lamp, he and his father followed the campaign: in December 1899, the Australian and Canadian volunteers landed at Cape Town and the war looked as though it was going well. In February 1900, General Sir Redvers Buller lifted the siege of the town of Ladysmith; in May, Mafeking was relieved and in June, Buller's army took Pretoria. Then, in August, a postman arrived one afternoon on horseback and gave them a letter. It was a cablegram: Fred had died two months earlier of pneumonia.

Five

Maria was sandsoaping the table top when the knock came at the door. It was an unfamiliar sound and it was probably the Indian hawker, for no one else called. She wanted nothing, could afford nothing, and prepared herself to send the man away. She moved across the floorboards of the kitchen. If it was the Hindu, where was the sound of his horse and cart? When Maria opened the door, a strange man was standing on the threshold: he was tall, wearing a slouch hat, a collarless shirt and braces. His hair was fair and his eyes as blue as agate. The man took off his hat and smiled, stooping awkwardly in the doorway. In the fowl yard, a rooster crowed and the noonday sun beat down. 'My name is Frank Cameron,' the man said.

'Good day, Mr Cameron.'

'I am your new neighbour.' He looked at the tall woman, with her black hair pinned back, her long dress, apron and boots. Her mouth was wide and her features handsome, and she was wearing a heavy gold ring on the third finger of her left hand.

'I am Mrs Hoffmayer.' Maria put out her hand in the European way and took him by surprise.

Frank shoved his hat under his arm and gripped her strong, cold fingers. 'I thought I should make myself known.'

'You will come in,' Maria said. 'My husband is absent.'

'Thank you,' Frank answered; he bent his head and stepped inside.

The kitchen seemed cool after the heat outside as he stood in the centre of the room. Maria's copper and cast-iron pots hung in rows; the table top gleamed white; the German crockery sat on the dresser; the floorboards were spotless and the grandfather clock chimed the quarter-hour. Somewhere from the back of the house came the sound of someone crying, but Maria Hoffmayer appeared not to have heard. Above the dresser he saw the hand-written scroll: GOD IS LIFE.

'Please put your hat on the table, Mr Cameron.' She lifted the hot plate on the range, poked at the coals and took the kettle from the hearth. 'Would you like some tea?'

'Thank you, I would.' The crying ceased and the dark red curtains drifted at the entrance to the hall.

Maria opened the stove door and tossed in several small logs, then filled the kettle from the enamel pitcher. 'We have very few visitors.' She straightened up and stared at him. 'Mr Hoffmayer will be in shortly; he will have his dinner.'

Why did this attractive woman wear a long black dress, and why was there no electricity and running water? He guessed the house had been built in the 1880s. Frank sat at the table while she arranged the cups and saucers. 'I've taken up a lease on the Kurnbrun block.'

Maria stood at the stove and considered the visitor. He was a soldier-settler, a returned man, and he appeared to have injured his leg in battle. What would he think of Germans? And what would Julius think of him? Mr Cameron looked very strong and determined. He was wearing a sheath knife and his boots were new. 'I wish you luck,' she said. 'That is hard country up there, but perhaps no harder than here.' Once more came the sound of crying. 'You will excuse me: I have a sick stepdaughter.'

As Frank rose, she bowed and disappeared down the hall. A door creaked and he heard the sound of voices, more crying and then silence. He remained at the table: it was hand-adzed and had been scrubbed a thousand times. A leg of boiled mutton and a home-made loaf of bread sat on a plate under a muslin flycover; the black kettle started to steam on the range and the clock ticked. Rows of four-pound biscuit tins sat on the shelves and a besom made of twigs was leaning against the wall by the back door. He was reminded of the peasants in France and Belgium, but the war was behind him now. Frank thought of the sisters in the German military hospital, the Christmas of 1917, the chocolates and the carols sung in German. It was as though the Hoffmayers were living in the nineteenth century and he was puzzled.

Then he heard her coming back up the hall and she appeared at the door. 'My stepdaughter has a summer cold,' she said.

'They are the hardest to get rid of,' Frank replied.

'You are a returned soldier?' Maria made the tea and put the pot on the table.

'Yes.'

'We have had two bad seasons. These are difficult times, I am told.'

'There is a depression.' Frank stirred his tea, drank and wondered if he could light a cigarette.

'Is your block cleared?'

Frank laughed. 'No. But there's a cottage of sorts and a home paddock.'

'Is there any water?'

'There's a windmill and pump. I think I can get it going.'

Maria raised her head. 'We are very short of water here.'

Frank took the hint. 'I'm sure I can get the well working.'

Maria was curious and thought of asking him about his wife and family, but decided not. That was his business. 'Do you want some bread and liverwurst?'

Frank got up from the table. 'No thank you, I'd better get going.'

She did not attempt to persuade him to stay. 'How did you get here? I did not hear your horse.'

'I've got a truck. I parked it on the road – some animals don't like them.' He took up his hat and stood by the door. 'Thanks for the tea.'

'I wish you well, Mr Cameron.'

'Thanks. I might meet your husband next time.'

'I will tell him you called.'

Frank turned on his heel by the doorstep, hit out at the flies, put his hat on his head and walked down the track to the road. The parakeets swooped from the gum trees and went for him. As he waved them away, he saw a man watching him from the far end of a fallowed paddock where the dust rose in swirls. Frank stopped and saluted, but the man did not respond.

Maria sat in the kitchen and thought about Mr Cameron: at last they had a neighbour – even if he was a mile to the north. But she wasn't sure whether to be pleased or not. While Julius would be aloof and suspicious, Carl would hate the newcomer on sight. She, too, was disturbed and wondered what the new man might do. He would clear his land, go into Rubicon once a week, drink with the other men at the Returned Soldiers' League and she might not see him for months. If that was how it turned out, so be it. They did not need neighbours – they were self-sufficient, Julius would see to that. When she looked at the clock and saw it was almost one o'clock, she knew the men would not now be home for their midday meal, and went into the front bedroom, where the curtains were drawn against the summer sun.

Maria stood in the dark room, with its stone fireplace, and looked at the iron double bed where each night she lay listening to Julius talking and groaning in his nightmares. The bed had been brought out from Saxony and transported from South Australia by ox-cart. She wished she could move into the other bedroom, but he would never permit that. For the past ten years she had slept with her husband on the horse-hair mattress beneath the patchwork quilt which had been made by Julius's mother. Their room smelled of camphor; their clothes were neatly folded in the drawers of the cedar chest – his best suit he used to wear when they used to go to church, her long summer dresses, his striped shirts and her wedding gown wrapped in tissue. Maria thought she had loved him once, but that was long since gone. Hoffmayer family photographs hung on the bedroom walls – there were Johannes and Elvira; their children, Ernst, Paul and Wilhelm; but no sign of August. Julius had removed every photograph

41

of his father from the house, and all that remained was his Bible.

Insects crawled and buzzed against the windowpanes as Maria stood in the shadowy room; then she opened the bottom drawer and took out the box of photographs. They were fading now and being eaten by silverfish; there were no photographs for the last seven years as Julius had even sold his father's Hasselbad camera. The pictures Maria liked best were those of the picnics at the lake with the men in their panamas, the women in their flowery hats and the boys in their cream summer trousers. The lake was full for five years then and they paddled with their trousers rolled up and their dresses hitched up to their knees. The men fished and they had freshwater lobster and redfin for tea; even on the hottest of days, a cool wind blew across the blue water where seabirds ducked and swam and ducks nested in the reeds.

She spread the photographs on the counterpane, blew away the borer dust and looked at the cars – the Fords, a Panhard, a Hupmobile – the picnic spreads of smoked ham, the bottled fruit, the pumpernickel and pots of liverwurst. Then, there were sailing boats and long walks on the shore in the summer evenings when the dragonflies hovered and the frogs croaked in the warm dark.

Maria looked once again at Aunt Matilde who had raised her since she was a baby; Sophie Hoffmayer; the uncles, some in bowler hats and others in wide-brimmed straw deckers; the beautiful, sad Carlotta; but of Carlotta's husband, August, there was no sign. By that time, he was already spending his time in the bars of city hotels and the beds of whores. Maria would visit the lake again, even though it was dry, with trees growing in the salty bed, and where bush rats ran in the picnic spots.

As Maria was putting the photographs back in the box, she heard the sound of Louisa crying once more. She put the box back carefully in the drawer of the chest and took her time, for there was nothing she could do. Julius forbade the doctor, saying the girl was in God's hands; and she was Sophie's daughter, not her's. Although Maria sometimes thought of the wicked stepmother, she knew she was not like that.

As she went past the umbrella stand and the photographs in their heavy black frames, it seemed as though the eyes of all the Hoffmayer family were upon her. She saw that the kerosine lamp on the hall wall was black and needed cleaning and once again opened the door to her stepdaughter's room. This time, Louisa was sitting upright in bed, her eyes vacant and recognising no one. Until recently, she had wandered through the house and garden; she had sat on the front verandah and looked at the gazebo, the overgrown terraces and the dead rose bushes; but now she lay in bed in her room with her childish toys and Dresden figurines.

At seventeen, Louisa Hoffmayer was very beautiful, with blonde hair falling to her shoulders, china-blue eyes and skin as pale as milk. She had not been outside for three weeks now and her face was an unblemished as those of the elegant, coiffeured ladies promenading on the Boulevard des Italiens pasted to her bedroom wall. Louisa sat quite still, her hair lying between her breasts, her nightgown rumpled and her legs up under the sheets. She smelt of musk and rose water and there was a faint trace of sweat glistening on the down of her upper lip. Maria dipped the sponge in the water in the pitcher and wiped Louisa's forehead; the small room was stifling and the branches of a dead rose bush scraped against the windowpane. The child's face was empty of all guile, her neck long and her body flawless, but Maria thought of the terrible line from Romans: *As it is written, there is none righteous, no, not one.*

Suddenly Maria heard the tramp of boots on the verandah outside and a man passed by the window: it was Carl. She left Louisa's room and went quickly down the hall to find him standing in the kitchen: he was taking down the carving knife to cut a slice of mutton. He looked at her with his pale eyes and said: 'I have come back for the rifle – there is a wild pig around.' Maria did not reply, and then her stepson asked: 'Who was the visitor?'

43

'A returned man – he has leased the Kurnbrun block.'

Carl cut the cold meat carefully: the knife was razor-sharp and the slice curled on to the plate. 'What did the soldier want?'

Mr Cameron was a soldier no longer, Maria thought – he was like them: a farmer. 'He came to introduce himself.'

'Ah.' Carl ate the meat. 'So we have a neighbour.'

'He is a mile to the north.'

'A neighbour, nevertheless, and a soldier.' Carl left the kitchen and then returned with the Mannlicher under his arm. Even at twenty, he was one of the best shots in the district. 'My father and I,' the young man said, 'will be home at six.'

The door creaked shut and he was gone. Carl had not gone into his sister's room since the illness had started. He had been taught to believe that the degeneration of human nature was inevitable, that it was God's will and nothing should prevent it.

That night, after tea and the Bible reading, they were in bed by nine. Maria lay under the calico sheets and listened to her husband muttering and groaning in his sleep as the hot north wind blew, ghost-like, through the eaves and posts of the verandah. Julius was sweating and dreaming of his dead father, August.

When she got up at six in the morning and lit the lamp, the first thing she looked at was the wedding photograph of her mother and father. She had looked at it for as long as she could remember; and during the summer, she put it in the top drawer of her chest to make sure it didn't fade. Aunt Matilde and Uncle Ernst were kind to her and, because they could have no children, treated her as their own. She could not remember her mother and father, both of whom had died of diptheria, quickly, one after the other.

Although Ernst and Matilde Ampt were descended from an aristocratic family in Saxony, and were entitled to use the suffix 'von', they had little money and life was hard. Their farm was only five hundred acres and was in the poorer part of the district where the soil was sandy and sterile and nothing seemed to grow. It may have been that Uncle Ernst was an indifferent farmer, for he spent much of his time reading books and playing the Bechstein piano: he liked Mozart and Brahms. Nor was he as devout as his neighbours – for some reason he had not inherited his mother's fierce beliefs. Try as he might to make money from his property, he was often seen dreaming and watching the eagles as he leant over the back-yard gate.

Uncle Ernst said the evening prayers quickly, then poured himself a glass of Rhenish wine and read in front of the fire. She remembered one book he read was Discourses by Plato. He had a large library and played Verdi and Wagner on the Edison gramophone.

It was she and Aunt Matilde who kept the farm going: every morning while Uncle Ernst lay in bed, the two of them would start the household duties. They would feed the work horses, the cows and the ponies; the fire was lit in the kitchen stove; the water buckets were filled and on cold days a fire was lit in the dining room as a special treat.

Uncle Ernst had a big moustache which made him look like Friedrich Nietzsche, whom, he said, was a leading German philosopher.

'Philosophy?' Aunt Matilde used to say. 'Opera? That doesn't get the cows milked, that doesn't get the butter churned or the jam made; that doesn't make the wheat grow.' But she loved him, and they were very happy, even though they had few friends because Uncle Ernst wouldn't go beer-drinking and discuss pig prices, new farm machinery and the weather.

At seven-thirty, she left for school on her pony, taking three jam sandwiches for lunch. In the winter, she had chilblains, sore ears and feet that felt like ice. But she was proud and good-looking, and the other children respected her.

In the evenings, after she and her aunt had washed the dishes, Uncle Ernst sometimes played Nellie Melba on the gramophone. But one night, she heard them raising their voices in the darkness of their room. 'I'm not sure,' Uncle Ernst was saying, 'I'm not sure if I believe there is a God. I'm not sure at all.'

Six

Because the drought would end sooner or later, and because wheat prices would once again rise, Julius Hoffmayer continued to clear his land. He and Carl smashed down the stunted trees with a wooden roller mounted on cart wheels and drawn by six oxen. When that was done, they dug out the stumps by hand and stacked the roots in great piles which looked like the heaps of bones from a charnel house. Then, when the wind was in the right quarter, the piles of trees and roots were set alight: sometimes, when all the farmers were burning, the fires across the plains glowed like the lights of a huge city and the smoke rolled up to two hundred miles away.

Father and son worked from dawn to dusk, flies clinging to their backs, their arms cut by branches, dust in their eyes and noses and sweat running down their bodies. Julius drove the oxen and Carl cleared and piled the trees and dug the stumps. They were both powerful men and could clear eight acres a day.

At forty-eight, Julius's hands were as hard as iron-bark; he was still able to lift a four-bushel bag of wheat and his skin was pitted with the dust of a thousand sand storms. His black beard was streaked with grey and his eyes shone as hard and as bright as a piece of coal. In all four seasons, he wore a wide-brimmed felt hat, stovepipe trousers, a collarless striped shirt and a waistcoat. Although Julius Hoffmayer spoke as little as possible, he was feared – and disliked. Every second Thursday, he strode into George Ballantine's store with his basket of eggs, cheese and liverwurst, refused to negotiate a price, and was paid in cash which he put into a leather purse hanging from his brass-buckled belt. His step was heavy and the wheels of his German waggon crushed the gravel and raised the dust in Federation Street. His two black geldings were the strongest and most envied in town and the produce he sold was the best in the district. Julius was never known to take a drink; he insisted on cash for every bag of wheat, every brown egg, each one of Maria's creamy cheeses, and did not have a bank account. He borrowed nothing and owed nothing; he saluted no one as he rode into Rubicon, did his business and left, the wheels of his cart rumbling over the railway lines and creaking on the ruts of the Kurnbrun road. Some said Julius Hoffmayer was one of the richest farmers in Rubicon; but no one really knew.

Carl was as fair as his father was dark. His eyes were as pale as the sky at dawn; his hair shone like brass; his lips were thin and bloodless; his forehead high and his body as strong as the horse he rode. Every year since he was fifteen he had turned up at the Rubicon Show as silently as his father and won the shooting competiton – for both rifle and shotgun – and gone away. He was never known to have spoken to a girl and, despite his good looks, none was ever known to have spoken to him.

Even though the Hoffmayers were cast out of the church because of the infamy of August, both Julius and Carl still believed that faith alone ensured salvation and that man had to abandon himself to God without seeking to penetrate the mystery of His will. God would end or not end the drought; He would restore or not restore prosperity and He would heal or not heal Louisa. Furthermore, they believed that corruption had entered everyone: the life and death of August Hoffmayer had proven that. The depression and the drought meant nothing to Julius and Carl, and that made them the most successful farmers in the district: other men were mortgaged to the hilt – they were walking away from their properties with their belongings in hand carts, their crying babies in prams, their tractors and livestock repossessed by the banks, but this father and son owed nothing and could not be moved.

This long summer, even the rabbits and dingoes were

dying. When they were not clearing, Julius and Carl put down wells; they built fences; poured charcoal into the settling tanks to clear the muddy water; they cut the shoots from the stumps with a bill-hook as keen as a cut-throat razor; and, as the drought deepened, they tore the thatch from the barn to feed the horses and any grain or corn or wheat that did grow was given to the animals – for without them, they would not survive.

Although he was only two when the Archduke Ferdinand of Austria was assassinated, and three when the field-grey German infantrymen dug their trenches and redoubts in the waterlogged farmlands of Belgium, Carl knew all about the Great War and would have won the Iron Cross. He would have fought at Verdun and helped take the Citadel. For him, then, the intractable shifting land, the stumps as heavy as grave-stones and the drought were the next best thing. Julius had taught him well.

As was his habit, Julius consulted his silver watch and they stopped work for ten minutes at half past three. Even the oxen trembled with the hard work; the flies plagued the horses and the starlings picked at the broken ground. Both men filled their meerschaums, sat on the stumps, smoked and drank carefully from their water bottles.

'The soldier,' Carl said, 'will have a hard time of it.'

'What did he look like?'

'I could not see, Father, he was too far away.'

Julius put the cork back in his water bottle and looked back at the fallow paddocks. All they needed was a few drops of rain. 'Let us hope he is always far away.'

'He will owe money to the bank,' said Carl.

'That he will, and the money-lenders will get their due.'

'What do you think Stepmother said to him?'

'That, I cannot tell.'

They sat in silence among the debris until twenty-to-four, then Julius cracked his long whip, the oxen strained and the roller once more crashed through the bush. As the parakeets rose in droves, Carl wished he had brought his shotgun; of the wild pig they had seen yesterday, there was no sign.

If it had a beginning, the drought began in the winter of 1931: that year, less than thirteen inches of rain fell and that summer the dry land yielded less than four bushels an acre. Although the crop was wizened and spare, Julius and Carl collected every head of wheat; they saved every stalk, every broken straw, for the hard times ahead. Unlike his father, Julius was an expert in husbandry; and as he knew the weather patterns, each bag of wheat, oats and chaff was stacked on platforms away from the rats and mice in the barn. Their stock of feed had dwindled, but they would see the drought out; and, unlike most farmers in the district, they had not lost one animal through death.

At the end of the day when they had fed and watered the oxen and the horses, Julius and Carl washed themselves with a bucket in a tin bath in the yard. The water was saved to settle and to be used tomorrow. Although the north wind was gone, the sun was still hot and glared as it travelled west over the uncleared, wild country. As the two men stood, the water glistening on their hard bodies, even the parakeets were quiet. In the silence, the windmill creaked and the blades slowly turned.

'It may rain tonight,' Carl said. 'I feel it in my bones.'

His father laughed and put his hand on his son's shoulder.

'Your bones are too young for that. All we will have in the morning is the dew.'

When they were dry, they pulled their shirts on and went into the kitchen. Maria was at the stove as her husband and his son sat down at the table.

'Carl thinks it is going to rain tonight.' Julius laughed again. 'But he is wrong.'

Maria could think of no reply and looked at the kettle, hoping it would boil soon. All was soundless in the kitchen, save for Carl cracking his knuckles. At last, the kettle started to hiss and whistle and Maria made the pot of tea.

'Is there any cheese?' Carl asked, his strong hands now resting on the table. They had broken many rabbits' backs and quietened the most evil-tempered of horses. His beard was still thin, but he was a man nonetheless. Something stirred in the front of the house and Maria hoped to God it was not Louisa. She gave him the cheese from the meat safe.

Carl drank his tea down, scalding hot, wiped his mouth and said: 'There is still some light left, I am going shooting.' Then he, too, laughed in his dry way. 'Rabbit would make a change.' He rose from the table, took his .22 rifle, bowed and was gone.

'The soldier will buy a tractor,' Julius said. 'He will use all the modern methods, but it will be on hire-purchase and the money-lenders will beat him.'

'I expect so.' She took Carl's cup and saucer and put them into the washing bucket. Again, she found herself wanting to hear the sound of music, even a jig on a button accordian, but Julius had sold the piano because his father used to play it. She remembered the Johann Strauss melodies, the music drifting into the darkest and most secret parts of the house, as August sang and drank his brandy. He was a handsome man – no wonder the women loved him. He should have lived in the salons and beerhalls of Berlin, not the bush of Australia. Somehow, she had never felt the cancer of original sin growing within her.

'Did anyone call today?' Julius asked as he took out his leather tobacco pouch.

'No.'

'I have heard the Indian hawker is about.'

How would he know? she thought; he never talks to anybody. 'I have not seen him.'

'I am going into Rubicon tomorrow,' Julius said. 'Are the eggs ready?'

'They are.'

'How many are there?'

'Five dozen.'

'Ah, so. Sixty of Maria Hoffmayer's best eggs for our friend, Mr Ballantine. That man is a rascal, but he never tricks me.' Julius coughed. 'He will have tricked the soldier by letting him have credit.'

He rose, his chair creaking, tapped the barometer and left the kitchen to sit on the verandah.

No one knew where Julius's money was hidden – not even Carl. Maria had forgotten what a pound note looked like and sometimes she longed to hold a half-crown in her hand and run her fingernail down the milling. It was over a year since she had been into Rubicon, and then she had sat in the cart while Julius sold the eggs and cheese. The street seemed noisy with motorcars, horses and buggies and the train steaming at the station. They rode past the picture house and she tried to see what was showing. What were the moving pictures like? she wondered. As she set the table for the evening meal, Maria heard the creak of Julius's rocking chair on the timbers of the verandah and the echoes of gunfire from the bush. Carl never failed and always came home with half a dozen rabbits swinging from his belt: they were neatly shot through the head. This summer, they were small and stringy, the flesh tasted dry and the bones were as sharp as needles.

Julius sat in his rocker and looked out at his estate as the sun gleamed on the sides of the barn and the outbuildings. The drought was nothing: the farm was his and it was free of any encumbrance. This was his castle and it would be in his family forever, and he would keep the forces of darkness out. He, too, heard the sound of Carl's rifle echoing in the late afternoon and was satisfied. Then, as he turned in his chair to avoid the direct rays of the sun, he saw the curtains move at the window of the back bedroom: it was Louisa and she was staring at him.

He would never forget it: Sophie was in labour for seventeen hours. The midwife was nervous and inefficient; it seemed that his wife's screams penetrated every corner of the house and then echoed into the bush and the desert far beyond. During that long night, the thunder was ceaseless and the lightning flashed like the fire from field guns in some dreadful battle, but not one drop of rain fell. His mother was weeping and helpless and his father was away, consorting with whores.

51

Sophie screamed, twisted and rent herself, sweating on the horse-hair mattress in the iron bed and, at noon the following day, gave birth to a tiny girl so small no one thought it would live. And the midwife had torn Sophie so much she was unable to have any more children. Within a year, she was dead of tuberculosis, but Julius was sure it was the birth. Julius knew then that Luther was right: *It is faith that makes us masters, while love makes us slaves.*

Julius also would never forget the first night he had visited Louisa fifteen years later, when he lay with her in the darkness of that bitter winter. It was then he turned his back on God's will and purpose, and in his rebellious and sinful condition, stood helpless under the judgement of God. The sins of his father were visited upon him. He sat on the verandah until well after dark.

He remembered the morning he found Erich Stampfl hanging from the tree. It was cold and clear, the ducks were dipping and flying from the water, the breath streamed from his horse – he had ridden hard, German cavalry-style, to clear his head of the disgusting crimes of his father, the tears of his mother, the mounting debts and the sin that pervaded the house. The water was running in the creek as his horse galloped over the bridge, the sound of its hooves as sharp as gunfire.

The body swung from the branch and the crows were waiting in the tree-top. The man's trousers were hanging from his legs, his shirt was torn, his chest was bare and cut, the blood congealed, and his genitals crushed. The horse shied and bucked and, as he jumped down, he recognized the face of his one boyhood friend. His gorge rising and the tears coming, he tried to reach the dangling feet, but could not. Then he saw the notice pinned to the man's jacket: HUN SHIT.

The bad times didn't start until 1917: in one battle there were over 30,000 Australian casualties and, the year before, all people with German names were required to register as aliens. Before that, they hardly saw any local people: the

Germans had their own church and school, spoke their own language, married within the community – and produced the best wheat. The only person who mixed with the townsfolk was his father, and he was very popular. He spent money freely, was generous, was as handsome as a European count and spoke English perfectly. August reminded the women of Conrad Veidt and could have starred in the moving pictures with his impeccable manners, dashing style and knowledge of the outside world. If a local trader tried something new – a Tiffany lamp in leaded glass, a toy steam engine or a pearl-handled safety revolver – his father would buy it.

In the spring of 1917, the troubles started and the burnings began. At first it was outhouses and barns, then houses and finally wheat crops. That summer, over four thousand acres of German-owned wheat went up, but no arrests were made and no enquiries held. By the end of the war, most of the German settlers had moved out – most going to the cities where they changed their names, working in factories and living in tenements. Because of his popularity and free-spending, August Hoffmayer's farm wasn't touched, but Julius didn't go into Rubicon until 1920. He remembered it all and told Carl.

Seven

Wheat prices had fallen suddenly in the summer of 1930, and now it seemed that the banks owned everything. Some of the farmers turned to pig-raising, but the drought ended that; and when they failed to keep up their interest payments, the banks sent men out to seize their wheat. No one knew what was going on, except that the good times were gone and, for some strange reason, there were fewer buyers for wheat. One year they were getting 5/3 bushel, the next 3/- and it looked as though it would go lower. Don Mooney, the local police constable, said it was a Bolshevist plot, triggered by the dumping of Russian wheat, and a lot of people thought he was right. The Returned Soldiers' League was talking about forming a vigilante group.

There were more strikes than usual – the slaughtermen, the waterside labourers and the coal miners; and there were rumours that the Reds were causing trouble among the timber-workers. When the slaughtermen struck, thousands of lambs died looking like dirty scraps of fly-infested wool in the dusty yards of the country abbatoirs. Some farmers volunteered to do the killing, but were turned back by hostile, jeering men on the picket lines. Some of them had foreign accents and the papers said they belonged to a Communist organization called the Industrial Workers of the World.

There had always been vagrants and men looking for work as they walked the roads; but those men were swaggies with faces as brown as the earth and their belongings in hessian bags. No one minded them much as they were as familiar as the parakeets, dingoes and kangaroos. But the new men were a different breed – clerks and tradesmen from the cities who were hopeless at country jobs and cadged off the farmers.

By the summer of 1932, there were so many of them that they started to live in camps under the bridges and in the dry creek beds. A lot of farmers started to lose chickens and sheep, and as Mooney was hard-pressed to round the culprits up, the younger men of the district volunteered to patrol the roads with their horses and shotguns. And when the fires started, a lot of people started to keep their guns loaded during the night. What was happening? Although they were powerless to do anything about the drought, they could at least keep the invaders out.

Frank was working on the windmill when he heard the sound of a horse on the hard earth; and when he looked down from the top of the latticed tower, he saw it was Ray Stark. The sky was cloudless and the horse sneezed and stamped at the flies. Stark had his rifle in an old scabbard and, with his slouch hat and riding boots, looked for a moment like a soldier from the Light Horse. He sat easily and looked at Frank's cottage as the heat shimmered off the corrugated iron. 'That ain't too bad.'

Frank laughed. 'I wouldn't go in there now if I was you.'

'I don't want to. How's it going?'

'I think I can get this bugger working. There's water in the well – I know that.'

Stark dismounted, led his horse into the shade and sat on a stump. 'There's a bit to do.' Then he said: 'I've got a bottle of beer in me saddlebag.'

Frank climbed down the tower, coughed and blew his nose into the dirt. 'Are you offering me a drink?'

'Yep.' Stark got up and went over to his horse. 'It's a bit warm, I ain't got an ice chest.' He opened the bottle with his teeth and passed it over.

Frank drank, thought and said: 'What's the story with the armed men in town?'

'Aw, to keep the riff-raff out.'

'Vagrants, men on the track?'

'The Reds, the timber-workers.' Stark grinned. 'And blokes like me.'

55

'How did you get the beer, then?'

'I've got me ways. Is there any fences?'

'A few posts riddled with white ants and some barbed wire that wouldn't keep a baby out.'

'Like I said, Mr Cameron, there's a bit to do.'

'There is.'

'What did you think of Rubicon?' Stark's voice was as quiet as before.

'Not too bad, it'll do.'

'There's some tough buggers in there.'

'You mean men who don't like blackfellows?'

'I suppose.'

'How do you know I don't?'

'You didn't tell me to piss off, and you drank from the same bottle.'

Frank brushed at the flies. 'You aren't your ordinary black, are you?'

'You mean I'm not laying around drinking grog and I don't run away when I see a white man?'

'That's part of it.'

'My tribe, the Wotjobaluk, used to live around here, for a long time, and I reckon I've got a right to stay.'

Frank smiled. 'The Last of the Mohicans, you said?'

'That's right. The missionaries didn't waste all their time on me.'

'When do you think it will rain?'

'It'll rain when it rains, Mr Cameron.'

'That makes sense.'

Stark got out his tobacco tin. 'They didn't give you much for fighting for the country, did they?'

'They could have,' Frank replied, 'but it's better than nothing.'

'Something is better than nothing, eh?'

Frank thought about Ray Stark and his father employing the black, Henry. 'Do you want some work?'

'I reckon I might.'

'There's clearing, stumping, burning and fencing.'

'I reckon I know what's what.'

'I can pay you a pound a week and tucker.'

'That'll do. Why don't you give the work to the whitefellows on the track?'

'I've got no use for clerks and pen-pushers, they wouldn't last a couple of days up here.'

'Okay, then.'

'There's the drink,' Frank said.

'What about it?'

'You know bloody well what I mean. A lot of you fellows are prone to the booze. I'm not saying you are, but your mob can't take it. If I ever find you pissed, you're out on your arse. Right?'

'I reckon I can hold it.'

Frank got up. 'You can start whenever you want to. I've got work to do.'

'What will the people in Rubicon say when they find out you've got a blackfellow on the place?'

'I don't give a bugger what they say,' Frank replied. 'I'll employ who I want. And one more thing – don't let this leg of mine fool you. I know all about hard work.'

'I reckon you do, Mr Cameron. I'll see you tomorrow.'

'Daybreak.'

'No worries.'

Stark put the empty bottle on the top of a post, went over to his horse and rode away through the bush.

By the end of the afternoon, Frank had the pump working – the water was warm, hard and cloudy, but it would more than do.

First light was breaking next morning and Frank was making tea and porridge when Ray Stark turned up. 'G'day,' he said, standing at the door, 'I've brought a few tools of me own.' He was carrying an axe, a bill-hook and a grubber on his shoulder.

'Do you want a cup of tea?' Frank asked.

'Okay.'

'Have you eaten anything?'

'Had some grub on me way over.'

Frank wondered where Ray had come from, but didn't ask. He threw some tea in the billy and hung it over the fire. 'I'm going to buy a horse today and I want you to come with me to ride it back.'

'Okay.'

'And I'm buying a tractor.'

'Jeez,' Ray said, 'that'll be the first they've sold in bloody months.'

'That means I'll get a good price.'

'You will if you pay cash.'

Frank thought before he answered. 'We'll see.' There was £1000 hidden in the seat of his truck – it had taken him ten years to save and he would invest it well. 'I want all that shit and junk out of the yard, I'm getting some chickens.'

'I can get some for you.'

Frank laughed. 'I bet you can, but I want them legal.'

Stark was offended. 'I won't steal nothing.'

'I thought I'd get them off the Hoffmayers.'

'I wouldn't buy a thing off that Hun bastard – he's the toughest bugger in the district.' Stark got up and carefully poured his teaslops back into the bucket.

'And he hates abos?'

'He hates every bastard.'

Frank thought of Maria Hoffmayer working in the dark kitchen and the crying coming from the back of the house. 'I'll get the horse and the tractor first – one step at a time. I want the wheat crop in by June.'

'With the tractor,' Stark answered, 'we'll piss it in by then.'

'You aren't a full-blood, are you?' Frank wanted to get that straight.

'Nah, me grandmother was taken by an Irishman.'

God help us all, Frank thought, the bloody Irish. He swallowed down the last of his porridge. 'Right, we've got four hours before we go into town.'

As they worked in the yard, Frank watched Stark from time

to time and was pleased to see he worked like the proverbial nigger. But having all that cash worried him – Stark's thin body was as tough as rope and, if it came to it, he would be hard to put down.

Frank wiped the sweat off his forehead and counted the tractors in Farrar's yard: there were twenty-seven and some of them had dead thistles and weeds in their wheels. Although it was nine-thirty, no one seemed to be about and, apart from a waggon lumbering up Federation Street, the town was dead. What kind of a sign was that? Frank thought he knew: this place was sinking to its knees. He strolled down the rows of machines with Ray and looked at the merchandise. As they moved away from each other, a man appeared from a tin shed at the back of the lot. He was big and bald and about Frank's age; he was wearing overalls and had hands as big as fire shovels. 'G'day,' he said.

'G'day,' Frank answered. 'I want to buy a tractor.'

'Who's the blackfellow?'

'He works for me.'

'I'm sorry, pal, we don't allow blackfellows in the yard.'

Frank measured up the man: this must be Farrar. 'Why's that?'

'Company rules – they steal things.'

Frank eased his stiff leg. 'It's Farrar, isn't it?'

'Yep.' The man stuck out his hand.

'It looks as though we can't do business.'

'Why not?'

'My man's got to drive the machine I buy, and if he can't see it, no dice.'

Farrar squinted. 'That's Ray Stark, ain't it?'

'That's right.'

'And he's working for you?'

'Right again.'

'How long have you been up here?'

'Two days.' Frank was getting impatient now.

'I wouldn't employ him if I was you.'

59

Frank turned on his boot heel. 'Okay, mister, it's a pity, it was going to be a cash deal.'

Farrar scratched his head with his greasy fingers. 'Cash makes a difference.'

'I thought it would.' He swung around. 'Ray,' he called, 'come and meet Mr Farrar.'

Stark came up through the piles of rusting harvesters, but no one shook hands.

Frank narrowed his choice to a McCormick-Deering. 'What do you want for that?' he said.

'Five hundred pounds.'

It was in good order, and when he started it he found it wasn't burning oil and would do the work he wanted. 'I'll give you three hundred.'

'No way.'

'That's too bad.' Frank rolled a cigarette and looked at Stark, who was as still as the grave under his slouch hat. A cat looked at them from a fencepost and chickens scratched. 'Maybe we can do business some other time,' Frank said, 'but I'm not sure when that will be.'

'Are you a returned soldier?' Farrar was uncertain as he looked at the big, fair man.

'Yep.'

'For king and country, I'll make it four hundred and fifty pounds.'

Frank laughed – he was not impressed with Mr Farrar. He pulled out his wallet and said: 'Look, I've got three hundred pounds here, there's no mucking around with hire-purchase or the bank – it's that and you can chuck in free transport and fifty gallons of kerosine. Take it or leave it.'

Farrar scowled. 'You drive a hard bargain, Mr Cameron.'

'These are hard times, Mr Farrar.'

He hadn't sold a tractor for five months. 'Okay, then.'

'What do you think, Ray?' Frank asked.

'That looks about right to me.'

The deal was done: the money changed hands, a receipt was given in the tiny office where last year's calendar hung and Mr Farrar's dog slept, but no one shook hands.

Frank had asked Farrar where he could buy a horse and when they got to the dealer's yard, the owner let them both look around without objecting. A phone call had been made: Frank knew the drill – they tracked your every movement in a small town. The gelding he had seen on his first day was still there – it was strong, well broken and free of cuts and sores, so he bought it. He bought a saddle, bridle and blanket for two pounds and Ray mounted, saluted, rode to the top of Federation Street and disappeared down the Kurnbrun road.

It was noon and over ninety degrees as Frank crossed the street and looked at the new radios in a shop next to the Regal Cinema. He thought about buying a three-valve battery model, then decided against it – luxuries must wait. He would find out what was happening on the wheat market soon enough. And what was the stockmarket doing? His father always used to say, never go into the red, and he was glad he had taken his advice. The tar was soft under his boots as he passed two old men sleeping on a bench in the noonday heat; beyond the buildings of Rubicon, the ploughed paddocks reminded Frank of brown corduroy. Would this place grow wheat, year in, year out?

As he strolled toward the pub, he saw the sign in a vacant shop window, where an old Union Jack lay draped over some packing cases. *RETURNED MEN – DO YOUR DUTY! Volunteers are invited to see Senior-Constable Donald Mooney to help protect property. KEEP AUSTRALIA SAFE!*

Mooney was in the bar of the Royal – he was balding and overweight and in his shirt-sleeves; he was leaning over the counter, his foot on the rail, with a notebook stuck in his back trouser pocket. A pair of handcuffs hung from his belt and he was talking to Jim Banks. Although the local lawman looked tough, he was out of condition and Frank knew he would be no good in a scrap.

'G'day,' Banks said as he came down, 'what's your poison?'

Frank bought a beer and said: 'That's Constable Mooney, I take it?'

'Sure is. Do you want to meet him?'

Frank laughed. 'I'd better check in.'

'I think the town knows you're here,' Banks answered. 'Don,' he called, 'come and meet our newest settler.'

Mooney's grip was strong and sweaty. 'Welcome to the best little town in the bush,' he said. 'You've got the block next to Hoffmayer?'

'That's right.'

Mooney slid half a crown across the bar. 'The last joker up there got TB, poor bastard. Where are you from?'

'Gippsland.'

'Where it rains.'

'That's right.'

'Too much rain and the wheat don't grow. You a wheat farmer?'

'No, but I'll learn.'

'Don't ask Hoffmayer. He'll tell you nothing.'

'You're looking for volunteers?' Frank asked.

'Volunteers?'

'The sign in the shop window.'

'That?' Mooney grinned. 'I'm President of the Rubicon Gun Club. We can always do with new members. Can you shoot?'

'A bit.'

Mooney considered. 'I bet you can. I'm a bit short-handed so some of the blokes from the gun club help me out.'

'In what way?'

'Aw, there's a lot of thievery about, a lot of vagrants and no-hopers, and there's the Bolshies.'

'Is there?'

'You should know, being a returned man, I don't mind the trade unions, but a lot of blokes are being misled by the Reds. Do you want to join the gun club?'

'What do you do?' But Frank knew damned well.

Mooney grinned once more. 'Go out shooting, do a bit of gun drill and drink a few bottles at the end of the day.'

'I'm busy settling in, but I'll think about it.'

'Good on you, mate, we want to keep this town the way

it is.' Mooney thrust out his hand again. 'Look, I'd better get going – duty calls. We meet in a room here on Saturday nights. You couldn't meet a better bunch of blokes.'

When Frank turned around, Banks was back behind the counter. 'How's it going on the block?'

'It's a bit early to say – I'll tell you this time next year.' Frank thought of Stark and hoped he had arrived back with the horse.

'Have you met Julius Hoffmayer yet?'

'No.'

Banks tapped the counter. 'Well, when you do, look out for the son – he's the one to watch.'

When Frank got back to the farm, his horse was tethered in the shade; it was fed and watered and Stark was digging post holes for the yard. Late that night, Frank heard the sound of gun-shot echoing in the bush, lay still in his bed roll, but all fell silent. When he got up in the morning to find Stark already at work, he decided to let him sleep in the cottage, and to hell with men like Farrar.

He met her at a dance, and he remembered the band was playing Goodbye Dolly, I Must Leave You *and it made him think of his brother. She was small and dark with large brown eyes and a pretty figure. She was wearing a yellow dress and she had flowers pinned to her waist. That's the girl for me, he thought and went right up and asked her. It was as though she was expecting it, and she said, yes, on the spot. The night was cool – perfect for dancing in the tin hall; and halfway through the evening they went outside and stood in the long grass. The moon was big as it hung over the bush and they strolled down the patch to the picket fence by the earth tennis court.*

They hung over the gate, she quite close to him and he wasn't nervous at all. Her name was Irene and her father worked on the railway as a guard on the Melbourne line; her mother took in dressmaking, and she had four sisters of whom she

63

was the second eldest. She played tennis and was training to be a telephone operator – that, she said, was the latest thing these days. When he put his arm around her, she didn't seem to mind, and it was as though they'd known each other for a long time. And when somebody whistled at them in the dark, they just laughed and went on talking. He used up all the money his father had paid him and bought a motor bike so he could see her every Saturday night.

In the summer, they played tennis and in the winter, she watched him play football: his team were runners-up that year and everyone put in for a trip to Melbourne. Although the city was exciting with its emporiums and moving-picture theatres, he spent most of his time thinking about Irene and wishing she was with him. The coach worked at the abbatoirs and one night over a drink told him about trades unions and the Industrial Workers of the World. He said there had to be one big union and that the capitalists might start a war.

He and Irene got married at St John's Church in February 1908, and she gave up being a telephonist to work on the farm. She didn't mind and she and his father got on like a house on fire. Butter prices were up that year and they built a cottage nearby to be on their own. That summer was brilliant and they went for long rambles in the bush; and on the Labour Day weekend they went camping on the Macallister River, where he caught three brown trout. They made love on the ground outside the tent and next day climbed the spur to the top of Mount Useful where the bellbirds chimed in the forest.

That winter, Irene became pregnant, but miscarried: after the tears, they realized they were both fit and strong and would try for another. Shortly after that, he saw his first Model-T in town and they determined to save up for one. Then Irene's father was injured in an accident on the railways: he could no longer work again, but her sisters and mother could look after him.

Now that farm prices were good, his father felt confident enough to borrow from Loan & Mercantile: they increased the herd to thirty Jersey cows and the property flourished. The rains were good and regular and the soil rich. Irene made bread; she preserved fruit; made butter and cheese; smoked bacon; grew potatoes, cabbages, peas and tomatoes. Roses climbed over the front porch of their cottage, and they lived off the fat of the land.

Eight

Maria poured the washing water into the settling tank and carried the basket over to the line. The vegetables in her garden were long since dead, and from now on they would have to rely on the potatoes, turnips and pumpkin stored in the cellar. The sun was high, the weather calm and not a leaf moved. The fowls crouched in the shade of the trees, no birds were flying, the rooster was silent and beyond the dull green bush, the sandhills gleamed. As she pegged out the work clothes, she remembered a poem she learnt at school from the Australian teacher:

> *Not a sound disturbs the air;*
> *There is quiet everywhere:*
> *Over plains and over woods*
> *What a mighty stillness broods!*

The washing was almost dry already – she had used the mangle carefully, saving all the water as it was squeezed from the clothes. Not one drop was wasted. As she hung up Julius's worn trousers, she heard a branch snap, turned and saw a man moving out from the darkness of the trees. Unafraid, she waited for him to come closer and saw he was carrying a Gladstone bag and wearing torn and patched city clothes. He was tall and thin and, as he came up, she saw his face was badly burned by the sun – his skin in blisters and one eye weeping. Maria knew what he wanted – but what was the time and how soon would Julius and Carl be home for their midday meal? She looked down the long paddock over the stubble and the starlings foraging in the dirt, but of the men there were no sign. The man took off his hat and said: 'Good morning, madam.' His voice was so soft she could barely hear him.

Maria stood, clothes in hand. 'Good morning.'

'Would you, by any chance,' the man said, 'have any work?'

'I'm afraid not. It is hard to get in these parts.' Once again, she glanced across the paddocks.

'Would you perhaps know where I may find some?' He seemed to be in his late twenties, with his hair neatly parted and his boots tied up with string. In the heat, he seemed about to fall, but steadied himself.

'I'm afraid not.' What could she say to him? Even if there were work, she did not know where it was. Then, as he turned away, she said: 'I can give you a piece of bread and a cup of tea.'

'That is most kind of you.' He raised the ghost of a smile, followed her across the yard, but waited at the door like a well-trained animal.

'You may come in,' Maria said; and when she looked at the grandfather clock, saw it was a quarter to twelve. And when she turned, the man was sitting hunched at the table: it was too late to turn him away now. His hair was fair and the stranger reminded her of Mr Cameron – of what he must have looked like before he went away to the Great War. When she raised the hot plate on the stove, Maria found the fire was almost out, blew at the coals and thrust in some kindling. She filled the kettle from the water pitcher and put it directly over the flames so it might boil faster. Then, quickly, she cut off a piece of bread and put it on the table.

The man looked at it and said: 'What kind of bread is that?'

'German bread.'

'Ah, *schwartzbrot*, home-made, the best you can get.'

'Eat it,' Maria replied, 'eat it, you will find it nourishing.'

She listened for the thump of boots on the side verandah. The man ate, saving every crumb and chewing slowly as he held the slice delicately with his long fingers. He was not a working man, she thought. What did he do? He knew some German, but was an Australian. Perhaps he was a teacher or an artist of some kind? She remembered a violin player of her girlhood and the sounds of *The Merry Widow* drifting through the rooms of her aunt's house. His fingernails were long and torn and, when he had finished eating, he laid his hands on the table. There was nothing to say and she stood by the stove, waiting for the kettle to boil. Was that a sound from Louisa's room? She listened, but could not tell. 'Have you come far?'

'From Melbourne.'

Although she had never been, Maria knew it was a large city in the south: August had spent much time there: he said it was a fine city of boulevards, English parks, theatres and public buildings. 'That is a long way.'

'It is, indeed.'

Again, there was silence and Maria waited. At last, the kettle boiled, she tossed in a spoonful of tea, tipped in the water and without waiting for it to draw, poured him out a cup. She had forgotten to give him milk and sugar, but the man didn't seem to mind. 'Thank you,' he said, as he raised the cup.

Then boots thumped, floorboards creaked and Carl entered. He stood at the door, browned by the weather, his shirt sleeves rolled up and his strong arms covered with dust. 'Who is this?' he asked.

Maria's voice was low. 'He is looking for work.'

'He will find none here.'

'I have told him that.'

The man rose from the table, was about to speak, but Carl stepped forward, snatched the cup from his hand and tipped the tea into the bucket. 'Nor will he eat our food.' He took the man by the collar of his jacket, lifted him easily and pushed him through the kitchen door. As he fell, Carl pushed him once more and he staggered down the track like some drought-stricken animal. 'You will go,' Carl shouted, 'you will go.'

When Carl came back into the house, he said: 'I will take some bread and cold meat for my father. You will make enough for us both.'

As Maria prepared her husband's lunch, his son sat at the

68

table, cracking his knuckles, saying nothing and gazing at her with his pale, blue eyes. When Carl was gone, Maria went outside and found the Gladstone bag lying on the doorstep. The leather was dry and cracked and the fastener was broken. For some time she looked at it and wondered what to do. At last, when she opened it, all she found was the photograph of a baby, and a sheet of music and an ivory-handled cut-throat razor. She hid the bag in the back of the barn, where, she thought, no one would ever find it.

After Carl put the nosebags on the horses, the two men sat on the stumps and ate their cold mutton and drank their sweet tea. When Carl told his father about the visitor, Julius said: 'I will talk to her about it. First the soldier and now a vagrant – all this must stop. We will have no one coming here.' As he spoke, he thought he saw someone moving in the bush at the far end of the clearing, but couldn't be sure. If this went on, they would have to bring out their loaded shotguns. He thought of the decline and decay of the farm when his father was alive: that would never happen again.

Carl said nothing and the flies buzzed in the midday heat; Julius sat, big and heavy, the sweat running down between his shoulder blades and his flannel vest clinging to his body. *It is love that makes us slaves.* He dreamed last night that his father had brought a whore into the house and was using her openly, pulling at the buttons of her blouse and fondling her breasts. In the dream he was a small boy and tried to leave the room, but all the doors were locked, the room was stifling and his father and the woman coupled on the floor like pigs in the yard. The woman was big and as strong as a prize mare, and when she had finished with his father, she came over, laughing, seized him by the shoulders and pushed his head between her thighs so hard he suffocated in her sweat and juice. Julius shivered in the heat. God would stop punishing him in His own time. He sprang up, seized the mattock and said: 'You drive the bullocks – I will dig the stumps.'

Julius and his son worked all afternoon; they worked until

the sun started to go down and the bush cast a shadow on the broken trees and the torn earth. The evening star was rising when the exhausted animals were stabled, fed and watered for the night.

After tea, Julius sat on the side verandah: the sunset was like a huge, soundless explosion and, as it sank, the sun hung in the darkening sky like a massive star shell. He thought of the vagrants, the thievery and the settlers moving off their farms. This was the time to buy more land as the prices wouldn't go any lower – he had wanted to get the Kurnbrun block, but couldn't as the soldier was there. But, by the end of the summer, Julius was sure the man would have gone.

This summer's crop was poor – less than four bushels to the acre – and the wild life had taken half of it: kangaroos, rats, mice, emus and dingoes. And before the prices crashed, the wheat was worth less because it was tainted with eucalyptus from the shoots growing from the mallee stumps. In previous years, he and Carl had cut the shoots for oil, but now the eucalyptus factory was closed down. From time to time, Julius raised his eyes and glanced at Louisa's window, but the curtains remained still. He thanked God for that. Then Maria came out and he saw her gazing at the bush, her apron stained with dishwater and the work of the day.

'You will not let strangers in,' Julius said.

'I thought he would faint for want of food.' She continued to survey the land where she had spent all her life. She was starting to hate it now.

'You will not let strangers in, not the soldier, not anyone.'

'The soldier?'

'The man with the limp.'

'But you have not seen him.'

'Carl told me.' God had given him this farm, and by God, he would keep it. 'Do you understand what I am saying?'

'Yes.' She stepped off the verandah to feed the chickens. 'Do not give them too much,' Julius called. But she did not reply, as he ground his teeth and wondered about her.

He slapped at the insects in the gloom. If there was no water, why were there mosquitoes? Then, in the fastness of the bush, a dog howled as the moon rose, huge and yellow, over the sand hills. The silence was vast, the birds had gone to sleep in the branches of the ancient trees, the dog howled once more and Julius felt his back rising. The dingoes were the work of the Devil – they carried off lambs and ruined the crops: it seemed that it was a punishment for profligacy. Not his, Julius thought, but his father's and farmers and speculators who had come after the war. The blocks were too small, the settlers inexperienced and the banks had encouraged their greed. It was the money-lenders who were to blame for these hard times and the Lord would see that they came to nothing.

That night at prayer, Julius read from St John 12: *He that rejecteth me, and receiveth not my words, hath one that judgeth him: the word that I have spoken, the same shall judge him in the last day.* As they prayed, the wind got up and drifted through the house; it blew the curtains in the hall, and the dust under the door; the kerosine lamps flickered and the grease dripped and ran down the side of the candles. Carl sat as silent as a gravestone, his eyes closed and his strong fingers spread on the table; Julius's voice was low as he read from his Bible; but Maria felt restless, the words seemed remote and all she could think of was the strange visitor as Carl shoved him down the track. No sooner had Julius finished, closing his Bible and pushing his chair back from the table, than a cry came from Louisa's room. Maria got up, but the two men did not move.

She was bolt upright in bed, her long legs bare and the sheets thrown back. Her breasts were exposed and her skin the colour of ivory. Louisa was laughing, her pink tongue licking her lips. She looked like a beautiful, young harlot. 'Do you like that, Papa?' she was saying. 'Do you like that?'

Maria saw she had eaten her food and picked up the tray. She had been glad to leave the men in the kitchen, but now she was not and sat by the bed with her stepdaughter. Once again, she thought of Julius's visits in the night. God would punish him in His time. But would He? And was that true? Maria knew what was wrong with her husband and his daughter, but there was no one she could tell.

That summer was brilliant – the days were mild, the rain gentle and the wheat crops abundant. The land yielded eight bushels an acre and there was a building boom in Rubicon. William Withers put up his new emporium – a maroon brick and tile building with fancy iron lace; new horse stalls were built at the Royal – seventy-eight in number, with a dozen grooms for the wealthy farmers; she remembered Withers' opening window display of tulle, laces and chiffons, where the women gathered and tossed their gold sovereigns on the counter.

She remembered her fifteenth birthday. The lake had been full for many years, and she could not recall a time when it was not. The creek was flowing, the willows hung over the water and redfin were caught in their hundreds.

Prospects looked good – even for Uncle Ernst. He had bought a new pony and trap; a cousin had written saying he had been appointed chairman of the new Magdeburg electric railway, and cereal prices were the highest ever. That morning, Aunt Matilde baked scones and a sponge, cut corned-beef sandwiches, opened jars of pickles and preserved fruit; and after morning church service, they went out to the lake.

It seemed the entire community was there – the Krugers, the Konigs, the Heinrichs, the Schillers, the Aldermanns and many more. The beach was crowded with men, women and children wearing flowery hats and panamas; some of the younger removed their jackets and stood about in their shirt-sleeves. A regatta was being held on the lake with sailing boats and people were rowing and paddling canoes. There were home-made rafts and the children were running, laughing and splashing.

Her aunt and uncle found a spot under the trees, spread the rug, took out the hamper and spread out the food. Through the bush came the sounds of a violin, and she was sure some people would have danced had it not been for the Pastor. Uncle Ernst discreetly opened his bottle of wine, stretched out in the sun and read his German newspapers. Aunt Matilde said: 'You look the most beautiful young woman here. Go out and promenade in your new dress.'

Although she knew very few people, she was neither embarrassed nor afraid. As she walked through the groups toward the lake, some of the young men stopped drinking their beer and watched her; the music drifted and the ducks took off from the lagoon, the water rippling and spinning. She was very happy.

She stepped over some rocks, tripped and fell on the sand. When she was helped up, she found herself looking into the dark eyes of a handsome man with a greying moustache – he, too, was drinking wine, but quite openly. There were three other people sitting by the water: the handsome gentleman introduced her to his wife, his daughter-in-law and his son. Their names were Carlotta, Sophie and Julius Hoffmayer.

Nine

Among the pencils, docket books, knives and sharpening steels on Reg Bolger's office table, sat a small skull. And when trade was slack Bolger sat, his boots up on the desk, with his fingers stuck in the eye sockets. The skull was that of an aborigine and Reg had won it years ago in a poker game. A calendar of King George and Queen Mary was pinned to the wall next to a Uhlan cavalry sword, a steel helmet and a cartridge belt from a Spandau. Bolger served as company butcher in the 45th Battalion. saw action at Pozières and, when he was repatriated, bought a race horse with his collection of gold fillings taken from the teeth of dead German infantrymen.

Whatever happened the night before, Reg Bolger made it his rule to open his shop each morning at five. He was a popular man in Rubicon, extending credit to his customers, free of interest: he knew good times would return and, when they did, he would make a tidy sum. Bolger got his meat from small country abattoirs and had lots of mates in the slaughtermen's union. He bought carcasses at bargain prices, sold his chops, steaks and sausages at a good margin and entered every deal on the bloodied pages of his account book. He was a patient man and would collect one day. Reg was a keen shooter and President of the Rubicon Gun Club: he owned a .303, a German Luger pistol and a fancy Hollis shotgun. He coached the local football team; his knives were as keen as cut-throat razors and he had no trouble carrying in a three-hundred pound carcass from his Essex truck.

Reg was stubbing his cigarette out when the flydoor banged and Don Mooney came in. The policeman leaned across the counter and said: 'I've checked our friend, Cameron, out.'

'How?'

'A toll call to Melbourne.'

Bolger eased himself up. 'And?'

'He was an officer in the 21st Battalion, won the Military Cross and got hit at the Somme.'

'A good man to have around, then.' Bolger pulled out his paring knife and cut the fat off the chops. 'Is he the big fair-haired bloke with the limp?'

'That's him.'

'He should join the gun club.'

'I've already asked him.'

'What did he say?'

'He said, he'd think it over.' Mooney paused. 'He's taken on Ray Stark.'

Bolger looked up from the cutting bench. 'Go on?'

'That's what he's done.'

'Jesus, he's been here less than a week and takes on the bloody abo.'

'That's right.'

'Who told you?'

'Henry Farrar. Cameron bought a tractor and paid cash, and had the black with him.'

'Is that so? Somebody had better tell him the error of his ways. Where's his block?'

'Out on the Kurnbrun road, next to the Hoffmayers.'

Bolger tossed the fat into the bin. 'Christ, I don't know whether to laugh or cry – a returned man comes here, employs an abo and lives next door to a Hun.'

'I don't suppose he can be blamed for the Hun. There's not much we can do, is there?'

'No,' the butcher replied, 'not at this stage. Any other news?'

'There's riots in Melbourne and the miners are on strike.'

'Fucking Reds. We'll fix those swine.'

'And there's some Jewish financier here from London to tell us what to do.'

Bolger banged his chopper on the bench. 'Christ, those

75

bastards planned the whole thing. And we'll fix him, too, won't we?'

'Yeah. I'll see you at five.'

'Okay.'

Mooney strolled to his office at the back of the court house, opened up and sat down behind his desk. He looked at his in-file and saw the warrants; he shoved them to the bottom of the pile, thought about a beer, but got up and put the kettle on for a cup of tea. Evictions and bailiffs were his biggest problems. When a farmer went bankrupt, he had to get the warrant to evict sworn by Harold Withers, and if the bailiffs couldn't get hold of the assets, go out to the property himself. This had happened twice, but luckily Mooney didn't know the people who were scratching out a living in the desert, north-west. What would he do when it happened to someone he knew? Mooney hoped to Christ all his friends could hang on. Rounding up no-hopers was one thing, but helping evict your mates was another. He never dreamed it would get this bad: at times he wished he was back in town, rounding up the trouble-makers. That was easy and enjoyable. When the kettle boiled, he made the tea, tipped some condensed milk into the mug and drank. Why would the government get a Jew out? But one man he wouldn't mind evicting was Julius Hoffmayer.

'Good morning, Don.' It was Harold Withers standing at the door in his pinstripe suit, his watch chain gleaming and starched cuffs at his wrists.

Mooney rose. 'Good morning, Mr Withers. Would you like a cup of tea?'

Withers gazed at the office with its torn Wanted posters and worn-out furniture. 'No thanks. Are there any warrants?'

'There's two.'

'People you know?'

'Not really.'

'Do you know them or not?'

'No.'

'We don't want any trouble.'

76

'There won't be any.' Mooney drank the last of his tea.

'Are they ready for signing?'

'Yes.'

'Well, give them to me, then.'

Mooney rummaged and handed them over. 'They're both Germans.'

Withers sat down and looked at the eviction notices. 'That makes it easier – so the rot has spread to our Teutonic friends?'

Although it was only after ten, the office was like an oven and clouds of dust were blowing down the street. Mooney sweated and wiped his forehead. 'It looks like it.'

'Who's the new farmer, a returned man, I believe?'

'Cameron, first name, Frank.'

'Have you met him?'

'I've had a couple of drinks with him.' Mooney thought Withers was a bastard, but he had to get on with him. The King of Rubicon.

'What were your impressions?'

'He was an officer and was decorated.' He wondered if he should tell Withers about the abo.

'We need more men like that, don't we?' Withers signed the documents and tossed them on Mooney's desk. 'I'd like to meet him sometime.'

'I reckon I could arrange that.'

Withers smiled. 'You can arrange most things, can't you? I'll be at the court house until one o'clock if you need me.' He pulled the door shut and Mooney watched his Justice of the Peace walk across the dusty grass and disappear inside the stone building. There were expensive drinks in a refrigerator inside. One day, Mooney thought, he too would be a Justice of the Peace.

Harold Withers sat alone in the cool of the court house and poured himself a whisky and soda. He opened his valise, drew out the file and studied the bank statement. His overdraft stood at £15,500 – thank God for the bonds and mortgages. One of his companies had a lien over the two German farmers, but no one knew. Although the properties weren't worth much, every little helped and the Germans always had something worth taking – a piano, antiques and grain stacked away. In any event, there was some justice in this – they had started the war. He took out a cigar, rolled it, snipped off the end and smoked. If the worst came to the worst, the banks would never get his house – he would see to that. Withers gave himself a lecture: be aggressive, be positive, be cunning, someone had to profit from the crash. For every share sold, one was bought – it was a matter of timing and confidence. Borrow he must, for there was blue-chip stock going for a song.

Thirty-four properties were mortgaged to Withers' land companies and he owned seven buildings in Federation Street – apart from the emporium – and all were choice sites. If any more farmers went through, the bailiffs and Mooney could do the dirty work. This was his country – he and his father had financed it, and it would be the bread basket of the world. The problem lay with the gutless government, the communists and the Jews. At least the German farmers worked – no one could deny that. In some ways, it was a pity they had had to fight them, the Bolsheviks were the real problem.

Withers took out the letter from his friend in Sydney and read it again. The new citizens' army, the New Guard, interested him and it sounded far more professional than Mooney's cronies who spent most of their time drunk in the back room of the Royal. He must find out more about the New Guard: what Australia needed was backbone; the Reds would try for a takeover sooner or later, and when that time came, the rabble at the gun club wouldn't be of much use.

Harold Withers owned the largest house in Rubicon – the biggest by far. It had twenty rooms, stood on a rise and overlooked the wheatfields to the north. Built by a land-boomer in 1883, the Withers' house was Italianate with iron lace, stone facings and a broad verandah with view of what he called *la compagnia*. There was a rose garden, terraces, chauffeur's quarters and a gazebo. All the buildings were roofed with diamond-shaped tiles and there was a large underground room, where a family could retire to escape dust storms. The main house was built of limestone, bevelled and morticed. In the front room was a grand piano, a rosewood dining table, a chiffonier and bookshelves containing sets of the *Encyclopaedia Britannica*, the works of Arthur Mee and the poems of Alfred, Lord Tennyson. In the kitchen was a large electric stove and two refrigerators. Although *la compagnia* was once fertile and productive for many years, its produce going to Withers' flour mill, it was now barren and thousands of starlings picked at the dry, grey earth. The view from the front verandah might be depressing, but Harold Withers took heart that his money was invested in the best asset there was – bricks and mortar and broad acres that stretched to the horizon. Furthermore, he was the most powerful man in Rubicon – the town was his and nobody would take it away from him. His wife had left him five years ago; he had no children, but he had money and didn't care at all.

Withers had one more whisky, put away his papers, closed his valise and locked the court-house door. As he stepped into the glare of the day, he put on his homberg hat and waved to his driver who was waiting in the Hupmobile. Then he was driven to the north-east to look at some properties he had been told should be coming up for sale in the next month. Soon, Withers thought, you wouldn't be able to give farms away. He shrugged: one man's loss was another man's gain. As the bleached country rolled by, he saw black clouds bunching up from the south above the lake but, despite his confidence, he was not hopeful that they meant anything.

Julius Hoffmayer stood in the darkness of George Ballantine's store, his big hands resting on the egg crates. 'Eight pence a dozen,' he said. 'That is what I want.'

'Sixpence is my top,' George Ballantine replied. 'You know that.'

'I have the best eggs in the district.' Julius was unperturbed:

this was the ritual and he always got his way.

'You may have the best eggs, but it's not best any more, it's cheapest. There's a depression on, haven't you heard?'

'I know what's happening, Mr Ballantine. You have no need to tell me.'

This afternoon, the German seemed bigger than ever, his voice low and menacing. Even the storekeeper found himself thinking it might have been a good idea to clear the lot out when the war began. 'I can't go any higher than sixpence, Mr Hoffmayer, I can't afford to.'

Julius leant across the counter. 'Do you know why you can't afford to pay for quality? No? You give credit, Mr Ballantine. And that is not a wise thing to do.'

'You, sir, will not tell me how to run my business.'

'I am not telling you how to run your business,' Julius replied. 'I am telling you the dangers of giving credit. A man must pay his way. That is the rule.'

'I think you should go, Mr Hoffmayer, we cannot do business today.'

If Julius was surprised, he did not show it. Nor did he threaten to take his produce to Withers', for he knew he would get less there. He would take the eggs home and have Maria preserve them. He would have eggs and wheat and meat when every other farmer did not. God and hard work would see to that. He took up the crates. 'Good day, Mr Ballantine.'

'Good day, Mr Hoffmayer.'

Outside in the heat, Julius loaded the crates on to his cart, covered them with a blanket and climbed up. There was nothing else he could do, and he now knew the eggs would be stale before he got back to his farm. He wondered if he should try to sell them from house to house, but that kind of hawking was unthinkable – he would be on a par with the failures. Nor was he an Indian hawker. As he sat, immobile, a Hupmobile drove past with Harold Withers in the back; it stopped several doors up, the chauffeur let the businessman out and he strode into his buildings. Julius would never forget the day when he paid the mortgage off to the last penny, the money neatly folded in £5 lots, the coins rattling on Withers' office desk. *I shall repay.*

As Julius took up the reins, a Chevrolet truck drew up alongside and a fair-haired man leant from the window. 'Mr Hoffmayer?'

'Yes.'

'I thought it was you,' the man said. 'I'm Frank Cameron.'

'Yes.'

'I called the other day and met your wife, but you were not there.'

'I was working.' Julius released the brake, snapped the reins and the cart creaked forward. 'Good day, Mr Cameron.'

Frank watched the cart rumble over the gravel, turn and go past the war memorial toward the wheat sheds at the railway station. He shrugged, stepped down on to the running-board and walked over to the Royal for a beer.

The man who looked like John Barrymore was standing at the bar and bowed deeply as Cameron came up. He was drinking whisky.

'I, sir,' he said, 'am the proprietor of the local cinema, the Regal.' His voice was deep and his tea-strainer moustache was stained. 'The name is Carver, and you, I believe, are Mr Cameron.'

'News travels fast in bush towns,' Frank said as they shook hands.

'It does, indeed.' Carver dug into his hip pocket and produced his wallet. 'Will you join me?'

'That would be a pleasure.'

'Be careful of this old bastard,' Jim Banks said as he came up and pulled Frank a beer. 'He'll get you into trouble as soon as look at you.'

'Calumny,' Carver said as he took up his glass. 'Would you excuse me, James? My legs are not the best today.'

The publican snorted. 'I don't wonder.'

'Let's sit by the window,' Carver said, 'and contemplate the rich tapestry of life in Rubicon.'

They sat at the table, where Carver produced a packet of

Capstan. He pointed down Federation Street. '*Anus mundi*,' he said.

'What?'

'The arsehole of the world.'

'Why do you stay, then?' Frank warmed to the man: like a lot of drunkards, he could be entertaining.

'Because I have nowhere else to go – and one bush town is as good as another, is it not?' He offered Frank a cigarette. 'We owe our life and liberty to you.'

'Me and about ten million others – not including the Russians.'

'Our Slavonic friends are not too popular now, are they?'

'The Bolshies?'

'Indeed.'

Frank drank his beer. 'It's all a bit overdone. The Reds, I mean. Have you ever worked in a timber mill?'

'No, sir, I have not had that pleasure.'

'I reckon those poor bastards deserve every penny they get, Reds or not.'

'That's seditious talk in this patriotic town.'

Frank thought of Don Mooney and the gun club. 'Maybe. What's on at the flicks?'

'*Dr Jekyll and Mr Hyde*. A masterpiece.'

'I've read the book.'

'Have you?' He paused. 'You've employed one of our black friends, I believe?'

'That's right.'

Carver leaned forward. 'I wonder what our city fathers will say about that?'

'It's not their business, is it?'

'Not strictly. But every town has its rules and customs.'

Frank was annoyed and got up. 'It's been nice talking to you, Mr Carver.'

'John.'

'I'll see you around, then.'

'Come to the Regal and forget your cares for a shilling.'

'I might do that.'

'And give my regards to Julius Hoffmayer,' Carver said. 'I remember his father well. He was my best client but, alas, he never saw the talkies.'

He was amazed the recruitment march was so far from town. The leading man, a drummer, wore a topee, a waistcoat, a silver watch chain and medals from the Boer War. There were about thirty of them, and they looked a likely bunch – all broad-shouldered and sunburnt with their swags on their backs. At the back of the column, a regular army man was riding a bay mare. He was an officer in the Light Horse.

He threw down his fencing tools as the men stopped and the officer came up. 'Do you mind if we have our dinner here?' the soldier asked.

'No worries. Go right ahead.'

All the blokes were cheerful and said they were going to march right through to Glenmaggie and then on to Heyfield. They said they were ten when they started and now they were thirty-two. There were a couple of fellows from the football seconds and he felt awkward as he stood, watching them roll their cigarettes and boil their billies. A week before, he'd seen the recruitment poster at the railway station: WILL YOU FIGHT FOR YOUR KING AND COUNTRY? COME ALONG BOYS, BEFORE IT'S TOO LATE! That had set him thinking.

That evening, he discussed joining up with Irene and his father. They both said he should go, that they'd miss him, but they could cope, and that the war wouldn't last long anyway. When they saw him off on the train, Irene wept and smiled and his father was proud of his son, who was by far the tallest man in the group. The engine was decorated with the Union Jack and all the boys were hanging out of the windows and laughing. When the train left, Irene ran down the platform and he saw her waving until the carriage went around the bend into the bush where he had spent all his life.

At first they pitched tents, carted stores, built cookhouses and dug latrines. The training was a breeze for a country man: drill, route marches, rifle shooting, grenade throwing and learning to fire the Vickers. He was soon made a platoon commander, and all the blokes liked him. A regular army sergeant told him he would make a good officer. He was put into the 2/8 Infantry Battalion, and after three months they sailed from Port Melbourne on the HMAS Benalla. When they were steaming in the Indian Ocean, the Colonel told them they were going to fight in France.

Ten

As he drove his waggon past the railway station, Julius saw the train pumping water into the town dam and the farmers lined up with tanks on their carts. They looked like the refugees in the war, with their tired horses and old trucks; some were using hand-pumps, others buckets, as they stood up to their thighs in the muddy water. The one good thing his father had done was to build a large dam and sink bores – but that was nothing beside his carnal sins, his obscenities and his drunkenness.

The road home was long, and this time his visit to Rubicon was profitless. Despite himself, Julius found he was dozing in the heat, the dust and the flies. The swingletrees rattled and the waggon creaked as the dust rose from the geldings' hooves as he drifted in and out of the thundery afternoon.

He was still a boy when he learned that his father was disobeying God's law. His mother did not tell him – he learnt from the teachings of the church. August was a handsome man with a moustache like that of Count von Bismarck; his shoulders were broad, his eyes bright blue and his walk confident. Julius remembered his parents' wedding photograph in the front parlour above the piano. His mother, Carlotta, was fragile and beautiful in her wedding gown; his father in a bespoke suit, top hat and a blossom in his lapel. It was, he was told, the wedding of the season, with fifty guests, a red carpet, a five-piece orchestra, the verandah decorated with bunting and flowers, imported German beer, French champagne, venison, sweetmeats and dancing – despite the wishes of the Pastor.

In the first year of their marriage, August bought two carriages and pairs, had the house renovated with bluestone and the fireplace rebuilt with marble from Italy; he had water installed; bought a pedigree bull for fifty guineas; purchased three Arab stallions, a dozen Clydesdales, a grand piano, walnut dining-room furniture and a magic lantern. His father joined the Rubicon Gun Club, won many trophies, took prizes for the best stock at the Annual Show, had the garden landscaped and had his liquor sent up from the best wholesaler in Melbourne. When Julius was a child, the rains seemed plentiful, the harvests abundant, the wheat prices high and credit easy. The stock market was buoyant and the dividends generous.

Then when Carlotta found she could have no more children, his father started going away to Melbourne to see his stockbrokers – he stayed in a suite at the Windsor Hotel, returned with suits from London and dresses from Paris. But people began to talk: his father was seen at the opera and music halls in the company of strange women – then, later on, he was encountered in the saloons of provincial hotels with sluttish girls from the mining camps. This went on for years, and Julius saw his father less and less: he was a solitary boy. As he got older, August took to wearing a hair-piece and drinking brandy before midday. He left the running of the Hoffmayer farm to his manager and hired help.

When Julius married Sophie in 1910, money seemed no problem and even the Great War did not seem to affect the fortunes of August Hoffmayer. His grief seemed short when Carlotta died in 1916 and, in 1920, he bought the first automobile in Rubicon – a four-cylinder Mercedes-Benz and, after that, a generator for electricity, an Edison phonograph, a refrigerator and a four-valve wireless set. But by this time, August had refinanced the farm to James Withers – Harold's father – and interest rates were rising.

Everyone knew about August's women, but only six months after Carlotta died, he brought one home. The woman was a whore with henna-dyed hair, her breasts seemed about to burst from her satin blouse, her hips were broad and her mouth was painted bright red. Sophie was appalled and Julius outraged, but all he could do was to grind his teeth and pray as his father and the woman went into the parlour with a bottle of Napoleon brandy to sing and cavort at the piano. But it was the night that seemed endless: they rutted like the beasts in the field, groaning, laughing, she shouting, and asking each other for more. The woman stayed for a week when, for some reason, they quarrelled and Julius had to drive her into the station.

And all that summer, August brought a succession of women into the house: his drinking and behaviour became violent and although he brought home many toys for his grandchildren – spinning tops, lead soldiers, dolls and games-sets – Sophie tried to keep them away from him.

A drought struck in the winter of 1922, the crops failed in the following summer and when Julius dismissed the manager and his workers, his father had them brought back. Now, it seemed, all he could do was to pray for his father's death, but God in His mystery would not listen. August had given up attending church many years ago, and such was their shame, Julius and Maria became too embarrassed to go. The Pastor of St John's expelled the family in the spring of 1923 and the disgrace of the Hoffmayers was complete.

When the women would no longer come to the house, August drove his Mercedes-Benz each night to Rubicon to sit and drink brandy in the Regal Cinema. There, in the cavernous corrugated-iron hall, with its battered seats and cracked piano, he watched the silent films of D.W. Griffith, Lillian Gish, Charles Chaplin, Harold Lloyd and Theda Bara. Although Julius prayed for an accident on the treacherous road through the bush, his father always returned home to rummage through the sideboard for schnapps, wine or whatever he could find. The devil certainly looked after his own. At last, on 1 April 1924, Julius found his father dead in his filthy, rumpled bed – God had answered his prayers and the old man was buried in an unmarked grave on the northern boundary of the farm. Only the crows knew the spot and, within weeks, thistles and mallee roots covered the mound of earth. The extirpation of August Hoffmayer was complete: his clothes were burnt; the Mercedes-Benz sold; the water pipes torn out; the electric system dismantled – every sign and memory of August Adolph Hoffmayer was eliminated, the hired help sacked and the task of restoring the property begun. Now, the debts and the mortgage had to be repaid and, when that was done, the Hoffmayer farm would be impregnable. But each night, Julius was plagued with dreams of his father – and he knew the reason. The blood of his father pumped within him: he wanted to possess his own daughter, and there was no forgiveness for that.

When Julius awoke, he found he was being overtaken by a Chevrolet truck on the Kurnbrun road about five miles from his front gate. It was the soldier, Cameron: the man saluted, but Julius did not look up.

It was when she started to go to school that he had to accept there was something wrong with his daughter. Like her mother, Louisa was beautiful: his father adored her and every time he returned home, he would reach into his portmanteau and bring out dolls from France and Germany, dresses from London and chocolates from Italy. On cold winter nights, they both sat by the fire as they laughed and opened the parcels. His father drank his brandy and played childish tunes on the piano to his grand-daughter, but he sat alone in the kitchen as he wondered how much it all cost and where it would all end. It hadn't rained for a year and the wheat crops were poor.

At the end of that week, the Pastor came up the drive in his waggonette with Louisa by his side. Holding her hand, the Pastor strode up and said: 'Your daughter is possessed by the devil.'

He thought of his father and replied: 'Why do you say that?'

'Because,' the Pastor answered, 'she does unspeakable things, because she corrupts the other children. Your daughter is unclean.'

'What does she do?'

'I cannot tell you, but you have my word, Mr Hoffmayer, she cannot go to my school.'

'How can a six-year-old child corrupt other children?' He saw Louisa standing in the garden, her hair shining in the sun, her arms and legs bare, her lips open and her eyes the colour of the water in the lake.

'That, sir, you must find out for yourself.' The Pastor turned, his boots heavy on the grass. 'I cannot allow her back.'

Once again, he thought of his father and his women. 'Is there anyone to whom I can appeal?'

'No, Mr Hoffmayer, there is no one to whom you can appeal.'

In the hot summer months that followed, he prayed and prayed to God for guidance.

His father did not care for Carl, but took to teaching his grand-daughter – he said it was better she did not go to school, and that the Pastor was a narrow-minded peasant, only fit to teach the children of farm labourers and serfs. Together, his father and Louisa would wander through the lush garden and sit in the gazebo, shaded from the broiling summer sun. His father made sure his grand-daughter always wore flowery, broad-brimmed hats of the finest straw and her skin remained as flawless as alabaster. August taught her to sing and gave her French childrens' books.

One day as he was walking to the barn to yoke up the Clydesdales for ploughing, he passed the home paddock to see his father and Louisa standing by the rails. They were watching a stallion and a mare mating.

Despite the chill of the evening, Ray Stark was stripped to the waist as he drilled the holes for the fence strainers. He put down the post-hole borer, grinned and said: 'G'day. What's happening in town?'

Frank thought of his conversation with John Carver, but answered: 'Nothing much. I spoke to our friend, Julius Hoffmayer, outside Ballantine's.'

'What did he say?'

'He's a surly bastard – I saw him again on the road, but he didn't respond.'

'That fellow's got troubles, I reckon.'

'What do you mean?'

Ray lifted a post and dropped it into the hole. 'His old man used to fuck everything in sight and the church chucked him out. That's what I've heard.'

'Their house is strange.'

'Hoffmayer don't hold with modern things – he don't like progress. All the gear there is old-fashioned.'

As the two men talked, thunder cracked and a few heavy drops of rain fell. 'I'm going to shoot a few bunnies,' Frank said. 'Do you want rabbit for tea?'

'Do you want me to get it?'

'No,' Frank answered. 'You do what you're doing. I'll see you later.'

'Okay.' Ray watched his boss move off. It was the first time a white fellow had cooked for him.

Frank bagged four rabbits which he roasted over the fire with some potatoes. The food was good and Ray thought the white man could cook real well. He cleared the tin plates of the bones, tossed the scraps into the fireplace, and took out his tobacco tin.

'Tell me about Don Mooney,' Frank said.

'The copper?'

'That's right.'

'He don't like me. That's for sure.'

'Why?' But Frank knew the answer.

'He thinks I'm a thieving blackfellow and it gives him the shits I stay around. Why did you take me on?'

'My father,' Frank replied, 'employed a black once. All the neighbours complained, but Dad stuck to his guns and Henry gave his best. He worked as hard as any white. The local church wouldn't bury him in the cemetery, so my father held a funeral on the farm. I think it's worth another shot.'

'You doing me a favour, then?'

Frank looked at Ray squarely. 'No, I'm a good judge of men.'

'And you make your mind up quick?'

'Yep.'

'Where was your Dad's farm?'

'Gippsland. It rains down there – it's dairy country.'

'Why aren't you there?'

'The bank got it all.'

'They's bastards, aren't they?'

'Not necessarily, that's the system.'

'They ain't going to like you taking me on,' Ray said.

'Maybe. I'll pay anybody for a good day's work.' Frank got up and poured the water for a cup of tea. 'Who's the bloke with the Hupmobile and the driver?'

'That's Harold Withers – he's more powerful than King George. He owns all the country around here.'

'Except this place. An Englishman's home is his castle.'

'How did you get that leg?'

'I got hit – by one of our blokes.' Frank laughed again. 'There were no hard feelings.'

'Does it hurt?'

'Only when it rains.'

Ray smiled. 'It's not going to hurt for a bit, is it?'

'It doesn't look like it.' Frank got up and took off his jacket. 'We're going to start pulling that bloody bush tomorrow.'

That cold, starry night, a farmhouse burnt down about five miles away and in the morning Don Mooney went out to have a look; but the farmer was a friend of his and no one knew the causes. The number of insurance claims was increasing as the financial grip tightened.

Eleven

The days started to pass slowly for the shopkeepers of Rubicon. Henry Farrar did not sell another tractor after Frank bought the McCormick-Deering. George Ballantine found himself passing the time reading on his high stool behind the counter or leafing through the ledger as the unpaid accounts mounted. Often nothing moved before midday on Federation Street – not even a horse and cart – and it seemed that Rubicon was becoming a ghost town.

In the summer of 1932, conferences were held, State Premiers met, economists conferred, one government fell and another took its place, but it seemed no one knew what to do as farm prices slumped further and the numbers of unemployed grew.

The strikes had increased over the past year as men became more desperate: the miners, the slaughtermen, the wharf labourers, the timber-workers, the shearers and the railway fettlers. Some of the wheat farmers had wanted to strike, too. They argued that if they deprived the nation of its bread, the government would have to sit up and take notice. But the trouble was that their leadership was divided: in January 1931, the picket lines at the rail heads would not hold – neighbour was pitted against neighbour, friend against friend and father against son. Julius Hoffmayer had declared he would deliver his wheat, no matter what – a contract, he said, was a contract and that was that.

As the confusion and bitterness grew, railway lines were sabotaged, town water tanks were ruptured and farm buildings set on fire. There were reports of suicides and strange murders in country and town. In outback Western Australia, one farmer killed his wife and five children and then turned the shotgun on himself. There was a crime wave in Melbourne as bad, some said, as the gangland killings in Chicago.

Some communities thought they could do better by themselves, and in a number of provincial towns meetings were held to argue for leaving the Federation. It looked as though Australia was breaking up and the sense of national purpose was disappearing. In Neukirck, the birthplace of the Hoffmayers, brown-shirted men wearing swastikas burned down the Town Hall and smashed the windows of Jewish shopkeepers. The looms of the clothmakers were destroyed and the bank closed.

Men started to carry guns when they were working outdoors, and some organized themselves in groups. And Harold Withers' friend was right: the New Guard was well organized – they were led by distinguished officers from the Great War and supported by lawyers and captains of industry. They drilled at rifle and bayonet practice in the country north of Sydney and held meetings in the Returned Soldiers' Halls and Masonic temples. In the parched back-lands of New South Wales and Victoria, there were reports that the Bolsheviks were training an army of revolution in the bush, that the blacks would rise up and burn down the remote settlements and townships and that Russian agents had infiltrated the unions and the unemployed. Jim Banks and Reg Bolger were sure of this and spread the word each night over beers in the Royal. Women were raped in Yorktown, Darwin and Horsham; it was reported that blacks went on the rampage in Tarec, and bushfires were lit in southern Queensland. In Rubicon, several more young men volunteered and the mounted guards were strengthened. The Prime Minister gave a stirring speech for national unity on the wireless, but it all seemed hopeless. Even the sports news was bad: the English cricket captain, Jardine, was playing unfairly and the first Test in Adelaide was lost.

Frank followed all this closely and once a week drove into Rubicon for the papers, and in the evenings he sat by the fire and read while Ray played patience. Sometimes they had a game of poker, but the work was hard and they were usually in their bed rolls by nine.

In the next two months, they cleared and ploughed a hundred acres, built stables for the horses, repaired fences, started on a storage shed and prepared the garden for the next winter's rain. Frank bought two house cows and they had a little fresh milk.

The two men worked together from dawn to dusk, day in, day out, their bodies sweating hard under the eternal summer sun. They reblocked the tank stand, lined the house and dug a cellar outside the kitchen: they made it large enough to shelter from sandstorms, with an air vent and stocks of tinned food and cans of water from the well. When he closed the trapdoor and sat in the darkness, Frank was reminded of *The Swiss Family Robinson*. The farm was his, and no bank or mortgagee could claim it.

They did not work on Sundays, when Ray went rabbiting or sparrow-shooting. And one thundery afternoon, he took Frank out to the Moravian mission where he had been brought up. The mission lay about twenty miles east of Rubicon, at the end of a yellow road where the bush closed in and the sand hills crept over the cleared ground. Some of them were so high that Frank expected to hear the sound of the sea and the gulls wheeling and diving. But instead the locusts sang in the stubble and the parakeets went for them as they got out of the truck.

'There was gardens here once,' Ray said, as they strolled toward the ruined buildings. But of cultivation, there was no sign and the thistles grew, rank and tall, their seeds floating away on the gentle north wind. This land, Frank thought, would never be brought back: it was a potter's field now.

The church was made of sandstone with a thatched roof and a bell tower. It was buttressed on the outside walls and the school house stood next door. Among the bracken were graves with broken headstones, some with rusting iron fences; the inscriptions were faded and eaten away by sand.

The school buildings reminded Frank of the drawings in

Hansel and Gretel and he walked over, stood on the stone base and peered in through the long, narrow window. Inside all was dark, but he could see the raised platform and the high teacher's desk. Ray stood beside him, looked in at the familiar room and said:

> '*B is for blackfellow*
> *We can all see*
> *Lazily sleeping*
> *Under a tree.*'

He laughed. 'The Moravians were tough buggers. Have you ever heard of a bloke called John Huss?'

'Can't say I have.'

'He said all sin comes from Adam.'

'A lot of people have said that.'

'These buggers banged it into us with a stick, day in, day out. Do you want to see where me mother's buried?'

'Okay.'

But when Ray showed the grave to him, it was only a rough mound and could have been anything.

'Do you believe that all sin comes from Adam?' Ray asked as they walked back to the truck.

'No, I think life's what you make of it.'

'A bit of a battle, eh?'

Frank eased his leg into the cab. 'Sometimes.'

When they got back to the block, they found a black Ford sedan parked outside the front gate: it was Constable Mooney and a big man Frank didn't recognize. He saw a shotgun lying on the front seat.

'G'day,' Mooney said to Frank. 'Do you know Reg Bolger?'

'Pleased to meet you,' the butcher said as he gripped Frank's hand.

Frank was about to introduce Ray Stark, but decided not – best see what they wanted first. 'What can I do for you?' he said to Mooney.

'A woman at Netherby was attacked last night.'

'So?'

For the first time Mooney looked at Ray. 'She says it was a black.'

'This is Ray Stark,' Frank said. 'I expect you know each other.'

'We do.' The policeman drew out a notebook. 'There's not a lot of blacks around here.'

'Where were you last night, Stark?' the butcher said.

Frank turned. 'I didn't know you were in the constabulary, Mr Bolger. I thought meat was your trade.'

'I'm helping with the enquiries.'

Ray stood as still as a tree. 'I was with Mr Cameron.'

'In the house?' Mooney asked.

'In the house,' Frank replied. 'We played cards until half past nine, then turned in.'

'In the same house?' It was Bolger again.

'In the same house.' Frank measured the man, then said: 'That settles it.'

But Mooney still had his notebook in hand. 'The woman said it was a black. Are you sure he didn't slip out?'

'Look, Mr Mooney,' Frank said, 'Ray's told you where he was. We've got work to do.'

'Where've you come from?' Bolger said.

'Mind your own fucking business.'

'Hey, hey,' Mooney said, 'Watch the language.'

Frank laughed. 'Are you scared we'll offend the crows? Open the gate, Ray.' He climbed up, started the Chev and leaned out the window. 'Good hunting.'

When they got to the house, Ray said: 'There's going to be trouble.'

'I've been in some small towns,' Frank answered, 'but Rubicon's one of the meanest. What does Bolger do when he's not butchering?'

'He's President of the Returned Soldiers.'

'Is that so? I must remember to wear my badge when I'm next in town.'

'They know you're a returned man. I reckon you've got them confused.'

But Frank was hungry. 'It's your turn to cook tonight,' he said. 'And this time I want rabbit.'

Of all these developments, Maria Hoffmayer knew nothing. Julius did not buy the papers, nor did he have a wireless and did not hear the Prime Minister's speech. If he did pick up information, he passed it on to no one – except Carl, and then only when it suited him. All Maria knew was that it was hotter and drier than any summer she had known before, that the animals were getting weak for want of feed and her husband, for the first time, had failed to sell the eggs, that they had gone stale on the journey home and he had thrown them in the creek bed.

Julius made an inventory of the stores in the barn and cellar and decided to ration the food. Only Louisa was allowed fresh eggs and scalded cream: Julius, Carl and Maria started to live on old potatoes, pumpkin and turnip with two slices of meat a day. Every morning, Julius inspected the salted meat in the cellar.

The sun was now so bright that Maria drew every curtain and blind in the house, and the silent days dragged by in semi-darkness. The blowflies buzzed against the dusty window-panes, the moths lay dead on the floor and the centipedes crawled. Dead and dying insects lay everywhere and soft debris drifted down from the pine ceilings. When the men were gone for the day, the only sound was the grandfather clock ticking, and when Louisa cried out, her voice echoed through the darkness of the house. In the yard outside, even the chickens were listless and the rooster had stopped crowing.

Quite suddenly, for reasons she dared not think about, Maria had stopped making her daily devotions, and her prayerbook lay on the sideboard unread. It was as though God had left them, and the parched country, and she did not mind. This, she thought, must be what limbo was like.

In the candle-lit evenings when the moths fluttered and burned themselves to death in the flames, and the mosquitoes bit, it seemed to Maria that the evening prayers and Bible

97

readings were growing longer. Julius's voice was growing hoarse and the steel rims on his spectacles gleamed like silver as he concentrated on the Revelations and the Last Judgement. *And the temple of God was opened in heaven, and there was seen in His temple the ark of His testament: and there were lightnings and voices, and thunderings, and an earthquake, and great hail.*

It seemed that Carl spent all his spare time cleaning and oiling his shotgun, and sharpening his slashers and bill-hooks – it was as though he was preparing for an insurrection. One evening after prayers, he placed his empty cup on the table and said: 'A dead man has been found by the roadside.'

Julius looked at his son over his spectacles. 'Do they know who it was?'

'A vagrant, one of the unemployed.'

'It has nothing to do with us, then.'

'No, father, it does not.'

Maria thought of the young, sunburned man with the Gladstone bag and the sheet music. Was it he? And what would she do if more men called? She thought of the Pharisee and wondered.

Carl took out his pocket knife and opened and closed the blades. 'We will have the top paddock cleared and ready for sowing by the end of the month.'

It was the end of March now and, when it ended, it would be the sixteenth month with only the dew in the early mornings. 'That we will,' his father said, as he put the Bible back on the dresser. The leather was cracking and the back was breaking in the heat.

Carl closed the knife. 'I heard that the soldier has employed a black man.'

'Who told you?'

The boy smiled. 'I have my ears to the ground.'

'There is only one such person in the district,' Julius replied.

'That is the one.'

'That is a mistake,' Julius said, looking at his wife. 'A grave error.'

'Why is that so?' Maria asked. But she knew.

Her husband ignored the question. 'We will have to be doubly vigilant – these are indeed difficult times.'

He rose from the table and disappeared into the front of the house, where she heard him trying all the locks.

Carl looked at her over the table. 'What was he like?' he said.

'Who?'

'The soldier – you are the only one who has seen him.'

'He has a limp – I think he was injured in the war.'

'Ah, is that so?' Her stepson smiled. 'Does he find it difficult to get around? This is hard country for such a man.'

'I have no idea.' Maria hoped Carl would leave the kitchen as he always did after prayers, but this night he sat at the table.

'I would like a cup of tea, Stepmother.'

She got up and put the kettle on the fire. 'Mr Cameron is a big man with fair hair.'

'Is he? An Aryan? I wonder why he would employ a savage.'

Maria had never seen Ray Stark and thought he might be like Farozi, the Indian hawker. 'I do not know about these things.'

Carl stretched his legs under the table and scraped his boots on the floor. 'You will have to be careful from now on. You will have to take great care of Louisa.'

It was the first time he had mentioned her name for months. 'I take great care of her now.'

'That is good.' Carl took the cup of tea and drank. 'That is very good.'

When he had seen to all the locks, Julius sat in the chair on the verandah, breathed in the night air and dozed.

That winter's night it was raining and cold; they sat around the stove, he reading his Bible, Carl cleaning his rifle and Maria knitting. The house creaked, the rain beat against the windows and a door slammed. 'What is that?' he asked.

Maria put down her needles. 'It is probably Louisa.'

He got up. 'I will go and see.'

He went down the hall, and when he got to her door, he stopped and spoke her name. There was no reply, he spoke again, waited, then opened the door. The fire was burning, her room was stifling and she was lying on the bed. Louisa was naked with her legs apart, her hands playing between her thighs; her eyes were vacant, her breasts sweating and body gleaming. As he found himself looking at her, she smiled. He was powerless, could neither speak nor move, saw her back arch, and watched her shudder.

Then she spoke: 'I can do that to you.'

He gasped, then turned and closed the door. He stood in the darkness; his heart thumped and he thought of his father, his women and his nightmares.

When he got back to the kitchen, Maria asked: 'Was it Louisa?'

He sat down, saw his Bible lying on the floor and replied: 'It was nothing. It was nothing.'

That morning, Maria had changed the sheets on the bed. They smelt of camphor and were rough to the touch. For the first time for as long as she could remember, Julius slept well, not moving through the entire night. But she was restless and listened to the sound of the wind in the dry trees: now and again, a cow bellowed with hunger and a dog barked. Where would they have taken the dead man's body? Was there a special burial place for unknown men? She remembered reading about the Unknown Warrior. As was their usual habit, she and her husband lay apart, and their bodies did not touch. She did not dream often, but that night she did: she dreamed it was snowing. She had only seen snow on Christmas cards from a great-aunt in Leipzig. The snow fell all over the bush and the plains; it even fell down the chimney into the stove where it fizzled and melted on the hot plates. August sang carols and played on a small harmonium and Julius was dressed as Father Christmas. Everyone was excited when he brought huge, bulky sacks of presents into the house. August kept on laughing and singing and playing the harmonium, but when Julius opened the sacks, they contained nothing but thousands of mice that smelled foul and ran over the floor, down into the cellar, along the hall, into the front parlour and into Louisa's room, where she lay naked in bed, shrieking and screaming. When Maria woke up, all she could hear was the sound of the wind, still whistling through the dry trees.

Twelve

The hot weather continued into April and it seemed that autumn would never come. For weeks, the land lay silent under the eternal sun. It was a wilderness of scrub, sand and stunted trees, the bright sun above and not a sound of life to break the silence. Over journeys of a hundred miles, by truck, horse buggy or on foot, not a solitary bird or living creature was to be seen. Farmers walked off and their properties were left vacant; diseased and dying stock were shot or left to wander the roads; weeds grew on the earth tennis courts; thistles choked the vegetable gardens and dams dried up, the earth ugly, hard and as cracked as crazy-paving. In some places, the only sign of life was the barked stems of small trees and bushes where rabbits had been feeding and the dead carcasses of dingoes.

In the hope of a miracle, some farmers sowed their wheat, but the seed withered and dried away. The soil on the farms, pulverized to powder, joined the dust on the roads, and the brown of the countryside turned to grey. The windmills ground and cranked in the hot north wind, but the bores went dry and spiders and lizards lived in the water troughs. Salt pans crept across the dried swamps and cattle and horses staggered to their knees. The queues at the water trains grew longer and children ate bran and treacle for their supper.

In the cities, children scavenged the railway yards for coal; a man killed his baby with an axe; stevedores beat a mate to death for crossing the picket lines; communists held secret meetings in safe houses; street-side orators stood on boxes; spiritualism became popular with the rich and seances were held in dark front rooms; battles were fought in streets and lanes as furniture was loaded on to trucks and horse-drawn

102

drays, and in university common rooms the academics argued over the causes of the collapse. To some, it seemed, Karl Marx was right.

For John Carver, business at the Regal had never been so good. He started to show double features three times a week. Each night, the families of Rubicon watched Paul Muni, James Cagney, Lew Ayres, Mary Pickford and Rosalind Russell. The children shouted for the Cisco Kid, cheered Don Winslow of the Coast Guard and stayed silent when the projector broke down. Now, there were no more hoots in the darkness when Carver struggled with the machine and drank his whisky: they sat quiet and hoped the dream would continue. Carver extended the season of *Frankenstein* by popular request.

On Federation Street, Sissy Jones closed the Madre Hair Salon and disappeared leaving her creditors with debts; Mrs Chamberlain shut the doors of her Coffee Palace and went to live with her son in Melbourne; Charles Smith, the farrier, died of a heart attack; Arnold Temby of Vivian Studios gave the negatives of his portraits to his son and took the train to the south; and the town council declared the empty Rubicon reservoir a place of danger and out of bounds. In the north, the two German farmers were evicted and went peacefully, their furniture stacked in their waggons. All their livestock, ploughs, harrows, reapers and wheat were confiscated by a small Melbourne loan company whose chairman was Harold Withers. The bailiffs were considerate men and he did not get the household effects.

Someone discovered that a windmill and pump were still working on an abandoned farm on the outskirts of Rubicon; the word spread and within a week the unemployed men set up a camp there – tents made of hessian bags and lean-tos of corrugated iron, wood and cardboard. Some of the men had .22 rifles and shot rabbits; chickens were stolen and flagons of Tokay appeared. The men spent most of their time playing two-up, pontoon and poker: they were veterans of the road – their bodies as brown as the earth, raw-boned, bearded, with battered, wide-brimmed hats and hard faces.

103

These were not swaggies, but men from the cities, hardened by living in the open and with the cunning of the narrow streets and tenements. Don Mooney drove out in his black Ford to have a look, but when three beer bottles hit the car, retired to do battle another day. By the end of April, the days were shortening and there was still no sign of rain. The country lay grey and dead, farm prices fell even lower, men fought the coppers in the streets of the cities and the government was powerless.

Ray Stark saw the fire first: it was burning about two miles away, and there was a north-east wind coming up. He threw down his fencing tools and rode back to the house.

'You've seen the fire?' Frank said.

'I reckon it's at the Hoffmayers.'

'It looks like it.' Frank looked at the smoke, and then saw the rim of fire: it could take the homestead out. 'There's just the two of them – Hoffmayer and the boy.'

'What do you think?' Ray stood by his horse and watched.

'They don't like company.'

'A fire's a fire.'

Frank thought of Maria, working in her dark kitchen. 'It is. You'd better get the truck and the gear.'

They loaded shovels, bill-hooks and sacks and drove east up the Kurnbrun road toward the smoke as it billowed into the sky.

There was no one at the house, where a horse was snorting and whinneying in the yard; the fowls were huddled under the brush and the cockatoos were silent. The smoke was thick, cinders falling and Frank thought the signs looked bad. They drove down the track for a mile, past the pines and river gums, and found the head of the fire, which was racing through a half-cleared paddock where the broken timber was piled high and igniting. The three of them were there: Julius, Carl and Maria, working with shovels, slashers and sacks as the flames ran through the stubble like twisting, lethal streams.

When Frank sounded the horn, Julius looked up, acknowledged and went on beating with the shovel, the fire around his boots; he looked like some giant in a storybook, with his massive shoulders and his arms rising and falling. Further up was Carl, cutting down the blazing branches and starting a fire-break; Frank knew that was where they should work and jumped down with Ray; they grabbed the shovels and sacks and dashed across the smouldering ground. Where was Maria? Then he saw her further down the front, beating with a sack, her long dress hitched above her knees.

As he worked, slashing and beating in the smoke and heat, Ray Stark knew the fire was nasty, but not impossible – he had fought before. Several hundred yards away, Carl beat, shovelled and slashed, cinders burning through his shirt, his boots deep in ash, but gave no sign he was being helped. For three hours, they all fought the blaze until at last it burnt back on itself, the fire abating and the danger over. Julius, his arms blistered and burnt, his clothes in shreds, threw down his shovel and said: 'It is over now. Thank you, Mr Cameron.' He put on his black hat. 'I owe you a debt.'

'You owe me nothing, Mr Hoffmayer,' Frank replied. 'You would do well to have a tractor.'

'You have a tractor, Mr Cameron. I do not. That is the difference between us.'

Frank wondered at this taciturn man, while Ray stood apart, leaning on his shovel. Carl was standing as still as a stone and there seemed nothing further to say. Then Maria came up, her hair down, her clothes filthy and torn. 'Thank you, Mr Cameron. If you come up to the house, I will make us all a cup of tea.'

'That,' her husband said, 'will not be possible. There is much to do.' He turned and went back to the bush as it smouldered.

The flies clung to their faces and backs and the sun beat down through the haze.

'Thank you,' Maria said once more, her face impassive, her hair to her shoulders; her blouse clung to her breasts with sweat and her arms were bleeding.

'We'll be on our way, then,' Frank answered. 'Good day to you.' Maria Hoffmayer, he thought, was a remarkably handsome woman.

'Good day.' She turned to Ray. 'And to you.'

As they drove back through the stubble, Ray said: 'That man don't say much.'

'He does not.'

'But a fire's a fire, ain't it?'

Frank was working on the house next morning when he heard the sound of a horse on the stamped earth of the yard. It was Maria Hoffmayer on a black gelding. The horse was nervous and shied at the flies, but she sat easily in the saddle. 'Good morning,' she said.

'Good morning.' He was stripped to the waist and sweating in the clear heat of the day.

'I have come,' Maria said, 'to apologize for my husband.'

If Frank were surprised to see her, he did not show it. 'There is nothing to apologize for. We all help each other out.'

'Ours is a very closed family.'

Frank laughed. 'It takes all sorts. Would you like to come in for a cup of tea?'

She hesitated: he was tanned and fit, his eyes clear, his face cleanly shaven – a man who looked after himself, a man who must know much of the world outside Rubicon. 'Just for a moment.' Neither Julius nor Carl knew she had left the house. Maria swung down, tethered her horse and followed him into the cottage.

Frank had lined the ceiling with timber and the house was cool and dark. The kitchen was neat, the gear stacked and everything in its place; the earth floor was swept, biscuit tins in rows on the shelf, a hurricane lamp hung from the rafters and a child's teddy bear sat on the mantel above the fireplace. Maria sat at the table as Frank put the kettle on the stove. Despite herself, she was curious – she could not remember when she had last been in a stranger's house. It was unfamiliar and disturbing. 'You live here with the black man?'

Frank looked up. 'I do. His name is Ray Stark, he's out fencing. There is much to do.'

'There is always much to do.'

'It's a good life,' Frank said, 'despite the Depression.'

'The Depression?'

He was baffled. 'The fall in farm prices, the unemployment.'

'Ah.'

'There was a man found dead near here the other day.'

'Was there?'

Frank wanted to ask her why such an established farm as theirs had no electricity and machinery, but decided not. It was none of his business. The silence was becoming awkward as they drank their tea. Then she said: 'Where did you get the teddy bear?'

'I found it when I moved in here.'

'You have no children?'

'No.'

'Neither do I – Carl is my stepson.'

'Do you want some more tea?' he said.

'No thank you, I must go.' She rose from the table and he followed her outside; her back was square and her neck long.

'Maybe I will see you again?'

She mounted her horse quickly. 'I am not sure.' There was a faint smile and she rode away up the track.

For several moments, Frank stood and thought about Maria Hoffmayer. But the flies bit; he pulled on his shirt, threw a saddle on his horse and went down to work with Ray Stark.

That evening was cool and the two men sat outside and listened to the sounds of the bush. Ray took out his tin of pipe tobacco and rolled a cigarette; he lit it and the smoke hung in the still air. Would it rain?

'Your leg ain't aching, is it?' Ray asked.

'No. We had a visitor today.'

'Yeah?'

'Mrs Hoffmayer.'

'What did she want?'

'She came to apologize for her husband.'

'It ain't the father,' Ray said, 'it's the son. That young bloke's not right in the head.'

'Why do you say that?'

'That whole Hoffmayer family – they're round the bend.'

'Go on.'

'I told you: the old man, Hoffmayer's dad, he was crazy – rooting women, drinking, they had the best place in the district, but the old bastard just about put it under. It was the first place to have electricity and running water. That's all gone now. That young Carl – I wouldn't be surprised if he did someone in.'

'What did your father do?' Frank said.

Ray laughed. 'Just what all blackfellows did: stumping, shoot-cutting, clearing, living on the skin of his arse. He was a good bloke, but no one trusted him: he was a cheeky nigger bastard, don't turn your back on a coon, keep the abo in his place, boot him in the balls, but he worked hard. He was a good bloke.'

'What happened to him?'

'They say some blokes kicked him to death, but I don't know, I was at the mission then. He didn't show up any more – no one knew where he went.' Ray laughed again and ground his cigarette butt out. 'I was luckier than him – the Moravians taught me to read and write.'

'I've been warned about employing you.'

'Yeah?'

'Carver who runs the Regal,' Frank said.

'He's a fucking pisspot.'

'Mooney.'

'Look, I go any time you like.'

'No, you take each man as you find him, right?'

'Okay. You're like your dad, eh?'

'In some ways, but he didn't beat the bank.'

'No bugger can do that.'

Frank got up. 'We'll see. I'm turning in, I'll see you in the morning.'

During the night, it thundered; Frank woke up twice and

thought about Maria Hoffmayer, sitting straight on her horse. A wind got up and the old house creaked as he flicked on the torch: Ray was sleeping soundly on the other side of the room. Someone told him once that a black will go for you when your back is turned. Had he done the right thing? He thought he had.

He was lying on his bunk when the German officer came in; his leg was healed and he could get around with a walking stick. It was November and the guns had stopped, but he thought it was just a lull in the barrage. For almost a year now, the sound of the war was like a distant railway train, and at night the sky was lit up with strange lights which reminded him of the thunderstorms at home. Most of the prisoners were French – nobody was ill-treated but, for some reason, he had been treated extra well, and the German nurses and sisters were interested in Australia. Two had relations living there – they were not sure where, but they thought it was near a desert.

The surgeon was a young man from Heidelberg, and he'd done the job efficiently – he'd saved the leg, but had told him he'd have a limp for the rest of his life. This wasn't too bad; it was much better than losing both legs at the thigh, or having your jaw and lower face replaced. There was one man who, after three operations, still looked like smashed gargoyle on a medieval church. He had looked in the mirror and never uttered a word since.

There was one German nurse who was tall and blonde, who bent over him like a willow tree. She gave him sweetmeats and chocolates and called him Franch. *If it weren't for Irene, he would have come back to Germany after the war and asked her to marry him. He sometimes dreamed of her and wondered how she would like Australia.*

The young officer stood at the door; he was like an actor and suddenly ripped off his shoulder tabs and decorations. He was small and thin and looked no more than twenty. 'The war is over,' he said. 'There is a socialist revolution – and our comrades in the Navy have left Kiel to give themselves up. They are flying the red flag.' The officer stood and looked at the men in the silent barrack room. 'You are all free to go. Good luck.'

There was no cheering: the men all looked puzzled, but one by one, they packed their belongings in what they could find and went outside. The silence was terrifying, and as there were only enough trucks for the limbless, he decided to walk. The country looked like a vast, badly ploughed field in winter: not a building nor a tree was standing. But in the quiet, he heard a bird singing and he found a lone daffodil growing.

It was a long walk: he went from camp to camp, keeping by himself, looked at the thousands of weary soldiers wandering across the ravaged land, and finally found an Australian unit. They gave him bread, butter and eggs for breakfast. When he disembarked at Leith in Scotland, he was given a year's pay and new clothing; he got drunk, and was put on a train to Southampton.

Thirteen

'We got the numbers,' Reg Bolger said, 'no worries about that. And we got the guns.'

Don Mooney drank his third beer. 'There's the law, don't forget.'

Reg laughed. 'Harold Withers looks after that. How many do you think there are?'

'About thirty at a guess.'

'Any Bolshies?' Jim Banks served the beer and whisky from the bar. The blinds were drawn against the night as the men stood in the small back room.

'There's sure to be – these bastards are from the towns.' Bolger's arms rested on the minutes of the Rubicon Gun Club, but no records were being taken.

'Any niggers?' Banks asked.

'Nah, even these people have their rules.' Reg coughed. 'But I reckon it's a dead cert Stark's been poking around – fucking half-breed.'

'How do you know that?'

'Jesus Christ, the bastard's always been coming and going for as long as we can remember.'

'Even now he's working for Cameron?'

'We'll get on to that later.'

Mooney took control. 'I can get them for trespassing, putting up an illegal camp, disturbing the peace, sly-grogging, illegal gambling, you name it. I've spoken to Withers – he wants them out – it's bad for the town.'

'You mean,' Banks said, 'it's bad for his investments.'

The policeman shrugged. 'It's no good for all of us. What about the women and kids? Someone's going to get raped. Jesus, it's happening all over – I don't know what's going on, but it's bad. They'll be laying round the main street next.'

'Give us another beer, Jim,' Reg said, 'I'm as dry as a chip. Is Henry Farrar coming?'

'He said he'd be along.'

'What about Carver?'

'We don't need that pisshead – he's too fucking old and unreliable.'

'Who can we get then?'

'I'll tell you,' Mooney answered. 'There's us, the Smith brothers, Farrar, at least three from the Lodge and my dog. He'll scare the shit out of them.'

'What about Frank Cameron?'

Mooney stared at Bolger. 'What do *you* think? He covered up for Stark, I never thought a returned man would do that. Cameron's a queer fish, he may have been decorated, but I think he's not going to join us.'

'He's got that leg,' Banks said.

'That doesn't seem to worry him.' Bolger slid his empty glass across the counter. 'He's doing some job on that farm from all accounts.'

'Do you want me to ask him, then?' Mooney said.

'Yeah, ask him and we'll see which side his bread's buttered. But a man who has a coon in the same house, there's got to be something wrong.'

'When Cameron's next in,' Mooney said, 'give me a ring, and I'll come round.'

'Okay. What's the plan?'

'We'll do it at night – say about twelve – they'll all be sleeping it off, and I'll set the day. No shooting, right?' Mooney belched. 'Is there anything else?'

'When's the annual shooting competition?' Banks asked.

'November,' Bolger replied.

'I suppose that young bastard, Hoffmayer, will take the honours.'

'It's open to all – we can't change that.'

'One for the road, then,' Mooney said. 'I can't be too late, I've got another eviction tomorrow.'

'Who is it this time?'

'The Dolans.'

'Bloody Micks,' Banks said, 'they were never any good.'

'Nah.'

Mooney gathered himself together. 'I'll see you blokes tomorrow.'

'Okay,' the publican said, 'don't do anything I wouldn't do.'

'No way.' But Mooney knew he would pick up a young tart from the house-bar later.

Henry Farrar arrived and, as Reg Bolger put it, they got on the piss. They drank another dozen glasses each of Richmond draught, sang *Frigging in the Rigging* and Great War songs, laid plans for burning down the unemployed camp, pissed in the back alley among the old car tyres and firewood and went to sleep in one of Jim Banks' vacant rooms upstairs. But Reg was up at four and drove his truck out to the abattoir to get the carcasses. As he carved out the chops, steaks and offal, he considered it had been a most satisfactory night.

In the afternoon, Harold Withers and Don Mooney sat in the cool of the court house. Withers' portmanteau was at his feet as he got up and went to the cupboard. 'Do you want a drink?'

'No thanks, not while I'm on duty.'

Withers laughed. 'Ha. I was on the phone to Melbourne, and the stock market has collapsed again.'

Mooney didn't have any stocks and shares. 'So?'

'It's belt-tightening time.'

The policeman thought Withers was talking about running costs. 'There's only me as it is.'

'You're doing all right, Don, you've got the Gun Club to back you up. What are you doing about that vagrants' camp?'

'We move in at the end of the week.'

'At night?'

'Yes.'

'I don't want any blood, you understand, just nice, clean arrests, and the word spread that Rubicon is not the town to camp in. Okay?'

'Right.'

'I won't ask who's helping you, and I don't want to know.'

'Leave it to me.'

'Belt-tightening means that those people more than six months behind with their interest payments have to make other arrangements. Some have to go for the common good. We've all got a stake in this town.'

More evictions, Mooney thought, and this time it was sure to be a mate. 'I'm listening.'

Withers opened the portmanteau and drew out a folder which he placed on the oak table. His hair gleamed with brilliantine, his collar and shirt cuffs were spotless and he still smelt of pomade. 'There's a list in here of five mortgagors who've failed to make it. If you serve warrants and supervise the evictions as you did with the two Germans, I'll more than make it worth your while. Get all you can, but no crying babies, screaming women or angry men.'

A country policeman's pay was pitiful, and Mooney could do with the money. 'I'll do my best.'

Withers drank his Scotch. 'I'm sure you will. And keep me advised on those layabouts in that camp.'

'I'll do that.'

Withers put down the glass. 'Have you heard of the New Guard?'

'Can't say I have.'

'You should read the papers more carefully. The New Guard is a military organization in Sydney. It's run by some of our most distinguished officers to act in the case of a Bolshevist takeover. We could do with that kind of thing here. Didn't you tell me that man Cameron was an officer in the Great War? Wasn't he decorated?'

Mooney thought once more. 'I don't think he would be suitable.'

'Why not?'

'You know Ray Stark?'

'Of course I know Stark.'

114

'Well, Cameron's employed him. He even lets Stark sleep in the house.'

'Why on earth would he do a thing like that when there's plenty of white men searching for jobs?'

'We don't know.'

'Our man, Cameron, has made a grave error. Stark will go for him when his back is turned, or at the least he'll lose everything he's got.' Withers drained his glass. 'You learn something new every day. I think I'll be seeing Stark standing in front of the bench before too long.' He pushed his chair back. 'I've got a great deal to do. Keep in touch.'

Withers got up and left the building, his black shoes squeaking on the polished floor.

Mooney opened Withers' file and looked at the list. Cleary, Donovan, Costello, Snaith and Johnson – three Micks and two Prots. He knew none of them well, so Lady Luck was still on his side. All the same, he'd put in yet again for a transfer back to Melbourne – or any place just to get out of this mess. Mooney left the office, the blowflies beating against the flydoor and the west sun blinding him from the tin roofs.

On his way down Federation Street, Mooney saw Frank Cameron coming out of Ballantine's store with a box of provisions in his arms. There was no time like the present – he'd ask him now. He crossed the street quickly and strolled up to Frank's truck.

'How are you doing?' he said.

Frank put the case on the tray, turned and saw the policeman.

'I'm doing okay, and you?'

'Good. Thirsty weather?'

'You could say that.'

'Got time for a beer?' Mooney smiled.

Frank pulled out his watch. 'Just a couple.'

Nothing more was said as they walked out between the cars and drays and over the street. Frank wondered if it was about the woman who was supposed to have been attacked at

115

Netherby. If it was, he supposed Mooney was only trying to do his job.

Mooney bought two beers and they stood near the window, away from the other men in the bar. Jim Banks nodded and Frank replied. It was quiet enough, well before the six o'clock rush, but some customers were already eating sausages, steaks and potatoes. The cigarette smoke hung thick in the sunlight.

'Did you know that some unemployed men have set up a camp on the south side of town?' Mooney drank his beer which tasted cold and bitter.

'No.'

'Well, they have and it's a fucking eyesore.'

'The poor buggers have got to live somewhere.'

'Not outside Rubicon.'

'If you say so, you're the lawman.'

'Others think the same way.'

'Who?'

'Harold Withers, for one.'

'I must meet him sometime.' Frank wondered what all this was leading up to.

'You will. We're getting up a party to clear those men out.'

'A posse?'

'It'll be legally constituted – Harold Withers will see to that. I was wondering if you wanted to be in.'

Frank looked squarely at Mooney. 'You want me to be part of a group of vigilantes to kick the shit out of the unemployed?'

'I wouldn't put it quite like that.'

'Who's volunteered?'

'Jim Banks, Reg Bolger, Henry Farrar, two blokes you don't know and a couple from the Lodge.' Mooney was getting apprehensive now, but didn't know quite why.

'Why are you asking me?'

'You're a returned man, an officer I hear, and was decorated.'

Jesus, Frank thought, the bush telegraph was efficient. 'You can count me out – I want no part of it.' He put his glass on the window-ledge and was gone.

The night they chose was stormy, with dry thunder booming over the bush and sand hills; the wind was warm and as they rode along the track past the reservoir; the sand blew into their faces. Now and again, the late summer moon appeared through the clouds, racing. Lightning struck far to the north in the desert where ruined homesteads stood. They rode slowly, their shotguns cradled and hats pulled down over their faces.

'Do you think they'll have anyone watching?' Jim Banks asked.

'No,' Bolger replied, 'this is not an army camp, for fuck's sake, this is rabble. They'll all be pissed. If I had my way, I'd shoot the bastards.'

Nothing else was said and they rode silently with Mooney in the lead.

At the edge of the clearing, a large Indian palm tree grew and, as they sat on their horses at the roadside, they could make out the shapes of the tents and shanties. Save for the wind, all was still and the embers of a fire glowed. Their horses stood quietly as Mooney produced a torch and shone it at the fence, then over the ground. They saw the remains of piggeries and fowl runs, an overturned water tank, a dray and wood lying in the thistles. Then they could see a light shining in a tent near some trees. Someone was still awake. The gate was down and beer bottles gleamed in the torchlight.

'Right,' Mooney said, 'in we go. Knock the rubbish down and get rid of them. No shooting, just make them remember they can't sit on their arses around Rubicon.'

It all seemed easy: as Mooney and Bolger shouted, men came out of the tents and lean-tos, gaped in the flickering light, cursed, grabbed whatever they could and made for the track. Cooking pots were overturned; tent ropes cut; corrugated iron torn down; bottles and flagons smashed and rags and clothing tossed aside. But there were more men than they had counted on: they ran about, jostled and blasphemed in

117

the dark. A kerosine tin fell into the embers and the flames licked into the night; then there was a scream and the sound of a baby crying. 'Jesus,' Farrar called to Bolger, 'there's a woman here.'

'Probably a black tart, just mind out.'

Then Banks' horse went down, its leg twisted and bellowing; bottles were thrown and a shot rang out. The fire spread, a tent went up and the brush flared.

'Jesus,' Mooney shouted, 'dowse that bloody fire.'

A bearded man ran up and went for his horse's fetlocks with a knife; Mooney hit him with the stock of his shotgun, the man went down, then ran off, clutching his head. He heard more shouts and screams, torches flashed and another shot echoed. Whose gun was that? Things were getting out of hand. He tried to find Bolger and rode toward the tent at the back of the camp.

In the firelight, he saw a white woman, her face filthy and hair down, clutching a baby. Blankets were scattered, food tins lay on the earth and the canvas ripped.

'You fucking bastards,' the woman shouted, 'you fucking bastards.'

She ran into the night, fell, dropped the child and disappeared. Mooney sweated, cursed, sat irresolute, then shone his torch, trying to find the child. Two men rode by and glass broke: it was a shambles now. Figures ran about in the half-dark, the horses reared at the fire and the campers ran in all directions – some for the bush and others for the road. Then, after about ten minutes, all fell quiet – the moon shone full and the wind ghosted through the trees.

'Is anybody hurt?' Mooney called.

'No.'

They met by the fire and dismounted. Bolger pulled out a flask, drank, passed it round and said: 'That's that.'

But all the men were white-faced and shaken.

'Who fired the shots?' Mooney asked. The whisky burned his throat and his stomach was empty.

'Fucked if I know. One of them bastards must have a gun.'

'Did any of you fire your gun?'

'No.'

We'd better have a good look around,' Mooney said. 'There was a woman with a kid – God knows what happened to it.'

'Black or white?' someone asked.

'White.'

'Jesus.'

They moved off through the litter, poking around with the barrels of their shotguns. Mooney's heart pounded, his hands ran with sweat and his back started to ache as he searched. He hoped to God he would find nothing.

It was Charlie Oldfield from the Lodge who found the baby. It was dead, its head smashed by horses' hooves. Oldfield threw up, the vomit running down his shirtfront and trousers. He shouted and screamed until the others came racing up.

'Jesus Christ,' Mooney whispered as he stared at the dirty little body, 'I'll have to report this.' He looked at the grey faces of his mates in the moonlight. 'I'll have to report this.'

Nothing was said, then Bolger spoke: 'The woman dropped the kid, didn't she? Where is she now? It's not our fault.'

'Ten to one, she'll tell the police somewhere along the track.'

'So what?' Bolger answered. 'If she does, and that's not certain, they'll ring you and you know nothing about it. You're not in uniform and none of them knew who we were.'

'I don't like it – I've got to put in a report.'

'I think Reg is right,' Henry Farrar said. 'It'll be death by misadventure, or something. A coroner will have to come up and conduct the enquiry, it'll get into the press and we'll all be in the shit.'

But Mooney was not convinced and hung his head.

'For Christ's sake,' Bolger said, 'what's one bloody kid? The woman was probably a tart, living with all those jokers. It would have died of starvation anyway, No one's going to know. Look out.' He bent down, picked up the bundle and strode away toward the bush.

When he came back, Mooney said: 'What did you do with it?'

Bolger stood, big and heavy. 'Ask no questions, be told no lies.'

They rode back in silence, Banks leading his lamed horse and the others straggling along the track. Twice, headlights shone and a car passed on the main road. They kept to the trees, nobody saw them, and the streets of Rubicon were deserted. The men disappeared until only Mooney was left. When he got to his house, he turned his horse out into the back paddock; he stood at the back door and heard barking. He thought of the bloodied child: thank God he had forgotten to take the dog.

Fourteen

Once again, Maria sat at Louisa's bedside and looked at the walls papered with the *Illustrated London News*: 'Mr Charles Dickens' Last Reading', 'The Duke of Edinburgh in India', 'The Oudh Industrial Exhibition at Lucknow'. Louisa was asleep, looking like a princess, her hair spread on the pillow and her chest rising and falling under the sheet. The morning was hot and still, and from the window Maria could see the orange trees: only they had survived the drought, but had not borne fruit for as long as she could remember. A blowfly was dying on the windowledge, then all was silent. Then she saw a horse and covered cart pass by outside: it was Farozi, the Indian hawker – it seemed he knew the day and the time to call, for Julius and Carl were working this morning on the far western boundary and would not be home until nightfall. Maria stood up and listened for the gentle tapping at the back door. There it was – she was as still as a statue – there it was again. She closed Louisa's door quietly and went down the hall.

'Good morning, Mrs Hoffmayer.' Farozi's turban was dusty, his suit shone and his smile was wide. 'One more fine day? I hope you and Mr Hoffmayer are in the best of health?'

'I do not wish to buy anything, Mr Farozi.'

'Are you quite sure? I have many new things since I saw you last.'

'I do not wish to buy anything, Mr Farozi.'

The Indian pointed to his waggon. 'I have scented soap, bunches of lavender, perfume from Paris, ribbons and laces, silk from Siam, decorated eggs from Imperial Russia – all manner of beautiful objects.'

'You will have to go, Mr Farozi.'

'I have brassware from the markets of Meerut.'

'I'm sorry, Mr Farozi.' As Maria went to close the door, she found herself apologizing.

The Indian delved into his bag. 'I have fountain pens, the best Watermans, steel nib or five-carat gold. You can write to your loved ones in Germany.'

Maria had not thought of Germany for a long time, nor had she ever been there, but she wondered what was happening in the homeland. She thought of the Easter cards she received from her great-aunt in Nuremberg when she was a girl. *The Christ, he is risen.* 'I must close the door, I have a sick child.'

'A sick child? I have many herbal remedies, I am an expert, I graduated in herbal medicine.' Farozi stepped closer. 'I could inspect her? I am an expert.'

'No, no, the doctor looks after her.'

'The doctor? The doctor in Rubicon is by no means the best – we Asiatic people have other remedies.' The sun beat down and the hawker had his boot on the step. 'What is her condition?'

'She has a summer cold.'

'A summer cold? That is the easiest condition to cure. I have many herbs in my bag, I will see her, she will be made whole before the night comes down.'

As the Indian made to come through the door, Maria grabbed the broom and struck him in the face; his nose split and blood spurted from his nostrils; as he fell back and dropped his bag, she slammed the door and shoved the bolt home. She listened at the door, heard the Indian blowing his nose, he seemed to be picking up his bag; then she heard the creak of a harness and the rumble of the wheels as the hawker drove away.

The only sound now came from the grandfather clock; even though the Indian had gone, she dared not go to the window and stood by the door. Would he come back? She thought not – Julius always said that the Hindus knew their place. But the man was sneaky and unreliable, turning up when he was least expected and preying on lonely women. Should she tell

Julius? She would think about that later and went back down the hall to Louisa.

This time she was awake and lying naked, her legs apart and her hands stretched behind her head. The sweat on her breasts gleamed and her nipples were large; she looked at her stepmother and smiled, twisting her body. Her pubic hair was golden and Maria found herself looking at her longer than she should. Then as she tried to cover Louisa up, her stepdaughter laughed in her throat and cast the sheets aside. She seemed rational: 'Don't you like me like that, Stepmother? Papa does.'

There was nothing to say; Maria closed the bedroom door and went outside on the verandah.

For months now – or was it a year? – Julius had risen from his bed after his nightmares and roamed the house. How long he was up, she did not know, and she dared not follow him. What was he doing to her? A blackness descended as Maria looked at the bush and the burnt stumps of the fire. She thought of the last time when Julius had wanted her: he was as strong as one of his oxen, but she fought tooth and nail and, at the end of it all, they lay sweating in the tangled sheets like exhausted animals. In the morning, nothing was said; she fed the chickens, brought in the wood for the stove, cooked the porridge and lit the copper for the washing. Julius and Carl left for work with their slashers and bill-hooks, looking like soldiers in some endless war, and she was left alone in the house where the ghost of August still drifted. Although she knew nothing of other marriages, Maria was sure that hers was a devilish mistake, a pre-destined error arranged by her aunt, but there was no one she could turn to and it seemed she had to live with it. What were other families like? She did not know.

Again, she thought: what did Julius do to her? Where did he put his hands? Did Louisa like it? Maria guessed she did. Although this was a terrible sin, there was no one to tell – and there was envy in Maria's heart. What if Julius got his daughter with child? No one would know – it would be kept a secret she would have to live with for the rest of her life – but even she knew this was not possible. More people were calling: Farozi would be back as if nothing had happened; there was Mr Cameron and the black man; and there were the vagrants, tramping the roads. She saw a magpie watching her from a post in the garden – they were evil, fearsome birds which swooped on her when she was hanging out the washing. Maria left the verandah and went inside. She wanted to look at Louisa, lying on her bed, but dared not. No sooner had she walked into the kitchen when the back door opened: it was Julius. 'We have decided to kill the last pig,' he said, 'and you will help us.'

Her husband was carrying a butcher's knife, and Maria saw Carl coming up the track to the house. 'I thought you were working all day in the far paddock.'

Julius looked at her. 'We have decided to kill the pig. It is a good day for it – there is a south breeze and no flies. We will do it under the trees. I will want a kerosine tin of hot water.'

Carl arrived, carrying an axe and a block and tackle. 'We want hot water and bowls for the pig's blood,' he said. 'I will dig the pit.'

'I know that.' Maria turned and went back into the kitchen.

They had killed many pigs before and she made black puddings from the blood. But this time, she felt a sense of foreboding. Why, and what did it mean? As Maria filled the tin from the tank, she thought of Louisa: 'Don't you like me like that, Stepmother? Papa does.' As she lugged the tin inside to the stove, she saw Julius talking to Carl: he was testing the knife with his thumb and then he disappeared into the barn to sharpen the blade on the whetstone.

When the water boiled, Maria carried it to the tree where the block and tackle hung from the branch; Carl had dug the pit and lined it with straw. Then, for some reason she did not understand, Julius did not kill the pig in the sty, but was carrying it struggling in his arms. The animal knew it was going to be killed: it squealed and kicked as Julius carried it easily over the dusty ground. He trapped the animal between his knees and looked at his son. 'You may kill it,' he said.

Carl acknowledged, raised the axe and struck the pig on the skull; the animal fell to its knees, but still kicked and did not want to die. Carl struck once more; the pig collapsed and Julius stabbed it under the cheek with his knife. As the blood spurted and flowed, Maria collected it in the bowls. Julius, his trousers fouled with shit and blood, watched.

'You must stir it,' he said. 'It must not set.'

'I know that.' Maria felt Carl standing near as he still held the axe. 'You must give me room to work,' she said. Although her stepson moved away, she was unnerved; her hands shook and the blood spilt on to the ground.

'That is precious,' Julius said quietly. 'We need it all.' This time, it seemed like a sacrifice.

Maria gathered herself together and carried the bowls on a tray to the kitchen. The two men watched her go, carried the carcass to the pit, scalded it with the hot water and started to scrape the hair and skin off with their knives. When that was done, it was hung from the chain, washed, slit and cleaned, its entrails spilling into the bucket. The liver and kidneys were saved, the feet and head severed; the body was washed and left to hang until Julius would butcher it tomorrow. For the first time, Maria's gorge rose: she ran from the kitchen, vomited and rinsed her mouth from the water tank. As she dried her face with her apron, she heard Julius ask, 'You are ill, why is that?'

'It is nothing.' Maria's mouth was dry. 'It is nothing.'

He pulled out his silver watch and consulted. 'Watch out for the crows and the magpies. We will be home at nightfall.'

As the pig was valuable and would be their only meat for months to come, Maria did as she was requsted: when the crows and parakeets came, she drove them off with the broom and found it caked with Farozi's blood. From Louisa's room there was no sound and, later on that afternoon, the dry thunder cracked and boomed over the desert in the north.

The cyclone struck at four o'clock, when Don Mooney was having his first beer in the bar of the Royal. In less than an hour, the temperature rose to one hundred degrees, dust clouds rolled in like an enormous gas attack, lightning struck, trees were uprooted from the waterless soil, the shelters and tents of the unemployed men were ripped to shreds and the corrugated iron roofs of Rubicon flew through the dark sky like paper. Some townsfolk bent on their knees and prayed, thinking this was Armageddon. On the Hoffmayer farm, the tree fell, the block and tackle broke and the carcass of the pig rolled beneath the trees for the ants, the parakeets and the crows. After ten minutes, all became silent; the sun shone through the dust cloud and no rain came.

'Jesus Christ,' Jim Banks said as the dust floated in the afternoon light. 'Do you think anyone's been killed?'

'Give me a Scotch,' Mooney replied, 'and I'll go outside and have a look.'

'Right.' The publican poured a double jigger of Dewar's. Mooney drank it down and left the bar.

After Banks had served a fresh round of beers, Mooney was back. 'Everything's okay.'

'Are you sure?'

The policeman stared. 'You're asking me?'

'I was just checking.'

'No one checks on me.'

'I know that.'

But both men were thinking of the raid on the vagrants' camp and the dead baby. 'Have you had any phone calls?' Banks asked.

'Of course I have. Why shouldn't I?'

Mooney drank another beer and thought: the evictions, the raid on the camp, Harold Withers, the drought. It seemed it was all closing in on him. He glanced out the front window and saw two men on horseback go by; then a waggon and a Hupmobile. 'I'd better be going,' he said. 'I'll see you later.'

'Okay.'

Outside on Federation Street, the shopkeepers were cleaning up the debris from the storm, and Mooney saw one of the girls walking up to the Royal. He ducked his head and strode away. As he passed Ballantine's store, Mooney heard his voice being called and stopped: it was Harold Withers sitting in the back of his Hupmobile. 'Constable,' he said, 'I want to see you.'

This time, the two men met in Withers' office at the back of the emporium. And this time, Withers didn't offer Mooney a drink, nor did he refer to the sudden storm. The room was shady and a fan rumbled in the corner by the safe and an Italian sideboard.

'Did you clear the riff-raff out?' he asked.

'Yes.'

'What happened?'

'Nothing. We cleared them out.'

'Anything untoward?'

'No.'

Withers leaned forward. 'I heard there was a fire.'

Mooney shifted in his chair. 'One of the blokes threw away a cigarette – stupid bastard.'

'Have you heard about the mission?'

'What mission?'

'The Moravian – they've found guns there.'

'Who told you?'

Withers smiled. 'I do believe, Don, that my network is more efficient than yours. A local farmer found a cellar, shotguns and ammunition. Bolsheviks, and the blacks were taught there. Remember?'

'Yeah.' Mooney thought of Ray Stark.

'And the timber workers are out again.'

'I heard that.'

'Did you?' Withers thought about a whisky, but he would wait until his guest had gone. 'The IWW are about, the country's falling apart, we'll be under siege.'

'Is it going to be as bad as that?'

'It is. We'll need every able-bodied man before the year

is out.' Withers got up. 'Australia, Constable Mooney, is on the brink of civil war. If I were a superstitious man, I'd say that storm today was an omen.'

Fifteen

The sunset looked like a huge explosion, but all was silent save for the breeze running through the dead grass and bracken. The salt shone in the lake bed where the young trees stood, dying. Back at the bridge over the dry creek, Frank saw tree trunks caught in branches ten feet from the ground – a flood had roared through maybe fifteen years ago. Would this country ever come back again? He was sure it would.

As Frank looked north toward the uncleared country, his horse shifted and snorted. He looked around to see a horseman approaching up the track by the lake. As the figure drew closer, he put his hand on the stock of his shotgun, but it was a woman – it was Maria Hoffmayer. He was startled to see her and stared in the dusty sunlight. 'Good afternoon, Mrs Hoffmayer.'

'Good afternoon, Mr Cameron.'

The birds chattered in the branches of the old trees and somewhere in the smashed bush a cow bellowed. The sun was getting low now and she turned to shade her face. What was the woman doing here at this time of day? Maria looked white-faced and sat on her horse. 'There was once water in this lake,' she said.

'So I've heard.'

'There is a saying,' she went on, 'that it fills every seven years, but that is false.'

She dismounted, tethered her horse and walked down to the shore where the skeleton of a row boat lay in the gravel. Still puzzled, Frank followed her to the beach: Ray had told him of the lake and he wanted to see what the country was like. Why was Maria Hoffmayer not home doing the chores and preparing the tea for her family? He, too, swung down and said: 'If this country has little, it at least has beautiful sunsets.'

Maria looked at him. 'Yes, it does, but that is all.'

'You were born here?' Frank asked.

'I was.'

'Then it's your home.'

Maria did not reply, but bent, picked up a pebble and sent it spinning into the dry lake bed. He was about to look at his watch, but decided not. She seemed in no hurry and stood motionless, despite the flies. 'You are having a spell from work?' she asked.

'Yes, I am. Ray Stark told me about the lake and I thought I'd take a look. It seems all Rubicon has to offer.'

Maria laughed. 'And it's a disappointment.'

'Not altogether. There are signs of beauty – the river gums, the beach, it will fill again – I'm sure of that.'

'We used to picnic here in the old days – my aunt and I, and our friends.'

'Germans?'

'Yes. Do you not like us?'

It was Frank's turn to smile. 'The war,' he said, 'was not the common soldiers' fault. We all shared – both sides. I don't think about the past – it's the future that counts. I had a good run: I came back alive.'

Maria asked the question: 'What about your injury?'

This time, Frank laughed. 'I've got my own lot to thank for that – the 21st Field Battery – the creeping barrage didn't creep fast enough. And my leg was saved by German sisters.'

'The returned men of Rubicon do not like the Germans.'

'They'll get over it – there's no point in carrying the war on.' But Frank thought of the drinking after the Anzac Day services, the smoke concerts, the hard faces and the bitterness.

'Thank you for helping us with the fire.'

'It was nothing: we're neighbours.'

'Yes,' Maria replied with the trace of a smile. 'We are.' Suddenly, she turned and started to walk quickly back to her horse, 'You must excuse me, I must go.'

'I may see you again?' Frank said.

'I don't know, I am kept very busy.' Maria mounted her horse. 'We used to come to the lake often – it is my favourite place.' The horse trotted away in the dust and she was gone.

Frank took the west road home and passed the Hoffmayers' gate where, in the distance, he saw smoke rising from the homestead chimney. Maria was at her work. He wondered what life was like with the dour husband and son. *Watch out for Carl,* Jim Banks had said. And what of the sick daughter? As he sat on his horse, Frank realized someone was watching him from the shade of the pine trees. The man was carrying a gun: it looked like Carl Hoffmayer. Jesus, Frank thought, what were they running – some kind of fortress? Were they hiding something? He remembered the cries from the back room. And why had Maria broken what must be a strict routine to visit the lake? He saw the man bring up the gun, dug his heels into his horse and rode up the track. When he stopped once more, he heard the sound of a gunshot echoing in the warm evening air.

When Frank got back to his cottage, he found the fire was going there, too. Ray was standing at the stove. He grinned. 'G'day,' he said. 'I'm making damper and I've put some dried fruit in – not your usual stuff. And we've got a chook.'

'Where did you get it?'

'I found it, trespassing.'

'You're sure?'

'Yep. And I've got some beer.'

'A celebration?'

'I reckon so, I've been here three months and that calls for a drink.' Ray opened the oven door and tipped the damper onto the table. 'Have a go at that.' The bread was good and Frank ate it while Ray got the bottles. 'How was the lake?'

'Dry.'

'It was good once. My tribe used to hunt there before they went away. Christ, there was fish – redfin, trout, crayfish, yabbies and roos and wallabies. They lived off the fat of the land. The bush wasn't cleared then and there was no wheat. No dust storms in them days – that's what I've been told.'

'There's been a change up here, then?' Frank said as he drank his beer.

'I reckon so. You don't see the animals and birds you used to.'

Over tea, Ray asked: 'Did you hear about the raid?'

'What raid?' But Frank thought he knew.

'On the camp. They say a woman lost her baby.'

'Go on.'

Ray licked his fingers. 'That's all I know.'

'Don Mooney was involved.'

'That bastard – he's no good.'

'Mooney,' Frank replied, 'doesn't like blackfellows. That's the size of it.'

'He don't like some whitefellows either – the unemployed jokers, the farmers – he boots them up the arse.'

'That's his job because the banks want their money out.'

'Well, the system's crook, ain't it?'

As the light went down, they lit the hurricane lamp, cleared away and drank more beer. Then they sat outside and listened to the sounds of the bush. 'I reckon something's going to happen around here,' Ray said.

'What sort of thing?'

'There's lots strange happening – fires, jokers tramping around looking for a job, strikes at the timber mills, guns being carried. I reckon I know.'

Frank thought of Maria Hoffmayer at the lake, then the man with the gun on the farm. He thanked God he did not go on the raid. What had happened to the baby? He'd met men like Bolger during the war, and what of Harold Withers? Frank thought of his father and the loss of the farm. He didn't care for land speculators who rode in chauffeur-driven Hup-mobiles.

'Do you want to hear some music?' Ray said. 'Not abo music – the real stuff.'

'Okay, then.'

132

Ray got up, stretched himself and ground his cigarette butt under his boot. 'Hang on.'

When he returned, Ray was holding something shiny in his hands. 'Can you play these buggers?' It was a German harmonica.

'No. Give us a tune.'

'What do you want?'

'Anything.'

'Do you want some more beer? There's two bottles left.'

'You stay there and wet your whistle,' Frank answered. 'I'll get them.' He'd made a good choice: he was sure of that.

'Okay.'

When Frank came out with the bottles, Ray was playing 'Land of Hope and Glory, Mother of the Free . . .'

Frank sang the song and the thin music drifted over the bush; the moon was big and bathed the country and he sang two verses, remembering the shocked and weary officers in the dugout in the front line. He was hit and taken prisoner the following morning: it seemed a long time ago now, and he thought once more of Maria as she spun a pebble into the lake bed. He passed the bottle over to Ray. 'Where did you learn that?'

'At the mission. They taught us all sorts of songs there.'

'Do you think this is the Land of Hope and Glory?' Frank asked.

'Yeah. It's a great place – it'll rain and the hard times won't last.'

'What about your lot?'

'My lot – the abos? They'll survive, they're tough buggers.'

Ray took up the bottles. 'I'm hitting the sack, I'll see you in the morning.'

That night, they were woken by a dog barking; but when they got up and searched around the yard, they found nothing.

Don Mooney parked his Ford at Michael Costello's gate and stuffed the warrant in his back trouser pocket. He thought for a moment, then reached into the glove pocket of the car and slipped his .38 revolver inside his jacket. A bony house cow was grazing in the home paddock and the hens were picking in the pine needles of the trees. The dust blew in flurries as he walked up the rough track. The Costello house was unpainted, the weatherboards split and the roof sagging; the gates were broken and thistles floated in the wind. Mooney looked around the junk in the front yard, but of the Costellos there was no sign. His back itched, his hands sweated and he cursed Harold Withers. After this, he had to go out to the mission and see the farmer who had found the cache of arms. What the fuck was this country coming to?

The flydoor on the porch banged in the wind as he knocked; all was silent and the ragged blinds were drawn. Suddenly a cat ran over the broken timbers – Mooney cursed once more. He didn't like the feel of this. He went carefully down the steps and walked around to the back of the house. There, all was ruin: washing lay in the weeds and brambles and broken toys lay in the dirt. Did the Costellos know he was coming? The bush telegraph was efficient and the farmers these days were starting to come together as the banks enforced foreclosures. He walked further down the track between the pine trees and then into the open paddocks.

At last, Mooney saw two men working on a fence with post-hole borers and wire-strainers. As he approached, they didn't look up, but they knew he was coming. When he got closer, he saw it was Michael Costello and his son. A shotgun stood propped against a corner fencepost and the dust rose in clouds from the fallowed paddocks beyond. When he was about thirty yards away, Mooney called: 'Mr Costello?'

The farmer looked up, his face gaunt and his hands around the handle of his shovel. 'Yes.'

'I'm Constable Don Mooney from Rubicon.'

'I know that.'

Costello's son continued to work, twisting the wire around the post with his big hands: he was a strong lad, wearing hobnail boots, an old waistcoat, and a slouch hat. Mooney came up and stood in the stubble on the other side of the fence. 'I've got some bad news for you.'

'Have you?' Costello gripped the wire between the barbs.

'I've got to serve you with a warrant from the land company.'

'Is that right?'

'It's my job – nothing personal.'

'Is that right?'

Mooney came closer. 'I've got to hand it to you and see that you get it.'

'Mooney,' the farmer said, 'that's an Irish name, ain't it?'

'I suppose so.'

'Are you a Mick?'

'Of sorts.' Mooney wondered what this was getting to and saw Costello's son standing up straight by the corner post.

'It was bastards like you that threw me grandfather off his land in the old country.'

'I'm not responsible for that.'

'Do you know the worst kind of bastard?' Costello said. 'One who betrays his own kind. You're in league with the profiteers.'

Mooney's voice rose. 'I'm just doing my job.'

'My job, mister, is to run this farm, and that's what I'm going to do, ain't it, son?'

'I reckon.' The boy's long arms hung down by his side.

'You aren't going to be difficult, are you?' Mooney watched the boy and felt the lump of the revolver in his jacket.

'Nope. I'm not going to take that fucking paper, that's all. You can wipe your arse with it. Now get off my land.'

Mooney bent down, picked up a rock and placed the warrant on the top of the post. When he straightened up, he found he was looking at the barrel of the shotgun. 'I can charge you with menace,' he said.

'There's one of you and two of us, mister.'

As Mooney stared at the farmer, he heard the sound of a baby crying. When he turned, he saw it was Mrs Costello standing with a child in her arms. Her face was twisted with anger and she began to shout. Mooney thought of the woman in the vagrants' camp and lost his resolve. This was going to be a bugger of a job. 'I'll be back.'

'Just remember,' Costello replied, 'a man's got his mates.'

'You've got seven days to get out,' Mooney said.

'Jesus Christ.' The boy pulled back a hammer on the shotgun.

Mooney turned away, his back rising. and walked past Mrs Costello and her child. 'Filthy copper,' she said and spat. 'Filthy copper.'

When he was back in his car, Mooney made a record of the time of the visit in his notebook and took the road to the mission.

The collection of firearms was quite impressive: three double-barrelled shotguns, four .303s, a Webly service pistol, a Smith & Wesson handgun, a dozen cartons of ammunition and some dynamite. The farmer had found the cache in a disused cellar at the back of the church. Mooney spent some time with the farmer who was above board – he was a Freemason and on the local Shire Council. They agreed it was the work of the Bolsheviks.

The drive back to Rubicon was long and dusty; Mooney thought of Costello, the son with the shotgun and the dead baby in the camp. He'd have to get reinforcements – there was no doubt about that. What they wanted was men from the Great War. It was fucking shame about Frank Cameron. He'd arrange a meeting with him and Harold Withers: something might come out of that.

Sixteen

At sixty-seven, George Ballantine lived at the back of his store, alone. He had never married, and the one girl he was fond of died in the influenza epidemic of 1920. He was too old to serve in the Great War and did not belong to the Lodge; and, unlike Harold Withers, had no interest in speculation. George went to the Church of Christ on Sundays and believed that usury was immoral. Honest trading and the fair deal were best. Although he bought his meat from Reg Bolger, George did not care for the town butcher; nor did he like Harold Withers who, he thought, would one day overreach himself. But if he did, that was his business and no one else's – he also knew that Withers had many mortgages over farmers in the district. Again, that was their business: George's father had taught him to be an honest trader, and an honest trader he would be. His mother had died in 1928: he still kept her bed made with calico sheets and a hand-made eiderdown. Sometimes, he looked around for her when he was sorting out the daily newspapers.

George had not seen Julius Hoffmayer since the day they could not agree over the price for the eggs. He thought this was unusual, but Hoffmayer was a proud and solitary man, whom he knew would not take his produce elsewhere. George had known August and his profligate ways and understood what Julius had had to put up with. Maria, George had seen only twice in the past two years – and of all the women in Rubicon, she was by far the most handsome with her coal-black hair, her straight back and her dark eyes. George thought that Maria could have been the heroine of any one of the Waverley novels and should have been a Queen in medieval times. She was being wasted on a back-

137

blocks farm in Rubicon. How such a woman coped with no running water and no electricity, he did not know.

George was sitting, reading the newspaper behind the counter one morning when Frank Cameron came in, his stiff leg thumping on the wooden floor. As he rose, he said: 'Good day, Mr Cameron.'

'Good day, Mr Ballantine. I've come to pay my account.'

'Have you? I'll look in my book.'

'Okay.' As he waited, Frank glanced at the news. '*LANG GOVERNMENT SACKED IN NEW SOUTH WALES. FEARS OF CIVIL REVOLT*'. He looked around the store, saw the dusty, faded merchandise and wondered how long the business could last. Then he went over and looked through the phonograph records. *Lily of Laguna, Cruising Down the River*, he thought of his father at the piano playing on wet Sunday nights after milking and the sound of wet logs steaming in the grate.

'I make it you owe me £4.7s.2d.' George said.

'Right.' Frank took a £10 note from his wallet, handed it over and put the change in his pocket.

'How's it going?' George asked.

'Not bad. We've cleared over a third of the place, done the ploughing and all we want is rain.'

'You've got a good man there.'

'Have I?'

'A lot of people in this town don't like Ray Stark because he reminds them.'

'Reminds them of what?'

'They cleared his lot out in the old days, let the mission go to rack and ruin, but he stays around. And he's cheerful and looks you straight in the eye – some folks don't like that. I used to know his father: that was a bad business.'

Frank leant on the counter. 'How's trade?'

'A bit quiet.' George peered over his glasses. 'It's got to improve.'

'Did you hear about the raid on the camp?'

'Yes,' George replied, 'I did. The poor devils have got to live somewhere, haven't they? There'll be vigilantes soon, like a Hopalong Cassidy book.'

'Organized by our Police Constable?'

George looked directly at Frank. 'It might be more than that.'

Frank stood up from the counter. 'These are difficult times, Mr Ballantine.'

'They are, but they'll pass.'

'I'll see you when I'm next in town,' Frank said.

'You do that,' George answered. 'Good luck, Mr Cameron.'

Just as Frank was about to get into his truck, he heard his name being called. When he looked around, he saw a well-dressed man in a business suit wearing a homberg. The man walked up, put out his hand and said: 'My name is Harold Withers.'

Frank took the strong, cold hand. 'I'm pleased to meet you.'

'I always like to meet our new settlers,' Withers said, 'especially when they're returned men.'

'There's nothing that special about returned men,' Frank replied.

'I think there is.' Withers took out his watch. 'Have you got time for a spot of lunch?'

Frank thought. 'I'd be pleased to.'

'Right, then. We'll go to the Royal dining-room. The food's quite passable there.'

They crossed Federation Street as an armed man rode by.

The dining-room at the Royal, Frank thought, must have been magnificent before the War. Now, the walnut tables were scratched and wormy, the bentwood chairs rickety and the tablecloths stained; the dried flowers were dusty and the cutlery was battered. They sat at a table overlooking the street and the waiter came up and bowed. Frank stretched his leg under the table and put his hat on a chair.

'What will you have to drink?' Withers asked.

'I'll have a cold beer.'

Withers smiled. 'I take it there's no refrigerator on the property?'

'Not yet.'

They ordered their lunch, ate the steaks, drank their beer and talked about wheat prices, plans for irrigation and the drought. Over his port, Withers lit a cigar and said: 'The country's falling to pieces, you know that?'

'Do you think so?'

'I know so. Lang may have gone in New South Wales, but the Bolsheviks are still there, the American saboteurs are on the waterfront and in the timber mills and the vagrants are rioting.'

Frank smiled. 'What about the abos?'

Withers put down his glass and stared. 'I don't think they'll be a problem. Our police can't cope and the government is gutless.'

'I'm a farmer,' Frank said, 'not a politician.'

'There are things other than farming.'

'Such as?'

'The future of the nation, the future of this town.' Withers drank his port carefully. 'We're being invaded by the Goths and Vandals.'

'And the Huns?'

It was Withers' turn to smile. 'We've beaten them already – they've been taught their lesson. Mooney can't cope, the government won't give us any more men and we've got to look after ourselves. Don's a good man, but his helpers are rabble: farm boys, rural riff-raff, there's no discipline.'

'So you're thinking about a local New Guard?'

'You've heard of them?'

'I have: they admire Mussolini and the Fascists.'

'You keep abreast of the news, Mr Cameron.'

'Not all farmers are illiterate, Mr Withers.'

'I didn't say that. All I'm saying is that there are tough times ahead – strikes, disobedience, foreign meddling. You were an officer in the War, I believe?'

'I was.'

'What rank?'

'Lieutenant.'

'And decorated?'

'Yes.'

Withers leant over the table. 'This town could do with officers like you.'

'This town's got me already,' Frank replied, 'and I'm a farmer now, not a soldier.'

'There are higher duties, are there not?'

Frank remembered the battle-weary men staggering around the bullring. 'I'm through with fighting.' He thought of the bush and the drought: he was another kind of soldier now.

Withers was insistent. 'I'm not talking about fighting – I'm talking about discipline, training and preparedness.'

'What you're talking about, Mr Withers, is training a bush army outside the law; it's happening in Germany and Italy now, and I don't like it. If you're asking me to get involved in that, you'd better find someone else.'

'You could be letting your country down.'

Frank got up. 'Look,' he said, 'when war broke out, I didn't sit on my arse, I volunteered; I spent three years up to my neck in mud and shit, while your lot stayed home and made big profits; and when we got home, all we are given is seven hundred acres of desert you couldn't even run dingoes on. It turns out the war was a big mistake, it achieved nothing, and you want to train some tin-pot army when times get tough to save your own bacon. Go and ask Reg Bolger: he's your man. Leave me out of it.'

Withers looked at Frank, standing over him, but stuck to his guns. 'Let me give you some advice, Mr Cameron. We don't employ niggers in this town – you've made a mistake.'

'You mean I've broken the rules?'

'You could put it that way.'

'I'll employ who I fucking well like. Have you heard a woman lost her baby in that raid on the camp?'

Withers' eyes were blank. 'What raid?'

'Jesus Christ. Why don't you stick to your mortgages and land dealings. That should keep you busy.'

'It seems there's nothing further to discuss,' Withers said.

'I won't thank you for the lunch,' Frank replied. 'I'm sure

you'll get it back out of some poor bastard's pocket.'

As Harold Withers watched the big man take his hat and walk to the door, he knew the first people he would see this afternoon were Mooney and Bolger.

This time, Withers offered his guests the whisky. 'It seems,' he said, 'that we have a Judas in our midst.'

'What?'

'Judas,' Withers replied as he passed the glass over to Bolger, 'was the man who betrayed Christ. I learnt that in Sunday School. I'm referring to Frank Cameron who will not join us in defending this town.'

'Ah.' Bolger looked around Withers' office, with its ornate Victorian furniture. One day, he would have a place like this. 'We'll get Cameron. We had a bloke like him in the war.'

'Get him for what?'

'Something will turn up.' Bolger thought. 'There's lots happening – strikes, fires, evictions, street marches. He'll get involved in something. Or Stark will.'

Withers turned to Mooney. 'We're all relying on you to maintain law and order.'

'I can do that. What's going to happen?'

'I told you, Don, the country's falling apart.'

Bolger drained his glass and slid it over the walnut table. 'It's the Bolshies, wogs and Jews.'

Withers laughed. 'Your politics were always uncomplicated, weren't they?'

'Yep, I know what's what.'

Withers looked once more at Mooney. 'The banks are drawing their horns in – have you had to serve many warrants?'

'A few.'

'Any trouble?'

'There was one the other day who wasn't very keen.'

'Who?'

'A man called Michael Costello.'

'Christ, I know him,' Bolger put in, 'dirty Irish, a no-hoper, a peasant. Old Costello made trouble in the war.'

'What happened?' Withers asked.

'His boy produced a shotgun.' Mooney glanced at the whisky bottle. 'Not to worry, I'll get around that.'

'Let me know if you have any more trouble.' Withers poured out three more whiskies. 'If the farmers gang together, I wonder what our friend, Cameron, would do.'

'Aw Jesus,' Bolger said, 'it's up to us, isn't it?'

'No, it's up to Constable Mooney, and then me as Justice of the Peace. He stood up as if the talk was over; but, suddenly, he looked hard at the policeman. 'You didn't tell me about the woman and the baby.'

Mooney paled. 'It was nothing.'

'Did you see the child?'

'It was in the dark.' Mooney glanced at Bolger.

'Did you see it?'

'Yes.'

'How old was it?'

'It was a baby.'

'Was it dead or alive?'

'It was dead,' Bolger said. 'The woman dropped it, she was a whore living with the men. They were the dregs.'

'Do you know how it died?'

'No.' Mooney shifted in his chair.

'What did you do with it?'

'I chucked it into the bush,' Bolger said.

'You threw it into the bush?'

'Yep.'

'And you didn't report it?' Withers asked Mooney.

'No.'

'We've got a case of unreported manslaughter on our hands, haven't we?'

'You could put it that way.' Mooney wondered what Withers would do.

'Well, the woman was a slut, the men were communists,

vagrants and saboteurs. There's no problem, is there?' Withers went to the door. 'My advice to you both is to keep your powder dry.'

When they had gone, Withers phoned his stockbrokers in Melbourne. The day's trading had been bad and the market had gone to a new low: it looked as though the bottom hadn't been reached yet and Withers had lost another £3000. He would have to refinance.

Seventeen

George Ballantine woke up to the sound of smashing glass at three in the morning. He struggled into his dressing gown and ran down the hall, past the bags of cement and shelves of boots and shoes, into the store. There he found men with torches ransacking the stock. In the half-light, there seemed to be about six of them – big, with cloth caps, their heavy boots scraping and thumping on the floor where the merchandise lay scattered. They were carrying sugar bags and clearing the shelves of tinned food, flour and oatmeal. As he stood helpless in the doorway, one of the men saw him. The big fellow tore the phone from the wall and said: 'Stand where you are, grandpa, or you'll get your head bashed in.'

George found himself shaking as the men carried the goods on to the street: there must be a truck outside. Who were these men? Were they an organized gang? From the way they were stripping the shop, it seemed they were.

There was nothing George could do: they were powerful and methodical. One of them pushed past him and came out carrying a four-bushel bag of wheat; another took a side of bacon; and another loaded jars of jam, potted meat and pickles into a wooden crate. George saw a man standing outside on Federation Street to see if anyone came. Nobody was abroad in Rubicon this dark and cold morning. The stars shone and the horses slept standing in the stables of the Royal Hotel; the crickets sang in the dry grass of the roadsides and the mice ran among the stacks of wheat at the railway station.

When they had finished taking the goods out, the men set about destroying George Ballantine's emporium. They tore down the shelves, turned over the wooden counters, smashed the jars of sweets, ripped open the packets of stationery and tipped the drums of kerosine on to the floor. They poured out bottles of metholated spirits, stood back and tossed a match. As the flames licked and ran, the big fellow came up to George and said: 'Okay, grandpa, we've got all we want, but here's one for the road.'

He struck George in the front of the throat, he fell, the men left him lying in the spilt wheat, the broken eggs, the workingmen's boots and the smashed toys as the flames leapt at the pine walls of his store. By the time the fire cart got to Ballantine's Emporium, it was too late and the night air reeked of celluloid, fertilizer and creosote: they managed to save the buildings next door and Harold Withers' store was unscathed. His was the only store in Rubicon now and the fire would be blamed on the Reds.

That week, the timber-workers struck in the mills all over the bush; three were burnt down and two men were killed by the police in a street riot. In a settlement south of Darwin, an aborigine accused of rape was castrated with a razor blade and hung by a mob. Hunger marches were held in the streets of Melbourne and Sydney; creditors met in the boardrooms of finance companies and banks; and mortgaged farmers who sold their stock were convicted of selling stolen property. When Michael Costello was evicted at gun-point by Don Mooney and two bailiffs from out of town, his neighbours met and resolved to resist the next foreclosure with violence.

When tea was done, Carl Hoffmayer pushed back his plate, lit his pipe, looked at his father and said: 'I found something interesting in the barn today.'

Maria sat quite still as she heard Julius ask: 'What was that?'

'It was a bag – they call them Gladstones, I think.'

'A bag?' his father said. 'Does it belong to this family?'

'No, I don't think so.'

'Do you have it here?'

'I'll go and get it.' Maria watched Carl leave the kitchen. When he came back, he was holding the dead man's bag, which he placed on the table.

'Have you looked inside?' his father asked.

'Yes.'

'Let me look.' Julius took the bag and opened it. He took out the sheet music, the photograph and the cut-throat razor. 'Offenbach.' He thought of his father and his music as he placed the photograph before him. 'The child is blond and good-looking. And the razor is of high quality.' He turned to his wife. 'Have you any idea how this bag came to be in our barn?'

'No.'

'You are sure?'

'Yes.'

Julius played with the razor and the blade gleamed in the light of the kerosine lamp. 'This is indeed a mystery.' He closed the bag and slid it over to Carl. 'You may put it back where you found it.'

As Maria cleared the plates away and started to wash up, Julius came up, seized her by the shoulders, turned her around and said: 'A man has been here, hasn't he?'

'It was the unemployed man – the man whom Carl turned out. He left his bag.'

'And you hid it?'

'Yes.'

'Why?'

Maria spoke up: 'Because I was ashamed of what happened.' Her laugh was bitter. 'There was no room at the inn.'

'Did you know,' Julius said, 'that Ballantine's Emporium was burned down two nights ago, and that Ballantine is dead?'

'No.'

'This district, the town, this farm is under siege by the rabble – the unemployed, criminals, the Bolsheviks, the scum from the cities – and we will keep them out.'

'Including our neighbours?'

'You are referring to the soldier?'

'Yes. His name is Cameron.'

'That man has employed a black – and we all know what blacks will do.'

Maria picked up the poker and stirred the fire in the stove. 'Are you afraid of what he might find out?'

'What is that?'

She held the poker. 'Louisa.'

Julius stood over his wife. 'What are you talking of?'

'She spoke about you the other day – of what you were doing to her.'

'Louisa is mad, she has lost her mind.' Julius thought of Romans: *For all have sinned, and come short of the glory of God.* After all this time, it was being revealed; but his lust was not his fault – the blood of his father ran in his veins, and there was nothing he could do about that. He would have to wait on God for deliverance.

'She may be mad, but what you are doing is evil.'

Julius found himself asking: 'What am I doing?' The fire in the oven glowed; the kitchen was stifling; he felt dizzy and clutched the end of the table. It seemed that Maria was the master now. He glanced around for Carl, but the boy was nowhere to be seen.

'You are going to her in the night and doing obscene things to her.' Maria's voice was low. 'You are taking pleasure, and a father is forbidden to do that to his daughter.'

Julius raised his hand and struck hard, but Maria did not fall – she stood at the fireplace, her face stinging and swelling and said: 'If there is a God, He will have his way with you and I do not care.'

He watched her as she hung up the poker and left the room.

From the verandah, Carl heard the conversation. As he listened, his back prickled and his hands sweated; he heard Maria's accusations, his father's voice and knew that his sister was evil. He was sure she was possessed by the Devil – she was sinful and would be struck down by the hand of God. Carl stepped off the boards, walked down the path past the water tank and placed the bag on the bench in the barn. If he placed it on a fencepost, it would make a good target. Once again, he would be the champion marksman of Rubicon, but his father had told him to put it in the barn. He took up his shotgun, loaded the barrels, glanced at the silent house and strolled toward the Kurnbrun road.

Julius locked the bedroom door and sat on the iron bed. The springs creaked and the room smelt of dust and camphor. He stared at the furniture which he had bought for Sophie – it was wormy and faded by the sun. Julius slipped the key from his watch-chain, opened the bottom drawer of the cedar chest and, like Maria, took out the envelope of photographs. There were the Hoffmayers: his great-grandfather and grandmother posing by a marble urn in a studio in Hamburg, his great-uncles, Friedrich and Ernst, who went to Ohio, family groups taken in backyards on farms in South Australia and his mother, Carlotta, when she was a young woman – before she met his father. He looked at the photograph carefully and saw a sloe-eyed, beautiful young woman as she sat composed, her hands on her lap. Her lips were full, her cheekbones high and her long black hair curled around her neck. Her breasts were full and her waist tiny; she looked like a houri – a courtesan. Alone in the room, he stared at his mother for a long time, then suddenly pushed the picture away. Louisa was as beautiful.

There was one photograph he always returned to: it was a family group, sitting and standing on the flagstoned steps of a house owned by one of his uncles. There were pot-plants on a carved table; ribbons hung from the verandah; one man was wearing a pill-box, military hat; another, a posy of flowers; the women were seated with needlework on their laps; the doors were louvred, roses bloomed and climbed on the posts and all were the signs of wealth and respectability. Sitting between the knees of his mother was a young, stern-faced boy in a lace shirt and knickerbockers. He was staring straight at the photographer – it was himself and he was the image of his father. He cursed the memory of August, his women, his fornication, his profligacy and his wantonness. He was building a new property and if he worked hard, God would expiate him.

Julius put the photographs away carefully and looked out

of the window. Tomorrow, he would clear more bush, drag out the stumps, repair the fences, and work with Carl from dawn to dark.

'When's the funeral?' Jim Banks asked.

'Tuesday.' Mooney wore his revolver in a holster and had his boot on the bar rail.

'The store was ripped apart before it went up, wasn't it?'

'It was. Withers is right – it's on for young and old now.'

'It looks as though Rubicon could be the last bastion of civilization.' John Carver lit another cigarette and drank his brandy.

'Withers has talked with Cameron,' Mooney said.

'And?' Banks looked toward the door – the bar was filling slowly now. It was late Friday and the farm hands were coming in for their fun. The afternoon was dark and the smell from the fire still drifted.

'He's not interested and gave Withers the arse.'

Carver laughed. 'He's the first one to do that.' He dropped his cigarette into the tray. 'Judge Jeffreys reviled.'

'Who was he?' Banks asked.

'The legendary hanging judge.'

Mooney seized Carver by the collar. 'Listen, you drunken old shit, Withers has hung no one. He can't do that.'

But Carver was undismayed. 'There's always a first time the way this town's going.' He coughed and laughed again. 'It's a long way from the regular courts, ain't it?'

The Royal was quiet as the three men talked, but at five-thirty, the bar was suddenly full with men, jostling and pushing. The air became thick with smoke and sweat – they drank beer, whisky, brandy and stout. Some of them were mean-faced, wearing patched waistcoats, braces, oily hats and hob-nailed boots.

'Jesus Christ,' Banks said as he worked at the bar, 'this is good for business. Who are these blokes?'

Mooney left the counter and pushed through the mob. He was glad he was wearing his gun: it was the biggest Friday night mob he'd ever seen. In one corner, he looked for familiar faces, but now saw none. These men were from out of town – he looked at them as he moved through. He didn't like the feel of this.

'Fuck you, copper.'

Mooney turned, but couldn't see the speaker. Suddenly, there were hands on his back, fingers at his belt, elbows in his chest, someone hissed and spittle ran down his neck; he turned and saw Jim Banks besieged at the bar. Who were these men, and where were they from? This was as sudden as last month's cyclone.

'Fuck you, copper. Have you killed any more kids lately?'

As Mooney swung to see the man, a horse shrieked on Federation Street, a car back-fired and a gun-shot rang. Fearful now, Mooney pulled out his gun as the men stood laughing at him. 'I want this pub cleared out,' he said.

'It's ten minutes to closing time, copper,' someone said. 'It ain't the law.'

'I'm the law,' Mooney said.

'Aw, shit.' The men stood, then dropped their glasses on the floor, tramped on the broken glass, laughed and made toward the door. 'This town's looking down the barrel,' a man said. 'No one's safe. You'd better lock up your valuables. And your women.'

'Not while I'm here,' Mooney said. He leant against the door so they couldn't see him shaking.

'You couldn't pull the skin off a rice pudding.'

'This town's on the list,' someone else said.

What list? Mooney watched them as they got into their old trucks and started up their engines. Some of the men looked like timber-workers, with their cloth caps and grimy neckerchiefs.

'I'm telling you to get out,' he shouted as the motors raced and the exhaust billowed.

'Aw, go and fuck yourself, copper.'

It was then that Mooney saw a dark man standing on the running-board of a Ford truck – he was an aborigine.

Jim Banks pulled down the blinds and they went into the house bar. His hands trembled as he poured out the jiggers of Scotch.

'Jesus Christ,' he said, 'who were those blokes?'

'They were the fucking commos, the fucking proletariat. Timber-workers – Withers is right again. Did you see the darkie?'

'No.'

'Well, I bloody did.'

'It wasn't Ray Stark?'

'Nah, but those black bastards are mixed up in it. I'm going to need help.'

Carver laughed. 'You'll have to swear in deputies à la the westerns.'

Mooney stared. 'Maybe I can. I'll have to ask Withers.'

'I don't think so,' Carver replied. 'This ain't Dodge City.'

'Listen, Carver,' Mooney said, 'don't tell me what I fucking can and can't do.'

'Well, you're going to need good men, tried and true.' Carver stubbed out his cigarette. 'Gentlemen, please excuse me – I have the world of entertainment to attend to.'

Banks and Mooney watched him walk out the door. 'That bastard,' Mooney said, 'gives me the shits. Who the fuck does he think he is?'

'Did someone mention the kid?'

'Yes,' Mooney answered. 'They did.'

Eighteen

Frank and Ray stood apart from the others at the graveside. Frank looked at the gravestones, the iron railings and the small mausoleums: Schram, Webber, Macdonald – it seemed that whole families had disappeared in the 'flu epidemic. Sometimes two children were buried in the same grave. He wondered if Ray was thinking about this mother and father. The crowd was large, over three hundred, and they stood about, heads bowed, as the minister took the service. George Ballantine had been a very popular man.

Harold Withers was at the graveside with the Grand Master of the Lodge, Henry Farrar, the bank manager and other traders of Federation Street. All were dressed in black, their boots in the fine, freshly dug earth where the wreaths and flowers lay. George's aunt, old and doddering, clung to the arm of her other nephew – a big, stooped man who had come up to Rubicon for the day. As the gentle north wind blew the leaves from the gum trees and the crows called from the branches, the minister intoned the service, the coffin was lowered, the earth thrown and the flowers scattered. The women wept and the men stood silent. *RIP. George Albert Ballantine.*

When the service was ended, the men lit up their cigarettes and hung about the cemetery gates, where their cars and trucks were parked.

'I'm going to the Royal for a drink.' Frank said. 'Do you want to come?'

Ray smiled. 'I don't think it's the best time for a blackfellow to be in a pub like the Royal.'

'Maybe you're right. Why don't you come past the pub in a couple hours and pick me up – I'll be outside.'

153

Ray put his foot on the running-board of the Chev. 'Okay. Watch out for that joker, Withers.'

'I will, I'll see you later.'

Ray watched his mate walk along the road back into town.

'It's war, now, isn't it?' Henry Farrar said. 'Civil, fucking war.'

They all stood at the bar: Withers, Mooney, Bolger, the men who were in the raid on the camp, the traders and the farmers.

'Gentlemen,' Withers said, 'I want you all to charge your glasses and drink to the memory of George Ballantine.'

They swallowed the liquor down and wiped their mouths. Outside, the street was silent, the shop doors were closed and the flag at the post office hung at half-mast.

'We've got to arm more men,' said Bolger. 'We're on our own up here – the nearest help's two hours' drive away. If you want something done, do it yourself.'

'Do what?' one of the men asked.

'Any strange bastard gets it.' The butcher ran his hand across his throat.

Withers lit a cigar. 'The enquiry will be held on Friday.'

'Aw shit.'

'There are legal processes and they will be upheld.'

From the door, Frank saw the group and strolled over to the bar.

'G'day,' he said, touching his hat. He took it off and laid it on the counter.

'I wouldn't put that there, if I was you,' Banks said. 'It takes up valuable space.'

'Okay,' Frank replied as he put his hat back on. 'You can give me a beer if you like.'

They watched him drink. 'I didn't see your neighbour at the funeral,' Bolger said.

'Who was that?'

'Hoffmayer.'

'He doesn't have a truck.'

'He could have come in on his waggon. Those Huns live in the Dark Ages.'

154

Frank put down his glass. 'If they prefer to live that way, it's their business.'

'It was a bad business, was it not?'

Frank considered Withers once more and saw the kind of man who had driven his father off the family farm. 'Of course it was. I found George Ballantine an honest man, and honest men are hard to find these days.'

'What do you mean by that?' Withers thought of the lunch. No one would ever know about the fire.

Frank laughed. 'Just what I said.' He knew damned well that he had been talked about.

'Fucking Hun,' Bolger said. 'He couldn't even turn up to George's funeral.'

'That was his business.'

'We should have put all them bastards to the sword.' It was Farrar now.

Frank laughed again. 'Did you go?'

'I was medically unfit.'

'There's nothing wrong in not having gone,' Frank said. 'It's just that *I* did. Not all Germans are bastards. They're like us – some are, some aren't.' This, he thought, had all the makings of a bust-up.

'I hear you won't join us.' Bolger said.

'Join you?'

'To keep the Bolshies out. They killed George Ballantine.'

'You mean, some tin-pot mob managed by our local J.P.? You've been going to too many of Mr Carver's westerns.'

Bolger persisted. 'The Bolshies killed George.'

'I think I know,' Frank replied, 'why Ballantine's was burnt down.'

'That's a matter for the enquiry,' Withers said.

'Last month,' Frank went on, 'an unemployeds' camp was raided, and a woman lost a baby. There could be a connection.'

'You're talking shit,' Mooney said. He was white-faced: the secret was out and only God knew what would happen now. Cameron was a puzzle – he didn't fit the rules.

'Maybe,' Frank answered, 'but I don't think so.'

'Aw Jesus.' They turned their backs on him and ordered more drinks.

But Frank found Bolger standing beside him. 'How's the farm doing?'

'Good.'

'Working hard?'

'Yes.'

'Nothing going missing?'

Frank turned to face the questioner. 'No.'

'Stark's got a bad reputation in this town – did you know that?'

'He's okay by me, Bolger, and someone else thought so, too.'

'Who?'

'George Ballantine.'

'A nice bloke, but too trusting.'

'As I said, Bolger, honest.'

'What's this "Bolger" stuff? Do you think you're still a bloody officer?'

'I don't believe we're on first names; you can call me "Cameron", if you like.'

The butcher was close now. 'You might have made a mistake coming up here, with your attitudes.'

'I don't think so, but if I've made mistakes I've got to live with them.'

'It looks as though you're the odd man out, employing a darkie and not helping us.'

Frank slid his glass down the counter toward Jim Banks. 'I've got work to do.'

'You be careful, Cameron. You might find it hard to live with your mistakes.'

'Is that a threat?'

Bolger coughed and laughed. 'Nah. Just an observation.'

As Frank turned away, he saw the others watching him go.

Frank stopped in the lobby and pulled out his watch: he would have to wait for Ray. He went down the corridor to the outside lavatory, past the beer barrels and junk in the back yard. When he came out, he found Bolger standing in the alley. 'So we meet again,' he said. 'I forgot to ask you – how's your leg?'

Frank sized up the butcher: he hadn't killed a man since he was in the army, and didn't want to do so now. 'Fine.'

'It doesn't stop you from getting around?'

'No.'

'Look, Cameron, I don't know what makes you tick, but you ain't one of us, so you'd better drink elsewhere.'

'There's only one pub in town.'

'That's your problem – you'll have to drink with the abo.'

The path was narrow and the beer barrels rose on either side. Jesus Christ, Frank thought, Jesus Christ. 'I'll drink where I like.'

'No you won't.' Bolger put a big hand on Frank's chest.

'I wouldn't do that,' Frank said.

'You're a fucking traitor.' Bolger pushed.

Very fast and very hard, Frank brought his knee up into the butcher's groin and, as the man collapsed, hit him on the bridge of the nose. The blood ran on to the pavement as Frank stood back. 'I won't kick you,' he said, 'I don't want shit on my boots.'

As he went back through the lobby, Frank was trembling. He stopped by the door, saw Withers and his friends still talking and went out the front door.

After the smell of the beer and piss, the air seemed fresh and people were strolling on Federation Street. Frank looked around for Ray in the truck, but it was too early and he was not there. By this time, Bolger would have dragged himself back to the bar and Mooney would come out to make an arrest – Frank had no doubt about that. Then, presumably, he would come up before Withers. In this situation, he was better off on home ground. He pulled his hat down and walked quickly up the street in the hope of seeing Ray. As the cars, trucks and horse-drawn waggons rattled by, he could

157

see no sign of the Chev; he glanced back toward the Royal and saw Mooney standing on the pavement; he ducked into the draper's, stood for a moment or two among the bolts of material, then went out and continued walking. Luck was with him: he saw Ray, flagged him down and jumped in. 'Okay,' he said, 'get out of town and make it quick.'

'What's up?' Ray asked.

'I tangled with Bolger in the Royal.'

'Did you hit him?'

'I did.'

'Hard?'

'Very.'

'Oh, shit.' Ray said. 'Oh shit.'

Julius's uncle had fought in the German 5th Imperial Cavalry; he was an Uhlan, but had not raped nuns, nor had he cut off children's ears. He was killed in the tank battle of the Marne in 1918 and the Hoffmayer family in Neukirch sent them a funeral card. His father showed it to him, and was drunk for a week on the finest Napoleon brandy; he drank in bed and insisted that the bottle be brought to him on a silver tray with a selection of sweetmeats, pickles and wafer-sliced pumpernickel. Julius once had a photograph of his uncle, dressed in his officer's uniform – he had a curling moustache, sabre scars and looked like Kaiser Wilhelm. He remembered that as a child, he thought all young German officers looked like the Kaiser. Why, then, had they lost the war when they faced a mob of English street urchins, the descendants of convicts and natives from Africa and India?

As he worked with Carl in the bush and on the powdery, cleared paddocks, he often thought of his Uncle Johann – he had all the correct values: discipline, honesty, bravery, loyalty and a belief in God. Had his uncle come to work in Australia, it would have been a better place. His uncle would have disowned his brother August and his filthy ways – at least he, Julius, had done that. Once Carl had seen the overgrown mound of August's grave on the far boundary of the farm.

'What is that, father?' Carl asked. And he replied: 'It is some native's grave – it is nothing.'

In the good seasons, when the rains were plentiful, Julius sowed the wheat by hand – broadcasting it from the back of the dray. Maria drove the dray for him, keeping a tree at the far end of the paddock between the horse's ears to make a straight line. Julius Hoffmayer sowed the straightest lines of wheat and ploughed the straightest furrows in the whole district of Rubicon: those were his benchmarks, his standards, and he would keep them that way. Then he, Carl and Maria would water, feed and groom a dozen horses and have the plough on the move at sunrise. Seven horses were abreast of a five-furrow plough and they would plough six acres a day. Then, the land yielded ten to twelve bushels of wheat to the acre, and he took his waggon loaded with four-bushel bags to the station where the stacks at the siding were over thirty feet high. Then, Rubicon was the bread-basket of the world. He was the farmer who supported the tradesman, the soldier, the doctor and even the man of God – without him, they were nothing. But now, with the civil commotion, the strikes, the bad prices and the pestilence of the drought, it seemed that his work was worth nothing.

Today, while Carl was cutting the shoots from the stumps, Julius had decided to farrow; and for five hours now, he had walked in the dust behind the horses. Of all the tasks, this was the most miserable: the dirt and the flies clung to his sweat, he walked like a blind man across the earth – a vast potter's field that would yield nothing until the rain came. *You are taking pleasure, and a father is forbidden to do that to his daughter.* It was a month since he had seen Louisa, but how long could he stay away? And how long could the secret be kept? In the dust, Julius thought of his wife standing in the kitchen in the heat of the oven. *If there is a God, He will have His way with you and I do not care.* Sooner or later, she would confide in someone; but whom he thought, could she tell?

The explosion shook Rubicon at half past two in the morning: Frank and Ray heard it, as did the Hoffmayers and the other farmers. Mooney's house creaked, glass smashed and, from his back window, he could see the glare of flames at the railway depot. As he struggled into his clothes, he heard the sound of the fire bell and people shouting. He strapped on his revolver, ran into the yard and got into his car. The Ford wouldn't start, he cursed, grabbed the crank handle in the back, turned the motor over and at last it fired. When he drove around the corner at the back of the Royal, he saw the blaze was big, had taken hold of the goods sheds and was racing toward the stock yards.

Within fifteen minutes, it seemd the whole town was there, but nothing could be done. The heat drove the people back to the perimeter of the yard and they heard the screams and bellowing of horses and cattle as they burned to death. In the crimson light, Mooney saw the Hupmobile draw up and ran over to see Withers. 'Sabotage.' he shouted.

Withers was calm. 'It looks that way.' He looked at the station as the roof caved in. It was government property and only God knew when it would be replaced. 'Have you seen anybody strange?'

Mooney threw his hands up. 'In this shambles?'

'I'm going home then,' Withers replied. 'You can report to me in the morning.'

'Okay.' The policeman caught sight of a group of men struggling with someone under some trees near the siding and dashed over.

When Mooney got there, he found them beating a man around the head. 'All right,' he said, 'you can leave it to me.'

'It's a bloody abo,' someone said.

When Mooney dragged the man to his feet by his braces, it was the black man he had seen on the running-board of the truck when the hooligans arrived in the bar of the Royal.

Nineteen

Ray Stark knew the blackfellow who was taken at the station – he was a brother, but not in the whiteman's sense. As he worked on the northern boundary fence, he wondered if he should tell Frank. But he had enough troubles of his own with Bolger and Mooney. The cop hadn't been out yet, but Ray was bloody sure he would; Bolger would lay charges – he was that kind of bastard – and Christ knew what would happen when Frank went up before Withers. Maybe nothing: there was a law for the Rubicon whites and another for the rest. God help the blackfellow captured at the explosion. They would probably beat him in the balls, hit him in the belly where it wouldn't show, Withers would pass sentence and he'd be taken away to some country prison where nothing more would be heard of him. When most blackfellows were put in jail, they disappeared and no one did anything about it. Ray thought of other white farmers he'd worked for. The crack of the shovel handle over the shoulders – *You cheeky nigger bastard.*

Why was Frank different? There were some good white jokers, and he'd been lucky enough to strike one. But Frank might have to pay, and what would happen then?

Ray was unrolling the barbed wire when Frank rode up. 'How's it going?'

'Good.'

Frank got down stiffly and eased his back. 'Did you hear they got a blackfellow at the station?'

'Yeah.'

'Do you know him?'

'Yeah.'

'A relation?'

Ray grinned. 'We're all related.'

'I shouldn't think he'd get a fair trial?'

'Nah.' Ray rolled a cigarette. 'You going back to town?'

'When?'

'Any time.'

'I think,' Frank said, 'I'll wait for developments. Do you think that black was with the men who blew up the railway?'

'Dunno. There's some tough bastards around and some of them have joined the unions. They've got things to pay back.'

Frank worked on the fence and thought: he was being forced into a corner. There was the bricklayer on the road up, Withers and Bolger. There was the death of Ballantine, and the Hoffmayers – something was happening on that farm and he could get involved. He tore his finger on a barb and cursed. Jesus, and a drought and the Depression to boot. And there was Rubicon – you have made an error, my son. He looked up at the sky and saw the familiar afternoon clouds drifting from the north. If it didn't rain in the next month, there would be no crop next season, and that meant failure. He was following the footsteps of his father.

After an hour, Frank tossed the pliers and wire-cutters into the saddlebag and led his horse down the fence-line. 'I'll be away for a couple of hours,' he said.

'Okay.' Ray grinned. 'Watch out for the baddies.'

'I will,' Frank answered as he mounted. 'See you later.' He rode toward the house, down the track and turned left on the Kurnbrun road for the lake.

Maria Hoffmayer *was* there – he saw her sitting on her horse at the end of a small headland overlooking the lake bed. As she heard him coming, she did a strange thing – she raised her hand. Frank acknowledged, his spirits rising, and rode out along the narrow path where the old gums drooped over the rocks. Then an aircraft appeared in the northern sky, its engine drumming in the still air. It was a biplane, flying south to Melbourne – to the suburbs and streets of a city he had last seen when he came home on the troopship in 1918. It seemed a long time ago.

They both looked up until the aeroplane disappeared beyond the bush line.

'That could have been Amy Johnson,' Frank said.

'Amy Johnson?'

'The aviatrix.' Then he saw her bruised face. 'What's happened to you?'

Maria turned her head away. 'It was an accident.'

Frank wondered if he should ask further, but said: 'Haven't you heard of Amy Johnson?'

'No.'

'She was an intrepid woman pilot who flew here from England two years ago.'

'We do not get the newspapers.'

Frank thought of the story about the Hoffmayers Ray had told him; then he realized they were having a conversation, almost that of friends. 'Why are you here?' he asked.

'I wanted to get away, I wanted to re-live my memories. Why are you?'

'I like this lake, even though it's dry. It's a sign of hope.'

Maria faced him. 'You are not like other men.'

'There's nothing special about me,' Frank replied. 'Do you know many men?'

'I know very few people – we Hoffmayers keep to ourselves.' She wondered what she could tell him – if anything. 'The station was blown up two nights ago. What does it mean?'

'It means Rubicon is under some kind of attack.'

'Why?'

'There are desperate men around – it's the Depression and the drought.' Frank paused. 'I thought I might find you here.'

'Did you?'

'You said it was your favourite place.'

They both dismounted and stood on the shore. 'There were cormorants and mallard ducks here,' Maria said. 'We used to feast on the game.'

'How is your husband?' Frank asked.

'Working hard.'

Frank took the plunge. 'I know a little about his father.'

'Who told you?'

'Rubicon is a small town: people talk.'

She was proud. 'Do they talk about the Hoffmayers?'

'Sometimes, as I told you – there are some men who are still fighting the Great War, and they find your husband hard to understand.'

Maria stood motionless. What *did* Frank Cameron know? 'Julius is a very independent man.'

'How is your daughter?'

'My stepdaughter – Louisa and Carl both belong to Julius.'

'Your stepdaughter.'

'Why do you ask?'

'When I first called to see you,' Frank said, 'she was ill – summer cold, I think.'

'Her health,' Maria answered, 'continues to be poor. It is in the Hoffmayer family.'

Her hair was drifting around her neck and she pinned it back with her long fingers. Frank had not been with a woman for a long time now and he found himself looking at her body. 'If you have any trouble,' he said, 'you can tell me.'

'That is kind of you, Mr Cameron.'

'Frank.'

They tethered their horses and walked along the shore.

'Tell me about Amy Johnson,' she said.

'I don't know much about her, except that she's good-looking and brave.'

'And you admire her?'

'Yes,' Frank replied, 'I do. I admire anybody who takes risks and succeeds. I took a risk coming up here to Rubicon, and I intend to succeed.' He looked at her face and dark eyes. 'Sometimes you have to break the rules.'

'What rules are those?'

'The rules of the past, attitudes, ways that no longer work.'

'Like employing Mr Stark?'

Frank laughed. 'That's the first time Ray's been called

"mister".' He thought of Banks, Farrar and Bolger. 'They call Germans, Huns; Withers chucks farmers out of their houses; Mooney and his mates bash the unemployed. It's unjust and doesn't help.'

Maria wondered if she should tell Frank about Louisa, Julius and her life. Would that be disloyalty? Instead she said: 'We do not get the newspapers, so I know very little of what is going on.'

'I can give you mine.'

'Julius would not allow that.'

'Well, I'll tell you.' Frank smiled. 'I'll give you a weekly news bulletin.'

'You are not married?'

'I was once, but she went away during the war.'

'While you were fighting?'

'Yes.'

Maria stopped on the path. 'And you came home to nothing?'

'I was still a young man then,' Frank said, 'but I've forgiven her. It was *her* life.'

'You think we should control ourselves?'

'Yes – as much as we can.'

'What about God?'

'I'm not sure about God.'

Foxes and rabbits ran through the brush; they came to a fallen log and, as Frank was about to swing his leg over, she put out her hand and helped him. Frank felt her fingers and gripped them. 'At least,' Maria said, 'you are not a *mutilé*. That's what the French call them, is it not?'

'How did you know that?'

'There were postcards of the war in my aunt's house. I remember a folding one of the battle for Verdun.' She let his hand go, slowly, sat down and, for the first time in years, unpinned her hair. It fell to her shoulders. 'You are right about this lake.'

Frank sat close. 'It will rain, and plants will grow again.'

'You are sure?'

'Yes.'

'Are you happy in Rubicon?' Maria asked.

Frank laughed. 'It's a tough town in hard country, and a hard country breeds hard men. Like your husband, I get misunderstood.'

'You do not hate the Germans?'

'That, and other things. Do you know a man called Withers?'

'Yes, Julius's father mortgaged the farm to his father.'

'I have the feeling Withers is owed money by many farmers in Rubicon.'

'Julius says that is their fault.'

'Maybe, it's the way he gets it back I don't like. Families should not have to walk on the roads and live in camps.'

'Do men call at your door?'

'Yes,' Frank said, 'they do.'

'And do you give them something to eat?'

'Yes, do you?'

'When I can. It is sometimes difficult.' Maria knew this was a good man, and she wanted to see more of him. She was glad he had come to the lake – the bush seemed less menacing, birds flew in droves and the sky looked beautiful. Then, as she turned toward Frank, she saw a man on a horse watching them from the shade of the trees in the ruined camping ground. Maria raised her arm. 'A man is up there,' she said.

When Frank looked, he saw a rider disappear into the bush. 'A local farmer,' he said.

Maria ran to her horse. 'I must go.'

As she rode up the track, Frank called: 'Don't forget what I said about trouble.'

'I will remember.' Then she was gone.

Mooney was in a reasonable mood. 'All right, blackie,' he said, 'you've had twenty-four hours to think it over. Now tell me why you were at the station.'

'I've got a name,' the aborigine said as he stood, handcuffed, in the small office.

The policeman doodled on the charge sheet. Angus McIntosh – some Scot had fucked his mother. 'All right, Angus, we know you're a member of the timber-workers' union, and *I* know you were with that mob in the Royal last week. Are you a Bolshie?'

'Eh?'

Mooney was a changeable man. 'Listen, you black bastard, don't do the dumb act with me. Timber-workers are commos, therefore you're a commo, and worse than that you're a black commo. You were apprehended at the scene of the crime of sabotage.'

'I'm not saying.'

'You're not saying what?'

'I'm not saying.'

Mooney came up close. 'Do you know a blackfellow called Stark?'

'Not me.'

'Come on, Angus, all you black people stick together like shit to a blanket. You all fuck each other.'

'Not me.'

Mooney sat down behind his desk. 'Do you know what I've got you on, boyo? I've got you on breaking and entering, arson, causing a civil commotion, disturbing the peace, sabotage, wilful destruction of government property and intent to commit murder. This town is forty miles away from the nearest settlement, and we make up our own rules in Rubicon. Where are you from?'

'Wilcannia.'

'Wilcannia? That's fucking hundreds of miles away.'

'I move around.'

Mooney rose and picked up his truncheon. 'Listen, you cheeky young bugger, I normally give a man a fair fight, I don't hit a bloke when his hands are tied – that's the white man's way. But your case is different: I want to know who those blokes were who came into the Royal, I want to know who burnt down Ballantine's, and I want to know who blew up the railway station.'

'I don't know nothing.'

'Okay, Angus, I'm going to have to beat your black belly and balls until you tell me.' Mooney laughed. 'There's going to be one very sore black boy in Rubicon tonight.'

The door opened and Harold Withers walked in. 'You're not going to belabour our aboriginal friend, are you? You'll give the town a bad name.'

'Just exercising.'

'Aha.' Withers sat down in Mooney's chair. 'I've read your report, Don – a masterpiece of English prose; but I must lend you my thesaurus. I've not got the power to try and sentence this man for such offences; he'll have to be sent down to Horsham. Has he made a statement yet?'

'He's about to.'

'Is he?' Withers glanced at the charge sheet. 'Have you asked him if he has any colleagues in the district?'

'Yes.'

'And what did he say?'

'He says he doesn't know anything.'

'It's sad,' Withers said, 'drink seems to affect their memories. Or maybe it's their natural cunning.' He folded the charge sheet neatly. 'If he makes a statement this afternoon, you can do the necessary paperwork and take him to Horsham in the morning. You'll have to excuse me – I've got a power of things to do.'

Withers left and the flydoor banged.

Mooney picked up the truncheon again. 'That, Angus', he said, 'was our local Justice of the Peace – a good man, firm but fair. Tell me: who were those blokes at the Royal?'

'Fuck you, copper.'

Mooney swung the truncheon and hit the aborigine in the stomach and, as he doubled, he hit him in his testicles. Then he struck him in the kidneys, on the kneecaps and in the stomach again. The man collapsed; Mooney dragged him to the cell, pushed him in, bolted the door and left the office. Reg Bolger was shutting his shop door as Mooney came up. 'How's our black mate?'

'A bit sore. He says he doesn't know anything.'

'Fucking Christ, it's like a cracked gramophone record. Have you charged Cameron yet?'

'I wanted to talk to you about that.'

Bolger turned the key in the padlock and looked up. 'What's there to talk about? The bastard attacked me.'

Mooney was careful. 'Knowing you, Reg, there could have been some provocation.'

'He was in the way and I put me hand on his shoulder – I told you that.'

They stood by the verandah post. 'I've got enough trouble as it is – there's the black, the station, Ballantine's, the evictions. Cameron could still be useful and the last thing we want is to arrest a returned man.'

'*I'm* a returned man.'

'But you weren't an officer, and you weren't decorated.'

'For fuck's sake, Don, the bugger attacked me.'

Mooney thought. 'I've never met a man like Cameron before. But as you said, something's going to happen – things will get worse before they get better. Cameron's bound to get it in the neck one way or another.' They crossed the street, past the war memorial and the garden. 'And,' Mooney said, 'if you want to arrange something without me knowing, it's up to you, isn't it?'

At half past seven next morning, when Mooney opened the cell door, he found Angus McIntosh hanging by the neck from the rafter. He had used his belt and his neck was broken. Mooney cursed, cut him down and drove over to see Withers, who was having breakfast. They talked in the dining-room, overlooking Withers' estate; Mooney drank tea and Withers gave him half a grapefruit from the refrigerator. He said it was unfortunate, but not really a problem; who would come forward and say he was the mate of a black man in the timber-workers' union which was involved in destroying a railway station? The best thing to do was to dump the body down a well, and there were plenty of those about.

Mooney did the job carefully. He drove out west to an abandoned gypsum mine, heaved the body down a shaft and went back to Rubicon past Frank Cameron's gate. He saw Frank and Ray fencing; they looked up, but Mooney didn't acknowledge them.

Twenty

The autumn days were shortening, the kitchen was dark and the kerosine lamp smoked.

'Why are we having cold meat for our evening meal?' Julius asked as he sat at the table.

'I have been busy,' Maria replied, as she set the thin slices of mutton before him.

'We are all busy,' he said. 'It is our lot.'

'I have been looking after Louisa.' She mentioned the child openly, but Julius said grace and dug his fork into the mashed potato.

'I will get a wild pig soon,' Carl said. 'I will keep looking.'

'How far did you go today?' The meat was stringy and Julius chewed carefully.

'Round and about.' Carl got up, trimmed the lamp and went back to his meal.

'Did you go near the soldier's farm?'

'No, I went the other way.'

'Toward the lake?'

'In that direction.'

'I think Louisa should be seen by a doctor.' Maria did not look at Carl, ate her meal quickly, took the plate to the bench and put a kettle of water on for tea.

'There are wild pigs around,' Julius said. 'I have seen their droppings. You would do best around the water-holes.'

'I agree,' his son replied. 'Please have patience.'

'That, I have plenty of, but remember we have only one pig to see us through the winter.'

As she put on more water to wash the dishes, Maria wondered if it were Carl who was the rider watching her and Frank Cameron at the lake. If it were, would he tell his father?

171

She should have been afraid, but she was not. She thought of Louisa and Julius – not of the disgrace if other people found out, but of the sickness in the Hoffmayers, of August, of Carl, of the isolation. It was as though they were the last family in a lost tribe, struggling to survive in a wilderness of drought and cruelty. Maria found herself thinking, thank God for Frank Cameron; he believed in friendship, knew it would rain and that the lake would fill once again.

'Tomorrow evening,' Julius said, 'I would like a hot meal. A man needs it after a hard day's work in the bush.' He was standing close behind her and it was as though the conversation about Louisa had never happened.

'Tomorrow night,' Maria replied, 'you will have your hot meal. Do not worry about that.'

'Your horse has been worked today,' Julius said. 'Why is that?'

'I went riding this afternoon.'

'Riding? Why?'

'Because,' Maria replied as she turned to face her husband, 'I wanted to leave this house.'

'Have you thought of the consequences?'

'What are those?'

'You are leaving a young woman unattended, and there is a black man but one mile away.'

'The woman,' Maria said, 'is your daughter, and she may be safer with the black man than she is with you.'

Again he went to strike her, but Maria stood firm and said: 'You will not hit me again. If you do, I will hit back and then we shall be like animals.'

'You will not leave this house.'

'I was once your *hausfrau*, but I am your *hausfrau* no longer.'

In his anger, Julius turned to Carl, but he was gone.

Maria sat on the verandah and listened to the sounds of the animals and insects of the bush. Where were Julius and Carl? She now knew that life in the house had been better when

172

August was there, despite his drinking and his women. He was a civilized man: he played Strauss and Lehar; he could speak French as well as German; he knew European history and what was happening in the world outside. Frank Cameron, too, had been to France, even if it were to fight a war. Maria thought of the French ladies, promenading on the Boulevard des Italiens: once her aunt had told her about the French balloonists, taking out messages when Paris was besieged by the Prussians. Then she thought of the aeroplane, flying over the lake south to a large city she had never seen. Where, she wondered, was August buried? Maybe, one day, she would visit his grave. Maria remembered listening to August playing the piano at a wedding long before she married Julius; there in the front parlour of a large house were Carlotta, Sophie and the guests listening:

> *Pretty girls are made to love and kiss,*
> *Who am I to interfere with this?*

She thought of Frank Cameron as the moon rose above the bush line.

The Bank of Australia gave Harold Withers thirty days to refinance; if he did not, they would sell him up and he would be in the same position as his mortgagors. The irony did not escape him and he began turning the screws on all his debtors, many of whom were in neighbouring country towns. Shopkeepers, garage proprietors, farmers, boarding-house ladies – all were served warrants and the bailiffs moved in. They were dispossessed and disappeared into the larger towns and cities to feed in soup kitchens and sleep in refuges. It was still possible he might have to sell his house and car, but such a course was unthinkable.

In neighbouring settlements, farmers were clubbing together at repossession auctions, buying the property and selling it back to the owner. At Netherby, a bailiff was badly beaten with axe handles and the auctioneer shot in the arm with a twelve-bore shotgun. Withers now feared that if he moved on farmers in Rubicon, there would be violence, but there was nothing else he could do. It seemed that all he had planned and worked for was disappearing in the dust clouds drifting over the bare and broken land.

Withers had Don Mooney to lunch upstairs at the Royal. 'No enquiries about our black friend?' he asked.

'No.' Mooney was in a confident mood.

'And none about the raid on the camp?'

'No, again.'

Withers stuck the wafer into his ice-cream. 'It looks like we're winning the war.' But he thought of the bank. '1932,' he went on, 'will go down as the worst in the century. And there's still months to go.'

'A lot of blokes are walking off,' Mooney said.

'The ones that walk off show some sense: they face up to reality. It's ones who stay and make trouble that are the fools.' Withers drank his port. 'We're going to want more armed men – I think those timber-workers will be back. We'll get no help from the politicians. I'm beginning to think that democracy brings out the lowest common denominator. Have you been following what's been happening in Europe?'

'I've been a bit busy.'

'There's a man in Germany called Hitler. He seems to have some of the answers. Trust the Huns – they're good at organization. Which reminds me: any news of our friend, Hoffmayer?'

'Nah, he keeps himself to himself.'

'Hoffmayer may be anti-social, but I can remember the day he came in and paid my father back every penny of the debt his father had run up. He works all hours God made, doesn't owe a thing.' Withers laughed. 'I can't see any of our socialist friends getting the better of our Julius. It's a pity he's a German.'

'Why?'

'Because,' Withers replied, 'he could set a fine example to the younger generation, to the red-feds in the unions. Think of Julius Hoffmayer patrolling the town with his rifle at the ready.' He laughed once more. 'We could mount a Spandau on the back of his waggon – that would keep the Bolshies away.'

'Ray Stark's laying low.'

Withers slid the bottle over. 'I think he would have known the black.'

'Probably.'

'Does that worry you?'

'Christ, no. Who gives a stuff about a black? But Cameron does – worry me, I mean.'

'Why?' But Withers knew.

'He's not your usual returned man, but he's also dangerous. He gave Reg a good going over.'

'You're not going to charge him?'

'No,' Mooney answered. 'We've been all through that.'

'Patience, Don, is a virtue seldom held by many.'

'That's what I told Reg.'

'I've got more warrants.'

'Christ.'

'Look, what the Depression is doing is to sort out the men from the boys, the strong from the weak. People have to learn that if they borrow money, they have to pay it back. If it's good enough for Hoffmayer, it's good enough for everyone else.'

Mooney's thoughts wandered. 'What will we do about Cameron?'

'Nothing. The man's not broken any law; he was decorated; he was an officer.' Withers thought of the lunch. *Why don't you stick to your mortgages and land dealings?* 'His time will come.' Withers wiped his mouth with his serviette. 'I'll give you the notices tomorrow.'

'Okay.'

Withers put his arm around Mooney as they walked toward the door. 'Keep your powder dry.'

John Carver's favourite film was *Dr Jekyll and Mr Hyde*. He had seen it nine times and watched the scenes where Fredric

March took the potion, carefully: he drank whisky as he sat by the projector, the talking picture echoing through the corrugated-iron building, where the rats ran and the pigeons warbled in the eaves. As he changed the reels, he put the bottle of Johnny Walker down carefully and thanked God this was a night when his cinema was closed: no dirty kids in the front seats, no clod-hopping farmers with their grotesque wives and no hoots when the film broke down.

When the film was over, he put the drums away carefully, sat down and had one for the road. He chain-smoked, coughed and considered recent events. Carver had lived in Rubicon fourteen years now: he had come north when wheat prices were high, the rains plentiful, and had once owned an Essex 6. He remembered August Hoffmayer drinking brandy in the grand circle as he watched Theda Bara, Lillian Gish and Gloria Swanson. August was the only man who understood *The Cabinet of Dr Caligari* and liked Conrad Veidt. Carver admired August Hoffmayer, his style, his women, his choice of cars and, most of all, his choice of drink. Would that man, he thought as he drained his glass, were alive today. He would have cleared the town of such savages as Bolger, Mooney and the *nouveau riche* Withers.

Carver stuck the bottle in his jacket pocket, turned off the light and climbed down the steep stairs to the lobby below. He tripped on the worn carpet, steadied himself and peered out the glass doors on to Federation Street. All was dark and silent and no lamp gleamed. He cursed the place and walked through the stalls to his sleep-out at the back. Once again, he almost fell, saved the bottle and made the back of the cinema.

He unbuttoned his fly, pissed on the gravel path, looked up at the Milky Way, said a half-forgotten prayer from his childhood and opened the door. The man sitting in his armchair was wearing a balaclava pulled down over his face and had a pick-handle over his knees. He saw the bottle of Johnny Walker and said: 'G'day, Dad, I could do with a stiff one to keep the cold out.'

176

Carver was a proud and brave man. 'This, sir,' he said, 'is my house. I have the sole right of occupancy.'

'If you don't give me that bottle,' the man said, 'I'll make your balls into jelly.'

Carver passed the bottle over. 'That is good whisky.'

'And a glass, Dad, I ain't no savage.'

Carver stood and watched the man drink. His hands were huge and his index finger was missing. 'To what,' he asked, 'do I owe this pleasure?'

'The pleasure's going to be mine, Dad. This building's the next to go.'

Carver thought of George Ballantine. 'Go?'

'Up – whoosh. You've drawn the short straw.'

'I'm not responsible,' Carver replied, 'for the actions of our Police Constable and his cronies.'

'So you know about what happened at the camp?'

'Yes.'

'In that case,' the man said, 'I reckon you're all in it – the whole fucking town.' Carver couldn't think of a reply; the man drained the bottle and got up, holding the pick-handle. 'We're going to burn this whole fucking joint down, building by building, but I'm going to do you a favour, Dad: you may get singed a bit, but if I do it right, I'm going to let you tell Mooney. That'll scare the shit out of him. And I ain't a black man – I won't be bashed in the knackers and swing.'

'You're going to set fire to my cinema?'

'It's a shame, ain't it? The good old Royal – I went to the flicks here once. You put on some real good shows.'

Like George Ballantine, John Carver was powerless. The man swung the pick-handle, Carver collapsed and the man picked him up like a baby, carried him outside into the night and tossed him over the paling fence. He lit a candle, set fire to the curtains, closed the door and walked down the path. In the cinema, he climbed the stairs to the projection room, tore open the cans of film, dowsed them with kerosine, threw a lighted match and descended to the lobby. When the smoke and flames burnt through the pine ceiling, he opened the glass doors, looked at the advertisements and walked up Federation Street.

The corrugated iron burnt so hot it glowed like the metal in an iron foundry; the windows exploded; the concrete and plaster façade collapsed; the roof fell in and the paling fence flared like a huge fuse through the dry grass. When John Carver came into hospital, he had a face worse than that of Mr Hyde. But he didn't tell Mooney about the man in the balaclava. He couldn't speak, was taken to a hospital in the south and never heard of again.

Twenty-One

Frank sat with Ray at the table and drank his tea. 'How well did you know him?' he asked.

'A bit, he was from Wilcannia, a good bloke.'

'What was his name?'

'Angus McIntosh – his father was from Scotland.'

'Do you think he was with the timber-workers?'

'He was a tough bugger, he moved around a lot, bad company.'

'Why would he hang himself?'

'Fucked if I know, I reckon Mooney would have bashed him. You shove a joker like that in a cell.'

'How do you feel?'

'About what?'

'The man's death.'

'Aw, tough, eh? I reckon those bastards will get it one day.'

Frank poured out another cup. 'What bastards?'

'Mooney, Bolger, Withers – all them that run the fucking town.'

'What do you think happened to the body?'

'Dumped somewhere, down a well or mineshaft – there's plenty of those about.'

'It's all getting dodgy,' Frank said.

'What?'

'Dangerous. Two buildings gone, the station, the black man, Ballantine dead, Carver in hospital. It's as though the place is under siege.'

'I reckon that baby belonged to some joker in the union. The town's in the shit.' Ray got up and took the plates over to the bench. 'They won't give up easy.'

'Mooney can get more men in.'

'I know those blokes,' Ray replied. 'They're like blacks – they hit and run off, they'll take some catching, and the timber-workers let black jokers work with them.' He grinned. 'Like you.'

'What do you think will happen?'

Ray stood by the bench and rolled a cigarette. 'This is real tough country up here. A lot of real wild men. I reckon the whole town will go up in flames.'

Frank thought of Maria and the bruising on her face: he was sure she had been hit. Was it Julius? He didn't want to discuss it with Ray. 'All we can do,' he said, 'is to wait and see.'

'Yeah. We ain't seen Mooney, have we? Next time you go into town, you better keep your back to the wall.' Ray poured some water into the bucket. 'I want to take a couple of days off. You needn't pay me or anything.'

Frank considered. 'That's okay.' Never ask a man where he's going.

'I want to see some of me people.'

'You see them.'

'Thanks, mate, I'll go in the morning.'

The next day, Frank rose at dawn, but Ray had already gone – with his horse and his gun.

For the first time in two months, Louisa sat on the verandah and considered her stepmother's garden. Even though the days were growing shorter, nothing still grew, save for the thistles, brambles and dandelions. She watched the thistle-down floating like tiny, fragile umbrellas toward the pine trees and the bush beyond. Louisa thought of the balloons on the pages of the magazines pasted on her bedroom walls. Where did the tiny parachutes go? What was beyond the bush line? She moved slowly down the rows of dead vegetables, where the stakes were stuck in the ground like strange bones. Then she saw a snake curled up asleep in the pumpkin patch; she pulled out a stake, poked at it, watched it strike at her legs, then disappear into the brambles. Louisa was unafraid.

The garden was empty; the fowls crouched in the shade and the horse stood motionless at the gate. As Louisa gained her legs and wandered up the track toward the bare paddocks, the locusts sang and the distant trees moved in the heat. When she got to the barn, she considered the building and wondered why some of the thatch was torn away. Was it being eaten by birds? A magpie watched her from a fencepost as she moved into the shadows. Inside, all smelt of hay, bran and chicken droppings; horse-shoes hung on nails; a rake was propped in a corner; and a saddle sat on a wooden horse, the stirrups dangling. Louisa smiled, hitched her dress and sat astride the saddle: she rocked and swayed on the old leather as the mice ran in the broken straw – she would ride away, she would ride down the Boulevard des Italiens.

It was then she saw the Gladstone bag sitting on the bench. She got off the horse, went over and opened the clip. Inside, she found a picture of a girl child, a sheet of music and a cut-throat razor. In the dusty silence of the barn, the sunlight streaming through the broken roof, she took out the sheet music, placed the razor carefully on top, put the picture in the pocket of her dress, closed the bag and left the barn. Outside, southerly clouds drifted: her body was hot and sticky; Louisa undid the buttons of her bodice. The breeze was as soft as a feather's touch on her bare breasts and she started to sing quietly to herself as she walked down the track. It was the music of her grandfather: *Pretty girls are made to love and kiss.*

Beyond the trees, the cleared paddocks rolled forever to the smudge of the horizon. The sky was infinite as Louisa, her hair flowing and dress drifting, walked to the edge of the world. Now, the locusts were deafening, the parakeets fluttered and the dust on the horizon rose in huge columns like the spires of a cathedral. On she dawdled toward the grey bush line where the eucalyptus shoots grew from the gargoyled stumps; the crows watched her from the fenceposts and, as the sun beat down, Louisa heard the sound of cutting, then saw a man stripped to the waist, the blade of his bill-hook rising and falling and gleaming.

When Maria came outside, stood and looked from the verandah, she saw nothing but the horse standing at the trough. She put the washing basket down and walked around to the front of the house. In the distance, dust rose from the road as a truck went by on the Kurnbrun road. Was that Frank Cameron? Apprehensive now, she went out on to the track and looked down toward the barn, but of Louisa there was no sign. After all this time in bed, the girl could barely walk – where was she? Maria glanced at the shadows of the trees on the ground and guessed it was after two o'clock.

When she got to the barn, she saw the sheet music and the razor on top of the bag on the bench. The bag was closed. Carl must have done that. But why take the man's belongings out – and when she looked, she saw that the photograph of the little girl was missing. Maria stood at the door, she called out Louisa's name several times, but there was no reply.

It was five when she sat down in the kitchen. Then she got up, strode down the hall and opened Louisa's bedroom door. The bed was as she had made it this morning and a blowfly buzzed at the window. Maria closed the door: there was nothing to do now but to wait until Julius and Carl returned.

'What time was it?' Julius asked as he stood, filthy and sweating in the kitchen.

'About half past two.'

'Ah.' He seemed calm and had not turned upon her. What was going through his mind?

Carl took up the hurricane lamps. 'We shall have to search. It will be dark in less than an hour. I will go and get the horses.'

'I would like you to go along the road,' Julius said to Maria. 'Carl and I will go to the north and west. You had better wear your coat as the night will be cold.'

'Should we get help?'

'No, we will find her by ourselves – this is our affair, and no one else's.'

Outside, they hung the lanterns on the pommels of their saddles. Both the men had their shotguns, the sun had almost gone and Maria left a light burning in the kitchen so they could see their way home. '*Auf Wiedersehen* then,' Julius said. 'Carl and I will be out all night, but you may come home when you get weary.'

Maria watched them ride toward the barn, waited, then turned her horse to the Kurnbrun road.

In the darkness, Maria saw a light gleaming through the trees at Frank's house. She dismounted, opened the gate and rode up to his cottage. He came to the door, dressed in his bushman's shirt and braces. He was surprised to see her and said: 'There's something wrong?'

'My stepdaughter is missing, and we are trying to find her.'

'Do you want me to help?'

'Yes,' she answered, 'yes, I do, but you are not to tell my husband.'

'I understand.'

'Where is Mr Stark?'

'He's away, seeing his people. If anyone could find her, it would be Ray.'

'But he is not here.'

Frank got his coat and they went to the stable, where he saddled his horse. 'Do you want me to come with you?' he asked.

'It makes more sense for us to search separately.'

'I think,' Frank replied, 'that it makes just as much sense for us to go together.'

She smiled. 'We go together.'

They rode south and searched the bush for six hours, but found nothing. The moon was high, the weather clear and the dew heavy. At eleven, they decided to stop and return to Frank's cottage. He tossed some sticks into the stove and they warmed themselves as he put the kettle on for some tea. Maria sat at the table. 'I have something to tell you.'

'What is that?'

She told him about Louisa, then her life and marriage and

ended saying: 'Julius does not like you – he does not like any returned man, he does not like any Australians except, perhaps, poor Mr Ballantine.'

Frank passed the mugs over. 'You can't blame your husband for that. Your community was badly treated in the war. And what of Carl?'

'He is a very strange young man; I'm not sure what will happen when you meet him.'

'Are you worried about Louisa?'

Maria turned on him. 'Of course I am – it is a human life. She may be mad, but she is a woman lost out there.'

'What about Julius and Carl?'

'What about them?'

'They'll be wondering where you are.'

'They are searching for Louisa; Julius said they would be out all night. I think Carl was the man who was watching us at the lake the other day.'

'Will he cause trouble?'

'I don't know. Do you believe in original sin?'

Frank looked up. 'No – you're the second person to ask me that.'

'Who was the first?'

'Ray Stark.'

'The Lutherans do.'

'I told you at the lake,' Frank said, '*we* control ourselves.'

Maria bent her head. 'I'm pleased you have come to the district, Frank.'

He reached across and took her hand. 'I'm pleased, too.'

She gripped his fingers. 'This is no sin?'

Frank found himself steadfast. 'No, it's not – it's complicated, and dangerous. I suspect it doesn't happen often.'

'Maybe it does, but it is always kept a secret. My life has not been as narrow as you think – when we next meet, I will tell you about Julius's father.'

'August Hoffmayer?'

'Yes,' Maria said, 'the man whom my husband hates most of all.'

'There will be a next time?'

'Yes.'

'How will I know?'

'I will leave the flag up on the mail box near the gate. I must go now – perhaps Julius and Carl have returned home. Perhaps there is news.'

As she rose, Frank put his arms around her; he kissed her on the mouth and smelt her hair. After a moment, she returned the embrace and they held each other in the centre of the room. 'You get home safely,' he said.

'I will do that.'

She kissed him again, picked up her coat and left.

Frank watched her ride up the track, bolted the door and lay on his bed.

Of all the stages of the trip, the train home seemed the longest. It stopped at every station, where crowds gathered to welcome the boys. The buildings were strung with bunting and draped with Union Jacks; the girls and mothers were laughing and crying; the children were waving flags and the town bands were playing. The carriage was littered with bottles, the men were drinking and singing, some had been sick and others were asleep. Evn though he was an officer, he didn't mind and didn't try to stop them. The poor bastards, he thought, it was the least they deserved. He was lucky – he had missed out on the final show.

After the grey and ruined countryside of northern France, the paddocks and the rain forest were unbelievably green. The cattle were fat and the grass was high; and as he thought of Irene and his father, a boy riding bareback galloped alongside. He was shouting and waving his hat then, as the train gathered speed, disappeared among the trees. 'Would you like a beer, sir?' the young soldier asked. His right arm was missing, but he seemed cheerful enough. The drink was warm and bitter and the boy sat down. 'I don't know what Mum and Dad will say when they see this.' He touched his pinned-up sleeve. 'But it don't matter, we're all alive, ain't we?'

185

Yes, he thought, we're all alive and I will have children and produce the finest cream in the district.

When the train steamed into the station, it seemed the entire town was there. He couldn't see Irene or his father, but grabbed his kit and stepped on to the platform as the people ran forward, their arms outstretched. Suddenly, he felt cold: was there no one to meet him? Then his father appeared, smiled, shook his hand and put his arms around him. 'You look fine,' he said. 'How's the leg?'

'As good as new, the German doctors were great. Where's Irene?'

His father looked down. 'Let's get out of here – I'll tell you on the way home.'

'What's happened? Is she ill?'

His father took the kitbag and swung it over his shoulder. 'I'll tell you on the way home.'

As the cart rumbled through the bush, his father told him that Irene had gone, that six months ago she had packed her bags and left, that she had taken up with another fellow. The afternoon was brilliant and the sun shone through the trees like the shafts of light in an English cathedral. But as he listened to his father, the bush seemed menacing and the birds' cries unearthly and mournful. The road wound through the country above the river where the ferns hung over the rapids and the journey seemed endless. At last he saw the smoke rising from the stone chimney and the cows standing, ready to be milked, at the shed.

He jumped down and walked through the grass to their cottage. When he opened the door, it was as he remembered it: there was his armchair at the fireplace, the dresser with the willow-patterned plates, the hand-made rug on the pine boards and the leather-bound classics on the shelf. But when he looked further he found there was no sign of her. She had taken all her clothes, all her linen, all her photographs; he searched for a note, but found none.

That night, he sat by the fire and warmed his hands as the darkness came down. He heard the sound of his father

186

*banging the cream cans in the dairy and the cows bellowing
in the pasture. Later, when the moon had risen, he got up,
closed and locked the door and joined his father. He pulled
the cottage down and used the timber to build a new barn.
He smashed down the stone chimney with a sledge-hammer
and used the rubble to dam the creek.*

Earlier that afternoon, Harold Withers leafed through the
mortgagors' files and did his sums – he was owed almost
£10,000, but nearly all of it was from farmers in the district.
If he foreclosed and sold the stock and equipment, he would
be lucky to raise a quarter of that amount, and the land was
worthless until times improved and the drought broke.
Although he could employ out-of-town bailiffs, the operation
would be expensive and tricky. He was right about one thing,
though: the country was sliding into chaos; the revolution-
aries had Rubicon in their sights and something had to be
done – and done damned quick. What if those bastards fire-
bombed his house? He started to curse the town, then
remembered the good old days when he had taken over from
his father and made a small fortune. By God, he'd do that
again.

There was a knock at the door and Mooney came in. Withers
closed the files. 'Any leads?'

'No.'

'How's Carver?'

'Too burnt to speak. Jesus, I've never seen anybody like
that. Maybe he doesn't want to, he's being sent south – our
people can't cope with a case like that.'

'He was probably drunk when it happened.'

'I don't think that makes any difference.'

'Maybe you're right. Any chance of more men?'

'No. I've been on the phone to Melbourne – it took me
ages to get through – and there's nothing doing. They're
stretched to the limit.'

Withers stretched back in his chair. 'God only helps those
who help themselves. We'll have to get our own men together.

And I want a guard put on my house.'

'Your house? Why?'

'Because, Constable Mooney, it's probably next in line – we're all being blamed for that raid by your drunken mates.'

'They weren't drinking.'

'For Christ's sake, a baby's killed, Bolger throws it into the bush and someone spreads the word.'

Mooney stood squarely on the carpet. 'You gave us the okay.'

'Did I? I can't recall that.'

'If you're backing away . . .'

Withers went over to the sideboard and got the bottle and two glasses. 'Look, Don, let's not argue – there's much to be done. You've got to recruit reliable men to look after the place and bring this scum to justice.'

'Who's going to lead them?'

Withers spread his hands. 'You are, and Bolger – he's always saying what he did in the war. Here's his chance to prove it.'

'A private army?'

'No,' Withers said, as he poured out the whisky, 'just concerned citizens looking after their families and property. If we can't do that, we can't do anything. That's what the unions do.'

Mooney drank. 'I suppose I can find the men.'

'Of course you can – just improve over the present lot. That shouldn't be too hard.' Withers sat on the leather couch. 'And I've got problems of my own – temporary, but problems. I've decided to employ bailiffs from out of town, but you'll have to accompany them.'

'Jesus.'

'You're doing your duty, Don – no more, no less. You can't be blamed for that.'

'I don't like losing friends.'

'Your friends don't pay their bills – any honourable man does that.'

'Costello's back: someone's seen him around the place.'

'If that Mick causes trouble, lock him up.'

'An abo's one thing, but a white man's another.'

'Everyone knows Costello's got connections with the Sinn Fein. Or his father did. Jesus Christ, Don, if we don't get organized, we're all down the drain.'

I'm down the drain, Mooney thought, not you. 'Okay, I'll see what I can do.'

'Good. Talk it over with Bolger – he's tough and reliable: he'll have some ideas.'

By the end of the evening, Bolger had come up with the names of men from farms and backyard abattoirs whom, he said, would break the heads of any bastards who caused trouble and guard Withers' house; they would provide their own guns and transport, if they got paid.

The next morning, Mooney saw Withers, who did some quick calculations and gave his approval. At lunch-time in the Royal, Bolger said he had plans to visit the unemployeds' camps, the gypsum mines and the timber mills to, as he put it, 'cut out the canker' and get the place cleaned up once and for all.

Twenty-two

Julius and Carl sat on their horses and looked at the country from the crest of the sand hill. It was noon of the fourth day and the search had been fruitless. They drank from their water bottles and lit their pipes. 'I think,' Julius said, 'that by now she is in the hands of the Almighty.'

'Do you want to go on looking?' Carl asked.

'No, I do not think so.' Julius screwed up his eyes against the dust. 'Maybe it is better this way.'

'Do you think so?' Carl was relieved it was ended.

'God made her imperfect – we do not know why – but that was His way.' He thought to himself: The burden has been lifted and I should be thankful. 'She did not know what she was doing, but God will forgive her.' I am cleansed, he thought, I am cleansed. He was no longer turning his back on God.

'We do not report it?' Carl said. He waited for the reply.

'No, we do not. We live by our own rules – not those of other men. There are only three of us who know, and it will be kept that way.' Julius swung down from his horse. 'Let us pray.'

Father and son stood bare-headed in the wilderness and Julius said: 'I am come a light into the world, that whosoever believeth in me should not abide in darkness.

'And if any man hear my words, and believe not, I judge him not: for I came not to judge the world, but to save the world.

'He that rejecteth me, and receiveth not my words, hath one that judgeth him: the words that I have spoken, the same shall judge him in the last day.'

As they turned for home, Julius thought once more of his

190

father: where had he buried him? He was finding it hard to remember. The sins of his father had been within his daughter and God had seen fit to extirpate them. As they followed the track to the south-east through the bush, they heard a horse snorting and the snap of breaking twigs. They stopped, looked at each other and continued, slowly. Julius and Carl heard the sound once more and at last saw the rider through the leaves and branches: it was Frank Cameron.

'Good day, Mr Hoffmayer.' If he were surprised, he didn't show it.

Julius sat stiff and still. 'Good day, Mr Cameron.'

'I don't know your son,' Frank said.

'This is my son, Carl Hoffmayer.'

Carl said nothing, but merely touched his hat.

Frank saw that their horses were tired and knew from their swags they had been sleeping in the open. They obviously had not found the girl. 'It seems we are both out of our way,' he said.

'My son and I have been looking for wild pigs,' Julius replied. He tapped the stock of his rifle.

'Any luck?'

'Not yet, but we will find them.' Julius did not ask Mr Cameron why he was out this far – it was none of his business.

'It is a dry season.' Carl spoke. 'The lake is empty.'

Frank thought of the rider watching him and Maria. He also wondered what they would do about Louisa: would they report her disappearance? He thought of Mooney, the dead black and the burning down of the Royal. Was there a point to a wholesale search? 'It always rains,' he replied. 'It's a matter of patience.'

'My son and I are patient men,' Julius said. 'We are very patient.'

'The Regal was a bad business,' Frank said.

'The Regal?'

'Mr Carver's cinema – it was burnt down.'

'I take no interest in the affairs of Rubicon,' Julius answered. 'They do not concern me.'

Frank considered the big man who, one day, could well be his adversary. But he knew Maria was unhappy, that the marriage was barren and she had to leave these two dour, strange men on a place that offered nothing but unrelenting work, suspicion and fear. The Hoffmayers were, he thought, some kind of small, forgotten tribe living in a desert of guilt. A cloud crossed the sun, the light darkened and the two men's faces were in shadow. 'I must be on my way,' he said.

'Good afternoon, Mr Cameron.' Julius touched his horse's flanks with his boots.

'The lake is empty,' Carl repeated. 'It is no good to anyone.' As he rode away, he pulled the shotgun from its scabbard and cradled it on his lap.

The bailiff was built like a front-row forward and wore a shoulder holster under his left arm. He drained his beer in two gulps and said: 'You ought to do what we done – arm yourselves, that's the only way.'

'That's what I keep saying,' Bolger replied. 'Return fire with fire, that's the only language they know.'

'Isn't your business to serve summonses and see they're carried out?' Mooney said.

'That's right, but a lot of these farmers are getting infected with the wrong ideas – Bolshevism, the Irish troubles, they can pay their bills, but won't. I've seen it down my way. Is there any Huns?'

'Several families.'

'Is that so? They're the best payers – the Huns. They work all hours God made, and one more; they live off the smell of an oily rag, but they pay.'

'We're organizing ourselves,' Bolger said.

'Christ, it's about time. You've lost three buildings, one bloke dead. Get out and knock a few heads together – show the bastards you mean it.'

'We've got men on watch, we know what we're doing.' Mooney didn't want free advice.

'Right. Any strange bastard that don't belong, or who won't

move on – kick him in the balls and shove him in the fucking clink. Who do we see tomorrow?'

'The Dolans and the Carrolls.'

'Micks, eh.' The bailiff looked at Mooney. 'No offence meant.'

'And none taken,' Bolger replied. 'Would you like another?'

The bailiff grinned. 'I never say no.' He had hands as big as shovels. 'What's there to do in a town like this at night?'

'There's the pictures,' Bolger said.

'No there's not.'

Bolger looked at Mooney. 'There's not now, but I could fix you up with a tart. She'll be a bit dingy, but you never look at the mantelpiece when you stoke the fire.'

The bailiff cheered up. 'That'll do. Have you got any niggers in the neighbourhood?'

'Just the one,' Mooney said.

'Well, you want to watch him, don't you? If there's any trouble, you can bet your bottom dollar that a nigger or a dago's at the bottom of it.'

Bolger thought of Frank Cameron. 'This abo works for a white bloke – he even sleeps in the same house.'

'Jesus, that's rum. You'd better watch the white bloke, too, hadn't you? I never heard of that before.' The bailiff wiped his mouth. 'How do I get the tart?'

'They're in the cat-bar,' Bolger answered. 'Do you want me to come with you?'

'Nah, she's apples, I can pick one out. I'll see you blokes in the morning.'

'I'm glad that bloke's on our side,' Bolger said, 'he'll help you out.'

'I don't need any help.'

'I think you do, Don. If there's any trouble, you can always blame it on the bailiff, can't you? Have you got any plans?'

'Plans for what?'

'Plans to catch the bastards, plans to clean the shit out of the system, plans to make Rubicon safe for our wives and daughters.'

'We'll have to wait,' Mooney answered.

'Wait? Not on your Nelly. We should cruise around the district and bring in suspects.'

Mooney thought of the black man hanging from the rafter. 'I don't know about that.'

Bolger put his arm around the policeman's shoulder. 'Where's your fighting spirit, me old mate? I'll tell you what we'll do: we'll go out to that mission where the arms were found; we'll go out to Netherby where that woman said she was molested; we'll look in on Cameron; we'll poke around and show them who's who.'

Mooney thought: there was no point in staying cooped up in town. 'Okay, then, but I've got the evictions tomorrow.'

'You'll shit them in,' Bolger said, 'with that big bastard.'

The evictions weren't too bad: the Dolans had their cart half-packed, and were going to walk off, anyway; the Carrolls shouted and argued with the bailiff – Mooney didn't say much, and the family somehow thought he was on their side. The bailiff got them on to the road, chained up the gate and put up a repossession notice. He said it was like taking a bottle away from a baby, and when they arrived back in town, got into his car and drove off.

That afternoon, Mooney and Bolger drove out to the mission: the road was bad and the country grey. 'Jesus, it's gone back,' Bolger said. 'I've never seen it as crook as this.'

The mission was deserted: they killed a couple of snakes lying on the marble slabs and drove further west. 'There's a mine out here,' Bolger said. 'Let's take a look at that.'

'I've been out there recently,' Mooney replied. 'There's nothing.'

'What did you go out there for?'

'Just part of me rounds.'

They saw the smoke rising through the trees at about half past three. And when they drove off the road and down a rutted track, they came upon a large camp in a dry gully. It was almost a shantytown with tents, lean-tos, outdoor ovens, washing hanging from the trees, children playing and dogs running. 'Jesus,' Bolger said, 'it's a big country. What have we got here?'

When they stopped the car, the children ran up: they were ragged, thin and snotty-nosed. But the women went on carrying water and washing, and the men didn't look up from the fires.

'G'day, mister,' a small boy said. The children gathered around Mooney's Ford and began fiddling with the wheels.

'Stay away from the car,' Bolger said. 'That's government property.'

Mooney looked around. 'Where's your dad?'

The boy pointed. 'Over there.'

The walk seemed long as they avoided broken bottles, fires, rubbish and dog shit. The women, hands on hips, looked at them and the men stood, idle. The boy ran ahead and went up to a tall, thin man wearing a waistcoat and cloth cap. 'There's two blokes here,' he said.

The man looked up – he had bright, green eyes and a scar across his forehead. 'G'day,' he said.

'Who runs this place?' Mooney asked.

'Nobody. We all run it.'

'Who's in charge?'

'Nobody – we all put in.'

Mooney felt Bolger standing close to him and took a chance.

'Don't you know this is private property?'

'That's news to me, mister.'

'I'm Constable Mooney from Rubicon.'

'Yeah?'

'I want to look around.'

'Okay.'

'This place is a piggery,' Bolger said. 'There's health regulations.'

'We're carting water,' the man said. 'The bore's half a mile away.'

'We've had two fires in Rubicon,' Mooney said. 'One man dead and another seriously injured.'

'That's no good.'

'You know nothing about it?'

'Nope.'

As Mooney and Bolger looked around, they saw men standing on the edge of the camp in the shadows of the trees. It looked as though they had pieces of wood in their hands, but they couldn't be sure. The smoke from the fires drifted as the children played and the dogs ran and scratched themselves.

They moved away toward the tents and lean-tos.

'Did you bring your gun?' Bolger asked.

'Yes.'

'Thank Christ for that.'

'These people are shit,' Bolger said, 'I reckon that bloke had dark blood.'

'He had green eyes.'

'Maybe his grandmother was fucked by an Irishman.'

Mooney bent down and picked up a stout stick and started to poke around the rubbish. They walked from tent to tent and the children started to follow them: they laughed and spat and farted.

Bolger swung around. 'Look, you little bastards,' he said, 'piss off.'

At last, Mooney found something of interest – a couple of four-gallon petrol tins and some oily waste. 'Here's something,' he said.

'Evidence.'

Mooney laughed. 'Maybe, but we've got to pin it on somebody.'

'Somebody here's responsible.'

'Could be.' But Mooney was starting to realize that the whole thing was beyond him.

The children laughed and jostled; the women watched and the men started to come down the slope and into the clearing. The sky was dark, the fires glowed and Mooney began to lose his nerve. 'I think,' he said, 'we'd better come back another day.'

'Why?'

'Because there's not much we can do, and there's more of them than us.'

Bolger looked around. 'Okay, let's get back to the car.'

The walk back seemed even longer. The camp was silent, the children were silent and even the dogs slunk through the debris. Somewhere, someone was playing a fiddle, but the music stopped. When they reached the Ford, they found a back tyre had been let down. They both cursed and Mooney stood against the mudguard while Bolger worked the pump. When they threw it in the back and opened the doors, they saw a man standing near a cardboard shack. It was Ray Stark.

Twenty-three

It was about eight-thirty when Mooney and Bolger pulled up outside Frank Cameron's gate. 'You stay here,' Mooney said. 'I've got enough trouble as it is.'

Bolger grinned. 'I can wait.'

Frank was carrying a hurricane lamp when he came to the door. 'Well, Constable Mooney,' he said, 'what can I do for you?'

'Can I come in?'

Frank opened the door wide. 'Make yourself at home.'

Mooney sat down. 'This is only going to be a question.'

'Okay.' Frank went over to the cupboard. 'Would you like a drink?' He knew by now the policeman wasn't going to charge him over Bolger. Maybe Louisa Hoffmayer's disappearance had leaked out, but he doubted it. 'It's Scotch.'

'Thanks, I could do with that.'

Frank poured two glasses and put the bottle on the table. 'What's on your mind?'

'Where's Stark?'

'I don't know – he took a few days off.'

'Did he say where he was going?'

'No.'

'You've got no idea?'

'No.'

'Didn't you ask him?'

Frank drank his whisky slowly. 'That's his business.'

'You know about the Regal and Carver?'

'Who doesn't?'

'I've got reason to believe it was unemployeds and Bolshies.'

'Didn't you arrest a man?'

198

'I did, but the stupid bastard hung himself.'

'What's this got to do with me?'

'If you'll wait, I'll tell you.' Mooney fished in his tunic and pulled out a packet of cigarettes. 'We found an unemployeds' camp today, out near Netherby.'

' "We" ?'

'Reg Bolger and me.'

'Right.'

'It was a bloody disgrace – rubbish and shit everywhere.'

'Did you drive them out?'

'No, we did not. But we found a couple of petrol tins and some cotton waste.'

Frank was interested, but careful. 'What does that prove?'

'Nothing directly – you know that. But we saw Stark skulking around.'

'Did you? If it was Ray, he's got every right to go where he pleases, hasn't he?'

'Yeah, he's got a right, but I'd bloody well like to know what he was doing there.'

Frank moved his chair and got up. 'When he comes back, you can ask him.'

'*If* he comes back – he's probably gone walkabout – you mightn't see him for months. You know what abos are like.'

'He'll be back.'

'If he does, will you let me know?'

'I'll tell Ray you called.' Frank wondered. Should he tell him Louisa Hoffmayer was missing? He thought not: it was up to Julius to do that. 'There's been more evictions lately, haven't there?'

Mooney thought Cameron was a tricky bastard. 'One or two – times are tough.'

'How's our friend, Mr Withers?'

Mooney, too, got to his feet. 'I hardly ever see him.'

'How's his private army going?'

'I don't know anything about that.'

Frank was opening the door. 'I'll pass the message on. Drive carefully – there's lots of 'roos about.'

Mooney put his cap on. 'I'll see you later.'

Frank stayed at the door, heard the car drive away and went inside. He poured himself out another drink and sat down. Jesus, he thought, it never rains but it pours. He laughed at himself, cut a piece of lamb, smeared it with chutney and ate. If everything broke at once, Mooney would have his hands full. He thought of Maria: it wasn't at all like the way he met Irene, and maybe it would be better for it. Would she leave Julius? He thought she would – but that would mean selling up as he couldn't stay in the district. Would she go with him? He wanted her – of that, he was certain. One step at a time, his father always said. He had done one thing he thought he would never do again: he had fallen in love. But with the wife of a diabolical neighbour in a small country town which was fast going bankrupt.

The night was growing cold, he lit a fire and sat watching the flames. He had no feelings about Louisa. How could he? He'd never known her. If she *was* mad, maybe this was the best way. Was there madness in the Hoffmayer family? Judging by young Carl, there was. Frank thought of Ray's advice: watch out for Carl. Their religion, he thought, had buggered up the family. Except Maria – she was too strong for it. He hadn't met many women, but Maria was extraordinary. *The lake is empty. It is no good to anyone.* From now on, he'd carry his shotgun.

He rolled a cigarette and smoked. What was Ray doing in an unemployeds' camp? The stupid bastard – if he didn't watch out, he'd end up like his friend McIntosh. Like Mooney, Frank thought events were getting beyond him. But there was a depression and a drought, and men did all kinds of desperate things. Harold Withers, he guessed, might prove to be the most desperate of all: he had the most to lose. He had a third, and last whisky, dowsed the fire and went to bed.

They came in a Ford coupé about half past two in the afternoon. He remembered it had been a brilliant summer, with rain at night and clear, cloudless days. The growth was remarkable – some places the grass was knee-high, wild flowers grew everywhere and they had plenty of hay for the winter. It looked like the start of a very good season.

He was in the front paddock when the two men got out and opened the gate. One was Bob Maxwell, the local cop, whom he didn't know very well; the other was a heavily built chap wearing a felt hat and a business suit. He was holding a manilla envelope.

The policeman looked uneasy as he stood on the track. 'G'day,' he said. 'Is your father around?'

'He's at the back.'

'Would you mind getting him?'

'Okay.' He wondered what was up, and didn't like the look of the big fellow. He noticed the big man appraising the house. 'I won't be a tick.'

'That's all right,' the big man said. 'We've got plenty of time.'

When he told his father about the cop and the other fellow, the old man drove the axe through a log, tossed it on the wood heap and went round the house to the front. He didn't say anything.

'G'day,' the man in the felt hat said. 'Are you Mr John Cameron?'

'That's me.'

'I'm from Financial Services Ltd. We act for Loan & Mercantile and I've got a notice of eviction against you for not paying the interest on your loan.'

The policeman was embarrassed. 'I'm only here to see the notice is served, Mr Cameron.'

'You've got seven days to get out,' the big man said.

He remembered he was shocked, then angry, and came up close to the bailiff. 'You've got no right to do this.'

'The company's got every right, mister. If a man don't pay his debts, he's got to take the consequences. I'm just doing me job.'

'If you don't get off our land, I'll break your bloody neck.'

The bailiff looked at him. 'Careful, boyo, there's a police

constable standing here. You don't want any more trouble, do you?'

His father suddenly looked grey and stooped. 'Come on, Frank. It's the law.'

He wondered if he should tell them he was a returned man, that he'd fought for these bastards, but he didn't want to live his life on that kind of overdraft. And when the policeman and the bailiff got into the car, he and his father went inside the house.

'I fought for that fucking bugger,' he said.

'You aren't in the army now,' his father replied. 'I won't have that kind of language.'

It turned out that interest rates had climbed after the war, that his father was six months behind and that the loan company owned the whole place, all the equipment, all the animals – lock, stock and barrel. His father went to live with one of his sisters in a suburb of Melbourne and got a job, sweeping floors in a factory.

He went share-milking on a place where the people were as mean as cat-shit, where he lived on porridge and treacle, where the cows gave third-grade cream because of the weeds. He never saw his father's house, nor the farm, again.

'You are not going to report it?' Maria said.

'No, I am not.' Julius sat in his chair by the stove. 'It is *our* business and no one else's.'

'Are we not required to, by law?'

'The only law is God's law.'

'I do not think that is so.'

'You will not argue with me,' Julius replied.

'Do you have a feeling of grief?'

He stared at the flames flickering. 'From the moment she was born, she belonged to no one – perhaps she never left God.'

She belonged to her grandfather, Maria thought. Although Louisa was not her child, she wondered if the girl was still wandering through the bush. It seemed that the only person who could help her now was Frank Cameron. 'I think we should still search – if she is dead, do you not want to give her a Christian burial?'

'God has her already – there is no point.'

Maria knew that if Louisa were found, she would be buried on the farm, and not in Rubicon cemetery. She then wondered if *she* were to die, where would Julius bury her? 'Where is Carl?' she asked.

'He is still searching.'

'I still think we should inform the police.'

Julius turned around. 'What help,' he said, 'would we get from that drunkard, Mooney? It was people like him who persecuted us in the war. They hung my friend, Stampfl; they drove us out and put us into camps; they burnt our crops; those men are scum.' Julius laughed. 'We do not require their help.'

'The war was a long time ago, and you were not driven out.'

'That was because of my father – he showered them with money, he cavorted with their women, he was a traitor. Whatever is to be done in this life, we do ourselves.' Julius got up and put his pipe on the shelf. 'I am going to bed.'

'As you wish. I will wait up for Carl.'

'He will not be back tonight.' Julius closed the door and she took his place by the stove.

At twenty-five, she was still unmarried. Even Uncle Ernst, who generally didn't think about such things, was concerned. Sometimes he discussed the matter with his wife. 'She is the most handsome woman in the district,' he said to Matilde, 'but Maria has no suitor. She should not grow into an old maid. The Ampts are a fine family – one day she should return to Germany with her children.'

'Maria is a proud woman,' Matilde replied, 'we cannot force her to do such a thing.'

'I am not talking about forcing her, I am simply saying she will need to have a husband. What will she do when we pass on?'

But she, too, was becoming uneasy when she saw the young couples at church or at the picnics at the lake. Would she spend all her life alone on a small farm in the bush?

When Sophie Hoffmayer died, she was not surprised there was no public funeral: many families still buried their own on the property. It was sad that such a young mother should die, but death was commonplace in the bush. Sometimes she saw Julius Hoffmayer, his father and the two children at the lake. And although people talked about August, she thought he was an attractive and charming man – he was witty and lay on the rug with his waistcoat unbuttoned and his trousers rolled up. He was often seen, splashing in the water with his grandchildren; he had bought a new Mercedes-Benz and had installed electric light in his house. August drank champagne, bowed to all the girls and often sang at picnics, his tenor voice echoing through the trees. His son, Julius, was silent and handsome with his black beard – for a year, he wore an armband in mourning for his dead wife.

In the summer of 1921, she often sat with Julius and his father and watched that the children did not wander away into the ferns and trees. Julius was reserved – not like the other men – and he remained quiet when conversation was not needed. It was said that August Hoffmayer was spending far too much money on the farm, that he was borrowing heavily and that he consorted with loose women. But to her, he was always gallant and reminded her of the stories Uncle Ernst told her about the von Ampts of Magdeburg. Sometimes as she sat with them on those hot summer Sundays, it seemed that Julius and his father did not get on, but she put that down to the son's natural reserve.

That winter, Julius started calling on her and they rode their horses to the country south of the lake. Then August paid his respects when they would take the children motoring in the afternoon before they had tea at home. The Hoffmayer *garden was beautiful with rose arbors, European trees, crazy paving, rustic seats and a fountain with reticulated water. The* hausfrau *looked after the children and served fine meals; and in the evenings August played the piano. It was, she thought, quite unlike any other family in the district.*

In the spring of 1922, when Julius asked her to marry him, she said, yes. But when she told her Uncle Ernst, he looked up from his newspaper and said: 'August Hoffmayer is like Kaiser Wilhelm – he cannot be trusted, nor can his young son.'

But later, Uncle Ernst gave Maria his blessing. Was not the Hoffmayer farm the richest in the district?'

Carl returned home a day later, his arms bloodied with cuts from the spear grass and his horse exhausted. Over his cold meat and cup of tea, he looked at his father and said: 'I do not think we should search anymore. I think, as you said, God has taken her and we should not deny His will.'

In the evening, Julius prayed long and hard, his voice echoing through the silent house, his hands clasped to the Bible and his body swaying over the kitchen table, where the lamp flickered and gleamed. At the end of it all, he prayed for rain; and that night, he slept and did not move. The nightmares were gone.

Twenty-four

Ahmed Farozi had only been in the town of Rubicon once: that was ten years ago. One morning about nine o'clock, he had driven his waggon up Federation Street, past Farrar's yard and the bakery toward the war memorial, when suddenly he was pelted with stones and bottles. Children shouted and screamed and ran after his cart; the shopkeepers stood under the verandahs and laughed; his horse shied and bolted and he ended up in the scrub near the cemetery. After that, he kept to the roads and tracks in the bush, calling on farms and camping at night under bridges or in creek beds.

All the other Indians in the district had either gone home, or gone north to work on camel farms in Queensland and the Northern Territory. Now a solitary man, Farozi was from north-west Baluchistan and made a modest living selling from door to door. Because of the depression and the drought, this was by far his worst year, but like the European farmers who despised him, he clung on, hoping for better things.

Trade was so bad that Farozi decided to venture farther afield and he took the road west to Netherby, where the wheat farms had been cleared earlier and the powerlines looped to the horizon. This day was even worse than usual: he was run off two farms, doors were slammed in his face and he was set upon by dogs. By the middle of the afternoon Farozi was so dispirited he decided to call it off and made for the shelter of the bush to doss down and boil the billy for a cup of tea. The call he had made on Mrs Hoffmayer, when she had split his nose with the broom, was nothing compared with this.

The sun was low and the crows called from the branches as he spread out his threadbare mat. He gave his horse some oats in the nosebag and went into the bush to collect wood for the fire.

It was on his third trip back to the fire that he noticed the mound of freshly dug earth -- it was so large that he wondered why he hadn't seen it before. Ever suspicious and careful, Farozi picked up a long stick and prodded. These days people hid all kinds of things: money, jewellery, antiques, so the banks couldn't get them. But the earth was too fine and sandy and he went back to the cart and got his shovel. After five minutes, he became aware of a sweet smell, stopped digging and wondered whether he should continue. His back was cold, he thought not, and threw down the spade. This was not his business. But curiosity got the better of him and he continued digging. The earth was as fine as powder and he discovered an arm, clotted with blood where ants crawled; three fingers were severed and the nails split. Farozi shrieked, vomited, dropped the shovel and ran back to his cart. His back prickled, his limbs shook, he threw up once more, mumbled and prayed to Allah and crouched on the mat like a child. The earth seemed vast, the sky fathomless, the silence terrible. He prayed, he prayed. What should he do?

He could pack up and leave, go to some other district and never come near this place again. But he would be missed, the body would be discovered and he would be tracked down and arrested. Then Farozi wondered if he had been seen after the last call later in the afternoon, but couldn't remember. He got up, looked across the fallow wheat fields and saw no one. The western sun gleamed on the corrugated-iron sheds in the distance and the windmills stood on the skyline. Then he saw dust rising, heard the sound of a tractor and saw the starlings wheeling. What should he do? He also knew that by the morning, the body would be mauled by dingoes.

Farozi's throat was dry and he poured some water from the kerosine tin and drank. He gathered himself together and went back to the mound: was this a nightmare? But the limb protruded from the earth – and it looked like the arm of a woman. He seized the shovel, ran back to the cart and removed the nosebag from his horse. There was only one thing he could do: he had to go to Rubicon and tell Constable Mooney.

It was dark when he got there; Farozi took out his silver watch and saw it was almost half past eight. The town seemed empty as he turned off Federation Street past the Royal Hotel. Somewhere a dog barked, but that was all. The lights were off in Constable Mooney's office as Farozi stood in front of the door. A light shone in the church opposite and he heard the sounds of a harmonium. He went around the back of the court house, saw a light on in Mooney's house, stepped onto the front porch and knocked at the door. A dog ran to the side fence and barked, growled and slathered. Farozi stood his ground and knocked at the door again. As the dog disappeared, he heard the sound of a wireless and a woman's voice. Just as he was tempted to run away, Constable Mooney appeared at the door in his shirt sleeves. He looked at the Indian through the flydoor. 'Jesus Christ,' he said, 'what do you want?' But Farozi was speechless as Mooney opened the flydoor and stood in his stockinged feet. 'What do you want?'

'There's a body, sir.'

'What?'

'An arm, sir, a body.'

Mooney's braces were hanging down his trousers and his shirt was out. 'Listen, Farozi,' he said, 'have you been smoking that stuff?'

'No, sir.'

Mooney peered at the Indian, saw him shaking and cursed. 'Wait here,' he said.

The door closed and the dog started to bark again.

Mooney turned the office light on and sat down behind his desk. 'For God's sake, Farozi,' he said, 'sit down and tell me what you've seen, and if you're bullshitting me, you're for the slammer.' But the policeman knew the Indian hawker was petrified.

'There is a body in the bush on the Netherby road.'

Piece by piece, Farozi told the story and, when he had

finished, Mooney knew he was telling the truth and recalled what Harold Withers had said about the year: it looked very much as though it would get worse before it got better. He looked at his watch and saw it was now almost ten o'clock. Jesus, he thought, another bloody mess. 'Stay where you are,' he said. 'I'll be back in a minute.'

'I'm not going anywhere.'

'You'd better not.'

When Mooney came back, he was wearing his cap and his revolver; he was also carrying his old Kodak camera and a flashlight. If the Indian had discovered a body, he'd have to call the Criminal Investigation Branch in Horsham. Jesus, he thought, eternal bloody rigmarole: it never rains but it pours.

Farozi heard the dog outside; he got up and peered out of the window.

'Felix won't hurt you,' Mooney said, 'unless you make a wrong move. Where's your horse and cart?'

'Outside on the street, sir.'

'Okay, bring it round to the back yard – this is going to be a long night.'

'Where are we going, sir?'

'For Christ's sake, get your arse into gear, we're going out to look.'

'How, sir?'

'In my car, you bloody dingo. Chop, chop. And bring that spade. Can you remember where it was?'

'What, sir?'

'The body, you bloody black idiot.'

'Oh yes, sir. We Indians are good at tracking. Very good.'

'You'd better be, I don't want to be fucking around in the bush all night.'

Mooney went out the back, got a wheat sack and threw it in the back of his car; he found a pair of gardening gloves, a pair of overalls and a bottle of disinfectant, opened the trunk and tossed them in. He had handled bodies before.

As he drove out of town on the Netherby road, Mooney realized he had never been this close to an Indian. Farozi smelt of sweat and curry; his turban was filthy and his clothes were dusty. The Indians might have been useful for driving the camel trains, but it was about time they were all shipped back. He agreed with Withers that the country was full of riff-raff, and that was the core of the problem. And if this black bugger was leading him on a wild goose chase, he'd see he got six months. The night was pitch black, the road rutted and Mooney cursed as he avoided the potholes. A policeman's lot was an unhappy one.

Farozi peered out the window. 'It is not far from here,' he said. 'It is not far.'

Mooney slowed down. In the car lights, he could see nothing but the road and the endless bush. 'You'd better get it right, my friend.'

'I know, I know.'

After ten minutes, Farozi said: 'It is here – this is where I put my cart. It is here.'

Mooney stopped the car and got out with his dog. Within seconds, the Alsatian was pulling at his leash, Mooney switched on his torch and they stumbled over the rough ground. But Farozi hung back. 'Come on,' Mooney said. 'Don't fuck about – I'm going to need your help.'

Mooney saw the arm in the torchlight and knew straight away he would have to phone the Criminal Investigation Branch. He stood and looked at the phone lines – Christ only knew where the nearest telephone was. 'Right,' he said to Farozi, 'you stay here, I'm going to find a phone. I could be gone for an hour, and if you're not here when I get back I'll hunt you down even if I've got to go to the Himalayas to find you.' He got in the car and drove down the dirt road.

The third house he tried had the phone and he finally raised the CIB. The line was bad and he had to shout, but at last a voice told him to stay put and they'd send someone up.

When Mooney got back, he found Farozi hunched and sitting on the ground. 'Okay,' he said, 'we've got a detective-sergeant coming up – a bloody expert, who'll think he's Lord Muck. You'd better make yourself comfortable: we could have a long night.' He left the Indian, sat in the car and lit the first of many cigarettes.

It was dawn when Mooney saw the car lights. As the car pulled up, he got out to see a tall, thin man in plain clothes. 'Jesus,' the man said as he pushed his felt hat onto the back of his head, 'some drive. I'm Bill Broadbent – what have we got here?'

Mooney told him and the work started.

'Okay,' Broadbent said. 'I want photographs.'

'I've got a camera and flash in my car,' Mooney answered. 'Can you use it?'

'I wouldn't have brought it if I couldn't.'

Broadbent stared hard at Mooney in the dusty first light. 'Go and get it: I'll tell you what I want and we can start measuring up.'

Broadbent was thorough: he got Mooney to take a dozen photographs; he put specimens of soil and other debris into paper bags, took measurements and searched carefully through the surrounding bush. 'Aha,' Mooney heard the detective say, 'here's someting.' Broadbent had found something: a torn photograph of a little girl. He put it into another paper bag and they started to take out the body.

Mooney had seen some mangled bodies in his time – timber-mill accidents and men caught in farm machinery, but he wasn't prepared for this. It was a young woman – about seventeen, he guessed – and she had been cut to pieces, not with an axe, but something sharper, maybe a slasher or a bill-hook. The ground was soaked with blood, both arms were almost severed from her torso, her neck was cut and her chest was slashed. Broadbent stooped and took more samples. 'Christ,' he said, 'some job.' But Mooney, his gorge rising and body numb, didn't say a word as they got the broken body into the wheat sack. He thought of the bottle of whisky in his car. Who was the young woman? Now a girl had been cut to pieces – on top of everything else. At last he spoke, his voice thin: 'We've got a madman on our hands.'

'It looks like it.'

It was daylight now as the two policemen wiped their hands and smoked their cigarettes. Broadbent eased his back and looked around before they carried the sack to Mooney's car. 'I've not been this far north for ages,' he said. 'It's not too good, is it?' He squinted toward the bush line. 'It's a wonder any bloody thing grows.' Then he looked at Farozi, sleeping. 'You'd better wake our Asiatic friend up,' he said. 'I want a statement from him.'

Still terrified, the Indian told all he knew. Broadbent seemed satisfied. 'Let's take her to the hospital,' he said. 'And you can take the dago – he's not coming with me.'

By the time they left, it was almost eight o'clock. Mooney found himself shocked, tired and desperate to wash himself; the drive back to Rubicon seemed endless and the dog whined all the way. Farozi fell asleep again and Mooney had to kick him in the shins when, at last, they got back to the station. He locked the Indian inside and drove with Broadbent to the hospital. The caretaker was a talkative man and most of the town knew of the discovery by midday.

Twenty-five

While Broadbent was having a meal at the Royal, Mooney sat at his desk and looked at the torn photograph. The afternoon sun streamed through the window and the blowflies buzzed. He cursed the heat, got up and pulled down the blinds. The photo was of a little girl aged, he guessed, about eighteen months. She had dark, curly hair and was sitting in a photographer's studio. The signature of the photographer was missing and the picture had been torn from its mounting. It was faded and looked as though it had been carried around for a long time. He found his magnifying glass and examined the photographer's stamp to see if it had been taken by Vivian's Studio in Rubicon, but it was indecipherable.

Earlier he had typed up Farozi's statement; the Indian had signed it with a cross and Mooney let him go. Broadbent said there was no point in keeping the Hindu in the cell, and they could pick him up any time. The poor, black bastard was scared shitless. Then Mooney telephoned Withers with the news. Withers had cursed: he said that was the last thing they wanted, as if it was Mooney's fault. Withers said to ring him when the doctor's report was in, asked him who the CIB man was, and then told him to get off the line as he was expecting someone to call from Melbourne. It was money, no doubt.

Mooney rubbed his eyes, thought about last night and went over to the cupboard. He drew the cork from the bottle of Scotch, poured out a shot, put the bottle back and drank. Who on earth was the victim? He thought of seeing Ray Stark in the unemployeds' camp and wondered. It was too soon to jump to conclusions. There was rabble everywhere these days and it could be anybody. He supposed Broadbent would stay several days and investigate the town and district. Not that

213

there was anything to hide, but Rubicon was a tight-arsed community and did things its own way. It was a pity the dead girl wasn't black – then there'd be no bloody rigmarole. Mooney thought about the dead baby and the hanged black, then dozed in his office chair.

Later in the afternoon, there was a knock at the flyscreen. When he opened the door, it was Broadbent and Dr Anderson from the hospital – the doctor was new to the district and Mooney didn't know him very well.

'I've done a preliminary examination,' Anderson said.

'There's a bit more to do,' Broadbent said as he dragged up two chairs.

Anderson was tall and thin and in his forties. 'You haven't got a drink, have you?'

Mooney looked at the detective. 'Sorry, not during working hours.' Broadbent, he thought, surely must drink: all cops did.

Anderson pulled out his cigarettes; he coughed, lit up and tossed the match into the tobacco tin. 'She was about seventeen, five feet six, blonde, blue eyed, and killed with a bill-hook or a slasher. There were seven wounds on her body – chest, arms, stomach, but the one in her throat was fatal.'

'When do you reckon she was killed?'

'Roughly four days ago,' Broadbent said. 'It's strange no one's been reported missing.'

'Not really,' Mooney answered. 'A lot of people in the bush don't have phones.'

'I think it's odd,' Anderson said. 'What about the Indian?'

Mooney got up. 'You can leave the enquiries to the police.'

Anderson remained in his chair. 'There was no sign of sexual interference.'

'You mean she wasn't raped?' Mooney asked.

'That's right.'

'Thanks, Dr Anderson,' Broadbent said. 'We've got a lot of work to do.'

'There's a lot of strangers about these days.'

'You can say that again.' Mooney walked over and opened

the door. It was still like a furnace outside.

'Right then,' Anderson said. 'If I can be of any further help, let me know.'

'I'll do that.'

Anderson stood on the step. 'She's in the cooler.'

'We know that,' Broadbent said, 'we know that.'

Broadbent then announced he was tired and was going to get some sleep in his room at the Royal. Mooney waited until he heard the car pull away and then poured himself a fresh Scotch. He, too, felt weary. The flies still buzzed and crawled up the window. He dozed in the oppressive afternoon.

It was dark when Harold Withers came in. 'What does the detective say?' he asked.

Mooney raised his hands. 'It's a murder – no doubt about that.'

'This country, Don, is going down the plug-hole. We've got three buildings burnt down, one man dead, another disfigured, riff-raff camped on private property, people who won't pay their debts and now a young, innocent girl murdered. And the police can't cope – our society has broken down.'

'Yeah.'

'What we need,' Withers went on, 'is an army – a body of loyal men to put a stop to all this. There was one in Russia and if the Allies hadn't been so gutless, they would have crushed the Bolsheviks.'

'I reckon the girl was German.'

Withers look up. 'What makes you think that?'

'Blonde hair, blue eyes.'

'Those characteristics aren't confined to our Ayran friends.'

'It's a start. There's the Krauses, the Schultzs, the Schmidts, the Ubergangs, the Hoffmayers. I've told Broadbent and we'll go out to Hunland and see them. Reg and I saw Stark mucking around in a camp out near Netherby the day before yesterday.'

'Did you? Did you see Cameron?'

'Yep. He says Stark's gone away for a few days.'

'Did you tell Broadbent?'

'I did.'

Withers thought. 'It's a pity about Cameron.'

'It takes all sorts.'

The office was stifling and Withers rose from his chair. 'I've got to make a phone call to Melbourne.'

'You can make it here.' Mooney laughed. 'It's on the government.'

'I'll make it from my office.' Withers put his hat on. 'I know someone who can assist. In the bush we may be, but I've got a powerful friend.'

Mooney's back was aching and his mouth was dry. 'Yeah.'

'German or not, the town's not going to like this.'

Mooney raised a smile. 'Lock up your daughters.'

Withers picked up his valise. 'Keep me informed.' He went out into the dark, Mooney finished the Scotch, fell asleep in his chair once more, and finally staggered across the yard, past the lock-up, and crawled into bed.

Frank Cameron looked at the sky. It was cloudless. As he went to feed the chickens, a mob of sparrows took off from the ground he and Ray had dug for the vegetable garden. Not even a weed was growing. Thank God for the bore. He stopped at the trough at the windmill and tasted the water. It was salty, but still good enough for drinking. Then he went under the pine trees, picked up a couple of eggs and put them in his hat. What was Ray doing in an unemployeds' camp? Silly bugger. He had every right to be there, but with Mooney and Bolger poking around, it meant trouble. And what of Louisa Hoffmayer? He thought of Maria as he stood in the shade – there would be tragedy and violence, Frank was sure of that. He was certain that Carl was the man who had been watching them at the lake,

Frank worked around the house until lunch-time, and when he had eaten, he caught his horse and rode down to the front gate. As he stood by the mail box, he saw a dust storm gathering in the north; then thunder rolled and lightning struck on the horizon, but Frank knew it wouldn't rain. As he rode along the fence-line, crows and parakeets sat

216

on the posts and kookaburras laughed in the trees. Of Ray Stark, there was no sign.

By four o'clock, Don Mooney was in desperate need of a drink. They had been driving all day and none of the German families reported anyone missing. On several properties all the stock had been shot and the settlers were living on treacle and millet; in other places, the people were obviously close to starvation – the children skin and bone and dressed in rags. In all his years in the bush, Mooney could not remember a drought as bad as this. Broadbent kept on wanting to stop the car to look at the country, and it seemed to Mooney that he was more interested in the drought than the murder.

As the Hoffmayers' gate was padlocked, Mooney and Broadbent climbed the fence and walked up the track toward the house. When they reached the overgrown rose garden, with its upturned birdbaths and the staggering gazebo, Mooney realized he had never been this close to the Hoffmayers' house before. The ornamental trees were dead and the rails on the verandah were bare of paint. This, Mooney thought, had once been a luxurious house and he thought of the stories about August Hoffmayer. As the front door had not been opened for years, they walked around to the back yard.

Mooney knocked and they waited as the fowls perched in the shade of the trees and the horse stood by the gate in the back paddock. All was quiet and Mooney felt uneasy. At last, the door was opened and a dark haired woman stood before them. 'Mrs Hoffmayer?'

'Yes.'

'I'm Donald Mooney, the Senior Constable at Rubicon, and this is Detective-Sergeant Broadbent from CIB.'

'Yes.'

'We're making enquiries about a missing girl.'

The woman stared at them, then looked up the track beyond the house. 'You had better come in.'

The kitchen was hot and dark, and Mooney could see the coals glowing in the range. He took his cap off, held it under

217

his arm and stood in the centre of the room. Mrs Hoffmayer was wearing a long black dress and her face was white. 'We're making enquiries about a missing girl,' Broadbent repeated.

'Why have you come here?'

'We're trying to find out if anyone is missing,' Mooney answered.

'I do not understand.'

'The body of a young girl has been found,' Broadbent said. 'Is there anyone missing in the household?'

Maria Hoffmayer was silent as she stood by the kitchen window. 'Is there anyone missing?' Mooney asked once again.

'My stepdaughter is missing.'

Broadbent stared. 'How long?'

'Four days.'

'Why didn't you report it?'

'You will have to ask my husband that. He did not wish to.'

'How old is she?'

'Seventeen.'

'Does she have fair hair and blue eyes?'

'Yes.'

Mooney got up. 'Where is your husband now, Mrs Hoffmayer?'

'My husband and his son are clearing bush up the track about half a mile away.'

The policemen made for the door. 'You'll be asked to make a full statement,' Broadbent said. 'Good afternoon, Mrs Hoffmayer.'

Maria sat and stared at the dusty back yard outside, then got up and went into the bedroom. She reached down an old portmanteau from the top of the wardrobe and started to pack some clothes.

When Julius saw Mooney and the other man open the gate and walk up over the stubble, he turned his back. He cut at the shoots with his bill-hook and his broad shoulders ran with sweat. He knew that Carl was further up the paddock near a dry creek bed.

'Mr Hoffmayer? Mr Hoffmayer?'

At last, Julius turned and faced Mooney. He leaned on the handle of the bill-hook. 'Yes.'

'I'm Don Mooney from Rubicon and this is Detective-Sergeant Broadbent.'

'Well?'

'I've just been speaking to your wife,' Broadbent said.

'What has that got to do with me?'

Broadbent studied the big German. 'She says your daughter is missing.'

'If there is someone missing in my family,' Julius said, 'what does it have to do with you?'

Jesus, Mooney thought. Reg Bolger was right about this Hun. He was beginning to wish he hadn't left his revolver in the car. Hoffmayer was built like an ox.

'By law,' Broadbent replied, 'if someone goes missing, you have to report it.'

'There is only one law, Mr Broadbent.'

Broadbent came up closer. 'The body of a young woman has been found on the Netherby road.' He looked at Julius carefully. 'She was about seventeen, with blonde hair and blue eyes. And Mrs Hoffmayer tells me your daughter is missing.'

Although Julius returned the stare, his big hands were trembling. 'You wish me to come into Rubicon and look at the body?'

'That's right.' Broadbent took out his notebook and pencil. 'And I want some information.'

Julius threw down the bill-hook and pointed to some stumps. He could see Carl watching them. 'We will sit down, Mr Broadbent.' He thought of the body of Eric Stampfl hanging from the tree. *HUN SHIT.*

'What's your daughter's name, Mr Hoffmayer?'

'Louisa Sophia Hoffmayer.'

'When did she go missing?'

'Four days ago.'

Mooney thought: at least that tallied with Mrs Hoffmayer.

'How did you know she had gone?' Broadbent went on.

'My wife told me when I got home at six o'clock. My son and I searched for the next three days.'

'Why didn't you report it?'

'It was no one's business but ours,' Julius said. 'And my son and I know this part of the country better than anyone.'

Mooney was starting to feel easier until he saw another man watching, but Hoffmayer did not explain. Why was the German not upset? But then he saw Julius was sitting on his hands. They were a strange race.

'You'll certainly have to come to the hospital and view the body,' Broadbent said.

'I will come into town tomorrow, Mr Broadbent. I will be there by nine o'clock.' He rose from the stump as the sun was starting to go down over the bush. The birds were singing in the trees and somewhere a cow bellowed with thirst. Soon it would be dark. 'I will come in the morning.'

Mooney thought of the bar of the Royal: he needed a Scotch with his mates. He turned and saw a young man with fair hair and blue eyes, his shirt undone, his chest broad. It was Carl Hoffmayer who, every year, won the shooting. Mooney felt his back prickling.

'Who is this?' Broadbent asked.

'My son, Carl,' Julius answered.

The detective seemed friendly. 'G'day, Carl.'

'Good afternoon.'

'I'll want a statement from you, if the deceased girl's your sister.'

But the young man looked at Broadbent with his pale eyes and did not reply. Julius got up and father and son faced the two policemen.

'That about wraps it up then,' Broadbent said. 'For the present.'

'Christ, they're a weird pair,' Broadbent said as they walked back to the car. 'I've never seen a Hun that big, and I ought to know – I fought them. And I've got medals to prove it.'

'Do you want me to fill you in on the Hoffmayers?' Mooney asked.

'You'd better.'

Mooney told Broadbent all he knew of the family and ended, saying 'I'd almost forgotten there was a daughter – I don't think she's ever been into town, and I think she was taken away from school for some reason or another. Maria Hoffmayer was last seen on Federation Street about a year ago.'

'A good-looking woman,' Broadbent said.

'The second wife – those aren't her kids.'

'So you said.' Broadbent put his foot on the running-board.

'They keep themselves to themselves.' He opened the car door.

'What did he mean about there being only one law?'

'God, I suppose.'

Broadbent looked blankly at Mooney and was silent all the way back to town.

When she heard the sound of the men's boots on the verandah, Maria was ready. She stood by the table in the dark of the kitchen. The fire in the stove was out and the tea unprepared. She listened to the noise as Julius and Carl washed their hands in the bucket. Then the door was opened.

'You told the policemen,' Julius said. He stood large in the gloom, then produced a match and lit the lamp. 'You told the policemen. Why did you do that?'

'Your daughter is missing. I told them because they asked me: it is the law.'

Julius stepped up and hit her hard on the side of the face; her ears stung, her head reeled, but she did not go down. He hit her again, but she stood, her nose running with blood. It ran down the side of her face. 'You will not hit me,' Maria said.

'I will hit you because you disobeyed me.' Julius struck once more, but his wife still stood.

'Louisa is *my* daughter,' Julius said, 'and if she disappears, it is God's will.' He hit Maria again as Carl watched from the door.

But, her eyes streaming, her face cut from the knuckles of his big hands, Maria came up to him and said: 'Your guilt has gone, but you will not forget, may God damn you, Julius Hoffmayer.'

As Julius raised his arm a fourth time, Maria upset the kitchen table, seized the fire poker and struck. His mouth bloodied, he went down on the floorboards and, as Carl came forward, she said: 'You will not touch me, you will not touch me.'

As the boy knelt over his father, Maria left the kitchen, went into the bedroom, took up the portmanteau and was gone.

Twenty-six

'How long have you been up here?' Broadbent asked Mooney.

'Seven years.' Mooney was dying for a drink and it was now half an hour past closing time.

'Christ, it's the end of the world. What did you do – fuck the senior's wife?'

'I don't think that's funny.'

'It's not meant to be.' Broadbent ran his hands through his thinning, sandy hair. 'If it is Louisa Hoffmayer – and it's a pound to a peanut it is – we'll have to give the father, mother and son a real going over. I wonder why the daughter was never seen out and about. There must be some medical records – they can't be that self-contained – this is the twentieth century. They're a strange mob, the German farmers: we did right to intern them during the war. I'll stay until the end of the week, do my investigations, then go back. You can do a lot of it, can't you? You might think *you've* got problems up here, but they're nothing compared to ours. There's about a murder a day in Melbourne: riots, street marches, evictions, strikes, bashings – no fucking end to it. And it's the same in the other cities, I'm told. We're hopelessly undermanned and the government's sitting on its arse. There's rumours of uprisings in various parts of the State. Have you heard that?'

'Yes.'

'Well, if civil war comes about,' Broadbent said, 'the murder of a German girl in a small bush town will pale into insignificance.'

Despite his thirst, Mooney told him about Ray Stark.

'That's our second stage,' Broadbent said when Mooney was finished. 'Suspicious characters, undesirables, vagrants, men on the track, the unemployeds, the country's crawling with them. The Commissioner's right – they should all be put into barbed wire camps like we did with the Boers. Bring the black in on principle: they're always doing something illegal; but I needn't tell you that you've got to have evidence to convict even a black of murder these days. I thought they'd gone from these parts?'

'They have: this one's stayed on.'

Broadbent laughed. 'Then he deserves anything he gets, doesn't he?'

Mooney looked once more at his watch. It was seven o'clock. 'Do you want a beer? You could meet the locals; I've got an arrangement with the publican.'

'No thanks, mate. I'll do things my own way: there's an advantage in staying away from the townsfolk, and I've got an ulcer – I'm strictly TT. I'll have tea at the pub and go to bed with Edgar Rice Burroughs. Have you read him?'

'Not for ages.'

'You should – takes your mind off things.'

This man, Mooney thought, wasn't quite like the bailiff who came up to evict the Dolans and wouldn't be after the women in the house bar. At last, Broadbent got up and Mooney could have his drink.

The men all looked up when Mooney strode into the bar. 'I know who it is,' he said.

'Who?'

'The Hoffmayer girl.'

They all sucked in their breaths and put down their glasses.

'I didn't know there *was* a Hoffmayer girl,' Banks said, as he poured out Mooney's beer.

'Well, there is – she's the daughter of the first marriage.' Mooney drank. 'Jesus, that house of theirs gives me the creeps. They live like peasants.'

'Who did you see?' Bolger had been working late and was still wearing his bloodied apron.

'We saw Mrs Hoffmayer, then Julius – and the boy was

skulking about. They were cutting bush. There's something wrong with that place.'

Bolger laughed. 'You can say that again.'

'The girl's been missing for four days, and Hoffmayer didn't report it.'

'Why?'

'Fucked if I know. He said something about there being only one law.' Mooney slid half a crown towards Banks. 'You can give me a whisky now Jim – a double.'

'What's the CIB man like?' Bolger asked. 'Why can't we meet him?'

'His name's Bill Broadbent,' Mooney said as he looked around the bar. 'He's upstairs in the dining room; he's TT, got an ulcer and arrogant like all plain-clothes blokes. He's staying until the end of the week.' He coughed. 'If we don't make an early breakthrough – and I don't think we will – I'll have to do all the fucking leg-work. I don't *have* to – it's Broadbent's case – but he'll be on my back.' Mooney drank his whisky. 'He says there's all sorts of shit happening in Melbourne: riots, murders, just like up here – and England and Europe. Maybe the whole world's falling apart.'

'Any ideas as to who did it?' Jim Banks asked.

'Nah. The whole place is crawling with strangers, but I wouldn't underestimate our Mr Broadbent.'

'Well, she wasn't one of us,' Bolger said.

'She was white. Hoffmayer's coming into town tomorrow to identify the body. It's got to be her, Mooney thought. 'Just for a moment there, I thought the bastard was going to go for us.'

'I'd get him,' Bolger said.

Mooney looked at the big butcher. 'I don't think anybody would get Julius Hoffmayer, except with a gun. And even then, it would be like stopping a charging elephant.'

'What's next?' Banks asked.

Mooney's legs were stiff and he sat down on the bar stool. 'Hoffmayer identifies the body, there's not much doubt about that. Then we get statements from the Hoffmayers, and anybody else. After that we do the boarding houses and look out for undesirables.

'The girl wasn't raped?'

'Nah. But it's some mad bastard – she was really carved up.'

Bolger took off his apron and threw it over the bar. 'There's nothing to stop us making enquiries, is there?'

'In the circumstances, no; but do it on the quiet. I don't want Broadbent's nose put out of joint. Withers says the whole place is sliding into anarchy.'

'What?'

'No government.'

Bolger laughed again. 'There never was any up here, was there? Except our own – the fucking socialists don't want government, they want revolution. Did you tell the CIB man about us seeing Stark?'

'Yeah.'

'What did he say?'

Mooney thought. He didn't want a posse at this stage. 'Nothing much.'

'Blackfellows kill white women, don't they?'

'They used to, Reg.' Mooney got up. 'I think I'll go and put my head down.'

'Any theories, at least?'

'We found a torn photo of a little girl by the body.'

Bolger put down his glass. 'Did you? That's a start. Do you mind if we poke around?'

'We?'

'Me and the boys from the Gun Club.'

Mooney's legs were starting to shake with delayed reaction. 'You can do what you bloody well like, as long as you tell me.'

'Okay. Keep your shirt on.' Bolger looked hard at the two men. 'There's going to be a lot of scared people, isn't there? There's only one person that can help you, and that's yourself. That's what made this country great.'

The whisky was burning Mooney's stomach and he felt ill. 'Look, Broadbent will be in charge of the enquiry and we'll take it from there.'

226

'Meantime,' Bolger replied, 'there's this mad bastard running round the country, killing innocent young girls. It could be an Australian woman next.'

Mooney made one last try. 'You and I are old mates, Reg, but leave it to me. Okay?'

In the darkness outside, the wind was blowing and the air was thick with dust. Thunder rolled and lightning struck over the country to the north. Mooney got into his car and drove home. He knew it wasn't going to rain.

Frank was lying in his bed roll and listening to the thunder when someone knocked at the door. He got up, looked at his shotgun propped against the wall and wondered. It could be Ray. He flicked on the torch and opened the door: it was Maria Hoffmayer and her face was bleeding. 'I have nowhere else to go,' she said.

Frank got her inside to the table and lit the hurricane lamp. 'How did you get here?'

'On my horse, there's a bag on the saddle.'

'Right,' he said, 'I'll go and get it and put the horse in the shed.' He lifted the hot plates on the stove and tossed in some kindling. 'I won't be long.'

Outside, the wind was strong and dust stung his eyes; her horse was nervous as branches and leaves flew. Frank threw the bag on the step and took the horse by the bridle toward the shed. He tethered it, gave it water from the tank, closed the door and stood on the track as the wind gusted. Then he walked back to the house and beyond, toward the front gate. The thunder cracked, the dirt flew and somewhere a heavy branch fell. Frank shone the torch and peered into the darkness – there seemed to be no one around, but in the rising dust storm it was hard to tell. Where was Julius Hoffmayer?

When he got inside, Maria had put the kettle on to boil and two mugs were on the table. 'Do you have any milk?' she asked.

'Only powdered – it's in the cupboard. I've got some

brandy, do you want some?'

'No, I do not drink.'

'I'll get you a clean rag for your face.'

'It is nothing.' But her body was shaking. 'The policemen came and I told them about Louisa. They have found a body.'

'Policemen? There were two of them?'

'Yes. Constable Mooney and a man called Broadbent.'

Frank thought. 'He would be a detective from out of town who will do the investigations.'

'Will he? I do not know about such things.'

'And Julius struck you?'

'He has driven me out – I cannot go back. It is too difficult there, I have finished with him. This is not the first time.'

Frank poured the tea as the wind growled around the house. Sand and dust flew in under the door and the moths fluttered around the lamp. Although it was now after nine o'clock, the room was hot. 'A dust storm is coming,' he said.

'It seems there are many kinds of storms this year.'

'Why did your husband hit you?'

'For telling the policemen Louisa was missing, for disobeying him. He is still a tribal German and, for some reason, I am not.'

'And they think the body is that of Louisa?'

'Yes, and I am sure it is.' Maria looked up at him. 'I cannot grieve: she was not my child.'

'You've done the unthinkable,' Frank said. 'You've left your husband.' Then he thought of Irene and the empty house. 'It doesn't happen very often.'

'God has made me strong,' Maria replied. 'Do you believe in Him?'

'I'm not sure – after what I've seen in my life, I'm not sure.'

'I think there is, but not the kind Julius believes in.'

'You can stay here,' Frank said.

'I cannot do that.'

'You won't last half an hour in that storm; it will blow all night.'

'Where is Mr Stark?'

228

Frank spread his hands. 'That, I do not know. He's gone away for a few days. Have you eaten?'

'No.'

'I'll cut some bread and cold meat.'

'Thank you.'

Frank locked the door, lit another lamp and started to prepare the meal. What was he getting into?

The thunder boomed far into the night; the wind grew violent; huge trees fell and the dust clouds rolled over the battered country. It reminded Frank of a battle in northern France. The dust inside the house hung as thick as a London fog and he stuffed rags between the window frames and blankets under the doors.

As they sat at the table that long night, Maria told him of her marriage, of August Hoffmayer, of her childhood, of Carl and Julius and Louisa. At the end of it all, Frank considered her bitter, isolated life and said: 'There is no way you can return, you've given it your best and that's the end to it.'

'Who could have killed Louisa?' Maria asked.

Frank thought carefully. 'Any one of a number of people: these are bad days – there are all kinds of desperate men on the roads.' Then he said: 'It could be Julius.'

Maria sat quite still. 'I have thought of that. She was like her grandfather – all my husband thought was corrupt.' Maria remembered the nightly Bible readings and prayers, Julius's nightmares and his movements in the dark house at night. *He that rejecteth me, and receiveth not my words, hath one that judgeth him.* But would a father murder his own daughter?

Several times in the night, Frank went outside and shone his torch at the windmill and the latticed tower. He disconnected the drive-shaft: the last thing he wanted was a broken pump. Once more, he looked around the yard and the bush, but now in the storm he could see nothing. No one would venture out on a night like this, but when the storm lifted, it would be another matter. Sooner or later, he would have to face Julius Hoffmayer – and maybe Carl. Most murders, he seemed to remember, were committed by members of the family and friends.

'Tell me what is happening,' Maria said.

'Happening where?'

'In Australia.'

Frank told her about the Depression, wheat prices, the strikes, the violence and the repossessions. 'That man Withers,' he said, 'is driving families off their farms.'

'August Hoffmayer,' Maria answered, 'owed money to Mr Withers' father and Julius paid it all off.'

'I think,' Frank said, 'Withers is involved in some kind of secret army – this is going to be a time of rough justice and innocent men are going to be driven to the wall.' He looked at his watch: it was now after midnight. 'You,' he said, 'will sleep in the other room, and I will sleep out here.' He got up as the windows rattled. 'One step at a time – we'll face the music tomorrow.'

By now, Maria was too tired to argue; she slept on Frank's bed roll as the sand and dust choked the dams and creeks and filled the water tanks of Rubicon.

Frank knew the police would want to find Maria to talk to her. He would talk about that with her in the morning.

It was nine o'clock when Julius Hoffmayer's cart rumbled down the driveway to the Rubicon Bush Hospital. The woman at the desk looked up as a big, bearded man entered. He was wearing a black, broad-brimmed hat, black jacket and waistcoat and calf-length boots. His mouth was bloodied and his voice was deep. 'I have come about the body of a young girl,' he said.

The woman flushed. 'Your name?'

'Mr Julius Hoffmayer.'

'If you'll wait, I'll get Dr Anderson.'

Her shoes tapped on the linoleum and the swinging doors creaked in the silence. The room smelt of carbolic and the other women in the office stared at the big man as he sat on the bench. Then a clock chimed the quarter-hour and somewhere a baby cried. Already, the dust had been swept away, but Julius's beard was full of sand and his clothes were streaked with the red earth of Rubicon. He, too, felt no grief: if it were she, God in His wisdom had taken her away and released him from slavery.

The doctor had watery, grey eyes and smelt of drink and tobacco.

'I'm Dr Anderson,' he said. He looked at Julius: 'Have you hurt your mouth?'

'It was an accident.'

Julius followed him down two flights of stairs into the basement, and along a concrete corridor. Then Broadbent appeared.

'Good morning, Mr Hoffmayer.' He also asked Julius about his mouth.

'It was an accident,' he repeated. 'Life can sometimes be dangerous for a farmer.'

Broadbent did not reply and they stopped at a door. The doctor produced a ring of keys, turned on the light and they stepped inside. The room was badly whitewashed and reminded Julius of a cool-room in an abattoir. They passed two bodies draped in worn tarpaulins.

'Heart attacks from the hot weather,' the doctor said. 'The drought's hard on the old folk.'

Then, at the far end of the room, there was another door and a curtained window. Anderson pointed to a chair. 'Please wait there, Mr Hoffmayer.'

As Julius sat down, he was conscious of Broadbent standing behind him. The doctor disappeared and the two men waited at the window; the silence was so profound that Julius could hear his watch ticking in his waistcoat pocket. What if it were not Louisa? But he knew it would be – God had worked His will. Julius watched a blowfly crawling on the lintel of the door. This was an antiseptic place: how did it get in here? He thought of the country abattoirs, the pig-killing and Maria holding the cup of blood. The light bulb glowed brightly on the white walls, and somewhere from the floor above came the sound of thumping as something heavy was moved. The sound was louder than that of his heart. Julius found himself wanting to look at Broadbent, but he remained still on the hospital chair.

Then the curtains parted and through the glass Julius saw Dr Anderson at the head of a trolley, carrying a form draped in a white sheet. The doctor lifted the sheet and exposed the face. It was Louisa.

The face seemed perfect, the lips full and her hair spread upon the pillow. He had seen her like that many times before, but, thank God, he would never see her again. Dr Anderson looked up through the window, and Julius said: 'That is my daughter.' But despite the cold in the room, sweat ran down his neck and back; his mouth was dry and his guts convulsed. 'That is my daughter.'

Broadbent moved behind Julius's back. 'Do you want me to leave you with her for a few minutes?'

'No.' That was the last thing he wanted.

'Do you want a cup of tea upstairs?'

'No.'

As they went out, Broadbent said: 'I will want to see you again – you and your wife and son – do you understand?'

'I understand.' He would have to tell the detective his wife had left him.

On the way home down the Kurnbrun road, Julius did not see the uprooted trees, the sand piled high against the fences and the dead and dying sheep. All he saw was Louisa's white face and her hair upon the pillow. He wondered what she was like beneath the sheet. How had she been killed? Had she been killed by gunfire, or stabbed or butchered? But he did not wish to learn the killer; he did not wish to seek revenge – this was the unfathomable work of God. He remembered the night when his father died and the evil was buried with him: he was free. All that remained now was to work and see out the drought – and the return of his wife. He would see to that.

When Mooney and Broadbent returned to the Hoffmayer farm next morning, they found Julius working in the vegetable garden and Carl splitting logs on the wood heap. To Broadbent, the garden looked hopeless, with its powdery soil, dead weeds and collapsed trellises. He wondered why people would go on trying to cultivate and farm in such country. When Julius saw them, he threw down his shovel and walked toward the house; Carl came over with his double-bladed axe, propped it against a post and the four men sat on the back verandah. The day was hot, but the father and son didn't seem to notice the flies.

'Where is Mrs Hoffmayer?' Broadbent asked. He thought they might be given a cup of tea, but they were offered nothing.

'My wife is not here,' Julius replied.

'Where is she, then?' Broadbent looked at the axe and the scars on Carl's arms.

'She has gone away – I do not know where she is,' Julius said.

Mooney took out his cigarettes, lit one and looked at the starlings on the wires of the fences. The bush in the distance was black and he saw a hawk behind some pines.

Broadbent's voice was soft. 'When did she leave, Mr Hoffmayer?'

'Two nights ago, before tea.'

'For what reason?'

'There was a disagreement.'

'Over what?'

'It is our affair, I do not wish to discuss it.'

Broadbent stretched his legs, raised his hand and killed a blowfly crawling on his trousers. 'We will have to find your wife. Tell me about your daughter, Mr Hoffmayer.'

'What do you wish to know?'

'Did she have any friends?'

'We have no need of friends.'

'Why was she taken away from school?'

'There was a disagreement with the Pastor.'

233

'Another disagreement?'

'Yes.'

'This is an isolated farm,' Broadbent observed. 'There is no phone or electricity.'

'We have no need of those things.'

'Most people do.'

'We,' said Julius, 'do not.'

Mooney thought about Maria Hoffmayer. Where was she? He considered Carl and remembered the stories he had heard about the boy's grandfather. He was starting to respect Broadbent and decided he would not like to be interviewed by the detective. In the morning heat, Mooney's mind wandered – what was Withers doing about the private army, and should he tell Broadbent? It had nothing to do with the murder and it was the affair of the big-wigs: the Commissioner and the powers-that-be. When all this was over, the town would still be on its own and they'd have to look after themselves.

'Carl,' Broadbent was saying, 'what's in the implement shed?'

'The usual things,' Carl replied. 'We work hard on this farm.'

'I'm sure you work hard,' Broadbent said, 'but I'd like to know what's in the shed.' He turned to Mooney. 'Don, I'd like Carl to show you, and take a note of what you see.'

'Okay.'

The boy and the policeman walked away through the garden.

'Now,' Broadbent asked Julius, 'where were you six nights ago?'

'I was in the bush with my son; we were searching for my daughter.'

'Where did you go?'

Julius spread his big hands. 'To all four points of the compass – to all the boundaries and beyond.'

'How far beyond?'

'That, I cannot tell you: a mile perhaps.'

'Did you see anybody?'

'Yes.'

'Who?'

'The soldier, Cameron.'

'Frank Cameron: the man who employs the black?'

'Yes.'

'What time was this?'

'Three days ago, about midday.'

'Did he say what he was doing out in the bush?'

'No,' Julius said, 'he did not.'

Despite his suspicions and dislike of Julius Hoffmayer, Broadbent could pin nothing on the big farmer. Would a father butcher his daughter? Would a brother butcher his sister? The answer to both questions was, yes. But the country was rife with vagabonds and this was where the solution probably lay – it would take months of work, most of which would fall on that drunkard Mooney, whether he liked it or not. The next step was to find Maria Hoffmayer and to see Frank Cameron. Broadbent thought that Julius and Carl Hoffmayer were two of the most unpleasant men he had met, but that didn't necessarily make them guilty of murder.

When the interviews were over, once more the two policemen walked to the road.

'Whereabouts in the shed was it?' Broadbent put the Gladstone bag on the bonnet of Mooney's Ford.

'On a bench by the door.'

Broadbent opened the cut-throat razor and ran his thumb down the blade. 'It's an odd thing to find, seeing neither man shaves?'

'Aw, I don't know,' Mooney replied. 'Farmers don't throw away anything, do they?'

Broadbent examined the sheet music. 'Who's Offenbach?'

'Fucked if I know.'

Twenty-Seven

In Rubicon, Harold Withers waited for his mail to arrive. The post from Melbourne took a long time – the sorting was inefficient, transport uncertain and God only knew who was on strike. Was the murder of Louisa Hoffmayer, he asked himself, part of the train of recent events? There was no doubt that law and order were fast collapsing. The unemployed had their own movement now: they had set up Soviet camps all over the country; the Jews had engineered the financial collapse; the Catholics were behind the political unrest and he was certain that the Russians had agents as far afield as Australia. It seemed that all the principles they had fought for in the war had come to nothing.

Withers knew the Commissioner of Police slightly – he had met him twice at the Melbourne Club and, on the second occasion, the Commissioner had remembered him. All he had to do was to get things squared away with Mooney.

Finally, the mail came and there *was* a letter from the Commissioner and he was most encouraging. He hadn't heard of the murder, but he had heard of the fires. He said that the only alternative now, especially in areas such as Rubicon, was self-help. Withers was surprised to learn that there were now over 65,000 men in the State organized under arms. But in the circumstances, the Commissioner wrote, this was by no means enough and he would welcome a force in Rubicon. The problem always was to find experienced and reliable leaders. Withers thought once more of Frank Cameron, but told himself he could organize that. The Commissioner also wrote he would see that Mooney was advised and wished him luck. He added that uprisings were expected at any time and that the utmost secrecy was essential.

When Withers put the letter away in the office safe, he was satisfied – he had his own force; he would command it himself and give the daily running to Bolger. If he couldn't get his money back, at least he would have the land. And they could now clear the rabble out from Rubicon – and not be bothered about the niceties of the law. Then he phoned Mooney, but there was no reply: he had to be out with the detective. He wondered what they would dig up – nothing involving evictions, he hoped. He stopped himself worrying: it was all perfectly legal.

She was up at six: Frank saw her at the pump as he came back from feeding the horses. He stopped and watched her filling the bucket. Her black hair was down to her shoulders and her arms were bare. Maria lifted the bucket and went inside. Frank stood and thought of the meetings at the lake, of Julius, Carl and Louisa. Would she stay with him? It was most unlikely. She would be breaking all the rules; a married woman living with a man next door after the murder of her stepdaughter. What would Julius do? What would the people of Rubicon and the police do? He didn't give a bugger about that – he had broken most of the rules already. Despite the risks, he wanted her to stay, but he was sure she would go back. What else could a woman like Maria Hoffmayer do? She would return to her husband no matter how grim the life. Frank looked through the dusty, broken trees for any movement, but there was none.

When he opened the door, there was the smell of porridge and toast. Maria looked up from the stove. 'Well, Frank,' she said, 'you run a tight ship, don't you? Is that the expression?'

He stood on the step and looked at the table laid for breakfast. 'Yes,' he replied, 'that's the expression.'

There was a silence, then she pointed at the teddy bear on the mantelpiece. 'Sometimes,' Maria said, 'I regret not having a child of my own, but it is just as well, is it not?'

'The toy was there when I arrived,' Frank said, 'and I didn't throw it out.'

'I think you are a good man, Mr Cameron.' She smiled. 'I have decided not to return to my husband. That is over, despite the laws of God. I will not be struck and I will not be treated in that way.'

'What will you do?'

'That depends on you. If you want me to stay, I shall; if you want me to go, I shall go. If I stay, things will be difficult for us both.'

Frank came up to her. 'I want you to stay.'

'What about Mr Stark, when he returns?'

He laughed. 'I shouldn't think that would worry Ray.'

Maria turned and they held each other: she was nervous and he could feel her trembling. 'It is going to be difficult,' she said. 'Julius will come, and Carl – they are vengeful men. Julius will not be disgraced.'

'I think,' Frank said, 'that I love you.'

She stood still. 'Have you loved before?'

'Twice. I was married, but she left me; and there was a German nurse in the war.'

'You are a lucky man.' Maria lowered her arms and stirred the pot. 'I do not want the porridge to burn.'

Frank sat at the table: he had not felt this way for a long time. 'When your husband comes,' he asked, 'what will you say?'

'I will tell him I have gone.' Maria, too, sat down. 'I am a steadfast woman, Frank Cameron.'

'You know Mooney and Broadbent will be trying to find you?'

'Yes.'

'And you know they will want to get a statement from you?'

'I do.' Maria looked at him straight in the face. 'I will not betray either Julius or Carl, despite all that has happened.'

Julius Hoffmayer sat in the kitchen and thought of Broadbent – it was the first time in twenty years he had not been working on his farm throughout the day. When he had told Carl it was Louisa, he had looked straight at him and said:

'It is God's will, Father.' Then he picked up the cutting gear and walked toward the bush. Carl was right.

He thought once more of Broadbent: the man was cunning and treacherous and would do all he could to find out about Louisa. Let them find the killer, but he wanted no part of it.

Where was Maria? She was essential to run the house, to get the meals, to make the cheese and *bratwurst* and to look after the poultry. Furthermore, Maria was *his* wife and, when the news got out, he would be disgraced in the eyes of other men. Strong she might be, but she would not survive more than several nights in the bush: and there was nowhere for her to go – she had nobody. He would let her sweat it out, and she would return.

Then Julius did as he had done before: every sign of corruption would be removed. He rose from the table, went down the hall and opened the door to Louisa's room; he gazed at her bed – the counterpane, the sheets; he opened the doors of the walnut chest and tossed out her dresses, her underclothes, the trinkets and toys of her childhood, and smashed the water jug, the mirror and the china figures from Bavaria. Julius worked hard and within an hour Louisa's room was stripped and bare. When he had heaped all his daughter's belongings – all sign and memory of her – in the thistles and weeds of the back garden, he went to the barn, took down the tin of kerosine, poured it over the pile, stood back and watched it burn. He stored the bed frame and the chest in the barn, and only the ladies on the Boulevard des Italiens remained.

By three o'clock, Julius was working with Carl. When he told his son what he had done, the boy nodded and then said: 'If you want to find out where Stepmother is, you should ask the soldier, Cameron.' Then he told his father he had seen them together on the shore of the lake.

It was late in the afternoon when Frank saw the dust from the hooves of a horse. When it got closer, he saw it was a tall, black gelding – and Julius Hoffmayer. The big man was carrying a shotgun.

Julius sat straight on his horse and stopped a few yards away on the freshly ploughed ground. Frank leant on the handle of his shovel and said: 'Good afternoon, Mr Hoffmayer.'

'There has been a tragedy in my family. I think you may know where my wife is.'

'I do, Mr Hoffmayer.'

'And where is that?'

'Back at my cottage.'

Julius did not reply, turned his horse and rode off. Frank thought about riding after him, but decided not: this affair was between husband and wife; and he was sure Maria could look after herself. Then he thought of the shotgun, but he still remained at the fence line. In the shadows of the bush the crows and the sparrows picked at the broken earth.

Maria was not surprised to see him. Julius looked bigger than ever, wearing his black hat and mounted on the gelding, the sun behind him. Horse and rider were both quite still despite the flies and dust. She stood by the broken rail fence and waited for him to speak.

'A wife does not leave her husband,' Julius said. 'It is God's law.'

'And a husband does not beat his wife,' Maria replied, 'and he does not desire his daughter. If there is a God, they, too are His laws.'

'Are you sleeping with the soldier, Cameron? You are committing adultery.'

'I am not sleeping with him. Unlike the man whom Carl drove away and who died, Frank Cameron has taken me in. He is not a Pharisee.'

Julius dismounted and came forward. 'I have had enough of this.' He held her by the arm. 'You are coming back where you belong.'

As he went to strike her, she twisted from his grasp and seized a paling from the fence. 'May God damn you again, Julius Hoffmayer. I've suffered you and your son for ten years;

I've seen you lust after your own daughter; I've seen you reduce the farm to the place of a German tribe in the Middle Ages; the only way you will take me is to use that shotgun.'

'My God.' Julius pulled back the hammer. 'My God.' He raised the gun as she stood, defiant, on the track.

Then a horseman appeared from the bush; he was black and wiry, wearing dirty moleskins and had a rifle cradled in his arms. 'I wouldn't do that if I was you, Mr Hoffmayer,' he said. It was Ray Stark.

As Julius turned, Ray put up his gun. 'This ain't your property,' he said. 'I think you should piss off.'

'You're nothing but black scum,' Julius said. 'You come and you go, you're not fit to pull a plough, you molest women, you're the last of a tribe of savages that should be extirpated from the earth, you've got no business in this community.'

'I got more business here than you might think, mister.'

'I'm not leaving my wife in the hands of a nigger.'

'Don't get me excited, mister,' Ray replied. He smiled as he cocked his gun. 'Us blacks got no control, remember?'

'No decent white man would employ a savage like you.'

'Who I employ is my business, Mr Hoffmayer.' It was Frank now. He rode up and faced Julius. 'If your wife wants to stay here, I think it's her business. You'd best put that shotgun down before there's an accident.'

'Mr Cameron,' Julius answered, 'you are a wife-stealer and an adulterer: God will vent His wrath upon you.'

'We'll have to wait and see, Mr Hoffmayer.'

'God punishes all sinners and He has His chosen agents on this earth. I will be back, Mr Cameron.' Julius suddenly turned his horse and rode away toward the Kurnbrun road.

Frank dismounted and went toward Ray. 'Where have you been, you stupid bugger?'

Ray raised his hat and wiped his forehead. 'Aw, round and about.' He looked at Maria. 'I'm up with all the bush gossip.'

'Maria,' Frank said, 'this is Ray Stark.'

She hadn't seen a black since her childhood – this man

looked straight and strong and could have saved her life. 'Thank you, Mr Stark.'

'No worries, Mrs Hoffmayer, I heard about your step-daughter.'

This was a good-looking woman and Ray wondered about her and Frank. This could be a real mess and they could be driven out of the district. 'I don't reckon I'm a savage, I was brought up by the Moravians.'

Maria was not afraid of the black man: he was direct and cheerful. 'Did they teach you about original sin?'

'Yeah, but Frank here doesn't believe in that.' Ray thought before he asked the question: 'Are you going to stay on this farm?' He knew she had been driven out.

'I've told her, she can stay as long as she likes,' Frank said.

'Okay, a good-looking woman will cheer the place up a bit and keep us on the straight and narrow.' Ray touched his hat. 'I think I'll go out before it gets dark and shoot a few bunnies.'

Frank and Maria sat in the shadows of the kitchen. 'So that's Mr Stark,' she said.

'That's Ray – he's a good man.' Frank touched her arm. 'And you're a brave woman.'

'That may be: after what has just happened, do you still want me here?'

'I told you – yes. What do you think your husband will do?'

'He will come back with Carl.'

'Will he get Don Mooney?'

'No, he says there is only one law – and that is God's.'

'So he'll go it alone?'

'Yes.'

'So after ten years of marriage and your religion, you're throwing your lot in with me?'

Maria touched his fingers. 'When you came into my kitchen that hot morning, my life started to change. With Julius I was a slave: with you, I am not. In a strange way, you remind me of my Uncle Ernst – although he was no farmer.'

'Your Uncle Ernst? In what way?'

'He was fair-minded and intelligent.'

'You're an unusual woman.'

Maria smiled. 'And, Frank, you are an unusual man.'

He leaned across the table and kissed her on the lips. Maria held his hands hard and kissed him back.

Maria enjoyed the evening meal. She found herself waiting for the prayers, but there were none. The two men spoke freely and Ray said he'd been visiting relations in New South Wales – in a town called Wentworth near the River Murray. She thought that Ray might have been doing other things, but Frank didn't press him. Then Ray, directly, asked her about her stepdaughter – who, he said, could have done such a thing? Although she had her own ideas, she said she didn't know. Ray said all aborigines were related and would share the grief. But Maria replied it wasn't the same with Europeans and that Louisa was her husband's daughter, not hers. When she said she could not grieve for her stepdaughter, but did not want her dead, Ray couldn't understand. 'There's going to be a hunt for the killer,' he said at last, 'all them men in Rubicon.'

'There will be a hunt,' Maria replied, 'but I want no part of it.'

Ray then told Frank that he'd seen many camps, many desperate men, and whitefellows armed with guns, riding around the countryside – that there was big trouble coming up. He reckoned there was an army of whites about to take over the whole State. As Frank listened, he thought of the Russian prisoners of war he'd seen; he thought of the young German officer announcing the beginning of the revolution; of the White Army trying to put down the Bolsheviks; he thought the Czar deserved what he got. Then he thought of Withers dispossessing farmers; of his father sweeping the floors in a Melbourne factory; of Bolger and Mooney raiding the camp; of Withers' plans to arm men. He wanted no part of that. He thought the political situation was like the drought and the afternoon thunderstorms: lightning must strike and men would die. When all this was over, he thought, life in

243

Australia would never be quite the same again.

At nine o'clock, Ray pulled his watch from his waistcoat and said he was going to doss down in the shed. Suddenly, he was gone and Maria and Frank were left alone in the cottage in the candle-light. The night was silent and warm.

Frank looked at her. 'I'm going to have a wash and turn in now,' he said. 'You will have my bed and I will sleep here in the kitchen.'

Maria lay in the dark and listened to the sounds of the night. She thought of Uncle Ernst, his advice and the terrible mistake she had made: ten years with a man she found she neither loved nor respected – and a man who did not respect her and who was obsessed with guilt for his father and daughter. She thought of meeting Frank by the lake: the grip of his hand, his clear blue eyes and his body, and wondered what it would be like to have him lying with her. No man had made love to her. What must it be like? Animals simply fornicated to reproduce themselves and all Julius had shown was merely lust.

In the dark, Maria felt her own body – her breasts and her thighs. What did Julius do to Louisa? Would Frank do the same? Once she had heard Ernst and Matilde in their bedroom – they were both laughing and sighing and, every morning, her uncle would kiss her aunt full on the mouth before he went out to work. Often in the evenings when they listened to the phonograph, they would sit on the sofa and hold hands, as the sounds of Wagner drifted through the house. They were a loving couple. Unlike Julius, Uncle Ernst did not believe that sexual lust was part of the punishment for Adam's sin.

Later in the night, Maria heard Frank moving around in the kitchen and the back door creak. Then she saw candle-light and heard the sound of water being poured from the pitcher. What was he doing? Then the door opened and he was standing with the light behind him. 'Are you awake?' Frank asked.

'Yes.'

'It's a warm night and hard to sleep. Do you want a cup of tea?'

'Yes, I'd like that.'

Several minutes later, he was at her side. 'I've found you a china cup,' he said.

They drank silently and, when he leant to take the cup, she smelt his body; he put the cup on the floor and they held each other in the dark. He kissed her on the mouth and, as she shivered, on the neck, ears and throat. She pulled him down on to her bed and felt his hands touching her. 'I want to look after you,' he said. She, too, touched and felt him – his face and chest. 'Have you ever loved before?' he asked.

'I told you, no.'

As they lay, she put her fingers in his mouth, his were in her hair, he touched her breasts, then her belly, he was gentle, and she with him. 'I think I am loving now,' she said.

He found her strong and beautiful; her hair fell over his face; her fingers gripped his; she rose to meet him and held him tight as they loved each other in that tiny room. For both it seemed it would never end, and when it was done, they lay side by side and listened to the barn owls calling in the dark.

'I don't think we're committing a sin,' Frank said. 'Do you?' It was the first time he had heard her laugh and her voice was soft. 'I think this may, too, be God's will,' she said.

Twenty-eight

'If the Commissioner approves, of course it's got to be right with me,' Mooney said. He was relieved now that Withers' plan had the seal of approval. 'It's about time something was done – we've got three buildings burnt down, vagrants and a murder. What else do we want? I want all the help I can get – we all know that.'

'And the Commissioner *has* written to you?' Withers asked.

'Yep. There was a letter waiting for me when I got in last night. Do you want to read it?'

Withers nodded and Mooney passed it over. The letter was headed TOP SECRET and it told him to give every possible co-operation and assistance to Harold Withers, as Justice of the Peace in Rubicon, in raising an efficient force of loyal and dedicated men to maintain law and order in the district. 'Right,' Withers said, 'I think I should command the force myself and I'm asking Reg to look after the day-to-day running – that's recruitment, training and operations in the field.' He looked at Bolger. 'Is that satisfactory?'

'Too right.'

'And no buggering about,' Withers went on. 'No drinking while on duty, no larrikins – I want an efficient body of men who will protect property and lives. I don't want a repetition of the last show – we may be dealing with Bolshevist rabble, but there are limits.'

'Right.'

'As I see it,' Withers said, 'there are three main areas of concern: property, the unemployeds and our Irish friends. The murder of the Hoffmayer girl is out of our hands.' He turned to Mooney. 'What did you and Broadbent learn yesterday?'

Mooney told him about the visit to the Hoffmayer farm and ended by saying: 'And Maria Hoffmayer's gone missing.'

Withers looked up. 'Does anyone know why?'

'Hoffmayer said it was a domestic disagreement. We're going to track her down today – she can't be far away – with some other Huns: they all stick together like shit to a blanket.'

'That will take you far and wide – our German friends are scattered.'

'We'll do it – and we're going to bring in Stark as soon as we find him.'

'What does Broadbent think of all this?'

'It's hard to tell – he doesn't say much. Still waters run deep, but he says to lock up the abo.'

'How long will Broadbent be here?' Withers asked.

This time it was Mooney's turn to look at Withers: he knew why the question was asked. 'I'm not sure – he'll want to question the Hoffmayer woman, make all kinds of enquiries and then if nothing comes up, he'll leave the leg-work to me.'

'But it's Broadbent's case, isn't it?'

'Yeah, it's his case, but with what's going on in Melbourne, and all over, I'll have to pitch in.'

'But your first responsibility is to law and order in Rubicon? There's much to do.'

'There sure is.'

'Have you got any ideas?' Withers asked.

'Not really – it's hard with all the strangers in the area. A lot of murders are within the family – so we were taught.'

'So,' Withers said, 'you're thinking of Julius or the son? Does a father hack his own daughter to pieces?'

Mooney spread his hands. 'Anything's possible – you know what a queer mob the Hoffmayers are. Your father dealt with August, and he was as mad as a snake. Maybe it's in the blood. There's something wrong with the boy – everyone knows that.'

'I think,' Withers replied, 'that there's something wrong with the whole damned race.'

'Maybe Stark will know something, when we find him. We

can sweat it out of him.'

'I'd like to work over that black bastard,' Bolger said.

'Be patient, Reg,' Withers answered. 'All in good time.'

'How many men do you want?'

'It's quality, not quantity. I'd rather have twenty good men, tried and true, than forty yahoos. And I want you both to remember that our operation takes precedence over the murder of a German girl – that's for the CIB, not us. Okay?'

'Yes.'

Withers leaned back in his office chair. 'The first thing on my agenda is that camp out near Netherby. To borrow a word from our Russian friends, we want a purge, a cleansing – of undesirables – to show everybody that Rubicon's a tight, clean place where a man can work hard with no interference and invest in the future. That's what it's going to be all about when things come right. These times will pass and we want no Bolshies or Sinn Feiners spoiling it for the ordinary, law-abiding people – or the investors. If the government won't do it, we will.' He stood up. 'Don't let that CIB man ride you, Don. I think we should meet three times a week to discuss progress. Some people in the town are shocked by the murder, but I can dampen that down; the first thing is safety and property – for Australians.'

Outside in the street, Mooney and Bolger compared notes. 'It's the go-ahead, then?' Bolger said. 'You've got to say Withers gets things done and sees the priorities. I'll start phoning blokes after work.'

'Yep.' Mooney looked at his watch. 'I'd better get moving and try and find the bloody Hoffmayer woman.'

'What's your mate doing?'

'Who?'

'Broadbent.'

'I'm not sure – he'll probably poke around the town. He's not such a bad bastard, so tell the customers not to get worried if he interviews them.' Mooney opened the door of his car. 'It's good to know that the Commissioner's behind us.'

That afternoon, Mooney saw all the German farmers he knew and came up with nothing. No one had seen Maria Hoffmayer. In Rubicon, Broadbent talked to the shopkeepers, visited Rubicon's only boarding house and had a session with Jim Banks. He thought that, for a publican, Banks didn't seem to know much: Rubicon was turning out to be the tightest little town he'd ever been in. Broadbent had lunch by himself in the Royal dining-room, then went to his room where he lay on the bed and read some more Edgar Rice Burroughs. At four-thirty he phoned Melbourne from Mooney's office. He was told that there had been yet another violent street march: two demonstrators were dead, a dozen men badly injured, four policemen hurt and two police horses put down. State cabinet was meeting to discuss a State of Emergency.

That evening, seven powerful men, including the Commissioner of Police, met in the cool, marbled dining-room of the Melbourne Club; and after steak and kidney pudding, red wine and cold stewed fruit, they decided to put the secret army on full alert.

Mooney and Broadbent arrived at Frank's farm at half past seven next morning. Mooney opened the gate and they drove up to the cottage. Mooney was wearing his Smith & Wesson .38 and there was a double-barrelled shotgun in the back of the Ford.

They got out, stood in the dewy grass and nobody seemed to be about; but when they went around the back, they found Maria hanging out some washing.

'Well, Mrs Hoffmayer,' Mooney said as they both stood stock still, 'what are you doing here? I've been looking all over the place for you.'

Maria looked at the two men and didn't answer the question. Then she gazed at Broadbent and knew who he was. 'Do you wish to see me?'

'Yes, Mrs Hoffmayer, yes I do.' He was disconcerted by this woman with the long, black hair.

'Well?'

'You know that the dead girl is your stepdaughter?'

'I do.'

'May I ask you why you are not with your husband?'

'He struck me once too often, so I have left him.'

'That's unusual, Mrs Hoffmayer.'

'What – a husband beating his wife, or a wife leaving?'

Broadbent had no answer.

As they talked at the back of the house by the shed and the windmill, Maria did not invite them inside, but made them stand among the washing as it flapped on the line. Broadbent asked her about Louisa, her disappearance, the search, but beyond the barest facts learned nothing. She had no information to give about the girl, except that she sometimes suffered ill-health and, for this reason, had been taken away from school. Broadbent knew this was nothing unusual in isolated communities in the bush. This time, however, he was puzzled and uneasy: he found the wife, in her own way, more formidable than her husband, and he knew he was dealing with no ordinary back-blocks woman.

Mooney stayed silent and looked around for Frank, of whom there was no sign. When he strolled over to the shed to look for the horses, he found them there, feeding from their nosebags. They hadn't been ridden. There were two: Cameron's gelding and the other he guessed belonged to Maria Hoffmayer. At the end of it all, Mooney chipped in and said: 'You'll have to sign a written statement, Mrs Hoffmayer.'

'If it is accurate and tells the truth,' Maria replied, 'I will sign it.'

Before he put away his notebook, Broadbent had one last question. 'I am told,' he said, 'that Mr Cameron was alone in the bush four days after your stepdaughter's disappearance. Would you know why?'

'You will have to ask Mr Cameron that.'

'Where is he?'

'He is farrowing.'

'Whereabouts?'

'Half a mile up that track.'

'Have you seen a black man called Ray Stark?' Mooney asked.

'No.' Maria turned away.

'What the fuck is that woman doing here?' Mooney said as they walked along the fence-line.

'You heard – she's left her husband.'

'Jesus,' Mooney said, 'if she's moved in with Cameron and the black, that'll be a turn-up for the troops – and with *her* background.'

'What does our friend, Cameron, look like?' Broadbent asked.

'He's a big, fair-headed bloke with a limp, tough, an officer in the war. He was decorated.'

'But not your usual returned man?'

'You can say that again.' Mooney paused. 'He did up Reg Bolger and that takes some doing.'

'Did he?' Broadbent had met the town butcher briefly yesterday. 'Do you think he's a Sinn Feiner or a Bolshie? Any political affiliations?'

'Nah. I don't think he belongs to anything – or anybody.'

'I wonder,' Broadbent said, 'if Hoffmayer knows.'

'What?'

'That his wife's shacked up with a neighbour.'

'If he does, Cameron's a dead man.'

Broadbent stopped on the track. 'Our job is to prevent homicides, Constable Mooney.'

'Just a figure of speech.'

'I wonder what made him employ a black?'

'Fucked if I know. If Cameron knows where Stark is, or can give us some leads, let's get *him* – it's a start.' Mooney thought. 'I don't think there's a law against screwing your neighbour's wife – except in the Bible.'

'It's called adultery,' Broadbent said. 'And it always leads to trouble. *I* know.

'We left the shotgun in the car,' Mooney said.

'For Gods' sake, Don, you've got your revolver – this isn't

251

bloody Chicago. And we're dealing with an officer and a gentleman.'

Mooney laughed.

Frank and Ray were taking a spell in the dirt beside the tractor. 'Don't look now,' Frank said, 'but we've got visitors.'

'Jesus,' Ray said, 'Jesus.'

They watched the two men walk up over the stubble. Frank knew straight away that the thin, sandy-haired man was a police detective and that they had come about Louisa Hoffmayer. He also knew that they could not have failed to see Maria.

Mooney was grinning. 'Well, well,' he said, 'if it isn't Mr Stark.'

Frank got up and leaned against the tractor. 'Good morning, Constable Mooney, you're up early. What can I do for you – and your colleague?'

'This is Mr William Broadbent,' Mooney replied, 'from the CIB.'

'So?'

'We're making enquiries about the Hoffmayer girl.'

Frank took out his tobacco, rolled two cigarettes and gave one to Ray. 'Fire ahead, we'll help you all we can.'

'I'm told,' Broadbent said, as he considered this big blond farmer and the black man, 'that you were out in the bush, alone, four days after she was missing.'

'I was.'

'Why?'

'I was searching for her.'

'You knew she was missing?'

'I did – otherwise I wouldn't have been out searching.'

'Who told you?'

'Mrs Hoffmayer.'

'You had seen Mrs Hoffmayer before then?'

'She came over and told me the evening the girl disappeared. For God's sake, Mr Broadbent, this is the bush – we're all neighbours.' Frank laughed. 'Or supposed to be. If you want an alibi, I can't give you one – but neither could most people in the district.'

'Where have you been, Stark?' It was Mooney now.

'Round and about – visiting me folks.'

'In unemployeds' camps?'

'I got mates everywhere.'

Frank Cameron was standing now and Broadbent remembered an officer he had served under in the war. The man had always been fair to his troops, whatever their failings. In the second battle of the Somme he had charged a machine-gun post unaided and was awarded a posthumous VC; he was tall and good-looking, the son of a farmer in the back-blocks of New South Wales, but did not belong and would not crack. This man, Cameron, was like that. Broadbent made up his mind quickly and pointed at Ray. 'It's you we want.'

'What for?'

Broadbent pulled out his notebook. 'Suspected arson of three buildings and inciting a riot.'

Frank threw down his cigarette and ground it with his boot. 'This is all bullshit, Broadbent.'

'I don't think so, Mr Cameron.'

'Have you got a warrant?'

'Yep,' Mooney said, 'we have.'

'Sworn by who?'

'A Justice of the Peace, Mr Harold Withers.'

'Holy Mother of God.'

Mooney stepped forward as Broadbent looked on. 'I wouldn't make trouble if I was you, Cameron.'

'Look, Mooney,' Frank said, 'I don't know what your colleague knows – but you're in the shit: the raid on the camp, an aborigine dying in custody, the body disappearing and Withers setting up a tin-pot army to get rid of innocent people to feather his own nest.'

'Mr Cameron,' Broadbent said easily, 'I'm not here to get mixed up in local politics. Constable Mooney's got a warrant for the arrest of Stark and that's it.'

'Do you know what you are, Mooney?' Frank said. 'You're a bloody arse-licker, you've got shit all over your mouth,

253

you're in the pay of a bloody viper who chucks people off their farms, you're all fat and fart.'

'You'd better watch yourself, mister,' Broadbent said.

Mooney was shaking. 'Are you fucking that Hun woman?' As Frank came forward, Mooney pulled out his gun. 'You watch it, Cameron.'

Frank controlled his anger and knew there was no point in this. 'Just serve the warrant, Mooney, and get this farce over with.'

He turned to Ray. 'I'll do my best for you, you know that?'

'Thanks, mate.' Ray grinned. 'You can put away that gun, Mr Mooney – this blackfellow's coming quietly.'

Frank then knew what had to be done. 'Okay, Ray, I'll be seeing you. Look after yourself.'

When they had gone, Frank lit another cigarette and thought. This was like some moving picture – what would they do to Ray in the cells? Would he end up like Angus McIntosh?

'They've taken Ray,' Frank said to Maria.

'What are the reasons?'

'Trumped-up charges. Mooney had a warrant sworn out by Withers. What did the detective ask you?'

She was calm and told him as they sat in the kitchen. 'I have nothing to worry about,' she said.

'I'm going into Rubicon to see Withers,' Frank said. 'What will you do if Julius comes?'

'Defend myself, defend my rights. I'm not going back.'

'Do you want me to leave you the shotgun?'

'Won't you need it?'

'Ray's left his rifle.' Frank took her hand. 'Can you use a shotgun?'

'My dear Frank Cameron, I'm a farmer's wife: I can shoot game, build fences and dress a pig.' Maria thought of the last pig-killing. It was Carl she feared. 'What will you say to Mr Withers?'

'I'll tell him that an innocent man's been arrested.'

Frank got to Rubicon just after eleven and parked the truck outside Withers' Emporium. He looked around Federation Street, went into the store past the racks of merchandise, and again thought it convenient for Withers that there was now only one general store in Rubicon. The next time he had to stock up, he must trade with the man. He looked at the locals at the counters and heard a cash register ring. When Frank climbed the stairs, he saw a door at the end of the corridor, pushed it open and walked straight in.

Harold Withers was putting the phone back, looked up and said: 'Mr Cameron – an unexpected pleasure.'

'Four hours ago,' Frank said, 'I was visited by Mooney, and Broadbent from the CIB. They arrested Ray Stark on a warrant sworn out by you. The charges are pure bullshit.'

Withers' shirt was spotless despite the heat and he smelt of imported brilliantine. He looked at the big, angry, filthy farmer. 'Any arrest in this town,' he replied, 'has nothing to do with me. You should see Constable Mooney.'

'You run this town, Withers, and Mooney's in your arse pocket.'

'I don't think so, Mr Cameron.'

'My father, Withers, was driven off his farm by bastards like you – you've got liens over most of the properties in this district – but not mine. Now you've got your vigilantes, and you've taken a man in because he's an abo, because he's a convenient scapegoat for the burnings and violence.' Frank took a long shot. 'Trade must be good now that Ballantine's gone.'

Withers sat quite still as the office fan droned. He now knew that Cameron would have to go – that he was the one person who could wreck his plans for Rubicon. Mooney had already called in and he was on the point of asking Cameron about Maria Hoffmayer, but decided not. 'I've got work to do,' he said. 'Go and see Mooney.'

'All right, I'll go and see Mooney, but I'm telling you that you're in the shit, my friend. You've covered up two killings – does the CIB know about that? You're running an illegal army and you're pitching farmers off their properties. I couldn't give a fuck about politics, but I can see what the socialists are on about. One day, Withers, you'll be where you belong – in the gutter with the poor bastards you've driven there – I'll see to that.'

As soon as Frank had gone, Withers made a phone call to Mooney. And Mooney called Bolger.

Twenty-nine

When Frank got to Mooney's office, the building was locked up and the blinds were down. He went around the back to find Mooney's big dog snarling and slathering against the wire netting. It was a big Alsatian and he picked up a fence paling lying in the grass. He looked at the neighbouring cottages, with their dead gardens and washing on the lines, scaled the fence and dropped down.

The dog stood off, its eyes red and its back raised. 'Come on, you bastard,' Frank said, 'have a go.' At the back of Mooney's office he could see the barred windows of the lock-up. As he moved to his right, the dog made its run. It leapt, grabbed Frank's arm, tore through the sleeve of his jacket and sank its teeth into his flesh. The blood flowed and he gasped with pain. 'Jesus,' he said, 'you bugger.' He struck it on the head with the paling, hit again, caught it on the muzzle and kicked it in the hindquarters with his heavy farm boots. The dog let go, then jumped and went for his face; he hit it again in the neck, it fell back and he struck it again in the eyes. As the blood pumped from his arm, Frank thought of beating it to death, but it ran to the far fence where it crouched, snarling. Christ, Frank thought, pity the poor unemployed sod bailed up by that animal.

He tore the sleeve from his shirt, wrapped it round his arm and walked over to the cell. Spiders' webs were growing between the bars and the high window was thick with dust and filth. 'Ray, Ray,' Frank called, but there was no reply. As the wind blew the dust around the yard, Frank kept his eye on the dog and wondered what to do. Then he looked at his watch – it was almost twelve-thirty – he had little doubt that Mooney and possibly Bolger would be drinking at the Royal.

He hurled the paling at the Alsatian, climbed the fence and drove back to Federation Street. All the blinds were drawn in the surrounding houses and no one saw him go.

They were there in the public bar: Mooney, Bolger, Banks behind the counter and three other men Frank didn't recognize. They stopped drinking and watched him come in.

'Hurt your arm?' Bolger said.

'You've got some animal there,' Frank said to Mooney. 'The next time I see it, I'll kill it with my twelve gauge.'

'I reckon you've been trespassing on government property,' Mooney replied. 'That's an offence.'

'Next time I see that dog,' Frank repeated, 'I'll blow its fucking head off.' He turned to Banks. 'Give me a beer.'

The men watched him as he drank and all was silent in the bar of the Royal.

'What brings you into town?' Bolger asked.

Frank ignored the butcher and faced Mooney once more. 'You've got an innocent man in that cell,' he said.

'That may be true: innocent until judged guilty by a Justice of the Peace.'

'Withers?'

'He's the only J.P. in the district.'

'If he's found guilty,' Frank said, 'there'll be trouble.'

Mooney laughed. 'I don't think so – no one's going to mind if a black's out of the way.'

'They tell me that Mrs Hoffmayer's a good-looking woman,' Bolger said.

Frank put his glass down. 'What's it got to do with you?'

'Nothing, just making conversation.' Bolger grinned. 'I suppose her old man's looking for her?'

'Listen,' Frank said, 'why don't you continue to sell your offal and keep out of other blokes' affairs?' He turned: there was no profitable business for him here.

'What's it like fucking a Hun tart?' Bolger said. 'Do they do it different?'

Be calm and be methodical, Frank said to himself, you got him last time, you can do it again. He measured the distance – he had to get in closer. He also considered the other men looking on and Banks behind the bar. It was doubtful if Mooney would join in. He stepped forward, his voice reasonable. 'I don't think what Mrs Hoffmayer's doing has got much to do with you.'

'There's public morals – this is a clean town.'

'Do you think so?'

'There's plenty of spare meat around,' Bolger said, 'but a bloke with your record should lay off the neighbours' wives. You were once a leader of men. Julius Hoffmayer might come after *you* with his twelve-gauge.'

'Do you think so?'

Bolger laughed. 'Oh Jesus, I think he will.'

Frank sprang, struck Bolger in the throat and brought his knee up into his groin. As the man doubled, Frank hit him in the teeth. Something cracked and blood spurted from his knuckles.

'Hey, hey,' Mooney shouted, shoved himself between, but did nothing.

But Bolger was all muscle: blood running from his mouth, he grabbed Frank by his injured arm, twisted so the wound tore open, then kicked him in the ankle. Then as Frank went down, the three other men started. 'Okay, Hun-fucker, nigger-lover,' one said. They were wearing hob-nail boots and they kicked him in the ribs, head and back; as he struggled to his feet, Bolger kicked him in the chest, then hauled Frank to his feet and hit him on the jaw.

'Okay, okay,' Mooney said as Banks came around with a bottle raised, 'that's enough. Don't kill him.'

Bolger wiped his bloodied face. 'My Christ, he's a strong bastard, what'll we do with him?'

'Get him out of here,' Mooney said. 'That's for sure.'

'Okay,' Bolger said, 'we'll take him out and chuck him over the back fence. The fucking know-all, officer bastard.'

'Just a moment,' Banks said, 'let's fill him full of cheap whisky.'

One man took a bottle, opened Frank's mouth and poured

it down. Then the four of them dragged him out as the blood congealed on the floor.

'Well,' Mooney said as they came back, 'I didn't see a thing.'

'I can vouch for that,' Jim Banks said. 'I sure can vouch for that.'

Bolger wiped his mouth. 'Next time I'll kill that shit, believe you me, I'll kill him.'

When Frank came to, he could hear the sounds of women laughing in the house-bar; someone belched and pissed against the tin fence. He lay in the grass and looked at the sky and the stars; his chest ached, his face was covered with dried blood and he reeked of whisky. Then a dog barked, a waggon went up Federation Street; a small church bell started to toll and a door slammed. A banjo played from an upstairs room as he lay on the hard ground. He retched and felt for his watch: it was almost seven o'clock. When he found his feet, he felt in his waistcoat for the keys of the Chev, walked slowly through a gateway, got into the cab and drove home.

The drive through the bush was slow and endless and after half an hour he saw the lamps were gleaming at the Hoffmayer house between the pines. He slowed down, but did not stop. Then, after a long while through the dust, he found his gate in the headlights, climbed down, opened it and drove up to the cottage door. Maria had heard the sound of the motor and was waiting.

'G'day,' Frank said as he stood in the opening. 'It looks as though the battle has started.'

Maria washed his face and gave him a cup of tea. She found he had a badly bruised back; his face was cut to the cheekbone; and he had two cracked ribs.

Ray Stark knew that he would not survive a third night alone in the police cell. The days were bad enough, but the night seemed endless and at times he felt he was falling into a dark, fathomless pit from which there was no escape.

He had expected to be beaten up by Mooney or, worse still, by Bolger, but apart from being given bread, cold meat and a mug of tea twice a day, neither man came near him. It was as though he had been left alone to die.

Ray had paced the cell out – it was eight feet by five feet, with a wooden bunk, a barred window and a shit can. It was built of stone, timber and corrugated iron and the walls were covered with filthy messages. Worst of all, there were the rafters from which Angus McIntosh had strung himself up. Ray told himself he wouldn't be doing that, but after the end of the second day, he was starting to have his doubts. Most of all he missed the sky and the smell of the bush.

He wondered what Frank would do and how soon he would come up before Mr Withers – he had no hope of getting off: he knew that. How would he explain being at the unemployeds' camp? It was none of their fucking business – a man could go where he wanted, but they might find out he had mates in the timber-workers' union and that would be the end of him. Would Frank try and get him out? After all, he was still a whitefellow and it mightn't be worth all the trouble.

Later in the morning he had been arrested, he heard a dog barking and he thought he heard a voice, but couldn't be sure. That evening Mooney came back late, shoved the food at him and shut the door. He didn't say a word. On the way into Rubicon, Mooney had slapped the handcuffs on and Broadbent sat in the front with the shotgun; he kept on looking around and smiling, but that was all. Ray wondered how he would go against Bolger – not too good in a cell. He wondered if he should pray, but his praying days were over. He had to get out and make a run for it. Another day and night cooped up would finish him.

There were two ways of getting out: to have a go at Mooney when he came in with the food, or to find a way out of the cell. Bashing a cop was the last thing he wanted to do, so he started to look at the building. The walls were of sandstone and timber: it would take him bloody months to get out by digging and scraping. Ray tried the bars of the window, but they were firm.

He looked at the rafters and the iron roof and again thought of Angus McIntosh strung up by his belt. They had not taken *his* belt – was that deliberate? Ray jumped, caught a rafter and swung up; he balanced on a beam and inspected the sheets of corrugated iron. The nail holes were rusty and with luck he could get the nails out with his pocket knife. Why hadn't Angus tried this? Solitary affected different men in different ways.

As he crouched on the beam, Ray heard a door creak and slam outside, then the sound of footsteps. It had to be Mooney; he jumped down and sat on the bunk. A key scraped and the cell door opened.

'G'day,' Mooney said. 'How are you doing?'

'Okay.'

'Well, you won't be – from what we know about you.' Mooney jangled the keys. 'I know a lot about abos. You don't like being on your ownsome, do you? It gets to your head – or neck. You thought there'd be some rough stuff, didn't you? Well, there might be, and there might not. Mr Withers is a very busy man and it might be weeks before he can hear your case, so in the meantime you'll just have to sweat it out in here. Sorry, chum.' Mooney peered. 'That's a nice old stockman's belt you're wearing – it might come in useful.' He closed the door and turned the key.

Ray then decided that getting through the roof by day was far too dangerous – he would have to get back on the beam, remember where the nail holes were, and try and escape at night.

He sat all through that day and waited for Mooney to come in with the evening food. At last the policeman came, shoved the plate at him and left. He waited another hour, then mounted the beam, remembered where the nail holes were and worked with his pocket knife.

The night was hot and the timber as hard as concrete. It was awkward in the dark and it took Ray an hour to get two nails out; he dropped down for a rest and sat on the bunk; he listened but could not hear the familiar and comforting sounds of the night. He got a third nail out, but cut his arm on the tin and felt the blood running down into the palm of his hand. Jesus, oh Jesus, he found himself praying. As last, in the depth of the black morning, he raised the tin and smelt the night. It was, he thought, better than any drink. Ray bent the tin roof back carefully and squeezed through, tearing his shirt and cutting his chest. Then, thank God, he was on the roof, under the night sky where the stars shone and the moon gleamed. Crickets sang, sheep bleated and a cow bellowed.

Ray dropped to the ground, heard a dog barking and made for the fence. The lights in Mooney's house went on, but Ray was away up the street and into the bush. He ran like a fox – he ran.

Thirty

In no more than three days, Bolger, for once, did his job well. He got twenty men, all of whom were good shots and riders, and eleven of whom had served in France or Palestine. All of them owned shotguns, six had a variety of stolen army service pistols; all were from Protestant families and half of them were Freemasons. Of the Great War veterans, three had been corporals and all were experienced men of the line. They met Harold Withers who swore them in and told them their objectives; they went target shooting in the bush, but didn't need much training. Bolger cleaned and oiled his German Luger, found a hundred rounds of ammunition and bought himself a new saddle from Henry Farrar. He was pleased with his success and since they had got rid of Frank Cameron, things, he thought, were on the up and up.

Bolger was cutting chops when Don Mooney came into the shop.

'That black bugger's gone,' he said.

'How?'

'Through the roof – he got out through the corrugated iron.'

'Jesus, is it your fault?'

'Yeah, he was in my custody; Stark was more resourceful than the last bugger.'

Bolger put his knife down on the chopping block and threw the bones into the bin. 'Not to worry, we'll soon get him – it's hard to hide a black face these days and we've got the men now.'

Mooney was anxious. 'He might have a horse at Cameron's.'

'He'd have to be fucking mad to go back there. Have you told Withers?'

'Yeah.'

'What did he say?'

'Nothing much,' Mooney answered. 'He seemed more concerned with the uprisings.'

'What uprisings?'

'There's apparently been Bolshevik activity in the south – and reports further north. He's had calls on the phone. We're all on alert.'

'Jesus, so it's on then?'

'It looks like it – Bolshies, the Irish, trade unionists.'

'What does Withers want us to do?'

'Move on that mob in the camp, for a start – clean up the district.'

'Good,' Bolger said, 'and we can look for Stark at the same time. That's his hunting ground.'

'We go tomorrow at dawn. Can you get the blokes organized by then?'

'No worries, I'll get on the phone tonight – they're all ready for a scrap. Where's the detective?' Bolger added.

'Gone back to Horsham. He's sure to be on the phone every bloody night: he'll come up and down until we make an arrest, and that could be weeks.'

'Any progress?'

'One thing at a time,' Mooney answered. 'I've got Withers on my back about the raid. I've got this, I've got that. Do you want to stick a broom up my arse so I can sweep the floor?'

Bolger laughed.

As they rode behind Mooney's car in the early dawn, they looked a formidable bunch, with their hats down and shotguns at the ready. The road was deserted, but already some farmers were up, smoke rising from the kitchen chimneys. The new day was grey and the rising sun shone through the clouds of dust. The country was black now.

Mooney stopped his car about a quarter of a mile from the camp and got out as they all gathered around. 'Right,' he said, 'this is a police raid of sorts, but you'll be under the command of Reg – and he's responsible to Mr Withers. We're looking after ourselves now – you all know that. No shooting unless you're attacked.' He laughed. 'And no prisoners – I don't mean kill them, just get the message home they can't camp around Rubicon, that the town's strong and won't be buggered around by Bolshies and riff-raff. We've already lost two buildings, one life and the railway station. We've got every excuse to be tough – if we're not, we'll lose everything we've got and have nothing to pass on to our kids.' He turned to Bolger. 'Do you want to say anything, Reg?'

'No, you've said it all. Just do what I say. Okay?'

'What if someone's wounded?' a man asked. 'What do we do with them?'

'If they can't walk,' Bolger said, 'we'll take them back to town and put them in the paddock behind the police station.' He got back onto his horse. 'Okay, off we go.'

It was the children who saw them first – they ran like rabbits through the dry bush, and by the time Bolger's men were at the camp, the men and women were standing in front of their tents and shanties. Bolger chose the biggest group he could see, rode up and said: 'This camp's illegal – you've ten minutes to pick up your stuff and get out. You can go anywhere, but we don't want to see you here – ever.'

'Who the fuck do you think you are?' a tall man said.

'Mind your language, mister,' Bolger answered. 'We're empowered by Rubicon's Justice of the Peace and the Senior Police Officer. It's all legal. You've got ten minutes.'

'What if we won't go?'

Bolger leaned forward on his horse. 'Then we kick you right up your smelly arse.'

No one moved and a baby started crying. Smoke from the fires rose straight into the still morning air; more men walked over and the children stopped playing. Bolger looked at his watch. 'You've got nine minutes.'

Bolger thought of the last time they had been in this camp: the sullen men, the dirty women and the larrikin children. This, he thought, was where they had seen Stark: they'd get him before long. Everything was organized now, and getting rid of this mob would be easy. No more scum around Rubicon. But they all hung around, and one woman was even boiling water for breakfast. 'You've got eight minutes,' he said.

'Listen mate,' the tall man said, 'you know what you are? You're a fucking fascist gangster – I've seen bastards like you in the coalfields, bashing blokes up and kicking women and children. When the revolution comes, you'll be put up against a wall and shot.'

'You're a Bolshie?' Bolger said.

'That's right, and bloody proud of it. I'm a member of the Communist Party and when the time comes, blokes like you will be the first to go in front of the firing squad.' Then he shouted: 'Long live the revolution!'

Bolger turned his horse round. 'Get that man,' he said. 'He's a fucking traitor to his country.'

Before anyone could dismount, the man produced a switch-blade knife, the blade glinting. 'The first bugger that comes near me,' the tall man said, 'get's it in the face or the throat.'

'Get your horses back,' Bolger shouted, 'we don't want to lose one.'

But the man was fast: he slashed a fetlock, the horse went down, screaming, and the rider toppled.

'Fucking Christ,' Bolger shouted as he pulled the Luger from the holster. The men and women ran for cover and some picked up fence palings and two were carrying pitchforks. Bolger fired his pistol into the air as the man ran for the bush. 'After that bastard,' he said, but the horses and riders milled in the dust and rubbish; the children shouted and the women screamed obscenities. Bolger sat on his horse, irresolute.

Powerless and worried, Mooney watched all this from the running-board of his car. God, he thought, another bloody cock-up. He jumped back into the Ford and drove over through the tents and heaps of rubbish. But by the time he arrived, horses and people were going in all directions. Mooney thought of the fires and the dead child in the first raid. 'Jesus,' he shouted at Bolger, 'get some order and shoot that horse.'

A man took his .303 and shot the animal between the eyes.

'Okay,' Bolger called, 'let's get organized. Come on, you blokes.'

The horseman gathered in the middle of the camp as the people watched them.

'Right,' Mooney said, 'we've lost a horse and that bugger's pissed off. Don't let that worry you – we're armed and they're not. Let's get methodical: I want five groups of four, go round the camp, give them half an hour to get their gear, then after that, pile up all the shit and burn it. But for Christ's sake, be careful and clear a space – the whole place is a tinder box. And look out for the mothers and kids.' Mooney was starting to wonder if all this was worth it, but he gathered himself together. 'We should have them all out by midday.'

'Midday?' Bolger said. 'Much sooner than that.'

The groups moved through the camp and some people started to take their tents down and put their gear in sugar bags. They had been moved on before. Mothers called their children, collected their pots and pans, dowsed the fires and threw their belongings into carts and prams. The wind got up and blew paper and rags over the bare ground as Bolger's men moved through. It was like the morning after a battle.

Like the blacks before them, the unemployed did not belong to regular life: in kitchens and drawing-rooms, in shops, factories and churches. They were a threat to ordinary Australians and had to be driven out; they were not fit to work and were lower than the farm animals. Some of the women wore crucifixes and rosary beads – these were the Sinn Feiners in league with the Bolsheviks and Jews, who were gnawing the heart out of Australia.

By eight o'clock, some families were already trudging up the dirt road to the north, their old bicycles loaded and their dole boots tied up with wire and rope. They would camp in the north by the Murray River and try to get work in the orange and apricot orchards until, once more, they were moved on.

'This is more like it,' Bolger said as he rode with his group. 'We'll get that bastard with the knife – no worries.'

All was quieter now – save for the children crying and the old men coughing and grumbling. The men from Rubicon worked hard, piling the canvas, timber and iron into heaps ready for the torch. But Bolger was wary and kept his eye out for the tall man and any evidence of the fires in Rubicon. Suddenly, a shot rang out and one of his men fell. Everybody shouted and ran for cover.

Mooney found himself shaking, cursed and looked at the man lying in the open. Was he only wounded? He hoped to Christ that was so. He crouched behind his car and looked toward the bush – it couldn't be the man with the knife, but some other bastard and, from the sound of the shot, it was a .303 – certainly not a .22. Then he saw Bolger crawling out from behind a pile of timber, watched, and saw his mate drag the man to safety. Would the man fire again – and what could they do? Were there other men, and was this the start of some kind of general uprising? He thought of Harold Withers – they had lost a horse and now one man was wounded. What would he say?

Another shot rang out, a flight of parakeets left the trees, but this time no one was hit. Christ, Mooney thought, they could be here for bloody hours, pinned down by this marksman. He sure knew how to shoot. The man was in the scrub on the south side of the camp and the only way to get at him was to send some men around the back – or go in the car himself. 'I'm going round,' he shouted to Bolger, 'I'm going round behind him. Do you hear me?'

'Okay. Jack's been hit in the shoulder.'

Mooney took a deep breath, ran round the side of the car, wrenched open the door and jumped in. As he started the motor, a rear window shattered, the glass flew and gashed his left hand. Blood dripping down his arm, Mooney drove toward the road, turned left, found a rough track and took the Ford down as far as he could. He pulled out his revolver and leapt into the dry grass.

His heart pumped – he hadn't used his gun for over a year. Mooney slipped off the safety, cocked it and waited. He remembered his training: let the other bloke move first – the rifleman couldn't stay there forever as he had no food, no transport and little or no water. Mooney looked at his watch and found it was almost nine. The blood on his hand was congealing and the flies crawling; but despite his forty-five years, the beer and the cigarettes, he didn't feel too bad; he tore the sleeve from his shirt and wrapped it around the wound. He would wait until the bastard moved. The sun was already hot and ants dashed over the ground. He'd be patient.

'G'day, copper,' the man said. Mooney jolted and turned and saw a small man with a Lee Enfield .303. He worked the bolt and the gun-barrel gleamed. 'The name's Sniper Donovan: 58th Battalion, 1st A.I.F. I can hit a man in the balls at five hundred yards, no worries. And at a thousand, I can take him in the chest.' He tapped the magazine. 'I've fired three rounds and there's five left, and one for you if you don't do what I say.' He stooped. 'Give me the Smith & Wesson. Nice little weapons, ain't they? But not as good as the Lee.'

Mooney handed over the gun. 'What do you want?' His hands shook.

The man ran his hands through his red hair; he had freckles and the little finger of his right hand was missing. A gold crucifix hung around his neck. 'I'm a timber-worker these days and done me bit for me country. You're no bush-trained copper, are you? Creeping up on you was easy; who's the big bloke who's fucking things up?'

'I don't know what you mean.'

'Come on, copper.' The red-haired man raised the rifle. 'He looks like a slaughter-man.'

Mooney knew he couldn't talk this man out. 'He's Reg Bolger.'

'What does he do? Is he the local carver-upper?'

'He's the butcher, yes.'

'And he's leading the vigilantes?'

'It's a properly constituted law-keeping force.'

Donovan laughed. 'Aw, Jesus, don't feed me that shit.' He fished in his jacket pocket. 'Do you know what this is?'

'It's a Returned Serviceman's badge.'

'Right, copper, just so's you know I'm on the level. I'm one digger who's on the side of the workers, one digger who came home to find cunts like Withers running the place. Here's what I want you to do.'

'What?'

'I want you to go back and call the raid off – I want you to get the carver-upper and his mates off the camp quick-smart. If you don't, I'll get you sooner or later – on a farm when you're serving a summons, in the street when you're leaving the pub, maybe in bed at night – you're never going to know.'

Mooney tried to play for time. 'Do you know a man called Stark?'

'No.'

'Or a man called Cameron?'

'No, that's a common name. Come on, copper, just go back down there and tell your blokes to go home. If you don't, you'll get it in the belly – real low in the dingle-dangles and you'll never know when it might happen. And tell the butcher I might have a go at him if I can't find you.'

Mooney got up, his joints cracking and his mouth dry. 'Okay.'

'Good on you copper. If you don't mind, I'll keep the Smith & Wesson. Remember, it could happen any time and tell your mate.'

Bolger saw the Ford and watched Mooney get out. 'Did you get him?' he asked. 'I didn't hear anything.'

Mooney looked old and grey. 'The raid's off – get the men out, we're going back to town.'

'Why?'

'Because I say so. Jesus, Reg, just get the blokes out.'

Bolger looked at Mooney's belt. 'Where's your gun?'

'For fuck's sake, Reg, get out of here.' Mooney came up close and Bolger saw he was trembling and sweating. 'I'll tell you later,' Mooney said, 'I'll tell you on the way home.'

Thirty-One

They heard someone at the door in the darkness of the early morning. Frank picked up his shotgun, drew the bolt and found Ray standing on the threshold. 'G'day,' Ray said.

Frank pulled him inside, then went out and looked down the track to the road. The sun was coming up over the bush line and the birds were starting to call. When he got back into the kitchen, Ray was lighting the kerosine lamp. 'All clear,' Frank said.

'What's happened to your face?' Ray asked.

'I can take on one or two,' Frank replied, 'but not four.'

'Where was this?'

'Where all the scrapping's done – the Royal. It was Bolger and his mates.'

'What was it about?'

'You.'

'Thanks, mate. I owe you a favour.'

'No you don't – it's all in a good day's work.'

Ray poured water from the pitcher. 'Did you come looking for me. I thought I heard something.'

'I did and got attacked by Mooney's bloody dog.'

'Where's Mrs Hoffmayer?'

Frank pointed to the other room. 'In there.'

'Is she okay?'

'Yes.'

'Any more sign of her old man?'

'Not yet.' Frank lit the stove. 'When did you get out?'

'About three hours ago. That fucking place was getting to me.'

'That's what they wanted.'

'Don't I know. I seen riders on the road – and Mooney's

273

car. All armed: it looked like a lynching.'

'Which way were they going?'

'To the west – there's a camp out that way.'

'Another one of Withers' clean-up operations, I should think,' Frank said. He watched the water boil, threw some leaves in the pot and made a cup of tea for Maria. He went to the door. 'Ray's back.'

'I will get up, then.'

'You can stay where you are.'

'No, I will get up. Put the tea on the table.'

Ray watched Frank with the cup: he was glad that Maria had stayed. 'I'm safe for a bit with all those blokes out there. Jesus, I wouldn't like to be at that camp.'

'I've got to ask you this,' Frank said. 'You weren't involved with those burnings, were you?'

'Nup. That's the truth – there's lots of ways to skin a cat, but burning ain't one of them. Not in my book.'

'But you've got mates in the timber-workers', haven't you?'

'Yeah. They're the only blokes who treat blacks anything like equal.' Ray smiled. 'Except for the odd joker like you.'

'You know that the timber-workers are seen as a menace, that they're Reds and Bolsheviks?'

'I don't know much about politics – except that most of the timber-workers want their rights. All I know is my mob have been driven out by bastards like Withers and Bolger and a bloke's got to take sides. There's good and bad, ain't there?'

'Good morning, Mr Stark,' Maria said. 'I'm glad to se you safe and sound.'

Ray got up from the table. 'Thanks, Mrs Hoffmayer.'

'Right,' Frank said. 'What do we do now?'

'I can get me horse and move on.'

'No,' Frank answered. 'No more running – you stay here.' He knew now that he was besieged: by Julius and Carl Hoffmayer on the one hand and by the men of Rubicon on the other. As he looked out of the window and saw the sun gleaming on the water tank and the blades of the windmill slowly turning, he saw there was also the drought. Only God could do something about that. Frank wondered, too, about the raid on the camp: Ray said he had counted twenty men with Bolger in the lead. Would there be killing? He thought so. All his hopes for himself – and Australia – were being blown away. He thought of the Four Horsemen of the Apocalypse, but stopped: that was being like Julius Hoffmayer.

They came mid-morning – father and son – both with shotguns. They sat on their horses with the sun behind them. 'I have come,' Julius said, 'to take my wife back.'

Frank looked up from the fence and stepped over the coil of barbed wire. 'I've told you before, Mr Hoffmayer, that if your wife prefers to stay here, it's her business.'

Carl looked at Frank's face. 'You have been in a fight, soldier?'

'Nothing I couldn't handle, sonny.' Frank was aware that Maria was in the house and Ray was in the paddock behind the shed. He knew, too, that Ray had his rifle with him. God only knew what young Hoffmayer would do, and he had to get at least one of them off their horse.

'You, Cameron,' Julius said, 'are a fornicator and a wifestealer. On the Judgement Day, you will roast in hell.'

'And you, Mr Hoffmayer, are a bigoted wife-beater.'

'You be careful of what you say to my father, soldier.' Carl raised his shotgun.

'Why don't you get off your horse, sonny?' Frank said. 'Are you scared without the gun?'

Carl looked towards his father, tossed him the shotgun and dismounted. He came across the dusty ground. 'My father, soldier, has come for his wife.'

'That's better, son, you're more like a man now than a boy with a pop-gun.'

'You're going to be sorry, soldier.'

Frank looked at Carl, the cold blue eyes, the sweat on the upper lip and the sand in the blond beard. He knew this young man was a killer and he thought of the dead Louisa. 'Listen, boy,' he said, as he let Carl come close, 'I don't want to fight you – why don't you and your father go back home? It's your stepmother's decision.' Frank's ribs ached and he couldn't let Carl get in the first blow. There were no rules in this game. He thought of the coil of barbed wire – better bloodied hands than another cracked rib.

'Stepmother belongs to my father.'

'No one belongs to anyone, son.'

'You will not call me that, you bastard.'

Frank seized the wire and threw it over Carl's head; the barbs bit his face and neck and the boy gasped and screamed. As Frank saw Julius raise his gun, he heard Ray's voice from behind. 'I wouldn't do that if I was you, Mr Hoffmayer.'

Julius could do nothing. As he turned and faced Ray, he saw his wife standing at the door. 'You should go, Julius Hoffmayer,' she said. 'Go back to your lost tribe; there is nothing for you here.'

Frank picked up the wire-cutters and stood over Carl. 'You better keep still.'

'You are a dead man, soldier.'

'Not at the moment – you're the stuck pig.' He used the handle of the cutters and turned the wire into Carl's face and throat. 'The next time you come on to my place, leave your guns at the gate.' He pulled the boy to his feet and began to cut. When the boy was free, Frank pushed him over to the water trough. 'Clean yourself up,' he said, 'and join your father.'

His hands bleeding, Frank went over to Julius. 'These may be bad times for us all, Mr Hoffmayer, but Maria left you – *you* drove her out. I'm afraid I've got to take that fancy German shotgun off you. The best thing you can do is to go back, work your farm and grieve for your daughter – and hunt for her killer – if you want to.'

'What do you mean by that?'

'I mean you may not want to know who killed your daughter, and if that's the case, it's your business. I know you couldn't give a damn about anything outside your farm, but there's no law now in Rubicon – except that made by Harold Withers.'

'The money-lender.'

'That's right, the money-lender, whose father almost took your property. It's anarchy now, but I don't see why you and I should add to it.'

'I am an agent of God, Mr Cameron.'

'You, Julius, are nothing,' Maria said. 'Once you had dignity, now you have none. Go back and think about that. You have lost me forever, and if you cannot control Carl, you may lose him, too.'

'I will see the policeman, Mooney – he will order you to return.'

'I don't think so, Julius,' Maria replied. 'As you have said: there is only one law and that is God's.'

Julius and his son rode toward the gate, the sun in their eyes and the dust rising from their horses' feet. They had both failed and it was going to be a long ride home.

'I am going to kill the soldier,' Carl said. The flies swarmed around the blood on his face and neck and he brushed them away. He looked at his father, who was sitting forward on his saddle, his beard grey and his shoulders hunched. 'That shotgun has been in our family for twenty years and I will take it back. He will pay for his immorality, his disgusting crimes, his fornication. The curse of God will be upon him.'

'Cameron is a stronger man than I thought,' Julius said, as he rode through the gravel, his black hat pulled down over his face. 'Maybe he will beat the money-lenders.'

'He is evil and corrupt and I will kill him. He has taken your wife. Have you not taught me, Father, that corruption must be extirpated?'

'That I have.' Julius stared into the bush. 'I wonder,' he said, 'what Cameron knows about the death of Louisa?'

'What should he know?'

'He knows a lot, he is a very resourceful man. He is not like the others.'

'That, he is not. He employs a savage; he steals a wife; that

277

man was responsible for the death of thousands of German boys.'

'Those days are over,' Julius replied.

'They are not – an eye for an eye, a tooth for a tooth.'

Julius stopped his horse, but did not look at his son. 'Do you think,' he asked, 'that Louisa was evil, that there is bad blood in us?'

'I think she was evil, but she has gone – it was God's will. Again, you have taught me that.'

'What *was* God's will?' Julius asked himself.

'I love you, Father.' Carl's voice was low in the evening breeze. 'I would do anything for you.'

But Julius once again remembered his Martin Luther: *It is love that makes us slaves.* Now he belonged to Carl.

Thirty-Two

It was the worst day Harold Withers could remember. While Mooney and Bolger were mounting the raid at the camp, the bank manager in Melbourne phoned to say they could give him no more accommodation and that he'd have to clear the overdraft within seven days. Withers had known the manager for fifteen years, but it soon became obvious from his voice that the days of trading on the friendship were over. The bank, too, was fighting for its life: there was yet another panic run on deposits; queues were forming at the doors at seven in the morning and there were violent scenes each day at the Stock Exchange as stocks and shares tumbled. It seemed that the market was bottomless and the exchanges in London and New York were a shambles. On top of that, Melbourne was rife with rumours of an insurrection; the government was on the point of declaring martial law; there was disaffection in the ranks of Melbourne dockside. All over the world, people were panicking and in Germany the value of the Deutsche-mark was so low that people were taking their money from the banks in wheelbarrows.

The manager's voice was grim and low: he had no advice to give Withers – except to try to realize his assets; but it was obvious that the customers for drought-ridden properties, and buildings in a bankrupt town, were few and far between. At last, Withers had to admit the truth to himself: Rubicon was no longer a place to invest in. When he went over Federation Street to the bank, Withers was told he had the princely sum of £43.3s.2d in his current account; and on his way back to the emporium, he was almost knocked down by a horse and cart.

For the first occasion he could remember, this time of the

279

morning, Withers poured himself a large Scotch, and considered what to do. He could call in no more money as his
debtors were bankrupt and evictions were pointless and
dangerous – the farmers, he had heard, were turning up with
shotguns, or block-bidding at auctions. In the face of the
banks and loan companies, they were starting to hold fast.
For Withers now, it had suddenly become a matter of personal
survival. As he drank, he thought of Frank Cameron: *One day,
Withers, you'll be where you belong – in the gutter with the
poor bastards you've driven there.* Since the Depression had
started, had anyone, he wondered, actually died of starvation?
He thought of selling the Hupmobile, until he realized it was
on hire-purchase and no one could afford to buy the petrol
to run it. Withers had a second and third Scotch, and found
himself starting to shake. Suddenly, his future was terrifying.
He couldn't even live off the food and clothe himself from
the Emporium as it and all the stock was mortgaged to the
bank. As he sat at his desk he dug his fingernails into his head
and drew blood.

Mooney and Bolger knocked at the door shortly after one
o'clock and Withers could see by their faces that something
had gone wrong. Mooney noticed the half-empty bottle of
Scotch on the table, but didn't remark on it.

'Well,' Withers said, 'you're back early. Was it a success?'
When he hid his hands under the desk, he saw smudges of
blood on the blotter.

Mooney, for once, came straight to the point. 'We lost a
horse, a man was wounded and the people are still in the
camp.'

'Tell me,' Withers said, his heart thumping, 'tell me.'

And Mooney did.

When Mooney was finished, Withers said: 'The sniper's
Irish, of course? He's one of the tribe.'

'If that's his real name. Who knows who he is? If you ask
me, none of us are safe.'

'For Christ sake, Don,' Bolger said as he looked at the
bottle of Scotch and Withers behind his desk, 'one fucking

shit of a traitor can't do this to us. One fucking Donovan can't do this to us. Let's ring up your pal, Broadbent, and get reinforcements.'

'We're on our own, it's self-help – remember? And it doesn't matter a damn if the sniper's Irish, Jewish, Russian or a defrocked Freemason, does it?' Mooney paused. 'He was an Australian, one of us.'

'It's civil war, then,' Withers said.

'I don't think one man with a Lee Enfield in the bush means civil war,' Mooney replied. He thought of the children and the old people in the camp.

'Any sign of Stark?' Withers asked. 'And what's happening about the murder?'

Mooney controlled himself. 'It's Broadbent's case – so you said.'

Withers wanted yet another Scotch. 'It may be best if we all stay in town,' he said.

'You must be joking.' Bolger shifted in his chair. 'What kind of stuff are we made of in Rubicon? We can't hide in our kitchens like bloody women.'

'What if there are more Sniper Donovans out there?' Withers thought of his debts. Was this the end?

'Are you all right?' Mooney asked.

'Just a headache, Don. It's this blasted weather.'

'Do I have your permission to take out the men and find this bastard – and Stark?' Bolger asked Withers.

The businessman looked up, his hands trembling, 'You have my permission, Reg, to do anything. I think that extreme measures are called for now.'

When Mooney got back to his office, he found that the wound on his dog's head was festering, the phone was ringing and the room was full of blowflies. His guts ached and he was starving. It was Broadbent on the telephone. 'What progress?' the detective asked. The line was uncertain and the voice thin.

'What?'

'I said: any progress?'

For the first time in his life, Mooney stood up to his superiors. 'It's your fucking case,' he said. 'Not mine.'

'Hey, hey, boy,' Broadbent's voice said, 'remember who you're talking to.'

When Mooney was about to tell him about the armed man in the bush, the line went dead. Bloody Jesus Christ, he said to himself, and went outside into the hot wind to inspect the dog. The wound looked bad and, as he went to touch it, the dog snarled and bit him on the hand. Mooney cursed and thought of Frank Cameron. There was nothing to it but to go to the Royal, have a feed and a few beers.

By six that evening, they were all roaring drunk, Mooney included.

'Why should we be cooped up by bloody rabble?' Bolger was saying. 'Why should we? We got the men and we got the guns. I fought for a better country, and by Christ, I'm going to get it. We should go out and round up every bloody Mick, every bloody Sinn Feiner, every bloody Hun and Jew, every bloody nigger, and put them behind bars. This is a white man's country – I'd get that bloody sniper's balls and use them for paperweights. If he's got any – and that's doubtful.'

But through the beer and whisky, Mooney thought of the sniper: *Remember – it could happen any time.* 'That was a dangerous man, Reg.' He remembered the crucifix around the man's neck.

'Dangerous? My arse, he was all piss and wind. With a name like that, he was a fucking Catholic – their first allegiance is to the Pope. You'd never trust a Catholic in my outfit: when the Huns came, those that were there turned and ran back to Ireland. They're full of spuds, and shit in the bath – they don't know what it's for. And they breed like rabbits; they're too tired from fucking to fight. If we're not careful, they'll outbreed us – Irish tarts have got cunts the size of buckets. They betrayed us in the war.'

Mooney, for the second time today, had had enough. 'I'm a Catholic, Reg.'

Bolger laughed. 'You're no Mick, you haven't been to Mass for thirty years, you've told me. You'll go to – what do they call it? – limbo. That's where you'll go. You're one of us now. You're no fucking Catholic, you're lapsed. You've got troubles with the Pope, but don't let that worry you.'

Mooney pulled himself together and went home. When he finally crawled into bed, he wanted to say the Rosary, but found he had forgotten the words.

In the bar of the Royal, Bolger told the company he had Withers' permission to do whatever he liked, and by the time the evening's drinking had ended, he had the names of fifty more men who would scour the shit out of Rubicon forever – and that included the Huns and that turn-coat bastard, Cameron. They would mount an expedition in the next couple of days. At midnight, they all raised their glasses: God, the King and the white men of Australia were all on their side.

Alone in his dark house, overlooking the barren wheatfields, Harold Withers moved from room to room. Although he had stopped drinking, his stomach felt sour, and he went to the refrigerator and poured himself out a glass of iced water from the pitcher. Then he went to the front door, stood on the wide verandah and looked at the moon. *La Compagnia*, his country: it was a desert now. He suddenly remembered a poem he had learnt at school:

> *My name is Ozymandias, King of Kings:*
> *Look upon my works, ye Mighty and despair!"*
> *Nothing beside remains. Round the decay*
> *Of that colossal wreck, boundless and bare,*
> *The lone and level sands stretch far away.*

Pigeons warbled in the eaves and the gazebo stood, ghost-like, in the garden. His wife had never liked Rubicon, and maybe she was right; his marriage had been as unproductive as the wheatfields. The moon was bright and he walked down the brick path, over the lawn past the tennis court and looked at his house. The bank owned it now. Then he went into the garage and looked at the Hupmobile – at least he could pay George, the chauffeur. He had seven children, an ailing wife and had been utterly reliable. That was one thing he could do. He laughed: the only debt he would pay was to a blacksmith's son who had never learned his father's trade.

Withers sat at the bureau, took out an envelope, wrote the address, folded a £5 note and placed it inside. Then he walked through the rooms as though he were in an art gallery: the rosewood table, the ten dining chairs, the Bavarian crystal, the grand piano, the library of books he had never read, *A Child's Book of England* by Arthur Mee, the thirteen volumes of the *Encyclopaedia Britannica*. He sat on the leather couch and looked at the porcelain electric light fittings, the parquet floors, and listened to the wind as it whispered around the verandah posts. This house was no longer his – he was the tenant now. For weeks, he had been reading the stories of the bankers standing on the window ledges of buildings in Wall Street. Having no money, he realized, was worse than death.

Withers rose, went into the billiard room and opened the gun cupboard. Dead moths lay on the baize of the table and he noticed that one of the cues had not been put back in the rack. When was the last game? And whom had it been with? In the gun cupboard were rifles – a BSA, a Remington, a Springfield, a brace of English duelling pistols and a Purdey shotgun which his father had owned. He remembered his father teaching him how to shoot at the lake – they had brought down many wildfowl and water birds. The lake had been full then, and they had gone shooting at dawn when the geese took off from the clear, cold water. He remembered his father talking to August Hoffmayer, the two men discussing business as they lay on a rug on the beach while the children played among the trees and ferns as the smoke from the picnic fires rose into the clear, blue sky. Like this house, the lake was worthless now.

With great care, Withers took the shotgun from the rack, broke it open, found the cartridges in the brass-handled drawer beneath, loaded both barrels and snapped the gun shut. He ran his fingernails down the ornate carvings of the stock and felt the coldness of the breech and the barrels. He walked back into the dining-room, put the gun down, lifted the carpet and found the ring-bolt of the trapdoor to the room below. This was the refuge from dust storms – and now other things. He found the light switch, turned it on, pulled the trapdoor over, locked it and went down the steep stairs. The underground room smelt of dust and, as he moved, it rose in clouds around him. Withers chose a high-backed chair, sat down, took off his shoes and socks, pulled back both hammers of the Purdey, put the double-barrel in his mouth and with his big toe depressed the triggers. The gun-shot rumbled with the thunder over the bush of Rubicon.

In the Royal Hotel, the glasses sat on the bar counter, unwashed, and in the dry country and the vast plains beyond, the vagrants slept uncertainly in their tents and cardboard shanties as the crows waited for the pickings of the morning.

Thirty-Three

'I think I know who killed your stepdaughter,' Ray said.

'Who is it?' Maria asked. But she knew the answer. They all did.

'That boy, Carl.'

'What do you think, Frank?'

'I think,' he said to her, 'that Ray's right.'

'Is there anything we should do?'

'No,' Frank replied, 'I don't think so. We've got no evidence: it's a matter for Mooney – and Broadbent, wherever he is.' He looked at Maria: 'Do you think Carl's father knows?'

'Yes. That is no ordinary father and son. Carl will never forgive you for disgracing him.' Maria thought. 'For as long as I can remember, he was sharpening knives and slashers, oiling guns, breaking rabbits' backs, beating horses. For Carl, killing a pig was a kind of sacrifice. If such young men are allowed to roam free in Germany, God help the Old Country.' She thought of Uncle Ernst and the opera playing on the phonograph: when all this was over, she would leave and go to Paris and Berlin and walk along the tree-lined boulevards she had seen in the postcards. There would be no more work, no more violence, no more ploughing, no more the silence of the bush. Would Frank leave, too? He had seen the old European churches and buildings. She had never seen the sea; she had never bought new clothes and she had never seen leaves falling in the autumn. Maria left the table, stood at the door and gazed at the dark horizon. There was no health in this place.

Frank wondered what had happened at the unemployeds' camp and whether he should try and find out. Had there been a killing? Of two things, he was sure: Mooney would come, looking for Ray, and Carl would return. He picked up his shotgun and moved to the door. 'I'm going to be out for a bit,' he said. 'And I'm taking the truck.'

Ray stood on the step. 'You be careful,' he said.

'I'll do that. What do you think happened at the camp?'

'If that was where they were going.' Ray put his hand on Frank's arm. 'Look, you know as well as me that there's men with guns all over the district – and some of them are bloody good shots. There's real hard jokers in the unions and the unemployeds and they're sick of being driven around, like I'm sick of being driven around, and you ain't popular with Bolger and Mooney and Withers and the rest. This is a kind of war. So be careful – that's all I'm telling you.'

As Maria came and stood beside Ray, Frank took her by the waist and kissed her. 'I'm not as good as my stepson with a rifle,' she said, 'but I know what to do.'

Frank held her hard. 'I'll be a couple of hours.' He walked over to the truck, climbed in and drove down the track to the Kurnbrun road.

When he saw the dust, Frank slowed, then stopped and let the riders come toward him. He looked at his watch and saw it was coming up to eleven o'clock. As they came, he thought he counted about fifty men, all on horses. Then he saw Bolger in the lead, riding a big brown gelding: some of the men he recognized from the bar of the Royal, and some he did not. They looked a wild lot – Frank thought of the rabble in the bull-ring in the army camps in France. They were the scum of the country towns and the cities: they were the men who thieved off the local farmers, took their daughters, brawled in estaminets, roved in packs like animals, refused to salute officers; but when it came to it, did not have the courage to obey the whistle and go over the top.

When the pack saw the truck, they stopped, then came on with Bolger out in front. Frank opened the cab door, stood with one foot on the running-board and looked at the country on either side of the road. It was shallow and undulating like the countryside in Belgium and northern France. It was barren and empty; the thistles blew and the sun climbed overhead in the dusty sky.

'Well, well,' Bolger said, 'if it ain't Mr Frank Cameron.'

The riders stopped, the horses sneezed and snorted and the flies buzzed and crawled. Frank glanced at his shotgun on the seat of the truck and saw the sun was still in Bolger's eyes – but not for long. 'Are you boys going on a picnic?' he said.

'Boys?' Bolger said from his horse. 'We ain't boys, Cameron, we're men.'

'Are you *men* on a picnic?' But when they started to laugh, Frank knew he had made a mistake – he recognized the faces of the veterans: the men who, like him, had fought hard and had come home to nothing.

'You're no officer now, mister,' someone said, 'you're a battler like the rest of us.'

Bolger leaned forward. 'We're going to clean the shit out of the system; we were fired on yesterday by some Irish Bolshie cunt and we're going to find him and string him up. Then we're going to make this place fit for hard-working white men. The war's on, mate – do you want Australia ruled by Sinn Feiners and Bolshies? Or do you want to join us?'

'Where's Mooney?' Frank said.

'Don's got other fish to fry,' Bolger answered. 'The murder of the Hun girl – what was her name? Louisa Hoffmayer? She's got a good-looking mother, so I hear. And we're looking for an escaped abo, called Stark. We're going right past your place and we thought we'd call in. You don't happen to know him, do you?'

Frank looked at the hard faces. Why weren't these men building fences and working on their farms? But as he looked at the dry land, he saw there was nothing to work for: there was nothing profitable to do, except to hunt down what they thought was the enemy and make him pay for the drought and the depression. Was this, he wondered, happening all over Australia? As he gazed at Bolger, he knew that he, too, was part of some terrible puzzle – as his father had been, and the Hoffmayers, the people of Rubicon, the government, the bankers and businessmen like Harold Withers.

'You'd better shift your truck, mate,' someone else said, 'we've got work to do.'

But Bolger got off his horse and came over, his boots crunching in the gravel. 'Have you hurt your face, Cameron? Did someone have a go at you?'

Frank stood his ground. 'Last time,' he said, 'it was four, now it's fifty. Under all that beef, you're a gutless shit.'

'Don't worry, mate, my men will do as they're told – I'm the officer now and you're the fucking traitor. You're the bloke who employs niggers, fucks neighbours' wives and who won't help his fellow countrymen. It was a bad day for Rubicon when you came in – but don't worry, Cameron, it's one-to-one now.' Bolger came up close. 'I'll let the cripple have first go.'

'Okay, then.' Frank kicked Bolger in the ankle and, as he fell, struck him in the belly. But Bolger was all muscle from years in country slaughter-houses. He grunted, got up from the dirt and hit Frank in the face, then hit him again between the eyes and kicked him as he staggered on the stones of the Kurnbrun road. The men sat on their horses and watched: they wanted the officer to be beaten. They, too, remembered the commands of the bull-ring, the endless days of marching and their mates tied to the punishment cross for insubordination.

'Come on, Reg, get the bastard,' a man shouted. 'Get him.'

It was like a bloody, prize-fighting film – Frank struck Bolger in the mouth; Bolger came in close, his fists working on Frank's chest and heart; the men watched, shouted and cheered: it was the War again. And Bolger knew where to get Frank: in his ribs – they were cracked, one could pierce his lungs and he would have this bastard beaten. But Frank, too, was strong: he struck Bolger's nose, smashed his cheekbones, feinted like a boxer, hit him in the throat and stepped back, then tripped and fell – the butcher stood as big as a church, his bulk as dark as any building. Bolger stood and laughed as the men cheered and smoked their cigarettes. It was all over now.

Bolger spat blood and wiped his face with his sleeve as he put his boot on Frank's chest. 'One move from you, digger, and your brains will be all over the road. I ought to kill you now, but there's too many witnesses – I can't trust all these bastards. Later on is the time, when we're alone and no bugger's ever going to know. We're going to get that nigger, then we're going to burn that camp down. It's all legal – I've got the authority.' Bolger turned. 'Right, you blokes, I want two of you.'

As two men came up and held Frank, Bolger struck him on the point of the jaw and he collapsed. 'Okay,' Bolger said, 'chuck him in the ditch.'

'What about the truck?'

'Take the bugger's shotgun, then set fire to it.'

One of the men rummaged in the back of the Chevrolet, found a piece of cotton waste, stuffed it down the fuel pipe and set it alight. Within minutes, the truck was ablaze; then it exploded. As Bolger got back on his horse, he called: 'The hunt's on – let's get that black boy.'

When Ray heard the sound of horses' hooves, and not Frank's truck, he knew what to expect. He ran inside, picked up his rifle and a box of cartridges, and went round to the back of the house. 'There's horsemen coming,' he said to Maria, 'and I've got the feeling they're after me. Do you want me to stay here with you?'

'For God's sake, Ray, you go, you go. I can look after myself.'

'You sure?'

'Yes.'

'Okay. I'll see you later. Hope Frank's all right.'

Ray ran up the track, vaulted the post-and-rail fence and disappeared into the darkness of the pine trees.

Maria stood by the windmill and waited as the riders came up. Some of them were drinking from whisky bottles and others were curious to see the German woman whose daughter had been carved up and who had left her husband. This had never happened in Rubicon before: Maria Hoffmayer was a slut – she was a threat to all their families, and to the good name of the town. Wives did not leave husbands. But as Maria stood, arms folded, the men fell silent.

'My name is Bolger,' the big man said.

'I know that.'

'We're looking for an abo.'

Maria looked at the man's cut face. Had he been fighting – and where was Frank? 'There is no one here,' she said. 'I am alone.'

Bolger dismounted. 'We're going to have a look around.'

'Do you have permission?'

'Permission?' Bolger laughed. 'You mean a warrant? We don't need no warrant, lady. We're the law.' He turned back to the men. 'I want you blokes to give this place a real going-over. We'll find the bastard.'

As she followed Bolger and two other men into the house, Maria decided not to ask about Frank. Bolger stood in the centre of the kitchen. 'A neat little place,' he said. 'Small, but neat. Where do you sleep?' He grinned.

'You mind your own business.'

One of the men put his whisky bottle on the table. 'Come on, love, everyone knows you're shacked up with Cameron.'

Bolger stared at Maria. Jesus, he thought. I wouldn't mind having a go at that. She was a good-looking tart. Then he saw a tobacco tin on the shelf and picked it up. It was Log Cabin cut-plug. He grinned again. 'Do you smoke?'

'No.'

'No, I don't reckon you do. Only dagos smoke this shit. They roll it in double papers, don't they?'

'I don't know what you're talking about.'

Bolger came up close. 'Listen, you Hun bitch, you're in deep trouble – I know Stark's been here and you're living with a traitor. Stark's wanted for murder and arson – Christ, he probably killed your daughter, and you're protecting him. It's all beyond me.' He put his hand on her shoulder. 'All the same, I can't blame Cameron.'

'Take your hand off me.'

'Come on, lady.' Bolger held her by the arm. 'You're a strong one, aren't you? Jesus.'

Maria broke free and dragged her fingernails down the side of Bolger's face. 'Get out, you pig.'

He stepped back and raised his fist. 'I ought to do to you what I did to your fancy man.' He stuffed the tobacco tin into his waistcoat pocket and went outside.

Bolger's men were thorough. They searched the barn, combed the bush, then spread out through the pines and over the paddocks. Their horses were strong and fast and the riders knew every track on Frank's property.

From his hiding-place behind a pile of timber on a rise, Ray could hear the sound of the horses' hooves; then he saw the dust and listened to the hoarse shouts, echoing.

These white bastards, he thought, were fucking mad. But, by Jesus, he'd give them a go when they found him. He looked down the slope and saw a bunch of men go into the half-cleared bush. With any luck, the rest might follow, then he could slip away. As he crouched on the straw, Ray wondered what Frank was doing. Had the buggers got him? Christ, it seemed he'd spent all his life on the run.

Ray knew a timber-worker who had been to America for the I.W.W. He remembered the joker well – a little Irish bloke with red hair, who was a crack shot and who had fought in the war. This Irishman had been to the South with a famous American labour leader and seen the Ku Klux Klan at work. Ray had never forgotten the story. The whitefellows had caught a nigger, sliced his cock and balls off, stuffed them in his mouth and then hung him from a tree. Would Australian white blokes do that? Bolger would, but maybe the other men would stop him. Frank Cameron – he was the bloke who would put an end to all this.

Then Ray saw three riders coming up the incline. He flicked off the safety and raised his rifle: they were an easy target. Although the Martini was an old gun, he could probably get two of them, at least. The riders stopped, then came forward, the dust rising from the stubble. Ray now had them in his sights, curled his finger around the trigger and took aim. Jesus, he thought, all the fucking around, all the running, all the beatings, God damn the Moravians, God damn the white bastards. But what was the point? If he killed these blokes, the others would come and they'd get him for murder. He remembered his father: *Don't let them get nothing on you, son.*

Ray stood up, tossed his rifle down and waited, as tall and as strong as a tree.

'Well, well,' the leading man said, 'if it ain't our black friend.' He turned to his mates. 'They're all the same – no guts.'

They laughed, dismounted and one of them produced a reel of fencing wire from his saddlebag. 'Don't worry, me little black cobber,' he said as he tied Ray's hands behind his back, 'we're just going to have some fun with you.'

Bolger was the last to leave. He raised his hat to Maria as she stood by the door. 'Like the Mounties,' he said, 'we always get our man. And your lover-boy's going to need some patching up when he gets back.'

As Maria watched the men go, she heard Bolger shout: 'Okay, you blokes, now for the camp.'

All she could do was wait.

Thirty-Four

Mooney phoned Harold Withers a second time, listened to the ringing, waited, then put the receiver down. He looked at his watch: it was odd for Withers not to be out and about this time of the morning. Maybe he had gone to the emporium. Mooney then phoned the office and a woman's voice told him that Mr Withers had not come in yet. He could have gone unexpectedly to Melbourne, or south, about some money matter.

Mooney lit the gas and put the kettle on for a cup of tea. Then he opened the office filing cabinet, looked at the half-empty bottle of whisky, found the biscuit tin and ate. His mouth was dry and the crackers stuck to his teeth and gums. He reached for his cigarettes, found he had run out and tossed the empty packet in the waste bin. The Louisa Hoffmayer file was lying on the desk; he opened it and looked at the records of interview. He thought of Ray Stark and wondered if they'd ever get him. Was he worth getting? Should he tell Broadbent? No, he would not – it was CIB's fucking case. Jesus, he thought, I'm getting tired. What a bloody mess. He seemed powerless now: events had overtaken him – the murder, the fires, the secret army, the sniper, the evictions, the drought. He now realized he shouldn't have been a party to beating up Frank Cameron. At least he was the one man who seemed to know what he was doing and what was going on in Rubicon.

Mooney rummaged through all the desk drawers for some cigarettes and, in a tobacco tin, he found a crucifix and beads. What were they doing there? He thought of Bolger last night: *You're no fucking Catholic, you're lapsed*, and he found himself suddenly weighed down with guilt. Should he go to

Confession? He didn't have the guts to sit in the box and talk to the priest. Mooney couldn't remember when he had last been to Mass – it was probably in some dreary suburban church in Melbourne. His wife was the devout one, and he didn't even know where she was living. Worse still, Mooney was an Irish Catholic, whether he liked it or not, and he was helping to chuck his own kind off their farms. Despite the sniper who called himself Donovan, Mooney knew that an Irish rebellion was bullshit. When the kettle whistled, Mooney made the tea, drank it down quickly, slipped the beads into his tunic pocket and went out to see Reg Bolger.

The butchery was closed; Mooney stood on the pavement for a minute, then went in next door to the barber's. Mooney bought two packets of cigarettes. 'Where's Reg?' he asked.

'Don't you know?' the barber replied.

Mooney lit up and inhaled. 'If I knew, I wouldn't be asking.'

'Him and the boys have gone on a raid.'

'What?'

'I said: him and the boys have gone on a raid.'

'Where?'

'Out near Netherby. I'd have gone, too, if it wasn't for me back. Those vagrant bastards deserve all they get.'

Mooney looked at his watch. It was almost half past one; he cursed himself for having slept in. He thought of the man with the Lee Enfield. What was Bolger doing? Why hadn't he been told? How could Reg have got the men so quickly? He could have picked them up on the way out. Most of the blokes had nothing to do these days. Jesus, this had all the makings of a bloody catastrophe. He remembered Broadbent: *Our job is to prevent homicides, Constable Mooney,* and Withers had given Bolger authority to do practically anything. He ran from the shop, got into the Ford and looked in the glove box for his revolver. It was not there. Mooney cursed again, drove back to his office, found the spare Smith & Wesson, tossed his shotgun in the back and headed up Federation Street, past the station and the blackened wheat sheds, for Netherby. After fifteen minutes, he realized he had forgotten to bring some extra shells for the shotgun, but it was too late to go back now. As he drove through the dust, Mooney found himself glad he had discovered the crucifix.

Mooney saw a truck burning in the middle of the road, and when he slowed down, there was a man sitting in the dry grass on the edge of the gravel. It was Frank Cameron. When Mooney had wound the window down, he said: 'G'day, what's happened?'

Frank looked at the policeman. 'It's your mate, Bolger, and about fifty men on their way to the unemployeds' camp; they burned my truck and went on to my place, looking for Ray Stark. What are you going to do about it?'

'Arson's an offence, Cameron. Is Stark on your property?'

Frank thought. 'He was.'

Mooney looked at the cuts and swellings on Frank's face. 'Have you been in a fight?'

'Yes.'

'Assault's an offence, too, isn't it? You'd better get in.'

Frank hesitated. 'I can get home.'

'Get in, Cameron.'

When he saw the revolver and the shotgun, Frank said: 'What's up?'

'I think you know, Cameron. The raid on the camp is fucking madness.'

'You've changed your mind, then?'

Mooney looked at Frank as he drove. 'Yeah, I've changed my bloody mind. It's law that holds us together, not anarchy. And I'm the law.'

'Stark's innocent.'

'Maybe. We'll call in at your place, okay?'

'For Ray?'

'No, he's probably gone by now. You've got a rifle?'

'I have.'

'Do you want to come to the camp with me?'

'Why?'

'To get some order out of this fucking mess. Look, Cameron,

you and I haven't exactly hit it off; you don't like me and I don't like you, but I'm sick of all the violence and the evictions. This is not the Australian way, is it? You were an officer – maybe you can get some sense into these crazy buggers.'

'What about Ray Stark?'

'He'll be treated fairly – I'll give you my word on that.'

'Why the turnabout?'

'For Christ's sake, Cameron, I've told you. There's no future in all this, is there?'

'No,' Frank replied as they bumped down the track to his house, 'there is not.'

When Maria saw Frank and Mooney getting out of the Ford, she stood still, then came forward. 'Men have been here,' she said.

'I know. Where's Ray?'

'He's not here.'

Frank took her hand. 'It's okay, you can talk in front of Mr Mooney.'

'They found him and took him away.'

'To a camp?' Mooney asked.

'Yes.'

'Right,' Frank said to Maria. 'Mr Mooney and I are going to the camp and I want you to stay here.'

'What is happening?'

'Killing,' Mooney answered, 'lynching, Christ knows what. We're going to try and stop it.'

Maria followed Frank into the house. 'Where is the truck?'

'Burnt. I met Bolger and his men on the road. Our friend, Mooney, has seen the light.' Frank took her by the shoulders. 'Maria Hoffmayer, you're all I've got, so you be here when I get back.'

'I will. Has Mr Mooney asked about Louisa?'

'No, and I've not mentioned it.' Frank raised the cellar trapdoor, went down the steps and came back with his rifle and a shotgun. Then he opened the drawer of the dresser, found a box of cartridges and tipped them into his pocket.

He gave Maria the shotgun. 'I'll be back by nightfall.'

'I will be here, safe and sound.'

'Stay inside.'

'I know what to do.'

Frank smiled. 'Yes, I know you do.'

Through the trees of the bush, Frank and Mooney saw smoke rising and then they heard the sound of men shouting. There was, thank God, no sound of gunfire. But the camp was a shambles. They found a dead dog on the side of the road; an old man was trudging up the track, his face cut and bleeding; tents and shanties were ablaze; children were crying and screaming; women were sitting on the earth, sobbing; and then they saw a group of men standing around a man sitting on a horse; he was tied to a rope, hanging over the branch of a tree. It was Ray Stark. 'Jesus Christ,' Mooney said. 'Jesus Christ.'

Mooney sounded the horn and drove down to the group as Frank grabbed his rifle. 'Careful, Cameron,' Mooney said. 'Let me handle this.'

Bolger and his men turned and looked as Mooney and Frank got out of the Ford.

'G'day,' Bolger said. 'So you've got Cameron as well?' He laughed. 'This calls for a drink.' The man was drunk. 'The bastard tried to kill me – you can get him on that.'

'What the fuck are you doing?' Mooney said.

'We're doing what I was told to do: we're cleaning up this camp, and we're having fun.'

Ray looked at Frank and raised a smile. 'G'day,' he said. 'This won't take long,' Frank replied. He looked at Bolger with the bottle and the men standing around, wearing their slouch hats, dirty waistcoats and patched moleskins. These were the dregs of the country, he thought. But for the grace of God, he could be one of them. He thought of his father, old and grey. *You're not in the army now, son.* Ray, on the horse, his black face and curly hair, looked part of the country, and the white men did not. This mob weren't hanging a blackfellow – they were hanging themselves. They were doing to Ray what they were doing to the land.

Ray's voice was as soft as when Frank had first met him in the tin house. 'I reckon these blokes don't know what they're doing.'

Mooney went over to Bolger. 'Get that man down off the horse.' 'Man?' Bolger said. 'That ain't no man. He's been burning and raping, he's in league with the Bolshies, he's nothing but trouble, he's part of all this shit here. You and me's seen him.' Then Bolger saw Frank was carrying a rifle. 'What's he armed for?'

Mooney raised his voice. 'I said, get that man down.' The men of Rubicon watched all this and shifted their feet among the empty beer bottles and debris. The vagrants stared.

'String him up,' someone shouted. 'The darkies take our jobs.' Mooney made one last try, for old time's sake. 'Look, Reg, get Stark down and get out of this camp. You're breaking the law, there's no point in this.'

'Breaking the law? You ought to talk – Jesus, you're part of all this, you're one of us. Don't give me that shit.' Bolger squinted at Frank. 'Don't tell me you and Cameron have teamed up. Christ, I was right – once a Catholic, always a Catholic; once an officer, always an officer.' He came up to Frank. 'When this is done, I'm going to kill you: we don't like men who fuck other blokes' wives in Rubicon. And we don't like men who protect nigger traitors.' Bolger threw the bottle down. 'Mooney,' he shouted. 'What kind of a name is that? A turn-coat, a Sinn Feiner in uniform, you can't trust any bastard.' He turned. 'This is the real stuff boys, let's top the bugger. This cop and this officer can't touch us. We make the rules – this is our country.' Bolger grabbed a riding crop and moved toward the horse.

There was one shot only, from a military rifle, and the bullet struck Bolger, dead-centre, in the groin. The big man screamed, jerked, then collapsed, the blood running through his fingers as he clutched himself, and then down his trousers as red as a summer rose. As he lay in the rubbish and filth of the camp, Bolger screamed again, then writhed and groaned as his entrails pumped from the wound between his legs. Ray turned his face away and found himself praying. He had never seen any man die in this way.

As the people of the camp fell flat, the men of Rubicon shouted and scattered like animals in a slaughter-yard and ran for cover. This was the uprising. They cocked their guns and squinted as they cursed and shook. But in the dusty afternoon sun, there was nothing to shoot at: no target, no revolutionary army in the shallow folds of the deserted landscape – nothing, save the crows and parakeets once more settling on the fenceposts and the branches of the ancient trees.

When he saw Bolger fall, Frank knew the next shot was not for him: this was a pin-point killing by a marksman. He stood upright on the earth. Mooney crouched and thought of the sniper, the cross hanging from his neck. For a moment, he dared not move, but when he put his hand in his tunic pocket, he felt the beads of the rosary.

Frank threw his rifle down, strolled across the open ground, climbed the fence and walked over the paddock toward a four-legged hay shed on the rise. He knew soldiers in his battalion who could shoot like that: they crouched in broken trees on the edge of no-man's-land and rarely missed their target.

When he got to the shed, Frank could see where the sniper had lain; and in the dust and straw, he saw what looked like a broken necklace. And when he bent down, he found a tiny, golden cross.

There was nothing now for the men of Rubicon to do. They got up, stood by their horses and watched Bolger die. The camp was silent and not even a baby cried.

Frank came back to find Ray standing by the Ford with Mooney. Ray had taken a blanket from a bed-roll and placed it over Bolger. 'There's not much you can do about him,' he said.

Mooney gazed at the landscape, then at Frank. 'No,' he said, 'there is not. Nor the marksman neither.'

Thirty-Five

The night seemed hotter than ever and Julius dozed uneasily, the sheets, stale, damp and heavy on his body. He thought of Maria: *You have lost me forever.* As far as he knew, no woman in his family or the district had ever left her husband before: he was humiliated. But Maria had disobeyed the word of God and the marriage vows and she would pay and repent. He thought of Carl, his neck and face bloodied, as they rode home along the endless, dusty Kurnbrun road. *I would do anything for you.* As Julius lay, he heard the sounds of the night: the birds scratching in the ceiling and the rats scuttling in the dirt beneath the floorboards. Yet again, he remembered his father, the tunes on the piano and the gleam of the chandeliers in the drawing-room. Luxury was the work of the Devil. Outside, the moon disappeared behind the clouds, the night grew black and Julius slept, and dreamed.

The young woman smelt of musk and rose water; her hair was dark, her body lean and strong; she wore a gold chain around her neck and two gold rings on the fingers of her right hand; her breasts were small, but the nipples large; she was standing before him, showing herself: her backside, then her genitals. He was tied to the iron bed – he was naked and could not control himself. The woman laughed, sat on his chest and pushed her genitals into his mouth; he felt her hair and tasted her juice. 'Your beard and mine,' she said. 'Yours and mine – you like that, don't you? You like that?' She thrust and swivelled; he was suffocating and could not speak. Then she turned the other way, raised her backside and grasped his penis. 'You're my lover,' she said, 'my lover and I can do anything with you. That's what you want; you live only for me.' He wanted to shout and say he was not her lover, that

301

his father was the fornicator and that *he* was in Hell for his sins and foul crimes, but he could not speak. Then the young woman started to pull his penis; she handled his scrotum, then bent forward and sucked; as she mouthed and sucked and bit, as he felt her tongue and teeth, he struggled, but he was powerless. She held his penis out, pulled hard, pulled hard, and laughed as he spurted, the semen running down her breasts and belly and over his thighs. 'You're mine,' the woman said. 'You're my property, you're mine until you die.' She turned and struck him in the mouth and he felt blood on his lips. 'Don't you forget,' she said, 'don't ever forget. I will not let you.' Then his father appeared and they fondled each other in front of him. They laughed and shrieked, and when she came into the light, he saw her hair was not dark – it was golden. Suddenly, a livid patchwork of slashes appeared over her face and neck, the blood seeping from the wounds. But it was not Louisa laughing at him – it was a naked man. It was Carl. 'You're my property,' he said.

When Julius rose at half-past five in the darkness of the morning, he lit the lamp, wound his silver watch, pulled on his shirt and sat on the edge of the iron bed. His loins smelt foul and he went to the water pitcher and washed himself. He thought of the dream and shivered. There was no sound, no smell of tea and porridge: the house was like a tomb. He went to the window, opened it, stared over the garden and saw the first light of the pale dawn. Not even a rooster crowed. It was as though it was the end of the world and he was the only human being left. Julius knelt to pray, but he could not remember the words of any text. What was God doing to him? He got up, his bones cracking, and listened for Carl. There was no sound. He would work in the bush with the oxen; he would plough and harrow and prepare for the rain. There was nothing else, but that was enough. He and his son were the providers of the staff of life, and, without work, the earth would produce nothing. The farmer was the key to God's plan, for without him there would be no harvest. He thought of the loaves of bread and the sheaves of wheat on the altar of the church.

Julius and Carl worked, without ceasing, until noon. The day was hot and thundery; lightning flashed; the clouds rolled in from the west; but there was no sign of rain. As Julius cut the bush with the slasher, he saw the shoots were sprouting from the stumps of last season's clearing. There was no end to it.

When he stopped to ease his back, Julius saw a mound of earth, covered with brambles. Beneath the blackberry, the yellow soil was bare and not even a weed grew. It was his father's grave. He stood before it and wondered if he should show it to Carl: when all was said and done, it was the Hoffmayer blood-line. Then he thought: if Carl produced no heirs, if he did not couple with a woman, the Hoffmayer line would finish and the property would be sold to strangers, or the bush would grow back and obliterate it forever. But Carl would never defile himself – Julius was sure of that. He thought of the woman in the dream, cursed, ran forward with his shovel and dug into the grave, scattering the sandy earth into the bush. No sign would remain. When he had finished his work, Julius remembered Chronicles and took cold comfort: *There is no man which sinneth not.*

At noon, father and son sat, facing each other in the clearing. The oxen stood by, flicking at the flies with their tails; the upturned harrows lay upon the earth and now a hot wind blew. The men had not eaten since dawn and their bellies rumbled with hunger. Suddenly, Carl said: 'She was corrupting you. God's will was within me.'

Now Julius looked at his son with his black eyes. 'You slew your sister, did you not?'

'Yes, I told you, Father, I would do anything for you.'

The works of the flesh are manifest . . . Julius tried to remember: . . . *adultery, fornication, uncleanness, lasciviousness* . . . How could a man get rid of evil without murder? 'You cut your sister to pieces with a bill-hook as

303

though she was a shoot growing from a stump?'

'That is it, Father: that is what we have done all our lives.'

Julius thought of the body in the hospital morgue, of his relief, but answered: 'It was a human life.'

'She was evil, she was corrupting you – she was like *your* father. There was bad blood within her.'

'You will be taken away by that man, Broadbent, you will hang for murder.'

'Not if he is not told, and no one will be told, will they?'

Julius looked at his son, his flesh and blood. 'No.'

Even now, despite the work, the heat and the dust, Julius could not erase the memory of her nakedness, her hair fallen on to her breasts, her lips parted and her fingers between his legs. *Do you like this, Father. You do, don't you?* It was the blood of his father and it was in him. God damn August Hoffmayer. *As it is written, There is none righteous, no, not one.*

'She was corrupting you.'

'She was.'

'What did she do to you?'

Julius thought of her hands touching, soft as a feather, then her fingers working. 'You will not ask me such a question. It is forbidden.'

'She can do it no longer. Maybe it is best that Stepmother has gone to the soldier – there is just you and I now. God has said that is how it should be.'

Julius looked at his son's clear, blue eyes, the blond hair and the strong body. He was stripped to the waist, the bill-hook between his knees. Carl's hard muscles gleamed with sweat. *You are my property.* The thought of living alone with Carl began to disturb him. 'I will go and get her back. What is a man without a wife? Look at us – we are hungry, and when we get home there will be no food on the table. Who will do the washing and cleaning? Who will look after the chickens? She makes the best sausages and cheese in the district.' Julius wanted Carl to tell him how he had slain his sister – what had he done, and where? But he already knew and he thought again of the mortuary, Louisa's face and Broadbent watching him. What did the detective think? And what would happen? Nothing – he would see to that: he and Carl would have to share the secret. But that bound him to his son until death. Julius rose. 'We should work, there is much to be done.'

Carl also got up and gripped Julius's arm. 'I think you are wrong, Father. We are better off by ourselves. There is no one to corrupt us. You have always told me that the outside world is evil: the money-lenders, the merchants, the scum from the cities, the soldier. It is the same with Stepmother – she, too, is corrupt. Do you remember her family, the Ampts? Her uncle did nothing, except listen to music and read strange books: their farm never paid. Now she is living with another man. God knows what he is doing to her, and God will punish them both.'

In the silence of the bush, Julius felt his son's hand gripping his arm; his fingers were strong and his face was close. 'I told you,' Julius said, 'there is much to do.'

'Louisa tried to corrupt me,' Carl said, his voice low. 'I came across her, wandering in the home paddock. She was half-naked and her body was exposed; she raised her dress and showed herself to me; she was like one of those women my grandfather used to bring to the house.' He paused and asked the same question: 'What did she do to you? Tell me.'

Carl was close and Julius could smell his body; sweat was running through the hairs of his blond beard and over his nipples. He looked like his sister. 'We must work, damn you.'

'Father, I must know.' Carl put his hands on Julius's shoulders, then gripped him, his thumbs under his father's collar bone. 'It is a secret we must share.'

Suddenly a flock of crows took off from the trees, their screeches echoing in the sky. Julius struck his son. He struck him hard, so hard that Carl fell back, stumbled, then fell on the upturned spikes of the harrow. The oxen bellowed and lumbered forward, the chains tangled; the dust rose; Carl gasped and screamed as Julius grabbed the yokes to stop the animals as they lowered their great heads and lunged. Julius was powerless.

When Julius lifted Carl from the bloodied harrow, the boy screamed and, when he went to carry him, he screamed once more. He screamed as his father carried him all the way home.

Julius had no need of a doctor: he was experienced with farm animals. From the angle of Carl's body and the boy's pain, it was obvious that his son's back was broken and that he would never walk again. It seemed God would never cease punishing him.

Thirty-Six

'There'll be no charges against Stark,' Mooney said to Frank as they sat in his office. 'But you tell that mongrel to behave himself – one mistake and it's curtains. Why he stays around here, I don't know – he'd be better off with his own people.'

'I'm thinking of leaving the district,' Frank said. 'There's no future here.'

'Future? Of course there's a future – it'll rain – it always does. Come the next season, we'll be chest-high in wheat and once we've fixed up the economic system, we'll get five shillings a bag. There's not going to be a revolution, is there?'

Frank laughed. 'No – as you said: it's not the Australian way.'

'Are you a Freemason?' Mooney asked.

'No.' Frank dug into his waistcoat pocket. 'I found something in that hay shed.'

'Did you?'

'This.' Frank placed the cross carefully on Mooney's desk.

'He called himself Donovan,' Mooney said. 'That's a common name – I can't arrest every Donovan in Rubicon, can I?'

'I don't suppose you can.' Frank paused. 'Bolger died hard.'

'That he did. But Reg was always looking for trouble – you should know that. He hated Catholics; there's quite a few of us in the Force.' Mooney put the cross in his pocket and passed the cigarettes over. 'Do you know anything about the Hoffmayer girl?'

'Not really.'

Mooney coughed. 'Nothing Mrs Hoffmayer might have told you?'

'No.'

'It was done by a very strong man; we know that. And that cuts out a woman, or the Hindu. A lot of murders begin at home, don't they?'

'Are you going to continue the enquiries?'

'No,' Mooney replied. 'It's Bill Broadbent's case – I've got my hands full quietening things down in Rubicon. And I've got a strong feeling that whoever did it won't strike again.' Mooney got up. 'Thanks for helping me at the camp.'

'That's okay.'

As Frank opened the office door, Mooney said: 'Stay in Rubicon, Cameron. It'll be the bread-basket of the world and you'll make a fortune.'

Frank felt the warm wind on his face. 'We'll see.'

After the door was closed, Mooney picked up the phone to ring Harold Withers. There was still no reply. Had the man done a bunk? Mooney hoped so – it would take the pressure off him. In the evening, when it was cooler, he would go round to Withers' house and have a look. Then he groaned: he would have to phone the CIB about Bolger.

Frank met Maria on the corner, where he told her about Ray. 'I'm thinking of leaving and I might ask him to run the farm,' he said.

'What about the Returned Soldiers people?'

'If Ray pays the lease to the loan company, I don't think anybody will care. This is the bush and we're a long way away.'

'Sometimes,' she said, 'I think this place is at the end of the world.'

They walked arm-in-arm past the cottages and iron sheds. 'This is the first time I've been in Rubicon for two years,' Maria said.

'Do you like what you see?'

'No. It's an ugly place.'

'But it's home.'

'Not for me.' Maria thought of Aunt Matilde's postcards and Uncle Ernst reading his philosophy. 'I want to see trees that lose their leaves. I want to see the ocean and I want to see snow.'

'Trees that lose their leaves are good,' Frank said. 'And after the snow and the winter, spring is a fresh start. I liked that. Do you want to stay in town? I wouldn't take you into the pub – and you don't drink anyway.'

'Let's get the horses and go,' Maria replied. 'We can visit the lake on the way back.'

'Yes,' Frank said, holding her arm tight, 'we can.'

The days were getting shorter and half the beach was in shadow as they strolled along the sand. 'If I go away,' Frank asked, 'would you come with me?'

She stopped, put her arms around him and kissed him on the lips. 'Yes.'

'Another rule broken: a wife leaves her husband and runs away with a separated man.'

'I think,' Maria said, 'that my uncle and aunt would have liked you. They were not tribal Germans like the Hoffmayers.'

'And Julius?'

'I have no sense of guilt. That was a bad marriage, and I don't see why any woman should stay in a position like that. You may think I wasted ten years of my life, living with Julius and Carl. Maybe that is so, but I hope I am wiser – they will work on that farm until Julius dies; then Carl will work after that – he, too, will die childless and the farm will be sold. All of August's dreams will come to nothing. He should have lived in Hamburg or Berlin, where he could chase pretty girls and drink in the beerhalls.'

'And stroll along the boulevards in the autumn?'

'Yes,' Maria said, 'and stroll along the boulevards in the autumn.'

'Do you think Julius will come back?'

'No, something tells me he will not. You may not be as big a man as Julius, but you are stronger.'

When they left the beach, the afternoon clouds were banking up from the south, but Frank and Maria did not notice them. All they saw were the dead trees, the bush rats, the emus and the rabbits. A lone duck flew over the trees in the dry lake bed and the wind vanished.

'Maria and I are going away,' Frank said to Ray.

'That don't surprise me – I reckon no white man's got any business here: only my mob.' Ray smiled. 'But that's the bloody trouble, the whitefellows *are* here. What are you going to do?'

'We might sail away to Europe.'

'Europe eh? Don't you like Australia?'

'Yes, Ray, I like Australia, but Maria's never seen her native country. Imagine if you lived in some other place and had never seen Australia – only in photographs and postcards.'

'That would be no good to me. I'd want to see the bush and the rocks and my old people. I can see why she wants to go.' Ray passed the bottle of beer over. 'Look, Frank, you're the best mate I ever had – I've had a few and I never thought the best would be a whitefellow. I'm sorry you're going away.'

'Would you like to stay on here and run the farm?' Frank asked. 'I think I can fix that.'

'That would be a mistake, mate. Even if it rains, this place ain't worth farming. I'm going to let the white jokers muck it up and go north. I don't know why I hung on so long.'

'Pride?'

'Yeah, that's it – I don't like to be beaten.'

'And you weren't, were you?'

'Aw, it was touch and go with Bolger and those bastards. Thanks, mate.'

'I owe you more than you owe me, Ray.'

'Why's that?'

'I know now where to farm and where not to. For a farmer, that's worth a fortune.'

'I thought you were going to Europe.'

'Look,' Frank said, 'it doesn't matter where I go, I'll always farm, won't I?'

'Yeah, Frank, I reckon you will.' Ray laughed. 'If you strike it rich, put it down to Ray Stark.'

'There's been no sign of the Hoffmayers?' Frank asked.

'Nup. I reckon the old man might have more trouble with his son than worrying about you.'

When Maria appeared from the front of the house, Ray got up and said: 'Frank tells me you're sailing off to Europe.'

'Yes, Ray, we are.'

'Home is home, Mrs Hoffmayer, and you've got to see it. The spirit comes from home: that's where everything begins.' He looked at the afternoon sky. 'Is your leg hurting, Frank?'

'Yes, it is.'

'Well, it's going to rain, isn't it?'

It was about five when the thunder started. It was distant at first; the lightning flashed; the thunder pealed and rolled and the horizon was lit up like some artillery barrage in the Great War. Within minutes, the light faded, the countryside grew dark, candles and lamps were lit, and as the lightning grew livid, animals started to run for cover under the yellow pines and beneath the eaves of empty hay sheds and vacant barns. Away to the south-west, the sky grew yellow and watery blue; the clouds were as black as the smoke from colliery towers; and the lightning was as bright as a thousand star shells. Then the rain started – a few drops as big as pennies fell at first – so heavy that some animals panicked and ran for the gates and fences. Then it began to drum faster and faster on the tin roofs of the homesteads, the houses and the public buildings of Rubicon. At first, the men and women waited; then, as the rain grew stronger, they ran into their back yards, streets and paddocks and looked heavenwards, the drops stinging their skin and blinding their eyes.

Now the thunder was as loud as the guns at Arras, Pozières and the Somme. The lightning lit up the embattled land; dogs barked and howled; cows bellowed and women ran outside with pots and pans. Before long, the sound of the rain was deafening. Rivulets ran along the clay roads and tiny creeks began to flow. Birds began to drink and wash their feathers in the puddles; the cracks in the dams started to fill; and the branches of the trees drooped before the coming onslaught.

311

By six, the night had fallen. The water ran between the dead trees in the creeks and river beds, and the tents and shelters of the vagrants had collapsed. The thunder rolled on, as loud as the Second Coming. The pious prayed and gave thanks to their Maker; the men in the country pubs threw down their glasses, rushed into every main street and stood, laughing and cheering, as the water cascaded from the tin roofs and public monuments. It rattled down the spouting; it ran down the bluestone gutters and poured through the ceilings of the cottages and warehouses. Now, the rain was as loud as machine-gun fire – and this time, it seemed there was no end to it.

The rain poured through the cracks in the bathing sheds of the lake; it poured on the lake bed and the ancient rivers started to flow. There was no wind – just the rain – and it seemed it would fall for forty days and nights. It was raining all over the land.

On his farm, Julius Hoffmayer dragged Carl's bed on to the front verandah – father and son watched the downpour, heard the thunder, watched the lightning, but said nothing. Each belonged to the other: that, like the rain, was God's will. Then Carl spoke: 'What did she do to you, Father?'

There was no one to see them off: Ray had gone early that morning and disappeared on his horse in the rain along the Kurnbrun road. The locomotive steamed and hissed, and a few passengers stared at the ruined station buildings through the steamy windows. Frank walked along the platform and threw their bags into the guard's van. He noticed that many of the windows were broken and patched up with brown paper; and, as he went back to Maria, he saw that the side of one carriage was daubed WORKERS OF THE WORLD UNITE. The paint was faded – so much for the revolution. He smiled, came up to her and said: 'Let's get on, there's no sense in standing in the rain.'

She, too, smiled. 'I still can't believe it – God moves in mysterious ways.'

'I think there'll be floods,' Frank answered. 'As they say – it's either a feast or a famine.'

As he tossed her small bag in the carriage doorway, he heard a voice behind him. 'I heard you were leaving – it's a country town.' It was Mooney, the water dripping from his raincoat. He grinned. 'A bit damp?' He proffered his hand. 'You saved my life – I never did thank you for that.'

'Saved your life?' Frank answered. 'I don't think I did that.'

'Yes you did, you saved it by changing it. Things will be different from now on.' Mooney turned to Maria. 'Good luck, Mrs Hoffmayer.'

'Thank you, Mr Mooney.'

'Look,' Frank said, 'we're getting drenched to the bone out here. We've got ten minutes – do you want to come into the carriage?'

'Okay. I've got a bit to tell you.'

'What's the news?' Frank asked, as they stood in the aisle.

'I found Withers.'

'Where?'

'In the cellar of his house. Dead. He killed himself with a twelve-gauge.'

'Christ.'

'Yeah,' Mooney said, 'there wasn't much left. He was bankrupt. It goes to show, doesn't it.'

'What?'

'That we all get our deserts. And I've got a visitor coming up.'

'Who?'

'Mr William Broadbent.' Mooney grinned again. 'I think he was a bit pissed off by the news.' Mooney put his cap on. 'I've got to go – see you around.' They watched him disappear through the ruins of the sheds.

The carriage was empty and they took their coats off and threw them on the wooden seats. 'Mr Mooney was a surprise?' Maria said.

'Maybe. There are cops who come good, just like the rest of us. He's a Catholic and hasn't lost his faith.'

'I think I've lost mine.'

Frank took her hand. 'I don't think you have.'

The carriage jolted and the couplings banged; a whistle blew and the train started to move. They travelled slowly down the line, past the fettlers working on the track, the rain streaming down their ragged oilskins. 'This place has been your only home,' Frank said.

'It has, but I want no more of it.'

'When we're in Germany, we could see Mr Hitler and tell him a thing or two.'

'From what you've told me, Frank, that might not be wise.' Maria thought of Carl – were brutal, young men like him the new breed?

'I don't think there'll be another war,' Frank said. 'Things are bound to improve; they can't keep good men down forever – or good women, for that matter.'

Within a few minutes, the train was moving through the bush – past the drowned paddocks, broken trees and farmers' houses. Frank rubbed the window with his sleeve and looked at the landscape: in a strange way, it looked as forlorn and desolate now as it did before the rain came. He saw a man driving a tractor through the mud, then a boy working on a wood-heap. Frank looked at the sky, the rain clouds, the creeks flowing and the soil running away as thick as blood. 'I think Ray was right,' he said. 'I think we're working against nature, we're working against ourselves. This is no place for towns like Rubicon; this is no place for farming. It's better left to itself.'

The train streamed south across the plains toward the sea.